PRAISE FOR LAURA GARDEN

"Queen of the flawed characters!"

—CHEYENNE BLUE, GOLDIE AWARD-WINNING AUTHOR OF *SWITCHEROO*

"Award-winning for good reason."

—JOAKIM BLYTT, *THE ARKIVE*

"*Queenslander* is a sweeping epic set on a farm near the Australian Outback, vividly described, a story about family lost, found and fought hard for. "

—ELIZABETH DE VEER, AUTHOR OF *THE OCEAN IN WINTER*

"There's few things I love more than messy queers, and *Queenslander* blends that into a moving story about family, identity, and belonging. Set on a sheep farm in Australia, *Queenslander* shows how people can atone for their past mistakes and discover who they're meant to be."

—MILO TODD, NATIONALLY BEST-SELLING AUTHOR OF *THE LILAC PEOPLE*

"This extraordinary debut from Laura Garden is so many things: a lyrical ode to Queensland and its people, an exploration of love in all its many forms, a double portrait of two women who only appear to be perfect opposites to one another, but in fact share a bond deeper than blood. *Queenslander*, like its protagonists Ronnie and Nev, never gives up its secrets easily, but the rewards along the way are well worth the journey. Lush and transportive, tender and fierce, this is a novel that lives on well after the last page."

—HESSE PHILLIPS, AUTHOR OF *LIGHTBORNE*

QUEENSLANDER

ALSO BY LAURA GARDEN

QUEENSLANDER

LAURA GARDEN

Merrimack
River
Press

Library of Congress Cataloging Data: LCCN: 2026904439

Cover art by Judi Parkinson

Cover design by Merrimack River Press

ISBNs: 979-8-9946062-1-6 (paperback), 979-8-9946062-0-9 (ebook)

First edition 2026

Merrimack River Press, Haverhill, MA

We acknowledge the Traditional Owners and Custodians of the lands on which we work and pay our respects to Indigenous Elders past, present and emerging.

For women

AUSTRALIAN LANGUAGE GLOSSARY

Akubra - Australian iconic wide-brimmed felt hat similar to a cowboy hat

Arvo - afternoon

Bikkies - biscuits, cookies

Blak - preferred spelling for Aboriginal Australians as a way of reclaiming Indigenous identity

Blundstones - a type of leather workboot

Bogan - redneck

Brumby - Australian wild pony or horse

Bush - wild land that isn't domesticated, the woods, the Outback

Drover - person on horseback who moves livestock

Dry season - May to October, includes bushfire season

Footy - can refer to Australian rules football (AFL), rugby, or soccer

Greenies - environmentalists

Jackaroo/jillaroo - cowboy/cowgirl

Mates - friends

Matildas - Australia women's national soccer (football) team

Never Never - the Outback

On country - On the lands of First Nations peoples, remembering that everywhere will always be Aboriginal land

Pademelons - adorable marsupials smaller than their cousins the wallabies and kangaroos

Swaggie/swagman - a drifter, possibly looking for work

Traditional Land Owners - Indigenous Australians, Aboriginal and Torres Strait Islanders

Ute - utility vehicle, pickup truck

Walkabout - a person 'on walkabout' has left and may or may not be coming back

Wet season - November to April, includes cyclone season

Wet Tropics in Far North Queensland - Biodiverse UNESCO World Heritage-listed tropical rainforest on the northeast coast of Australia

Wog – Racial slur for Italian/Greek immigrants, and other non-Anglo white people, etc.

Loitering there in an aimless way
Somehow I noticed the poor old grey,
Weary and battered and screwed, of course;
Yet when I noticed the old grey horse,
The rough bush saddle, and single rein
Of the bridle laid on his tangled mane,
Straightway the crowd and the auctioneer
Seemed on a sudden to disappear,
Melted away in a kind of haze —
For my heart went back to the droving days.

...

At dawn of day we could feel the breeze
That stirred the boughs of the sleeping trees,
And brought a breath of the fragrance rare
That comes and goes in that scented air;
For the trees and grass and the shrubs contain
A dry sweet scent on the saltbush plain.
for those that love it and understand
The saltbush plain is a wonderland,
A wondrous country, where Nature's ways
Were revealed to me in the droving days.

...

"Only a pound!" and was this the end —
Only a pound for the drover's friend.
The drover's friend that has seen his day,
And now was worthless and cast away

With a broken knee and a broken heart
To be flogged and starved in a hawker's cart.
Well, I made a bid for a sense of shame
And the memories of the good old game.

...

And now he's wandering, fat and sleek,
On the lucerne flats by the Homestead Creek;
I dare not ride him for fear he'd fall,
But he does a journey to beat them all,
For though he scarcely a trot can raise,
He can take me back to the droving days.

—A. B. "Banjo" Paterson, 1891
Abridged from "In The Droving Days"

PROLOGUE

LIONHEART, FAR NORTH QUEENSLAND

The bedroom light turned on. Nev took off the noise-cancelling headphones. Her elderly father and stepmother stood in matching pajamas in the doorway, visibly frightened. Now that the headphones were off she could hear what had woken them. Someone was in the living room smashing the furniture.

"Right," she said, pushing herself to standing. Her knees and lower back protested. She unlocked the gun cupboard. With steady hands she bent the double-barrel over her arm, slid two shells into the shotgun's empty chambers and locked it straight again. "Go back to bed."

"I called the station," her father said. "Wait until the police arrive."

Nev frowned at her father. Big man, white beard, thick glasses, meant well.

She walked into the living room, flicked on the overhead lights. The room was trashed: bookcases down, paper snow on the ground, waxed floorboards and Persian rugs sparkling with broken glass. Movement caught her eye. A skinny kid headed for broken windows.

"Oi! Wrong house, mate."

The teenager turned and froze. Nev expected the shaved head and the cricket bat dangling from the right hand, but she wasn't expecting the intruder to be a girl, and wasn't expecting her to be sober. It was hard to tell from this angle, but Nev thought she saw a round stomach protruding.

It was the eyes that got her—empty stare that held the world in it. After a certain level of exhaustion, predator and prey both have the look. The last time she saw it had been through a camera in Kigali.

Nev lowered her gun.

She watched to see if the girl's gaze followed. It did, which was a good sign. Curiosity was the last emotion to go and the first to return.

She opened the shotgun and extracted one shell, then the other, with steady fingers, tucked them in her chest pocket, snapped the gun closed and leaned it against the wall before raising empty hands on either side of her face, hoping to appear non-threatening. That shouldn't be hard given her size, but she had been told on multiple occasions that she sounded bigger than she was. Her parents peered out from behind her. Her stepmother moaned.

The intruder looked tired. Nev wondered if this was her first child or if she had more asleep somewhere in diapers and fuzzy blankets.

"What address do you think this is? We're not into drugs. I don't owe money except to the bank. I'm Nev." Niv, rhymes with give. "If someone sent you here to shake me down, they think you are expendable. Whoever sent you here is trying to kill you."

"Fuck. Sorry."

"Mistakes happen. You can work it off."

Work for me instead of them.

The intruder turned away to duck through shattered glass

sliding doors. Nev followed her out into the loud wet oven of a summer night to a pickup that had seen better days.

Under the floodlight, the kid made the ute look small.

The kid had to be in her upper teens. It was summer now and the girl's skin was brown, Southern Mediterranean if Nev had to guess. In the winter the kid would still be olive, what they called a 'wog' here. Dressed in a black singlet and men's gym shorts, trying to look butch instead of like a gangly teenaged boy. Drug addict or sleeping with one. People aren't that different, Nev thought. They all need a safe place to sleep and a job to do.

She had seen it too many times in too many countries. Everyone had the potential to be good or bad depending on circumstances. Kids didn't commit crimes in a vacuum.

"Oi! Wait." Nev pulled the wallet from her back pocket. Why she had been sleeping in jeans was a matter for contemplating another day. "How much for the bat?"

The kid looked wary. "Why?"

"Need it for all the violent crimes I'm planning," Nev said. "Reckon I might go on a spree."

The kid looked at her blankly, then laughed.

Gotcha.

Nev held out two bills. "I can do two hundred today and another hundred tomorrow."

The kid got in a dented black Ford pickup. Not being willing to part with the bat was a bad sign.

"Listen. I have your number plates," Nev said. "If you help me clean up this mess I won't report it. You can work it off. I have sheep. Horses. There's a shed and an air mattress if you need a safe place to crash."

"Not a runaway," the kid said behind headlights. "Sorry about the house. Should have guessed this was the wrong place. Thanks for keeping your lid on. I'll pay you for repairs when I can. Didn't mean to scare old people."

Nev wondered if that category included her. "They'll survive. Tell me what's going on. Whatever's hunting you out there in the dark, you don't have to return to it tonight." Nev felt strange as the words left her mouth. Other than the baby bump, the kid was too skinny. Nev's heart somersaulted behind her sternum, adrenaline arriving late. "Stay."

Echoes of Rwanda in ninety-four: teens with machetes wandering the night, mosquito soup, the smell of fire and rain. She hadn't saved anyone then.

She swallowed, hood of the truck warm beneath her palm. "I make a mean chicken parmi." The old tick-tick-boom feeling warned her that this was a test. It had been a minute since god gave her one of those. They never panned out, but they were gifts while they lasted, Stradivarii in the cosmic wood splitter. If she could convince the kid to stay, someone wouldn't die in the soup below the horizon. "Listen. Do that to any other house on a dirt road like this, you'd be dead. Farmers out here have guns. What's your name?"

The pickup backed out, turned, and the kid was gone.

Nev crossed her arms, rubbed her jaw. What a slow-moving train-wreck of a planet that put the capacity for violence in children. She sat down, rested her headache in her hands. She needed a drink.

Nev lifted the flask from her pocket, unscrewed the lid, inhaled caramel fumes of Bundaberg rum, hesitated, then poured it onto orange clay, where it pooled, refusing to sink in. Topsoil at Upsend Downs held the Bundy the way it rejected blood, sweat, and tears—silently, as if waiting.

Her failure sat on the surface, looking back at her, as if the land was asking her to offer something better.

This land was ancient, nestled in the oldest rainforest—it knew her, and her capabilities, so it required a greater sacrifice.

1

RONNIE

TEN YEARS LATER

On January 26th, Australia Day, also known as Survival Day, wedge-tail eagles dove screaming behind a plow on the coastal plain west of Cairns, and Ronnie Madonna was in a race with a storm. Light rain speckled her motorcycle helmet as she hugged her Kawasaki W800 and followed the highway west from the Pacific Ocean towards dark lumps on the horizon.

Right turn onto the Gillies Range Road leading uphill through the Gillies mountains. In her helmet headphones, she blasted "Edge of Seventeen," by Stevie Nicks. Switchbacks without guardrails through eucalyptus forest were so familiar she barely saw them.

Up ahead, butcherbirds fought over a green tree snake, jumping on the pavement, tugging opposite ends of it in their beaks. Good day for the birds, bad day for the snake.

Most people have a moment from which there is no coming back—a moment that lives in infamy, if only in their mind. At twenty-six, she had one regret, but she was trying not to think about it.

In a rear-view mirror she eyed the highway patrol car before glancing down at the speedometer, a hair over the speed limit.

Lights flicked on a moment before the siren.

"You've got to be kidding me," she muttered, pulling over to the edge of the cliff.

She took off her helmet, shaking out greasy black curls full of tangles before hanging the helmet from the handlebars. An officer she didn't recognize approached the motorbike. Luckily her nine-year-old daughter wasn't with her and wouldn't witness this—that would have been a million times worse.

"Speeding. License and registration."

Swearing inwardly, she turned off the engine, toed the kickstand, swung her leg off the bike and stood, resisting the urge to stretch out the tension in her neck and shoulders before reaching into the back pocket of her jeans for her wallet. She tried not to make any moves that might intimidate the officer who frowned up at her through mirrored sunglasses.

When condoms in cellophane wrappers fell out, she resisted the urge to pick them up as she handed over the documents. Her hands shook.

The officer walked back to his patrol car.

Ronnie's armpits prickled and she felt herself sweating through her shirt. She wanted to take off the leather jacket, but not in front of him.

The officer returned. "Walk on back with me."

With a sinking feeling, Ronnie did. The butcherbirds bounced back and forth across the road playing tug-of-war with the snake.

A second officer waited in front of the patrol car; *COLLINS* embroidered on a patch on his chest. "Where are you coming from?"

"Townsville."

"What were you doing there?"

"Surfing."

"Where you headed?"

"Home. Lionheart."

"Relax. You're not in trouble. Hands behind your ears. You know the drill." The cop patted her down. At six-two, she was taller than both officers. "Lift your shirt."

She lifted her leather jacket and men's XL tee, revealing washboard abs and tattoos that she knew they wouldn't like. Cops hated slurs against prison guards.

"Turn slowly."

She glanced over her shoulder.

He frowned, looking unimpressed by the "SAVE A NAIL, HAMMER A SCREW" tattoo on her lower back.

Shit... I should have that removed...

The cops stepped away to consult. When they returned, the Collins one stuck his thumbs in his belt. "Is there someone you can call to come get your bike?"

"Mate," she said. "Can I pay a fine or something? What the hell?"

"Relax, we just have to ask you questions and this is not a safe place to do it. We're not messing with you. We're not charging you with nothing."

She looked at the sky and bit her lip. A flock of Sulfur-crested cockatoos flew over. She refused to glance down into the backseat of the squad car. *Don't do this to me, mate. Give me a ticket, but don't take me in.* If they put her in a box again, she'd have a panic attack. Sweat dripping down her lower back tickled.

The officer walked away, lifting a cell phone to his ear. He didn't use the police radio. When he returned, he jerked his thumb over his shoulder. "Get out of here, Madonna. Vamoose."

She walked back to her bike, slid a long leg over it and turned on the engine.

"Stay out of trouble."

Mute, she put her helmet on, skin crawling.

She couldn't bring herself to thank them. She waited for a break in the cars before pulling out into traffic. In a side mirror she watched the patrol car pull out behind her and trail her from a distance.

She watched the speedometer.

After the patrol car disappeared, she felt a burning stab in the back of her neck—a knot in the muscles, her body holding onto stress. As predicted, she had sweat through her shirt. At the sign for Gordonvale she made an impulse decision and turned. A quickie on the way home would loosen her up.

On a shady residential street in Gordonvale lined with jacarandas she slowed before turning left into the open garage of a run-down white Queenslander with the world's tiniest greenhouse in the garden. She parked her bike and took off her helmet.

She had outrun the storm for now.

Ronnie tied her hair up in a messy topknot, then tapped a knuckle against the side door.

Her ex answered in beach clothes. Maude looked like a model, bangs framing green eyes, and subtle make-up that had probably taken an hour to put on. Maude rolled her eyes when she saw her.

Ronnie pressed her finger to her lips, glancing behind her past the pile of tiny pink sandals into the house where cartoons played. She stole a quick glimpse of the back of the nine-year-old girl's head. It wasn't much, but it was proof of life. The hot poker touched her between the shoulder-blades again. She swallowed.

Ronnie's ex sighed, stepped down into the garage and locked the door so they wouldn't be interrupted.

Maude was also heavily tattooed, but that was where all similarities ended. The pale woman ran manicured nails through heat-straightened auburn hair, fluffed it, releasing the familiar scent of expensive perfume, then managed to look down at Ronnie despite being a foot shorter. Maude reached up to press a soft palm against Ronnie's T-shirt over her sports bra, fisted the cotton and pushed her against the garage wall.

Ronnie picked up the smaller woman, carrying her to the hood of Maude's candy-colored Chevy truck.

Around Maude, Ronnie became fourteen again, hyped up on

first-job money, cheap booze, and joyrides in the back of awful men's cars. She always felt gross afterwards. Her footy teammates called it 'the putangover.'

Mountain air became colder as she rode the retro black Kawasaki up the Gillies Range Road higher in elevation through eucalyptus mountains. A sign, WELCOME TO THE ATHERTON TABLE-LANDS, preceded green hills. Ronnie leaned into a bend in the road and then straightened. Queensland's Wet Tropics contained several wildly different climates between the coast and the Outback.

The sun came out, revealing a neon green plateau. Gently rolling hills appeared between low-hanging rainforest clouds, materializing out of the mist like that other Oz, the one in the book.

Near Boar Pocket Road, a group of steers blocked traffic. Ronnie hit the brakes and slowed to a stop, smiling. Johnson's beef cattle had escaped again. Several cars in front of her sat parked in the road. Drivers had gotten out of their cars to watch the show.

She looked for and then found the familiar slender cowboy shape and Akubra hat.

Nev whistled, long and sharp. Gaia, a six-year-old collie, flew at the steers, who watched, unperturbed and enormous. Instead of veering off at the last moment, the dog hit the wall of cattle and began snapping and snarling.

"Get down!" Nev said, holding out the shepherd's cane she used for herding. "Get down, Guy. Get down!"

Gaia was a sledgehammer.

The steers saw that the collie meant business and began to move, slowly at first, then trotting, back up Boar Pocket Road toward home. Turning with a hand in her pocket, Nev finally noticed Ronnie and raised her crook in greeting.

Ronnie waved back, cheeks warm, irrationally happy. Her

boss's attention sparked a warm feeling in her chest. She envied the dog.

She turned the key in the ignition. The bike's engine roared to life.

In the center of town, Ronnie rode past the ancient Lionheart Hotel with Victorian wooden arches and wraparound second floor balcony, past rows of small, brightly-painted houses, and an athletic field where children in school uniforms played.

Coming back to her childhood home always felt like stepping back in time. The village of Lionheart was hay country, dairy country, and as her dad told fire department recruits when he toured them around, home of the Wadjanbarra Yidi and Bund-abarra Yidi Traditional Land Owners.

On the edge of town, the purple Queenslander on Pademelon Road waited for her in run-down Victorian coziness, the nostalgia place that decayed but never fundamentally changed despite a maelstrom battering the outside world—a refuge in more ways than one. An official-looking sign on the wooden railing read, "Licensed Wildlife Rehabilitation Facility."

Ronnie parked her bike on the lawn beside her dad's shiny new black Ford F-250, then climbed the staircase two steps at a time up to the wraparound veranda on the second floor and let herself in through the unlocked front door, through the screened-in sunroom with green plastic carpet to the inner front door, which had swollen from the humidity and was always ajar.

The old house smelled like a pet store: wood shavings, grain, and warm milk. Her dogs jumped on her, tails wagging. Matilda, a Jack Russell, snapped at Maya, the Blue Heeler. Ronnie picked Matilda up and carried her into the family room, which was full of wallabies.

Orphaned joeys peered out at her from large, clean cages. The smallest one sat on Ronnie's dad's lap, wrapped in a faded Little Mermaid towel.

Reg Madonna, chief of the volunteer fire department, sat in rugby shirt and cargo shorts watching the Matildas play the Black Ferns in soccer. Ronnie collapsed across from him.

"How was surfing with Mikey? Any waves this time?"

"Some cops pulled me over on the Gillies."

Reg glanced over at her between plays, beneath a framed picture of a man who looked Pacific Islander kneeling in Aussie military uniform on the deck of a battleship in World War Two. A newspaper clipping from nine years ago taped to the picture read, "Lionheart's Founding Family Bids Adieu to Beloved Patriarch".

"All right, baby?" He muted the telly. "They did what now?"

She told him.

He swore. "Those bastards... I'd have got you, Brum."

"Thanks, Da."

He set the baby joey down next to him and lifted his arms without getting up. "Come 'ere." Without fail, he made her feel like he was proud of her. When he hugged her, she felt like a kid who had won an award. She didn't know why he was still proud of her now. She hadn't been that kid in a long time.

He put the wallaby back in its cage and patted the cushion. "Blaise will fix up the guest room."

"Yeah, nah." Ronnie had her own temporary modular home in a caravan park in Tinaroo, a working-class tourist town on the west bank of Lake Tinaroo. It was good enough for now—near cousins and safe enough for her daughter to ride a bike around the neighborhood on the odd weekend Ronnie had her.

"I insist." Reg pressed the remote. The Matildas had won. Commentators reviewed the best plays. Ronnie loved that he was a super fan of women's soccer. He was a girl dad. She leaned against his side. If anyone had seen her, she would have been embarrassed and denied it.

She hoped telling him wasn't a mistake.

During the commercial Reg made a phone call, then put his arm around her again. She wanted to say thank you but her tongue was lead. She had won the dad lottery. Reg hadn't even been a real stepdad, just one of her "van life" mum's ex-boyfriends, but no one around here cared. He had thrown a bigger party when she was born than he had two years earlier for his biological son, her half-brother.

Maybe that was why when their mum went walkabout, she had taken her dogs but left the kids. No one had batted an eye.

When afternoon rainclouds rolled in, darkening the lawn, Ronnie went outside to move her bike under the car port. Rain pounded her stepmother Blaise's flowering succulents, bromeliads and bottlebrush grevillea—the same rain that on the other side of town grew sweet young grass for hungry ewes and lambs.

Clouds parted, and the sun popped out again. In the summer heat, anywhere rain had gathered on wet pavers and cement emitted a layer of white fog which swirled in low clouds. As was usual over school holidays, Madonna relatives trickled in, gathering in the kitchen and around the firepit. Reg was ablaze with the fire of civic protest, threatening to call elected officials to complain about police corruption.

Ronnie stayed quiet, tired of retelling the story.

The Madonnas—a dozen burly men and Ronnie, their messed-up baby cousin who wasn't a baby anymore—ate take-away pizza in front of the Wallabies men's soccer match and drank two slabs of Victoria Bitter. They cheered when a Wallaby with the ball got near the goal. Reg pointed to the cages, reminding them to keep it down so as not to upset the joeys who might be sleeping. The shot bounced wide off the goalpost. They all groaned.

Ronnie was the tallest on the couch, but a decade short of scoring one of the coveted ottomans. After the day she'd had, she felt bruised and a little numb, as if she had fallen, picked herself up and didn't know yet how bad the damage was.

After dark, her dad knocked on the guest bedroom door. "Oi,

Brum!" His fluffy hair was wet. In the kitchen Blaise blasted Abba's "Slipping Through My Fingers."

"Oi, Da…"

"How ya feeling?"

"Fine."

"Brilliant. First rate. Listen. We're going to file a complaint. If they call you in to talk about it, we'll all go with you."

"Oh?"

"Everyone's invested. Opportunity to prove a point we've been making for years."

"I don't know, Da."

"It's intimidation, Brum. Pure and simple. They mess with you, they mess with me. They know who I am. Mess with me, they mess with our family. Madonnas won't stand for it."

"I'd rather not."

"Eh?"

"They let me go with nothing, not even a warning. What if we complain and it bounces back on us? What if they punish me for it later?" She swallowed. Too late, she said it.

"Bloody hell, Brum."

She crossed her arms.

"You disagree?" he asked.

"It's complicated."

"Even if it was random, they have no right to bully you like that. They knew you had a record when they pulled you up on their scanner. You give them a pass when it's yourself, but you wouldn't let them harass a gay kid because he's gay or a woman because she's a woman or a person with a record…"

"I got lucky."

"It's not lucky to be threatened by pigs who treat you like scum. What about next time?" Reg asked.

She'd wondered the same thing. "No worries. No harm done."

"You would say that…" Reg swallowed. He cleared his throat, patted her arm.

Stomach rumbling, she went to the kitchen to stare at the

contents of the fridge. He followed her. "No worries, princess. Clean living for a week, deal? Just chill with us and relax. Don't get in your head."

She nodded. It could have been so much worse. Nothing bad had happened.

"Should we call Rainbow?" he asked. "First week of school. Check in?"

She shook her head. "You can if you like." Calls were tough for her. "I miss her too much to talk to her. Maude said she'll let me pick her up Friday after school."

Her dad frowned. "You better not have dropped in on them on your way home... Brum..."

She walked down the hall barefoot, finishing her lukewarm beer. Her childhood bedroom overlooked the pool; now it was her stepmother's office.

The guest bedroom used to be Mattie's. Dusty blinds looked out onto the front veranda. Beyond Blaise's potted hibiscus the neon-green lawn sloped down to a quiet paved road. The room still smelled like weed, though Blaise had changed everything except the mattress. Mattie, who played pro rugby for New Zealand, still slept here when he came home.

She logged into her account to see her balance. Her paycheck marked UPSEND DOWNS had come through on time, direct deposit. She transferred five hundred into the joint account she shared with Maude, then shot off a text.

paid feb early

2

ABOUT RAINBOW

At the soccer pitch behind the Atherton primary school, Ronnie ran five and six-year-olds through a practice game. Getting them to play in two teams and track the ball without all following it in a pack felt like herding kittens.

Dozens of sweaty little girls in school uniforms, tube socks and hair bows, glowing with pride. For some of the youngest girls this was their first practice match.

Was *ironic* the word for this? Had it occurred to her that she was getting something selfish out of this job? Yes, yes it had. Was it funny that she was hero-worshipped four hours a day by every pre-teen girl in town but the one she had given birth to? Yes, yes it was.

After practice, she walked over to her bike in the car park, put on her jacket and checked her phone. Missed call from the American turtle biologist intern she had been hooking up with on karaoke night, not important. She zipped her phone into a pocket of her leather jacket and started her bike.

Atherton was the local metropolis with a grocery, department store, Burger King, and a main drag with shops on both sides.

At the purple house in Lionheart her stepmother was blasting ABBA again. Ronnie tuned it out the way she tuned out her stepmother. Both were inoffensive, sentimental and nostalgic for the 80's. She wondered what the lyrics of *Slipping Through My Fingers* meant to Blaise. A mother watching a happy young girl grow up too fast, dearly loved but disappearing every minute. Blaise had no kids. Maybe Blaise was sad about Ronnie's daughter Rainbow growing up.

Thinking about Rainbow was uncomfortably close to missing Rainbow, which led to why Rainbow wasn't here, which smelled of a stinking pile of shit guilt and possibly some kind of horrible joke some bastard cops were laughing at in a station somewhere in the past. No, she didn't want to think about that.

Ronnie locked herself in the guest bedroom in preparation for the feelings incoming, scrolling through pictures she had taken that afternoon.

She wondered what Rainbow was doing now over in Gordon-vale. She hoped it was wholesome, whatever it was. Her daughter was probably watching telly, playing computer games or texting her friends.

Ronnie sighed, spread-kneed on the edge of the bed. She inhaled carefully. Exhaled to a count of five. She rubbed her face. Should shower before she fell asleep. She could already tell it would be an early night. Nowhere to go from here but call it and try again in the morning. Do a reset tomorrow.

Matilda and Maya barked. She didn't think anything of the arrival of another car until the knock on the bedroom door. Her chest hurt. A lump caught in her throat. She swallowed. Maybe they would go away.

Then again. Three loud knocks.

Three small soft knocks.

She blinked. The waterworks started, silent tears running down her cheeks. She wiped them away. "Come in."

The door remained closed.

Fuck, she thought, this hurts, this hope business.

The door swung open, revealing Reg standing behind a nine-year-old girl with pigtails and skinned knees. Ronnie smiled.

Rainbow was wearing the binoculars Santa had given her. She took them everywhere, even slept with them.

Reg whispered in Rainbow's ear. The girl held up a cardboard sign that said YOU ARE THE BEST MUM! in pink magic marker.

Ronnie chuckled, opened her arms. Rainbow went to her without any more encouragement.

Ronnie closed her eyes and smelled her daughter's head. "What are you doing here, angel?"

"Grandad brought me."

She cupped Rainbow's round cheeks and kissed her nose. "Did he kidnap you?" She feared he had.

He leaned on the windowsill. "Maude let me take her. She'll fetch her Monday."

Ronnie couldn't breathe. She must not have heard correctly. "Monday?"

Reg nodded.

The longest Ronnie had ever had her daughter was two nights every other weekend. Two nights out of every fourteen. She struggled to count how many nights there were to Monday. She glanced over at Reg. "What day is it?"

"Wednesday."

She counted on her fingers, then pressed the back of a trembling hand to her mouth, not wanting to upset Rainbow. The girl was too young to understand.

Rainbow would never have to pretend not to miss her own daughter. To pretend that a schedule was humane and bearable to protect a child from knowing what had been stolen from her. It had been stolen from not just her but from four generations of her family one grey day ten years ago—a house of cards brought down by a single careless flick of the criminal justice system.

That was one of the lessons she had learned. Never let them know they hurt you. If they know they hurt you, they win.

She took her daughter's hands. "Did you bring your things?"

A shy smile.

Ronnie grinned. "We are going to have so much fun! We'll go

to the park and ride bikes, swim at Lake Eacham, ride horses over at the farm… You can help me teach girls how to win at soccer! Are you ready?"

"Can I stay here with you and Grandad?"

"Until Monday. Unless the plan changes. I don't make the schedule. You know that, right?"

Her daughter looked unsure. "Who makes the schedule?"

Ronnie met her dad's eyes over the girl's head. "Maude."

"Oh." Rainbow looked confused.

She squeezed her daughter's hands. "We've talked about this before, babe. Did you forget?"

"I didn't forget."

"Who did you think made the schedule?"

Rainbow shrugged.

Ronnie had heard a story about a man who lived years with a piece of his left humerus missing and his arm in a splint. With the splint, he was able to regain full range of motion in his shoulder and even lift small objects. He lived a normal life. Except, when he took off the splint to shower, his arm hung at an unnatural angle.

This felt like that. She felt the moment something shifted. It wasn't broken, exactly, but she couldn't control it. A part of her suddenly separate and foreign, hanging by a string.

She studied the sensation the way the man must have studied his detached arm.

"Oh my god…"

"Steady, she'll be right," Reg said.

Reg was talking to Rainbow, shooing the girl out of the guest bedroom, reassuring her in a low voice and promising her favorite show.

Then Blaise was there telling Ronnie to breathe. Ronnie ignored her.

"It's all right."

"She thinks I did this… She thinks I did this on purpose…"

"She'll understand when she's older."

"I'm a bad mum…"

Blaise shook her head. "You're not a bad mum. She adores you."

"I fucked up..."

Her stepmother clucked her tongue. "You did the best you could at the time."

Ronnie reached for the empty trash can under the desk.

Blaise played with Ronnie's hair while Ronnie leaned over the bucket. Nothing came up. She blew her nose. "I'm not all right... I'm not all right with this schedule."

"Ask for a hearing. A judge will review the case."

Fat lot of good that would do. Adoption was permanent. If she challenged it, she would be the bad guy. She had given up her parental rights.

"I want her so much..."

"We know. We want that for you, too."

"This is a nightmare." She sat with her head in her hands. Every time she left the house she feared losing what little she was allowed.

This was a different kind of prison, one nobody talked about.

She rubbed her eyebrows. Only nine more years of walking on eggshells. The girl was halfway to eighteen. Baby steps.

"I don't know who to be angry at."

She should have fought harder to keep her daughter. Separation was too humiliating to name. Safer to set a lid on it and live with it, to pretend life started and stopped every other weekend. Every other weekend soaking up toddler giggles, birthdays, school years and lost teeth to pretend she wasn't missing time— to pretend Rainbow wasn't growing up six times faster than the girls Ronnie coached.

When Ronnie was alone, the nine-year-old snuck back into the room and sat beside her.

She pulled her shit together in front of her daughter. Rainbow had not missed six-sevenths of her own life. Rainbow would be fine.

Ronnie blew her nose. "I feel better. Sometimes adults need a good cry."

"Why can't I decide who I live with?"

"I don't know, baby. That's a good question. Someday you will."

"I want to live with you."

Ronnie forced a smile, knowing she had to be careful not to say anything that her ex called 'triangulation' or 'manipulation.' If she admitted to Rainbow that she wanted custody, Maude might punish her for it later. Maude insisted that they never trash-talked each other in front of Rainbow. Good idea, in theory. They had to be on the same team. Consistent messaging mattered.

But she couldn't lie to Rainbow. Well, she could, but if she did now, what would be the point of any of this?

She put her arm around her daughter. "I want that too, baby. I would take care of you and do everything for you if I could. You know I love you. We can't change the past, only the future. Right?"

"Mum, focus. How would it work? Like, where would we live? If I lived with you where would I go to school?"

"If you lived with me it would be half of the time, and where you went to school would be up to Maude." *Don't get her hopes up...* She had never asked Maude outright to share custody with her, only dropped hints which Maude ignored.

She should probably swallow her pride and ask, otherwise nothing would change until Rainbow was a teenager, when Rainbow would have to go through the traumatic experience of petitioning a judge in a courtroom, potentially standing across from Maude and losing, which would send the girl off in a direction of teenaged rebellion that Ronnie knew all too well. Ronnie would do anything to spare her daughter having to go through what she went through.

Even if it meant risking losing her.

Since Maude first let her babysit, Ronnie had never been late to pick-up or drop-off Rainbow. After her parole ended six years ago, she had been careful not to get so much as a speeding ticket. She had to stay squeaky clean. Easier said than done when all the police departments on the Tableland knew who she was.

"Can we watch Frozen and eat mac and cheese?"

Ronnie rubbed her daughter's warm back. "Or we could pitch a tent in the garden and roast snags over a camp fire! Wouldn't that be fun?"

The girl looked skeptical.

They watched Frozen and ate macaroni. Rainbow could read thick chapter books and could spell words like *especially* and *inconceivable*. She practiced her recorder before bed—a show both hilarious and baffling—and slept with a stuffed unicorn in her mum's bed despite being too old for that.

Ronnie wasn't concerned.

At bedtime Rainbow produced a glossy picture book from her backpack with a sparkly photo of a blue morpho butterfly on the cover. Rainbow began reading aloud.

Later, Rainbow closed the library book, clicked off the lamp and snuggled under the weight of Ronnie's tattooed arm. Ronnie inhaled the smell of fruity shampoo and farts, then sighed contented. She had the best daughter in the world. She loved this little dork so much.

This was safe; bedtime was safe.

Ronnie could love things that didn't happen every day. "Tomorrow morning what say we go to the farm?"

The girl nodded, small body a weighted blanket against Ronnie's side. "Can I ride Brighty?" Her child voice rising, light and sweet.

"Yes, you can ride the pony." She kissed the crown of her daughter's head. Absence makes the heart fonder. That's all love was: an urge to protect forever things that didn't belong to you.

3
FARMHAND

EIGHT YEARS EARLIER

Last week of March, end of the wet season. The gravel car park at the pub had flooded on one side. Nev parked there anyway. Inside, not too many people yet, a small crowd of regulars at the bar. No live music. If there was, she would be it. She hadn't brought her guitar or fiddle tonight. She hung her wet barn coat on the wall.

The barmaid who was the owner's daughter poured Nev a schooner: amber liquid, nectar of the gods, foam on top the color of teeth and eyes. Nev felt the question in the woman as soon as she sat down at the bar. Debbie Collins—pretty, middle-aged, smelled like jasmine. Nev had tried when she was twenty and Debbie was twenty-three, had been shot down, no hard feelings. Not a large dating pool in Lionheart: big families, everyone related, people stuck around.

"Nev Darlin'," Debbie said. "Looking for another hand on the farm?"

"That depends. Who've you got?" Nev asked.

"Reg Madonna's looking for work for his girl."

Nev sipped her Carlton Mid. That name again. Debbie's mother, Peggy, who in addition to owning the pub also answered the phone for the Lionheart police department, had helped Nev figure out the intruder's name two years ago.

Ronnie Peterson. Only girl in town who looked like that. Reg Madonna's baby mama's other child. Had the mother's last name but not the mother.

Pregnant kid with the cricket bat out on parole. Who was she without the baby and the bat?

"Oh?" Nev's breath slowed and her palms began to sweat. She had resisted the urge to follow up on the kid after the break-in. It had taken her a year to finish putting the family room back together, and by then there was no family left to live in it. Her parents' rapid decline had taken precedence over home renovation.

She hadn't asked Peggy at the station for gossip.

The paper had printed the details of the domestic violence trial and name of the victim—Maude—over eighteen. Unusual case.

Juvenile sentencing was strange. Four years sounded like a long time and yet not a long time for attempted murder. Two years inside, two on parole.

"Why isn't she looking herself?" Nev asked.

"You'll understand when you see her. Not a lot of prospects in town."

"She should be in school." Knee-jerk reaction. Manual labor's a bleak future. It gets old fast, like the people who do it.

Debbie shook her head. That was one thing Nev hated about this place, the casual disregard of higher education as a means to a better life. That rural mentality translated into a general lack of ambition. But who was she to judge? She hadn't done anything to write home about since '94. Managing a thousand sheep bound for slaughter wasn't glamourous jet-setting or saving the world. Now that her parents were both gone—step-mother dead of an aneurism two years ago, her father of heart failure two months later—she wouldn't know where to send that letter anyway.

"Bad kid, could be a hard worker," Debbie said. "The Madonnas are a tight bunch; she'll straighten out. The family's protective. My cousin's her probation officer. To talk to her he has to talk to all of them." You couldn't throw a stone around here without hitting a Madonna or a Collins. There were black Madonnas and white Madonnas, same as the Collinses.

Nev's people, the Bickermans, had only been here four generations, not enough time to spread out. She considered herself the only child of an only child of an only child. The last one. They waited too long to have kids in her family. At thirty-eight, she was turning out to be no exception, but her dad had guilted her into freezing her eggs before he died. Small price to pay for the peace of mind of a dying man.

"You must know Reg?" Debbie said.

"Not personally. Should I?" His name came up in the local rag sometimes for his intercultural advocacy work and his conservation efforts. He was on the board of directors of the tree-planting nonprofit that was always sending her passive-aggressive emails offering to replant trees along the creek in her sheep paddocks.

"He spent the last two years protesting in his camper outside the Youth Detention Centre down near Brissie," Debbie said, squinting. "They just elected him Chief of the volunteer fire department. He's a mover and a shaker. Grass doesn't grow on him."

High praise. Nev wondered what the kid looked like now.

"Tell him to send her around tomorrow." She could find something for the kid to do. She wasn't worried about the girl's temper. Even a good dog will bite if backed into a corner. She was concerned that the girl might be a drug addict. Nev didn't deal with addicts, as a rule, couldn't hack it, like talking to a potted plant.

Nev finished her Carlton Mid, slid the empty glass across the bar. What was in it for Debbie Collins, to help the girl? What favor did the bartender need from Reg Madonna? Maybe nothing. Nev was paranoid, jaded from living elsewhere for too long. People here didn't think that way. They were nice to each other for no reason. Karma was a close-woven basket here. It didn't take long to reap what you sowed.

The next morning a dual cab black truck pulled down the drive, parked in front of the barn—what Nev would call a ute if it was used for farm work. This truck had never been used hard, looked pristine. Three people got out.

Nev shook hands with Reg Madonna. She recognized him from community events. Good-looking man—stocky, tanned, with warm brown eyes and short black hair.

Reg was around her age, maybe a little younger. He had grown up here; she hadn't. Nev had moved to Christchurch, New Zealand, after her mother left her father when Nev was two. Nev's grandparents with tin-mining money had lived out in Ravenshoe, highest town in Queensland with Queensland's highest pub, in a different social strata than the Madonnas and Collinses.

"G'day, Madonna. Welcome to Upsend Downs."

"G'day, Bickerman. Appreciate your time. Gorgeous spread you got here. This all your place?"

"It belonged to my parents," Nev said, self-conscious of the wide view of the horizon from her front lawn. Upsend Downs looked like a rich person's estate, but was a working farm, and she was rationing her inheritance to keep it afloat one year to the next. "I came out here to shuffle the papers before they died, got trapped in the wheel."

"I don't believe it for a second," Reg said. He swiveled, admiring the view again. "My nan had a dairy farm out here somewhere."

"This was part of it. My dad bought this block in eighty from the bloke who bought your grandmother's farm in sixty-five."

Reg smiled behind dark sunglasses. "Small world. You look familiar."

Nev forced herself not to glance back at the girl. "Want a tour?"

Reg shook his head. "Another time. You're all right." He turned to his adult kids. "This was part of your nan's dairy farm." Reg turned to Nev. "My father passed away in July."

"My condolences. Mine passed away last year also."

"Sucks, doesn't it? Was that the original house?" Reg asked, gesturing to Stone House behind her.

Nev shook her head. "Your grandparents' homestead was down where lake Tinaroo is now. On the left-hand side, see the dead trees? That's where the homestead was, toward Kulara. Your grandparents moved the original farmhouse up to Boar Pocket Road in the fifties, but it burned down before we got here. Lightning. Wraparound veranda, ten bedrooms."

"Families were bigger then," Reg said. He eyed her thoughtfully, then turned to his kids. Nev heard him whisper to the young woman. "Don't be a dick to her. She's had hard luck."

Nev blushed. Even before Rwanda she had been a semi-tragic figure in town. She was the type of well-behaved person mothers wanted to take care of. She gestured behind Reg. "These your kids?"

Two young people behind Reg towered over him. He chuckled. "Their mum is a giant. They're both my kids." He introduced them. Mattie, young man in his early twenties, looked like Reg. Ron, the young woman in her late teens, did not.

Nev laughed. The scrawny girl who had done the sloppy B&E had gone the way of all things. The woman behind Reg had a large tattoo up the side of her neck that said KITTEN in graffiti letters, had gained half her body weight in muscle and grown a hand taller. Funny how juvie took scared kids and turned them into hardened criminals. She looked to be in her mid-twenties, but had to be younger.

"What have they been feeding you in that place? Fertilizer?"

The young woman wearing sunglasses like her brother and stepdad uncrossed her arms to shake Nev's hand and had a grip like a basketball player. Christ, she was tall. She hadn't seemed so tall before, but then, it had been dark.

"You don't want to know. Sorry to hear about your parents."

"Thanks. Old age gets us all in the end, if we're lucky."

Reg looked from one to the other, then back again. "You two know each other?"

Nev grinned. "Never seen her a day in my life." It had been nighttime.

"Sorry again about that," the young woman said.

"No worries."

"I'm afraid to ask," Reg said. "Mattie here is going to stay with her the first week. I assume you'll give her a test run. If it isn't a good fit, no worries. No harm in trying."

Nev addressed the younger man. "Keen to work, too? Plenty needs doing. I'll pay you."

Reg left in the black truck.

Nev and the Madonna siblings, half-siblings by the look of it, walked toward the horse barn. She addressed the young woman. "What do you want to be called?"

"Ron." Long vowel, rhymed with gone. Odd name for a girl.

"What's that short for?"

Ron raised an eyebrow.

Nev went out on a limb, hoped it didn't break. "Pronouns?"

The young man laughed loudly. He seemed like a nong.

Ron didn't appear to mind. "She. What about you?"

"Same. How old's the baby?"

"She's twenty-two months."

"Reckon she's cute. When was the last time you saw her?"

"Thursday."

Visitation, then, baby in foster care or with the ex.

"How did you know she had a baby?" the brother asked.

Nev ignored him. "Pictures?"

Ron took out her phone, showed pictures of a toddler with

curly black hair and dark eyes. The family resemblance was strong.

"Cute kid. Looks like you."

"Thanks."

"What does she like?" Nev asked.

"Music, animals…"

"Delightful."

"She is," the girl agreed.

"You have kids?" the older brother asked. Nev had already forgotten his name.

She shook her head. "Never married."

"You don't have to be married to have a kid."

"True. Never had time for it."

A week later Ron showed up alone in a beat-up black Ford truck while the dew was still cold underfoot and a cloud of fog erased the lower paddocks.

The Madonna siblings had been coming around her place early morning and leaving mid-afternoon—something about community service in the afternoons at the primary school, some sport. Ron had been released with two years of parole and a curfew. Youth sentencing was either lenient or draconian depending who you asked. Nev didn't have a strong enough grasp of Queensland's justice system to say whether the state was tough or soft on youth crime. She didn't belong to a political party and only voted on behalf of those who couldn't.

Ron hadn't destroyed the edges of the lavender with the whipper snipper yet, which was a good sign. She paid attention, head down, took her time. She was faster every day.

Coffee mug in hand, Nev brought her over to the machine shed where she showed her how to hose mud off the rear of the farm utes and blow grass off the hay mower and baler with an air compressor. She supervised for a while, then left her to it.

The girl found her in the machine shop an hour later. "I'm done. What else can I do?"

In the silver F-250 Nev brought her down into a low-lying paddock below Boar Pocket Road. Later there would be an epic sunset over the lake.

The grass in most of the lower pastures was short where she had baled hay and sold it already. Along the fences the grass was still tall where she couldn't cut it with the mower, gone to seed, golden tops bobbing in the breeze like wheat. Cicadas and other buzzing insects droned. It was lovely down here. No one ever spent time here, except scrub wrens, wallabies, brush turkeys, and sometimes three thousand sheep.

It was early April. That time again. The not good time. Travelling time.

Nev spent half an hour teaching Ron how to mend a timber and barbed wire fence: not complicated, but a perpetual chore. Storms blew dead trees and branches down on the wire. Pulling staples off a neighbor's posts had been Nev's summer job when she was thirteen. "He put the fear of god in me, specifically about losing staples. If I lost one a cow would eat it and cark it. I never lost one. It's best you don't either."

The girl had a low ponytail and a shaved undercut. Ron always wore sunglasses, a baggy black T-shirt and footy shorts with crew socks and work boots, and bench pressed more than Nev weighed on the old bench behind the barn. Kazi had told her that one evening over a beer with a big shit-eating grin. Nev had nothing to say to that.

He didn't know she had pointed a loaded gun at the girl, held her life in her hands, or that she still had nightmares about shooting the girl.

Gunni, her old German friend who fancied himself an amateur psychoanalyst, said her pain and pleasure synapses had been crossed during the war, and it was too late to do anything about it now. She figured he was probably right.

After lunch she taught the girl to drive a tractor. On, off.

Forward, reverse. High gear, low gear. "Don't ride across a steep incline or you'll roll over, crush yourself to death. Don't drive in mud or you'll tear up the grass." A tractor wasn't all that different than a truck. Ron picked it up so quick in the first lesson that Nev decided she was ready to slash an overgrown paddock.

At the end of the second week she handed Ron a tax form in the middle of the muddy gravel yard between the barns and shop buildings. It was the heart of the place, the spot through which everything with wheels or legs on the farm crossed. "Congratulations. You're hired."

Ron's eyes widened. She glanced down at the tax form, then back up at Nev. The girl looked down at the form, frowning.

Sudden tightness in Nev's throat, a sick feeling in her stomach as it occurred to her that the girl had never seen a tax form. Come to think of it, she didn't know if Ron could read. Had to be tactful about these sorts of things.

"Your dad will help you fill it out."

Ron nodded.

Nev cleared her throat. "Questions?"

The girl shook her head.

"Forty hours a week, minimum wage. Try not to spend it all. Have your dad fill that out and give it back to me."

"I appreciate it." The girl held the sheet of paper like a photograph, gently, by the edges. Nev knew the girl would put it in her truck right away. She didn't underestimate the importance of a first job to a person on parole. Ron's Adam's apple bobbed when she swallowed. "I meant what I said that night. I want to pay you back for the damages. Subtract it from my pay."

"Don't be silly. You're doing me a favor." Nev looked up the drive towards the back of her house. Inside the front door her suitcase was packed.

"I insist."

"You're not going to win this one."

In an hour a taxi would drive her to the airport. "I'll be gone for two weeks. Kaz's in charge. He's been here longer than I have. I trust him."

"Where are you going?" the kid asked.

"Kigali."

"Where's that?"

"Africa."

"Business or pleasure?"

Nev turned back, surprised that the girl was still talking. Eye contact was there, although it broke under her gaze.

"I go every year," Nev said.

"What is it like?"

"Green." And red. "They had a genocide there."

"Fuck."

Correct response.

"What was your favorite subject in school?" Nev asked.

The kid hesitated, probably didn't have one. "Band." Interesting. Not what she expected. "I was homeschooled. By my mum. But we didn't really do school."

"Lucky you. You've had an interesting life," Nev guessed. For someone so young.

"It's been a lot."

"Your dad's a good bloke?"

The girl nodded.

"You're safe at his place?"

Hesitation, averted gaze.

Shit... "You're not safe there?"

"I don't like my parole officer."

"Tell your dad. You can talk to Kazi and Barney, too. I don't know about Ric-Rac, he's kind of a nong. But they're good kids. Once you've been here a while they'll have your back. Teamwork makes the dream work, eh? Don't do anything stupid while I'm gone."

· · ·

Two weeks later Nev's plane landed back in Cairns on a Monday afternoon. The taxi from the airport raced to beat traffic, got her back to Upsend in record time, an hour twenty. A pile of papers on her desk welcomed her home. Kazi had not sorted the unpaid bills from the requests for charitable donations; Nev did it now. At the bottom of the stack of mail on her desk was a tax form, filled out in neat handwriting with small round letters.

She picked it up. Was it the great Reg Madonna's handwriting? Or the girl's? Hard to guess. Based on the birthday written on the form, the girl was eighteen. Nev let out a breath. *Thank god...* Dodged a bullet there. She was still a creep for finding her attractive. Her new farmhand was a Sagittarius.

How long would she last?

She found Ron poking around the machine shop early the next morning staring at chainsaws. "You like them?" The old boom box played gentle Scottish folk music from the seventies.

Ron shrugged, and turned off the music. Interesting. She hadn't been studying chainsaws, she had been daydreaming. "How was your trip?"

Terrible. Challenging. Sobering. Emotional. Horrifying. Same as usual. "Humbling."

"How many years have you been going?"

"This makes nine. You know how to ride?"

"I know the general idea," Ron said. In Lionheart, there were two types of country kids: those who grew up riding horses and those who grew up riding four-wheelers. Nev suspected her new employee fell in the latter category.

"Come on, then." Nev showed Ron how to saddle and put tack on Dreadnought, the great bay mare. Tighten the girth, the belt under the mare's belly. Put the toe of her boot in the stirrup and throw her leg over Dreadnought's back. Reins held between fingers and thumbs. Pressure from heels and tension on the reins told the mare to go forward, left, right, and stop, back up, or go faster.

Post in a trot or the saddle will slap your arse. A canter is nice, smoother.

"That's it. You're a natural."

She showed her the ice machine, electric kettle and coffee maker in the employee kitchen in the shop building that the other farmhands used.

"You ever been in trouble?" Ron asked. "Why are you so nice to me?"

Nev only knew one way to answer that question. She brought her inside Stone House on the hill, showed her the photos of Rwanda.

"Black and white, artsy fartsy." Ron stared at a picture of a Hutu man with a machete. "Did you take these?"

Nev hated that picture. She nodded, watching Ron move from one framed photo to another down the high-ceilinged corridor that led to Nev's bedroom. She hadn't thought this through when she had this bright idea. She stood in the foyer, her side towards the open door, not blocking the exit, but as close to it as she could be without losing sight of the eighteen-year-old. She had to wrap this up post haste, return to Upsend and the public side of the farm.

"Were you a professional photographer?" Ron asked.

"Nine years," Nev said. '87 to '95.

"Why did you stop?"

Nev pointed to a photo of the hotel in downtown Kigali, 1994. She couldn't tell if that meant anything to her or not.

"Do you still take pictures?"

Nev shook her head. The old SLR camera from her conflict photojournalist days gathered dust in the attic. She should sell it. No sense in holding onto an expensive toy she would never use again. She had come close to selling it on several occasions, but each time something had held her back.

"These are really good."

"Thanks." Nev didn't look at the black and white landscapes. To her, they weren't art or anything to be proud of, but windows into a reality most Queenslanders with their first world privilege refused to see. She had physically escaped every war zone she photographed, but carried them with her inside.

You ever been in trouble? Why are you so nice to me?

Nev didn't know if the pictures answered the questions, but the girl looked satisfied.

4
UPSEND DOWNS

Ronnie pulled into the carpark at Rainbow's primary school early. No traffic today. *Good.* Gordonvale, a cane-growing town on the coastal plain south of Cairns, caught a run-of-the-mill summer spill. Tourists didn't visit during the wet season.

Parents huddled under the awning, mums on one side and a few dads on the other. The dads wore the tradie uniform: dark sunglasses, tight T-shirt, work pants, meaty arms, dirty fingers. Ronnie went to stand with them. She had never been allowed to pick Rainbow up from school before, so she wasn't sure how this was supposed to go.

She had called the primary school in Atherton to let them know she would be late to soccer practice today. She shook hands with a man she knew from footy.

Rainbow ran into her arms. It was all worth it for this hug.

"How was school today?"

"Good."

Hand in hand, they turned and walked towards the carpark. "What did you do today?"

"Normal stuff."

"Like what?"

"I forget."

. . .

Athletic fields, Atherton. As she had suspected, the boys' assistant coach who had covered for her was visibly bored, frowning on the sidelines with his arms crossed. Girls dribbled balls in a circle.

Ronnie slipped her whistle around her neck. The girls looked relieved to see her. They stared at Rainbow. The teams were rivals, in a primary school way, more heated than adult sports rivals, with a ferocity akin to *Lord of the Flies*.

Ronnie set Rainbow's bag on the stands to shake hands with Jack Collins. "Thanks, mate."

"No worries." He ruffled Rainbow's hair. "Hi cowgirl! How was school?"

"Good."

He winked at Ronnie, touched her shoulder and walked towards the boys' soccer team that was practicing two fields over. Jackie was all right.

Ronnie walked into the center of the soccer pitch and was instantly swarmed by girls like chooks gathered cheeping and peeping around a feeder. "Did you miss me, Wattles?" Their school mascot was a wattle, an acacia tree with sunshine yellow flowers.

A chorus of 'yes'es, a few cheeky 'no's.

"I missed you, too. Let's start at the beginning. Matildas, to my left. Football Ferns, to my right." The girls separated into their scrimmage teams on either side of the pitch, then converged along the center line. They knew the tradition.

Ronnie stood between them, hand on her hips, scrolling through playlists on her phone. She set the speakers on the center line. "Ready?"

The girls nodded. No one smiled. They took the coin flip extremely seriously.

She pressed a button. The opening bars of "U Can't Touch This" by MC Hammer played over the speakers. The team on her left, the Matildas, began side-stepping, heel-stepping, in time to the music. Ronnie danced along for any of the girls who had forgotten the moves she had taught them. Left-right fist pumping. Criss-cross feet, grapevine, hands in the air, then slide. Walking in place, jogging in place, jumping side to side, spinning around. Ronnie mouthed the words.

The next track was for the Ferns group. "Obsession" by Animotion blasted through the speakers. Rhythmic synth and drums, followed by a haunting high-pitched synth line before the bass voice joined in. Ronnie shimmied her shoulders, side-stepping to the beat. The girls tossed their ponytails and pigtails, shimmying and clapping. They got down on all fours when she did, then rolled over and sprang up to their feet in a spread-eagle, jumping, clapping, and then shimmying in a circle, arms in the air.

Afterwards the primary school girls closed their eyes. "Raise your hand if you think the Matildas won. No peeking." Ronnie counted fifteen hands. "Raise your hand if you think the Ferns were better. Keep those eyes closed." She counted eight hands. "Open your eyes. Congratulations, we have a winner. Drumroll, please." The team patted their thighs.

Ronnie pointed her fingers, crouched, swung her arms in a circle, then pointed to the group on the left. "Let's hear it for the Matildas! Woot woot!" The girls all clapped. The team on the left side of the line shrieked and jumped up and down, hugging each other. "Well done girls! Better luck next time, Ferns. It was close. You were fire as well." Ronnie picked up a soccer ball, set it on the center line. "Matildas, your ball."

Farms collect broken things. Free from the limitations of space, they hoard. Upsend Downs was no exception—useful things came here after death to oxidize.

Unfixable things waited for resurrection.

She snapped a picture of Rainbow on her phone. Rainbow sat

on the seat of an unrecognizable lump of rusty metal in front of Stone House.

"What is it?" Rainbow asked.

"Horse-drawn potato harvester. Nev bought that thinking she would get it working again."

"But she doesn't grow potatoes."

"Not yet."

They walked to the horse barn. Inside was quiet and tidy, no one there except animals. It smelled like hay. Rainbow saddled Brighty the fat pony while Ronnie saddled Dreadnought the mare, her favorite.

On the wild side of the fence, Shadow grazed beside this years' foal, lazily flicking flies away with her tail. Feral ponies ignored fences. Brumbies belonged to no one, like rabbits and brush turkey. The name "brumby" probably originated from the Aboriginal word "baroombie," meaning wild. Australia had more wild horses than any other country, all descended from escaped thoroughbreds. Years ago, Shadow had been shy and skittish, but Ronnie had been feeding her carrots and apples.

Reg had affectionately nicknamed her "Brum" when she was still little and feral with a mane of thick black hair. Now Rainbow was that child, the one they all loved, the one they hung their hopes on.

Ronnie double-checked that the nine-year-old had tightened the pony's girth. She tightened the belt under his belly another notch until it was snug. "Good work, kiddo. You're a pro. We'll hire you soon."

Rainbow led the way. Ronnie's horse followed the pony up the perimeter trail uphill through the bush, towards the top of the mountain owned by the international Centre for Rainforest Research, then cut downhill towards Lake Tinaroo, through Nev's hay pastures and sheep paddocks.

Dreadnought and Brighty waded across Lazy Creek.

Miniature kangaroos called pademelons—Rainbow's favorite

because they looked like teddy bears—camouflaged against bushes in the shade.

The trail descended gently towards Lake Tinaroo. Barbed wire fence on their right—Johnson's cattle farm. No cattle in sight today, only empty paddocks with gum trees along fences and creeks. She had been fantasizing about buying that property for years, had even squirreled away a few thousand in the bank for a down payment in case any of it ever came up for sale.

The trail veered left at the marsh that formed the eastern edge of Lake Tinaroo. Below, water lay flat and brilliant. "Thirty-five square kilometers of surface area," Rainbow said. "I learned that in science class."

They rode uphill to the Upsend Downs Native and Exotic Plant Nursery, passing the potting shed, walking the horse and pony between rows of healthy-looking plants, through the lavender field and orchard of young trees in pots.

The view from top of the hill still took her breath away.

Below them lay gold and silver horizons, hazy in the heat. The nursery was peaceful, no customers yet. Careful to keep Dreadnought to the middle of the path, Ronnie led her daughter among ornamental plants, fountains and birdbaths, mahogany trees, and boxwood hedges. The air smelled like an herb cabinet.

An access road led behind neighbors' houses to the back door of Nev's horse barn.

Brushing down Dreadnought in the barn after dismounting and unsaddling the animals, Ronnie asked, "Has your mama been nice to you?"

"I hate her."

"Why? What happened?"

"She doesn't pay me to do chores, she won't let me sleep over at Lizzie's, and she doesn't let me watch R-rated movies."

"You're nine."

"So?" Rainbow lifted her horse's front foreleg to scrape the mud out of the horse's hoof with a pick. Ronnie watched, still brushing the bay mare, whose coat shone.

"Sounds like a normal strict parent. Gentle with that."

"Your mum let you do whatever."

"Look how that turned out." Necessity could force her to see her ex, but no one could force her to see her mum. "Other than that, is she nice to you?"

Rainbow appeared to be focused on her task. A glob of manure fell out of the cleft of the soft center of the horse's hoof. She shrugged. Another glob of mud fell out under the hoof pick, hitting Ronnie's leg before landing on the barn floor.

"Careful," Ronnie said. "Gentle with his hoof. Is she patient? Does she yell?"

"Not at me. She yells at the dog."

"Does she help you with homework?"

"Homework's easy." Lucky girl. Rainbow hadn't inherited that from her. "Besides, Nev helps me." That was true. Ronnie's annoyingly brilliant boss helped Rainbow with her homework every other weekend.

"Does she cook? Do you eat at the table?"

"Weekdays I stay with nan."

"Are you safe there?"

"Mum..."

"You would tell me if someone was hitting you or making you do icky stuff?"

"You sound like the social worker. You're not my coach or my social worker. You're just my mum."

"What do you think a mum is? You're awfully precocious."

Rainbow rolled her eyes. Where had she learned that? At school? She was acting like a teenager already.

At night after the nine-year-old fell asleep in the guest bed at Reg and Blaise's house, Ronnie texted Maude.

(Ronnie) Why does Rainbow have a social worker?

(Maude) The school gave her one.

(Ronnie) Why? What's wrong with her?

(Maude) I'm not having this conversation with you over text.

(Ronnie) ?

(Maude) She was fighting on the bus.

(Ronnie) When?

(Maude) Last year. It's resolved. Don't bring it up.

(Ronnie) You should have told me.

(Maude) Why? So you could give her tips?

Back at Upsend Downs the next morning while Rainbow was in school, Ronnie rode in front of the flock carrying a small plastic bucket of grain, driving a thousand ewes and two thousand lambs from one paddock to another.

The flock had to be moved every day.

At the rear, Kazi looked at home in the saddle, having a brilliant time. He was in his element, unconcerned about stragglers. She admired how straight his back was, how lightly he perched on the saddle, and she copied the way he held the reins in one hand and rested the other on his thigh.

Droving was surprisingly relaxing. The way the flock carried her along before it swept forward under its own momentum, enveloping obstacles in its path, swallowing, spilling over, reminded her of surfing.

Dreadnought rocked side to side above the white sheep ocean. When Ronnie tapped the mare's flanks with her heels the mare broke into a canter.

Sunlight glowed yellow ribbons through dust clouds churned

by twelve thousand tear-shaved hooves. More torrential rains would flood the neighbor's lowlands soon.

From the horse barn and gravel parking lot, Stone House appeared to be a squat, single-story stone box with a wraparound veranda, but it had been built on a hill—the back side was a two-story, open-concept, timber-frame and plaster villa with repurposed wrought-iron railings made of old Singer sewing machines and French doors looking down on a sloping lime-green lawn.

She found Nev in the kitchen fixing lunch. Nev looked like Robert Redford had walked off the set of *Out of Africa*. Ronnie's boss was one of those pink, weather-beaten people—old in the face, young in the body—who could be anywhere between thirty and fifty without surprising anyone.

Ronnie washed her hands, checking on the fingernail that had been black since she accidentally hit it with a hammer. A Christmas card smiled back from the windowsill behind the sink. On it Nev's kid sister posed in front of the University of Auckland, surrounded by large handwritten letters: "Happy birthday big sis! I hope you, Ronnie and Rainbow have a happy Christmas and New Year. Love, Taylor."

The kitchen looked down on Lazy Creek, Boar Pocket Road, and beyond that, hundreds of hectares of open eucalyptus scrub —Nev's sheep on the left, Johnson's cattle on the right—reaching down to the marshy shore of manmade Lake Tinaroo. Indigo mountains on the horizon.

Nev garnished with parsley before handing her two plates to carry out on to the veranda. Eating here was always posh. Today, lunch was salmon, wild rice, kale salad, mandolined radishes and baby rocket.

Flecks of hay coated the hair on Ronnie's forearms. "What's happening with the sheep in the paddock here?" A group of ewes stood grazing on the other side of an electric fence. One stared directly at them, hoping for a treat like the apple in front of Nev on the patio table.

"Their eyelids are pale. I'll deworm them after lunch." Nev walked over to the fence and gave the ewe the apple, scratching behind her ears and between her shoulder-blades. The sheep wiggled her butt and hind legs side to side like a dog.

Ronnie hadn't grown up on a farm and the idea of parasites still gave her the ick. "How old is Kazi? Who's replacing him?"

Nev wiped her hands on her pants and returned to the table. "He's a dying breed. They don't make men like him anymore." The drover in question was half-naked in the yard wearing nothing but wool, greasy cap and a splash of white hair, back bent at a ninety-degree angle to trim a hoof. "He got into this before child labor laws, shearing at the big stations with his dad. He would prefer to be a full-time shearer, but he doesn't have a driver's license and he's bollocks at swagging. You know how he is. Likes his creature comforts."

She snorted, trying to decide if she enjoyed the peppery after-taste of this arugula. Kazi lived by himself in the hayloft. He had worked for Nev's father, which had always struck Ronnie as sad. The idea of belonging to an estate felt old-fashioned at best and colonial at worst.

Ronnie forked a burger-sized wedge of salmon into her wide mouth and chewed. "No new drover, then."

"It's not the life," Nev agreed. "Stockmen are a dime a dozen and sheep people can't find work within a hundred kilometers of a city. It's not a transferable skill. Don't end up like that, Dain'y. Stick with horses and machines, you'll find work anywhere, Rome to Rio. If you can manage a barn or fix a car, you can support a family. It's called job security. You always want to be moving into a field in high demand, so you can take vertical steps to a higher paid job."

"Like you."

"Do as I say, not as I do."

. . .

Ronnie picked up Rainbow from school again and coached soccer. At her dad's house that night, Reg and Blaise had a meeting at the fire station, so she made lasagna, salad, rice, and beans for Rainbow. As usual she cooked way too much food for two people. Rainbow wiped tomato sauce off the snake.

A local Yidinji artist had handmade the elaborate tile mosaic of the Rainbow Serpent on the kitchen floor. As a kid, Ronnie had taken her dad's local art collection for granted, had been surprised when she went over to friends' houses and they didn't have Yidinji, Wadjanbarra Yidi artwork on the floors and walls. More than seventeen traditional owner groups and twenty thousand Aboriginal people lived across the Wet Tropics region.

After dinner, she piled leftovers into plastic containers which Rainbow stacked in the fridge. *Teamwork makes the dream work.*

"Can we go to the basketball court?" Rainbow asked.

"The one with lights?" It wasn't raining outside and she didn't have to return the girl to Gordonvale tonight. Ronnie was sore from lifting weights and exhausted from repotting hundreds of trees at Upsend Downs, but she would rally. "Put on your trainers and grab a ball from the shed."

At the basketball court, they shot hoops with neighborhood kids. After half an hour Ronnie dragged, barely able to jog around the court after the ball, but the nine-year-old still giggled and jumped, doing cartwheels, begging her over and over to take her camping, and she couldn't say no.

At bedtime they loaded camping gear into her dented F-150 and drove out into the bush. No streetlights out here. Upsend Downs was dark except for a floodlight on each of the barns. In low gear they rolled up the hill, around Stone House—one light on in Nev's bedroom—then down the hill again to Lazy Creek.

She parked under black trees. Rotten Davidson's plums littered the ground. The passenger door slamming interrupted water gargling over mossy stones. In the plum trees, a kookaburra laughed, 'ooo-ooo-aaa-aah!' and an Eastern Whipbird call cut through the twilight like a blaster pistol in a space opera.

Rainbow gasped. "Cool!"

Ronnie smiled and drew a deep breath, filling her lungs with unpolluted air. She would sleep like a baby here. They set up camp in the clearing next to Lazy Creek as they had dozens of times. She didn't mind the lack of light—they could set up camp just as easily in the dark.

In the Outback, she and her mum had often spent nights staked out with sniper rifles in treetops, hunting feral pigs. Those nights had been sleepless, but not dreamless. She had had the wildest dreams in trees, dreams that ran on and on when she recalled them the following day, one improbable fantasy blurring into the next like the snake that swallowed its own tail.

Her mother had taught her how to take a sniper rifle apart, clean it, and put it back together in the dark. Good fun at the time, but didn't age well. In hindsight, letting a child clean your guns was probably illegal. Ronnie would never take Rainbow hunting at night, when you could only see the world in black cutout shapes, shadow puppets across the horizon. Her mum had taught her to hunt by sound alone, but that wouldn't fly here in the real world.

Rainbow helped snap the tent ribs open and raise the nylon tent. While Ronnie hammered in the pegs, Rainbow carried their packs inside and unrolled the sleeping bags.

The tent lit up from within like a blue lantern.

Something in Ronnie relaxed. She drew a deep breath and let it out, before joining her daughter inside.

Rainbow had laid the sleeping bags together on one side of the tent, which made Ronnie feel a certain way. "You're so sweet, babe. Thanks for setting this up." They brushed their teeth. Snuggled up close at her daughter's side under the battery-powered lantern, she opened the library book that she and Rainbow were reading together. She read slowly, pausing after every other word, deciphering her handwritten sticky notes. When she pronounced a word wrong the nine-year-old corrected her.

"The Great Barrier Reef World Heritage Area is a national trea-

sure. Covering an area of 300,000 km2 on Australia's continental shelf, the Great Barrier Reef is home to vast amounts of biodiversity. However, sediment and nutrient runoff is damaging the reef, causing coral bleaching and increasing invasive predation, both of which pose serious threats to the future of the Reef."

She wondered if her daughter chose difficult books to challenge her as an act of preteen rebellion. Some nights Rainbow made fun of her for pausing and being slow. When that happened, reading became infinitely harder. Tonight, Rainbow didn't comment. Smart girl.

Rainbow read five perfect pages aloud in a fraction the time, turned off the battery-powered lantern and went to sleep.

The nine-year-old made it look like breathing air.

Ronnie lay awake in the dark. How come her daughter was a genius? The girl hadn't inherited that trait from her. Maybe schools were better at teaching now. Ronnie hadn't been reading advanced shit like this in year three in Lionheart. She had gotten as far as the Mrs. Piggle Wiggle books before her mum decided her days of mainstream education were over.

Rainbow was light years ahead of where Ronnie had been at that age. Either Rainbow was performing above grade level or Ronnie must have been under-performing before her mother pulled her out of school and into the Outback.

Something to chew on.

Her mum was out there in the bush now.

The thing about people like that who said they wanted to 'connect to the land' was that land was everywhere. You were always on land. What those people actually meant but didn't say, was that they wanted to get away from other people.

5
ABOUT MAUDE

Rainbow had begged her all weekend to try out the new board she got for Christmas, so here they were, Monday afternoon, at the crowded skate park, taking turns. Skateboarding, Ronnie quickly decided, was a form of exercise for teenagers who loved throwing themselves in the air to see what would happen. Most of the time when the teens at the skate park attempted a flip, they didn't stick the landing. When one of them managed to do it, the others cheered.

She was not a teenager anymore. She felt twice as tall as these kids and twice as heavy.

After she worked up a sweat, she started to enjoy the airborne thrill of it, the cool breeze on her face, limbs warm and loose, before a hard crash landing hurt worse than usual. Wipeout.

She picked herself up, retrieved the upside-down board and went over to sit on the bench. She had sprained a wrist before. This felt like that, but her hand didn't want to open or close.

"Are you okay?" Rainbow asked, concerned. She looked so cute in her little helmet and pads.

"Nah, yeah, no biggie." Ronnie had more broken bones than she could count, but never a wrist before. Getting home might be tricky.

Half an hour later, Rainbow looked tired and it was time to return her, so with one hand Ronnie drove her an hour north-east down out of the mountains and parked in front of the faded white house in Gordonvale. Inside and outside lights were on, and two cars sat parked in the drive—Maude's custom pink Silverado and an ancient Toyota Corolla. Her heart sank. Maude's mother didn't like Ronnie. Her stomach hurt, which she wished she could change, but unfortunately nerves were out of her control.

Her left wrist had swollen and stiffened during the drive, but she hugged Rainbow with the other arm, then kissed her on both eyelids and both cheeks. "Be good. You are strong."

She watched from the behind the wheel as Rainbow ran up the front steps and let herself in.

Maude stepped out onto the landing, gesturing that she wanted to talk.

Ronnie waved with two fingers as if she had someplace to go and was in a hurry, then when Maude approached, reluctantly rolled down the window. Under the steering wheel her left leg jiggled.

Maude frowned. "Why didn't you walk her to the door?"

"I was watching her."

"You always walk her to the door. That's part of the deal."

"She's nine."

"What's wrong with you? Are you drunk?"

"Keep it down. No, of course not. Are you?"

Maude had been drinking rosé with her mother. Maude's mother always brought a nice bottle to go with dinner. "What's wrong with your arm? Did you hurt yourself?"

Ronnie glanced down at her injured arm and then at her other hand on the steering wheel.

"I bought that board for her, not you. It's for a child. You're an idiot."

A curtain moved. Someone inside was watching. Maude's mother.

Ronnie hadn't done anything wrong. "Don't berate me."

"Wait here. I'll get some ice."

Maude returned with two bags of frozen corn. Ronnie leaned sideways, reaching for them through the truck window. Maude shook her head, opened the driver's door.

Ronnie reluctantly stepped out of the truck. Standing, she towered over her ex. Maude laid one bag of frozen corn on the bonnet of the truck. "Put it there."

She did. Maude laid the second bag of frozen corn on top of her injured wrist and pushed down. Ronnie yelped. The bags of corn had been defrosted and refrozen into solid blocks of ice.

She grabbed her ex's hands, curling her fingertips under them and pulling, but Maude leaned forward again, positioning the weight of her upper body over Ronnie's wrist again like a psychopathic paramedic doing evil CPR.

Ronnie's vision blurred. She swore. Everything Maude did to her was payback for what Ronnie did ten years ago.

"Stop. You're hurting me." She tried to extricate her wrist from between the blocks of ice on the hood. Rainbow appeared framed by yellow curtains in the window next to Maude's mother. Ronnie took a breath, trying to appear relaxed. "Not in front of Rainbow."

Maude released her. The bag of frozen corn that remained on the bonnet bore a faint imprint of Ronnie's hand. Ronnie shut the door, forcing herself not to look at Maude as she turned on the engine and twisted to make sure the drive behind her was clear. Her wrist made her eyes sting.

Ronnie's ex flushed, pupils dilated.

A relay race of questions appeared, ready and muscular, but Ronnie kept her mouth shut. *Are you being a bitch because your mother is here? Is this performative vengeance?* It didn't matter. Maybe it did, but anything she said now would only escalate the situation in front of her kid.

Ronnie put her truck in gear and carefully backed out of Maude's drive. She watched her hands grip the wheel, one limp and useless, the other white-knuckled and shaking. Sixteen again, ears burning, winded, sucker-punched. She should have seen it coming, should have known better than to let her guard down.

Rainbow disappearing in the rear-view mirror.

At the main road Ronnie pulled off onto the verge to get a grip. She smoked until she stopped shaking.

When she started the engine again it was nighttime, and the heat of the day had broken.

She drove with the windows down, summer night air warm and wet. Familiar roads became dreamlike after dark—no depth, no warning of what was to come. Maude hadn't seemed high. Her veins and skin had looked fine. Ronnie wondered, charitably, if Maude felt this way when Rainbow was with her.

Surely it must be more terrifying for Maude, co-parenting with someone who had tried to kill her.

6

THE BAD ONE

Sixteen-year-old Ronnie sat in her pickup truck outside the faded white Queenslander with the tiny greenhouse in the overgrown yard, smoking a cigarette with trembling fingers. She was still warm and tingly from almost being shot in the face by a stranger half an hour ago, and could smell her own stale sweat. She wondered if this was how her girlfriend Maude and Maude's clients, subordinate dealers, and drug-trapped working girls felt when they got high here in front of her. It was two in the morning but the inside lights were still on and a truck she didn't recognize sat beside her girlfriend's car.

Maude wasn't really her girlfriend—Ronnie realized that now.

Ronnie had been so stupid.

She should return in the morning to grab her things, but fuck it.

This ends now.

Maude wouldn't like what Ronnie had to say, and was probably drunk or high, but Ronnie had to get this feeling off her chest and break up with her now before she forgot the words she had rehearsed in the truck and chickened out. Her stomach burbled. She stubbed out the cigarette in the ash tray before slowly unfolding her large frame from the truck, clumsy from the baby bump stretching the waistband of her gym shorts, and climbed the front steps two at a time, cricket bat hanging loosely from her left hand behind her.

Not all monsters hit people. Some make others do their dirty work for them.

Bashing a house full of innocent people was too much. What if there had been kids inside? Shaking down criminals who owed Maude money was one thing. Being tricked into committing an actual crime was another.

The baby didn't deserve that.

No one deserved that.

Inside, Maude slumped on the couch watching Braveheart with a tall man more than twice her age, his arm around her narrow shoulders making her look like a child. When Ronnie froze in the kitchen doorway, wondering why she was here instead of at her dad's house, fear flickered in the tiny eighteen-year-old's eyes and Maude pushed the man beside her away. "Leave." The man took one slow glance up at Ronnie filling the kitchen door-way, stood, picked up his hat, nodded politely, and wordlessly let himself out the back door.

Ronnie grabbed a trash bag from under the sink and jogged up the stairs to the bedroom, snatching her clothes from the dresser.

Maude screamed up the stairs at her. "You fucked up, didn't you?"

Ronnie pawed through the pile of dirty laundry on the floor, separating out what was hers.

"If you steal from me, I will send Shaky-eyes after you, and you won't like it!"

Ronnie shuddered, stuffing into the bag unfinished home-work assignments from the high school she would never graduate from. "I'm not stealing! Don't call Shaky-eyes!"

"You owe me two thousand dollars! I need that money tonight!"

Heart racing, she shoved soccer cleats she hadn't used since the coach kicked her off the team into the bag. "I don't owe you anything! I didn't collect! Do you hear me? I don't have the money! I quit!"

Everything that belonged to her went in, no matter how cheap or replaceable. She was tired of starting over with nothing. Her shit was coming with her. She might be human garbage, but her daughter wouldn't be.

"You can't quit, you're fired! Get busy, because if you don't find the money you owe me by tomorrow, Shaky-eyes will become your problem, not mine!"

The last person Shaky-eyes had caught, a working girl, had been found dead in a dumpster. If Maude sent him to rough up Ronnie, there was no chance the baby would survive.

"I'm sorry, okay? I would have collected if you sent me to the right address!"

"What are you talking about? Where did you go? You retard! Please tell me you didn't bash the wrong house!"

She was used to that word, but it still bothered her. Ronnie would never call anyone that, ever. "Fuck you! I nearly got shot! I don't owe you money! Stop threatening me! I can't do this anymore!" No more of Maude's lies. The gaslighting made her feel insane.

When everything she owned was in the bag, she jogged down the stairs carrying it over her left shoulder, cricket bat tucked behind her in her right hand, dread tight in the pit of her stomach, armpits sweating in anticipation of the confrontation awaiting her below. White noise murmured on the television and the house smelled like pot cookies baking in the oven.

———

Fog near the ceiling. The house smelled like burning cookies. Pounding on the outside of the front door, a neighbor shouting.

Breathing hard, Ronnie dropped the cricket bat and felt lighter. Now that she was free to go, she found she couldn't. Her legs wouldn't obey her brain, perhaps because her reason to run had evaporated. She rubbed her face and leaned against the wall, trying to slow her racing heart by slowing her breathing.

Sirens outside. Flashing lights.

She opened the oven door, releasing a cloud that set off the smoke alarm.

In a daze, she turned off the oven, stepped over the motionless body that was too horrible to look at and the wreckage of a silverware drawer upended across the floor, found a loaf of bread, opened the fridge and made herself a sandwich. She couldn't remember whether she had eaten breakfast and she knew she hadn't had lunch or dinner.

Cops beat the locked front door and back door. They would break one or both down this time, for real. This wasn't a rehearsal. This was the last one.

Holding the side of her stomach made it hurt less. Hopefully it was only a muscle sprain, not something to do with the baby. She rubbed the sharp pain under her belly button.

Time stopped. The trash bag with everything she owned waited hopefully beside the front door like a dog that didn't know its owner had died. She felt bad for it.

Focused on eating the sandwich, she walked away as the front door splintered and flew off its hinges like in a movie.

Cops piled in with guns drawn—semi-automatic handguns, she noticed, Glocks. She liked those. Her mother had an illegal one. The van was more of a gun cabinet than a camper, didn't even have proper beds. She walked to the bathroom, locked the door, sat on the toilet and continued eating the sandwich. Turkey, ham, and cheese, with lettuce, tomato and mustard. It tasted bloody good.

"I don't mind shaking down drug dealers who owe you money, I mind being tricked into doing evil shit to innocent people! You sent me to the wrong house because I wouldn't have sex with that guy!"

She wondered what juvie would be like, wondered if it would be like television.

"You need to apologize to me and admit that sending me to bash a random house was fucked up!"

The ultrasound tech had said the baby was a girl.

"You know I'm pregnant! Why the fuck did you send me to get my head blown off? I could have lost the baby! You would sic Shaky-eyes on me and my baby?"

Sitting on the toilet, she wiped her cheeks with cold hands, cradling her burning stomach and the welt that would be a bruise tomorrow.

She took another bite of the sandwich. Maude had been her last vestige of a social life. There had been so many red flags. Maude would have pimped Ronnie's daughter out to pedophiles and convinced her it was her own idea.

Ronnie's life didn't matter now. If they locked her up, her daughter would be safe, escape this place and grow up anywhere else. That was all she could think of to do, to protect her kid. She could get her out of this bloody house.

Reg would be so disappointed. Ronnie's phone had cracked in spiderwebs, but miraculously still worked. She dialed with shaking hands, then leaned forward on the toilet, closed her eyes and pinched the bridge of her nose. The line rang.

A policeman opened the bathroom door and stared down at her. Ronnie held up her finger, then pointed to the phone.

Her dad answered, sleepily. "It's the middle of the night."

The officer shouted something back to the other officer.

Ronnie's eyes burned as she swallowed the sudden lump in her throat. "Dad, I fucked up." She hid her eyes with her hand. "I'm sorry."

"I'm not mad, baby. I'll come get you. Where are you?"

"Maude's house. Gordonvale. The police are here. I'm in trouble. I'm sorry."

"Remember what we talked about. Stay calm, do what they tell you, and ask to speak to a lawyer."

"I will. I love you, Dad."

"I love you, too, Brum. I promise it'll be all right. Just try to stay calm and think happy thoughts."

She wiped her eyes with the heel of her hand.

"Do you remember my phone number?" He recited it.

She recited it back to him, voice quivering. Now three police officers were in the doorway staring at her, talking to each other in low voices.

"Good girl! You memorized it! See! You are so smart! All that practice we did paid off. You can do hard things. I'm so proud of you, baby. Remember what we talked about. If they take you into custody, I probably won't be allowed to call you since I'm not legally your dad. They won't let me call you. You'll have to call me. Call me."

"I remember. I will."

"If you forget my number, you know my name. They can look it up."

"Okay."

"Don't be scared. They're not going to hurt you."

"I think I killed Maude."

The three officers in the doorway had been talking to each other but fell silent and looked at her when she said that.

Reg swore. "It was self-defense. Tell them it was self-defense."

"I don't know. I think I blacked out."

"It was self-defense. Whatever happened."

A female paramedic pushed between the three police officers to crouch in front of her. "Are you hurt?"

Ronnie nodded.

"Where?"

She pulled up her shirt to show the red mark on her stomach. The paramedic looked at it, then left.

One of the officers tapped his wrist. "Time's up. We're arresting you now."

"Is she dead?"

"Stand up slowly with your hands above your head."

Ronnie stood up but kept the phone pressed to her ear. Standing up hurt—cramp low in her belly. She steadied herself against the top of the doorframe. "I gotta go, Dad. They're booking me or whatever."

"That's all right, baby. You're safe, and that's the important thing. Remember to call me. I will always answer your calls. I will never stop fighting for you. You are so smart. You are strong."

"Thanks, Dad. I'll call you, when I can."

"We'll fight this in court."

In the kitchen of the old house, paramedics carrying a body on a stretcher out the front door pushed silverware out of the way with their boots. "I'm pleading guilty, Dad. They're definitely charging me with something."

She held the phone to her shoulder while a police officer patted her down. "Can I have my own ambulance? I think I might be going into labor."

"We'll take you to get checked out. Turn around."

She tried to stand still while they patted down her back. "Sorry, Dad."

"I love you, Brum. This was my fault. I knew it was bad, but I didn't know how bad. If I had known, I would have been more proactive. I should have parented harder."

"Don't be ridiculous." Now he was blaming himself. She didn't deserve him. The wall in front of her blurred and disappeared. She pressed the phone to her shoulder and turned her head away as an ugly sound leaked out of her mouth. She needed a hug. Suddenly the loneliest she had ever been, sensing she wouldn't see him again for a long time, she covered her mouth with the back of her forearm.

"Shh, baby, it'll get easier. One day at a time. I'll find you as soon as I can. I promise you'll be all right without me. If you don't see me, it's because they physically stopped me at the door. I'm never giving up on you, so you can't give up on yourself, right? You're a good kid and you have a bright future. No one can take that away. Remember that. This is not who you are."

A short, heavy-set officer with buzzed hair stepped forward. "State your name and address for me, please."

"Ronnie Peterson." She gave Reg's address, the purple house on Pademelon Road. "My dad is Reg Madonna. I'm sixteen. I don't have a legal guardian. If you need to call someone, call my dad. This is him." She held out the phone. "Do you want to talk to him?"

The officer shook his head. "I'm arresting you for assault and attempted murder. Do you voluntarily surrender?"

"Yes."

7
WRIST

The 24-hour clinic in Atherton was quiet coming and going. It was dark by the time she left. A woman had taken an x-ray of Ronnie's wrist, splinted it and sent her home. The doctor would see her in the morning.

For a few minutes she sat in the dark carpark. She could go back to the donga. She could go to her dad's. She could go to the pub. Her dogs were at the donga in Tinaroo. She should feed them.

She drove east. No need to make a decision yet.

When the road split, she made the selfish choice, turning right onto the Gillies Range Road toward the farm. Nev would know what to do.

Nev always knew the right thing to do.

Time went wobbly at night in the old truck, when she couldn't remember what year it was. She noticed she was disassociating and became emotional about it. Her splinted hand snaked inside her shirt, fingertips grazing a hard six-pack on their way up to where the broken rib had been.

Twenty-five minutes later she turned left onto Boar Pocket Road. The horizon opened and dropped to reveal a hidden valley between Lake Tinaroo and mountains. At night it became a series of overexposed two-dimensional images that only existed in the brief time they were illuminated by her headlights. The road followed rolling hills dotted with white Brahman-cross cattle in one paddock, sheep in another, improved pastures and tree-lined ravines, then past the large wooden sign for Upsend Downs. She had planted those azaleas.

She was a person who planted azaleas.

She pulled into Nev's drive without signaling, no one else in any direction—the way she liked it. If it had been daytime she would have let herself in through the open front door without knocking. Since it was dark, and Nev's collies were silent, she parked under the flood light beside Nev's silver F-250.

Never surprise a gun-owner in the country at night. She wouldn't make that mistake again.

The front step bent under her weight. She had been after Nev to fix it. Inside, Nev told the dogs to stop barking. "It's only Ron, quit."

Nev answered the door in a robe and slippers—she had clearly been drinking, but not too much yet—and gestured her in.

Inside, the telly in the bedroom talked. Nev had been watching a documentary.

Ronnie's eyes prickled, then blurred. This would be one of those nights they cleaned up with a mop and never talked about again. She tried not to fall apart all at once.

Nev frowned at the splint on her wrist. "Bit of a barney, was it?"

She had prepared a funny line about eating shite at the skate park, but it stuck in her throat. This felt like an allergic reaction, the way her body reenacted one of her old episodes. Even people who had been to therapy for a decade could get triggered sometimes. Nev was the only person who treated her like she was normal regardless of what shape she was in.

Nev disappeared into the kitchen. She followed. Nev opened the freezer, tossed a bag of peas on the table.

She looked at it for a minute, then reached for the bag, which was soft, and held it to her splinted wrist.

"Have you been round to your dad yet?"

I feel like I have a bag over my head, she thought.

Instinctively, she turned into Nev's shoulder, which was lower than she wanted it to be. Hugs from the older woman were rare, reserved for special occasions. Nev was a good hugger, although most people would never guess that from looking at her. One of Nev's secret talents was taming skittish horses, which came from the time she spent overseas in conflict zones working with children.

Nev patted her back. "Shh…"

Ronnie wiped her eyes. "Don't call anyone…"

"Shh… You'll feel better after you talk to your dad. Let's call Reg."

Ronnie shook her head. This wasn't something he could fix. She didn't want his help. She swallowed. "Can I sleep here?"

"Yeah." Nev flicked on the electric kettle without looking at it. "You can."

Beyond the kitchen, the living room with its arched timber-frame ceiling reminded her of ten years ago. No matter how hard she tried, she couldn't escape her mistakes. Everywhere in this town triggered embarrassing memories. She wondered, not for the first time, if she should move away. Start over somewhere else where she didn't have a reputation.

"What did that woman do this time?" Nev refused to say Maude's name.

The answer felt childish, insignificant, hardly worth saying out loud.

She watched Nev absently worry the electric kettle's on-off switch.

With her back against the kitchen wall, she explained the

bags of corn, explained how frozen food defrosted and frozen again could form ice. It didn't sound so bad. That was the problem with Maude—nothing she did to Ronnie sounded as bad as it felt, which made it hard to complain. Maude didn't need to touch her to hurt her, she could do that with a glance. Ronnie knew she had lost all sense of perspective when it came to her ex, which made her panicky and angry. Was Maude an evil bitch, or did Ronnie deserve everything her ex threw at her and more? She wanted to believe the former, but suspected the latter.

Nev listened. When Ronnie finished, Nev carried two cups of tea into Nev's bedroom and set one on each bedside table. Why were there two bedside tables? She had never had a roommate in all the years Ronnie had known her.

"She only acts like a bitch when her mum is visiting. Her mum's car was in the yard." It terrified Ronnie because there was nothing she could do about it. *I feel helpless.*

"You think she's using again?"

"I don't think so. I think she's still mad at me." Maybe rightly so. Maybe not.

"Want to call the cops? File a report?"

Ronnie shook her head. She could never do that. Maude wouldn't hurt Rainbow. Maude's mother was there. They loved Rainbow. The girl wasn't a hostage.

Rainbow wasn't a hostage.

Ronnie sat gingerly on the edge of Nev's bed, chest and arms tingling. Nev shrugged out of the bathrobe into a frayed jean shirt and put on a headlamp. "Ima get your dogs. You stay."

Ronnie lay down on her side and closed her eyes.

Rainbow. Fuck.

She should steal the girl. In another life she would have become an outlaw on the run. That life was so close to this one she could taste it. In that other timeline Ronnie was toothy and useful, unafraid of Maude, the police, and being put in a windowless box.

The compulsion to protect the girl remained, a decade later, as irresistible as it had ever been. Life would be easier if the state had taken that from her as well. Sometimes she wished it had.

No one said out loud that the place had broken them.

Ronnie had done this to herself—drank the Kool-Aid, sold out, stripped away her favorite part of herself—anything to buy herself more time on the outside where she could see the sky and feel the temperature drop at night.

Selfish. The need to be comfortable, to touch grass, to be loved, to never be alone.

She hugged a pillow, covered her head, forced air in and out of her lungs. Imagined she heard the buzzing of the fluorescent tubes in the ceiling that didn't turn off.

She wasn't tough like her friends from juvie.

She wasn't going to any correctional institution again.

Nev returned with Matilda and Maya, who promptly ran around the house wagging their tails and play-fighting with Nev's collies while Nev propped a baby gate across the bedroom doorway to keep them out for a while.

Ronnie had been tugging at the elastic band under her armpit with her good hand, wrestling with the sports bra that had become a straitjacket.

Nev disappeared into the kitchen, reappeared with scissors. She chuckled as she sat down behind Ronnie on the bed. "This brings back memories." Nev might have been referring to a war; Ronnie didn't ask. Nev cut the sports bra up the middle of the back. "Your bras are too tight. They aren't supposed to leave red marks."

Ronnie eased the loopy black elastic snake over the splint on her arm, shrugged back into her T-shirt, then sprawled across the duvet. "Sports bras are supposed to be tight."

"Depends who you ask." Nev paused the telly. "What do you want to watch?"

"That looks fine. What is it?"

"Documentary about the man who wrote *Shantaram*." Nev glanced over at her. "The book wasn't bad."

The made-for-television film by the Australian Broadcasting Corporation profiled the life of a bank robber born in Melbourne who escaped prison in broad daylight, fled to 1980s Bombay and set up a free health clinic in a slum before writing an international best-seller about his decade as Australia's most wanted man.

"How much of it did he make up?" she wondered.

"How the hell would I know?" Nev said.

Ronnie smiled weakly. Her arm hurt.

Nev kept unopened toothbrushes under the bathroom sink for when Ronnie and Rainbow slept over. Ronnie brushed her teeth. In Nev's bed, she propped up her wrist on extra pillows.

The floor-to-ceiling windows on the far wall were black, but in the morning there would be a view. She loved it here.

Stone House had a soul. Conceived in the eighties as a repro-duction of a stone-and-mortar country cottage in the Cotswolds, the structure had gradually morphed into something a third British, a third French and a third Australian. The country gardens had been inspired by formal gardens Nev visited when she lived in Paris.

Nev wasn't snobby. She didn't drive a fast car, get her hair cut and colored at a salon, or take luxury vacations. All of her trav-eling had been to conflict zones for work, most of it Agence France-Presse embedded with French armed forces, although she had briefly worked for the UN. Now she invested in sheep, alfalfa, and potting soil for her plant nursery.

When Ronnie rolled over, the older woman raised her arm to let Ronnie rest against her. Ronnie closed her eyes with a sigh. She was still uncomfortable, but she could sleep here.

Time had never moved the same since that night. As usual, she reminded herself that she wasn't that teenager anymore—Ronnie Madonna was a grown-ass woman with old feelings and old problems, trapped in a relationship she didn't want with a woman she hated, resigned to work minimum-wage jobs forever, like her mum, but it could be worse. Yes, it could definitely be worse.

"I can't believe it's been ten years since the night we met."

Nev rubbed her back, neither agreeing nor disagreeing.

Ronnie opened her eyes. "Why did she give me your address?" The taxidermized barn owl stared at her from its perch in the corner. Nev had inherited the owl from her mother, had it flown in from Christchurch. It had arrived in a box with a dead mouse; bizarre coincidence or a postal carrier's idea of a joke.

"No idea." *No eyed deer.*

"We would never have met, otherwise."

Nev held her loosely, looked thoughtful. "We would have met two years later when Debbie Collins told me you were looking for work. The real question is, why did Debbie tell me you were looking for work? Did she know your dad?"

Ronnie shrugged.

"Reckon I should put animatronics in it. Clap on, clap off, that sort of thing."

"What would it do?"

"Normal owl stuff. Turn its head, hoot, ruffle its feathers. What do you say?"

"It could have a remote."

"Nah, I'd lose it the next day. Better be voice-activated. Like Alexa."

Ronnie laughed. Nev did, too. The older woman's laugh was silent, a vibration in her ribcage. Ronnie closed her eyes, asking her neck and shoulders to relax. They sort of did. "It could be on a timer, but random."

"Only sensible suggestion so far. Maybe Deb was doing Peg a favor." Debbie was pub owner Peggy Collins's youngest child and lived with her. "Why would Peg..." Nev fell silent. "Ah."

"What? Tell me."

"I told Peg about the break in. She must have told Deb."

"That doesn't explain why Debbie connected us."

"Neighborhood karma," Nev said. "People like feeling they facilitated a resolution. We're probably overthinking it. They probably just thought 'there's a dyke, she should work for the other dyke.'"

Truth.

The documentary ended. On her request Nev put on the 1994 performance of Riverdance at the Eurovision Song Contest. The lead male dancer in the flowy silk shirt and blonde mullet looked like a younger version of Nev.

"This brings back memories," Nev said.

Ronnie checked her phone. A missed call from Reg, a text from her cousin and two texts from Mikey. Nothing from Rainbow.

"Why did you never have kids?"

"Reckon I never met the right person at the right time."

Ronnie understood. Plenty of incredible people never met the right person at the right time. Being single wasn't a reflection of any inadequacy or lack of desire—at any age. Nev's pajamas were buttery-soft, acid-washed chambray. Ronnie lay half-entombed by pillows, feeling lucky for this compassionate woman's affection and pampering, like she was doing something illegal and getting away with it. Truly, she was the robber who had never left. Nev leaned over to turn off the light. Ronnie complained until Nev came close again. Under normal circumstances Nev would have teased her about having mommy issues, but not tonight.

Nev was warm and soft. She smelled like sheep, lavender, and vermouth. Ronnie was not completely clueless. If Nev had been twenty years younger or Ronnie had been twenty years older they would have tried to be lovers. They might have dated. Class and education differences had never created tension in their friendship, maybe because Nev was in a different stage of life.

Flat on her back, eyes closed, Ronnie tried not to think about Rainbow. It was a strange feeling. Nev's hand was muscular and callous-rough in her own but smaller and colder. She didn't need to say thank you. Sometimes she did. It was obvious that she was grateful. Nev knew that she admired and looked up to her, although every time Ronnie said so, she threatened to have Ronnie committed. Ronnie didn't mind being the big dumb one who moved rocks. She knew she had the better end of the deal.

She couldn't understand why a powerhouse like Nev hadn't been scooped up yet. Ronnie's boss was the ultimate package: looks, brains, and personality. Ronnie only had the face the genetic lottery had given her, and had an easy time finding lovers.

Nev sighed. "Do you want the pep talk now or in the morning?"

"Morning."

"Love you, Dain'y."

She smiled against the older woman's flat chest in the dark. "Love you more."

Ronnie woke to a pounding headache and the smell of coffee. Nev set the French press on the end table near her head: the older woman's sense of humor in a nutshell, understated into oblivion, a nod to the years she worked for the French press.

"Take a leak and hop in the ute. I want to be back before noon."

Ronnie peered at the table. "Cup?"

Nev returned, placed a ceramic mug in her palm. Ronnie levered herself upright onto her elbow and poured herself a cup of coffee. "Cream?"

"In the fridge. Help yourself."

"Shitty room service." She sipped the coffee black.

Nev returned with the cream, poured a generous splash in Ronnie's cup.

"Ta."

"Don't get used to it. Up."

Nev opened the passenger side door for her. Now that the sun was hot, pushing nine o-clock, Nev's patience for what she called 'faffery' appeared to be in steep decline. "In case you haven't noticed, you're not a skinny little bird anymore who can fly loop-de-loops on a half-pipe and bounce off the ground like rubber. Gravity is not your friend. Your ex is out of line. Don't let her treat you that way."

Ronnie's wrist hurt.

"You are winning at life."

She felt a sudden pressure in her chest and swallowed. Maude would never hurt Rainbow.

"I feel better today."

"Knew you would. Magical how that happens." Nev glanced at her and back at the road.

Gum trees flew by the window.

"You're young. From where I'm sitting, you're a kid. I'm still bunging dings out at my age. You're right where you're supposed to be. Doing bloody well compared to other people."

"You think?"

"You're a hard worker, Dain'y. You're reliable and honest. You're a fantastic mum. You pay attention to your kid. It's normal to be off the rails in your twenties. You think Barney or Ric-Rac have it all figured out?"

She raised an eyebrow.

"You are winning at life," Nev repeated. "You just can't see it yet."

It was noon when Nev dropped her and the dogs off at the donga park in Tinaroo. The clinic had been cold and bright. A doctor in watermelon-patterned scrubs had fiddled with her swollen wrist, pushing and pulling bones back where they were supposed to be. Now it was in a black cast elbow to thumb and throbbed in a way that made it hard to think.

Nev walked up the front step of Ronnie's rectangular aluminum trailer. The cardboard door swung inwards. "Pound a glass of water, watch footy and eat something that doesn't appear through a window and come in a bag. No work on the farm today."

"I'll see how I feel later."

"Tomorrow I'll line you out with projects around the house."

Her truck, which she had left at Upsend Downs, had already been parked in front of her donga.

Small town magic.

8

DAINTY

FOUR YEARS EARLIER

If Nev didn't go, Reg would harass her about it later, so she made an appearance at the party. He did that for Ron's birthday every December, invited all his relatives, friends, and coworkers from the fire station. Two matching gold foil balloons tied to the front veranda. Ron was still only twenty-two, the age Nev had been when she graduated school, moved to full-time war photography and effectively became an adult.

Ron didn't have graduation ceremonies, so it was less clear when she was supposed to grow up. Maybe her family would coddle her and keep her eternally young, free of responsibilities. Nev caught herself. That thought wasn't fair. Rainbow was a responsibility. Could have been. Should have been.

Behind the purple Madonna house hid a tropical North Queensland paradise—a large pool, several shopbuildings, sheds full of off-road vehicles, a vegetable patch, archery targets, charred fire pit, a badminton net, and a playground, none of it visible from the road.

She found Reg at the barbeque flipping bratwurst and burgers.

His face lit up when he saw her. "How ya goin'?" He tapped his half-empty stubby of Carlton Mid against her full one. Behind him, Ron and her cousins played touch rugby on the lawn. Judging by the misty look in his eyes, this wasn't his first stubby. "Blaise is a Christian. It's her deal. Have to respect the wife's deal. Never question another man's religion, politics, or sports club, right? Anyway. I never understood the Prodigal Son story."

Be nice, Nev warned herself. *He's a sentimental drunk.*

He flipped a row of prawns on the top rack with his tongs. "You're lucky you don't have kids."

She took back every good thing she had thought about him.

He peered downish at her.

It was her turn to say something. *You're an arsehole. Why did Blaise marry you again?* "Christ, Reg. Don't ever tell someone that, you insensitive bastard."

He wasn't listening. "Thanks for taking a chance on her. It means the world to me. She's my world."

"Don't mention it. She's a good worker." Her irritation faded when she looked over at the lawn and saw Ron sprinting with a rugby ball, chased and tackled to the ground, laughing hard.

"She wants to be like you when she grows up."

Bloody hell… Cue the panic. "You're kidding."

Reg laughed. "She looks up to you. You're her role model."

"Bullshit. I know for a fact you are." Nev was no good at this conversation. Is this how he talked to his mates? Was this him including her in normal male bonding around the barbie? Maybe all the Madonnas were over-sharers? Was he buttering her up for bad news? Or was it a warning to be more careful?

The following morning, Nev sat at her desk as Ron leaned across her to see the new STAFF shirts on the computer screen. Ron sipped a Fanta. "What about that long-sleeve neon yellow one that says quick-dry?"

"It would turn brown immediately. We haven't had dark shirts in a few years. How about brown?"

"A light color would be cooler."

"Got it, boss." Nev clicked on the shirts Ron wanted. "Still a large?" The tag of the shirt Ron was wearing said XL. Nev sat down again, ordered three for each employee. "Your dainties are showing."

"My what?"

"Is that the style these days? Pants sticking out of shorts?"

"Bugger off. What's a Dain'y?"

"Daintys? Underdaks? Underpants?"

Ron laughed. "No one says dainties, mate. That's like two hundred years old."

"My exact biological age."

Something rested on top of her head. Nev froze in her desk chair. It took her a minute to figure out that it was Ron's chin. Nev patted one of the hairy forearms wrapping her in a hug.

"Go on, scram."

Ron left whistling, taking her fanta with her. Affection was a youthful affectation, a form of benign manipulation indicative of innocence or its opposite. Nev knew better than to be flattered by attention. If anyone caught her holding her cheeks she would be mortified.

It wasn't that Ron was a flirt—Ron didn't know she was boundary pushing, checking for moral weakness. If Nev did anything unprofessional, Ron wouldn't be safe. To feel safe, Ron needed proof that her boss' self-control was rock solid one hundred percent of the time.

Nev needed to be super-human.

If she admitted she didn't feel the age difference, friends would misunderstand. That was the oddest thing, feeling no superiority over this one, having to constantly stop herself from asking Ron for advice on how to do things.

Sometimes when the two of them were out fixing fences or

baling hay, she forgot her dad was dead, forgot she was the boss now. It was an easy mistake. Ron was easy to look up to.

Nev had to be careful not to let her guard down.

It was safe to want something she couldn't have. She hoped it wasn't a Freudian thing, although with her luck this professional relationship would end up having wholesome mother-daughter undertones.

The worst part about feeling young again was catching a glimpse of her reflection in the mirror and being surprised by the crow's feet in the corners of her eyes and the grey at her temples. So many wasted years... What had she accomplished since she was twenty-two? Nothing.

The problem with thinking too much was that it caused her to do too little. She couldn't let that happen again.

Someone had to protect Ron.

9
BLAME

The Lionheart Volunteer Fire Station was quiet in the middle of the day on a Tuesday. Nev walked in the unlocked front door and up cement stairs to the office.

Reg looked up from his desk, pushed back his chair and stood, extending his hand automatically. "G'day, Bickerman."

Nev shook it. "G'day, Madonna."

"How ya goin'?"

"I'm going to sit," she said.

The fire chief gestured to the empty chair. "What's going on?" He crossed his arms.

Nev sat down and rested a boot on her opposite knee before she explained about the frozen corn.

Reg rubbed his face and looked overwhelmed.

"Will you deal with it, or should I?" Nev asked.

"Definitely not you. Stay out of it," Reg said. "She wants to be more independent. I can't always swoop in and rescue her."

Nev stood up and put her hat back on. No one had ever swooped in and rescued Ron. That was the problem.

"Don't look at me like that," he said. "And don't do something stupid. This isn't time for heroics."

She frowned. It never was, was it? She glared at him. "I thought you changed."

"What does that mean?"

He knew bloody well. She tipped the brim of her Akubra. "Enjoy the rest of your arvo."

When she was out the door and halfway down the hallway, Reg called her back. He leaned forward on his elbows at his desk. "Shut the door."

She did.

He held his forearms. "How do you think custody is split?"

Nev raised her eyebrows. "Maude majority, Ron partial?"

Reg shook his head. "Did she tell you she has partial?"

"I know she does."

Reg sighed. "She gave Rainbow up for a closed adoption. She doesn't even have visitation rights. No contact. Maude was a caregiver when Rainbow was with her nan, then became foster parent and later adopted her. There's no way to undo an adoption unless they file a joint petition together. We've all researched it. Maude would have to consent to share custody with her. Maude lets her have every other weekend because Brum pays pretend child support and she's a free babysitter, but there's no paper trail. Maude doesn't have to let her see Rainbow. She could cut us off at any time and move away, not tell us where she went."

Nev swallowed. "Right." The idea of the Madonnas losing Gumball turned her stomach. "Why didn't you and Blaise take the baby?"

"We tried. I'm not on Brum's birth certificate and Matilda-Jane never married me—"

Nev couldn't help but roll her eyes. *Does this man think he's Ron's biological father? If so, god bless...*

"So I couldn't talk to her for two years when she was in that place, you know. I waved to her from the car park. You don't know how much you love someone until you can't see them. They arrested me for trespassing, it was a whole deal—that place is a bloody nightmare. I'm shocked no one's burnt it down yet. After she got out, I adopted her, but it was too late. Rainbow was in the system. I did what I could. You know, she's not the brightest bulb in the box, and without someone advocating for her..." He popped his knuckles.

The nuclear family was a scam. "We need to get Maude to sign papers."

"Brum does. She should have asked Maude to let her have some parental rights back years ago."

Ron must be terrified to lose every other weekend with Gumball. Nev would be in a constant state of anxiety if she was her. The situation was worse than she thought. How had Ron been functioning all these years?

"I wish she had told me."

"What could you have done?"

Nothing.

Reg made her a cup of tea in the firehouse kitchen. He should have gone into politics. He handed her a chipped mug with a fire department logo on the side. Nev cleared her throat. "Who moved her truck this morning?"

He shook his head. "Not me. I assumed you did."

"You know what they say about assumptions." Nev blew on the Earl Grey.

Reg also drank his tea without milk, but his was basic black tea that came in a big box. "Are you two dating yet?"

Nev snorted. "No."

Reg opened a bag of biscuits, offered her one which she refused, then dipped it in his tea and ate it. "What has she told you about the bloke who knocked her up when she was fifteen?"

Caught off guard, Nev uncrossed her legs. "Nothing. Why?"

Reg looked thoughtful. "She's still protecting him, then. I think he's older." They were alone in the firehouse, but he glanced at the door behind her before he continued in a low voice. "I'm afraid it's one of my mates."

Shit... Now she felt sorry for him. That must be a nightmare, not knowing who he could trust. She felt a pang of guilt that he didn't know about the break in, but it wasn't her story to tell, and it wasn't any of his business. Maybe he was trying to trick her into spilling the beans with a fake heart-to-heart.

Reg frowned and swore under his breath. "This isn't an interrogation, mate. Why is your guard up all the time? Who did this to you?"

It was a fair question, but the answer wasn't a person.

Reg continued. "I reckon we're two angels on her shoulder. On the other shoulder there's demons, but I don't know who they are. I think there's another bad influence out there, maybe the baby daddy. Someone worse than Maude."

Who could possibly be worse than Maude?

When he put it like that, he was probably right. Weird for him to say that to his daughter's boss over a cup of tea on a Tuesday afternoon. Reg was a bit of a drama hound, come to think of it. Nev snorted.

He got up and washed his mug, set it to dry in the rack next to the sink. "What would we talk about if Brum had her shit together?"

Good question. "Footy, obviously." Nev washed her mug. Her conscience pricked her again. It was generous of him to accept a stranger into their lives and make her feel like she belonged.

She set her mug in the drying rack and wiped her hands on a towel. Reg watched. She wondered what he thought about her.

She jammed her hands in the pockets of her jeans. "How old are you?"

He blinked, then broke into a wide grin. "Forty-five." She could believe that. He was lucky he still had a full head of hair. "How about you?"

"Guess."

He chuckled. "I was taught never to guess a lady's age."

"I'm forty-six."

He looked surprised.

Nev put her hat on. "Thanks for the tea. In the future, don't talk to me about Ron." *I'm not a member of the family and I'm not your friend.*

"You came to me, remember." His expression softened. "I'll see what I can do."

10

GOLDEN TICKET

Mosquitos swarmed Ronnie at dusk as light spilled out Reg's front door onto the raised veranda with the timber pillars and arched dollhouse trim. Cast in a sling, she awkwardly pulled open the screen door with the hand that was carrying a bag of ice and stepped inside. "Oi, Da! I got the ice for the esky!" Ceiling fans pulled a cross breeze through the drafty house, competing with the sports radio in the kitchen and the game on the telly.

Nonna had cooked spaghetti bolognaise and chicken parmesan.

Ronnie used the hand that wasn't in a cast to put the ice in the cooler, then bent to hug her grandmother and give her a peck on the cheek. "Ooo, spag bol and chicken parmi, my favorite!"

"What happened to your arm?" Nonna asked, visibly concerned.

"Skateboarding accident."

Nonna and Blaise winced in sympathy. Orphaned baby wallabies in the family room made rattling sounds when they licked their water bottles. Reg frowned across the dining room table. "Nev dropped by the firehouse."

Ronnie pulled out a chair with the hand that wasn't in a cast and sat down slowly. The table was silent. In the family room wallaby water bottles rattled.

"Are you all right?" Nonna asked.

"Yeah," Ronnie lied. Inside the cast, her wrist throbbed.

"You need to be more careful," Reg warned.

Ronnie scratched her neck. She needed a shower.

Nonna looked at Reg, then at Ronnie.

"I don't want to talk about it."

Reg glanced at his mother, then back at her. "Did you ask about sharing custody? Is that why she went off?"

"No." That wasn't a conversation she looked forward to having.

She had no appetite, but served herself chicken parm on spaghetti bolognaise anyway, to make Nonna happy.

Blaise met her eyes across the table. "I'll send you a list of lawyers tonight."

"Thanks."

Her grandmother reached over to pat her leg. "We're sorry that you have to deal with this, darling. We're here for you. We'll support you."

"Thanks, Nonna."

"I'll pay for the lawyer."

"No," Ronnie rushed to say. "Really. I have money."

Reg rolled his eyes. "Ask the lawyer if there's any chance they can get you full custody."

"They can't. I don't know how she's such a good mum. I keep expecting her to do something horrible to Rainbow, but she hasn't."

Divorce was like that sometimes, she had heard. Some shitty exes were okay parents. At least she and Maude had been in agreement from the start not to use Rainbow as a weapon. They had done one thing right in this dumpster fire of a relationship.

"Stay away from her, Brum."

Ronnie swallowed. He stopped going through her phone years ago. Hadn't he?

"Aunt Suki saw pictures of you two on a boat at Lake Tinaroo. Cover your ears, mum. No more booty calls. You're not like your brother. Now's not the time to sabotage yourself when your life is about to turn a corner."

What corner? "She didn't ruin my life, I did. I'd rather be who I am, where I am, than who he is, where he is." This was mostly true.

Reg scowled at her. The women passed parmesan and pepper around the table.

"If you're a masochist, join a BDSM dungeon or date a cop." Reg worked himself up. "If her mother sees those pictures she'll drive circles on my lawn. You're a good girl and you need to look good. Your reputation is in rehab. Protect your reputation like your life. Go on dates with nice girls."

"I went on dates last week." One didn't go anywhere, but the other turned into a second location and an overnight in a fancy hotel.

"How did those go? Any second date material?"

She shrugged. "They seemed nice." The doctor had been a fun time.

"But they live in Townsville? That's a load of nothingburger. That's not happening. Find a nice girl who lives five minutes away. Someone who likes animals, long walks in the rain and adores you. Someone reliable. No drama. Boring is good in a partner."

Blaise agreed.

"I'm not looking for a partner." Casual dating was one thing. Inviting a stranger into Rainbow's life was unthinkable.

"Because you have Nev."

"Come again?" Ronnie said.

"You're not looking for anything serious because you have... Forget it. Rainbow has to be your priority."

· · ·

When she got home she found another envelope in the mailbox and tossed it on the kitchen island to open later. Blaise had already emailed her a list of three lawyers. She looked at their websites, but didn't find their rates reasonable.

She picked up the white envelope that lay on the kitchen island and studied it. The return address said 'Australian Football League.' She ripped it open. Inside was a typed letter with half a page of text and a signature at the bottom.

Holding her breath, she resisted the urge to skip to the end, and focused on reading one word at a time.

"Dear Ms. Madonna, Congratulations on being awarded MVP of the South Cairns Cutters last October. We would like to invite you to try out for the Brisbane Lions Women's this October…"

No fucking way! A professional team! This must be one of Mattie's elaborate pranks, payback for the vegemite in his sneakers last Christmas. He would do something like this. She put a wooden spoon handle under the line she was reading and moved her fingers from one word to the next, reading it out loud to herself.

"Training camp week will be held at the Brighton Homes Arena in Springfield. Candidates are responsible for flights and ground transportation to and from the facility. Room and board are provided."

Holy shit! She covered her mouth and leaned on the kitchen island, staring down at the letter.

Ronnie slid her fingers into her hair and pulled it by the roots. "No fucking way…"

She called Mattie to ask if this was one of his pranks, but he denied it.

"Send me a picture. I need to see this."

She did.

A minute later, Mattie cheered.

She hung up and texted the photo of the letter to her dad and Mikey. Reg called her immediately.

"Is this a joke?"

"I don't think so?"

"Are you going?" Reg asked. "Might as well. You're a legend on the Cutters. The Lions should have scouted you years ago. I don't know why it took them so long. Maybe you wouldn't have to move there. Tryouts would be good for you. Give you something healthy to focus on."

Now that she realized she had a choice, she became frantic. "I have to, right? I can't say no. This has been my dream since I was five..."

A text came through from Mikey.

(Mikey) OMG CONGRATS!!!!!

She heard Reg sigh and blow a raspberry over the phone. "Yeah, you gotta go. You deserve this."

She could guess what he was thinking. If she won equal custody of Rainbow, she couldn't move three days south to Brisbane.

"I've been looking at lawyers. They're crazy expensive."

"The ones Blaise sent you do a sliding scale."

What if Maude said no? She probably would say no. If Rainbow was only with Ronnie every other weekend, she could swing travelling back and forth on an airplane. If Maude cut her off all together, she could definitely move to the big city. Rainbow was the only responsibility keeping her here on the Tablelands.

"I knew you'd get scouted eventually, Brum. You're fast as, and you're the best ruck the Cutters have had in a decade." She appreciated that her dad didn't rain on her parade.

"Thanks, dad. Love you."

"Love you, Brum. Congratulations. You should be proud. It's an honor to be invited, another notch for your belt, regardless of what happens."

She tossed the letter on the pile of paid bills. "Yeah." Her heart fell. She had never been on an airplane. Commuting across Queensland seemed wasteful and bad for the environment. She couldn't ask Rainbow to fly alone twice a month. Rent in Brisbane would be astronomical compared to here, but her salary there might be higher. Something to research.

No. She couldn't seriously consider it.

Could she?

11

MURPHY'S LAW

In the morning, she found Nev in the horse barn filling water buckets. Her boss did not appear surprised to see her.

"This better be a social visit," Nev said. "You're on sick leave with that arm."

"That could all be automated. Timers on faucets are a thing now. You said you had easy faff I could do?"

"Never said 'easy.' Said indoors."

Nev's office was a disaster. She hadn't been lying. Now that Ronnie thought about it, the tile floors could use a mop. Not her specialty, but she could figure it out.

"You had a cleaning lady."

"She retired, by way of death."

Ronnie swore. "I'm sorry. Was she nice?"

Nev shrugged.

Ronnie didn't know what else to say. "Want me to hoover?'

Nev looked around. "Yeah. Wash the windows with newspaper if you feel up to it."

Lunch at the kitchen table, turkey and cheese sandwiches with mustard, baby spinach, and pickled beetroot. They listened to the game on the radio. Barney, Ric-Rac and Kazi ate esky lunch on the veranda.

Ronnie had been waiting until she was off the clock to show her boss the letter. She took it out of the back pocket of her jeans now, unfolded it, and slid it across the table.

Nev raised an eyebrow, shot her a questioning look, then picked up the letter from the Brisbane Lions. "What's this?"

She watched her boss skim the letter, saw her inhale in surprise and push out her chair to stand up from the kitchen table.

Ronnie returned the bear hug. "Thanks." She sat back down at the table after Nev did and picked up the letter again. "Murphy's Law. This is happening now to test my resolve."

Nev didn't disagree. "When do you have to reply?"

"It doesn't say." She studied the letter again. "I can ignore this until I find out if I'm getting equal custody of Rainbow." She couldn't say out loud the alternative.

"You'll always have her, one way or another." Empty words, unusual for Nev. Ronnie's boss looked down at her sandwich. Reg must have told her how screwed Ronnie was.

"Thanks. I can't talk about it right now. It bums me out."

After lunch the lads went back to work on the farm and she washed more windows.

Nev eyed her up on the ladder with the cast elevated on one side and a bucket of water balanced on her knee and frowned. "Come down from there before you break your neck."

When it was time for her to coach soccer in Atherton, Nev gave her a glass of lavender iced tea. As always, she downed it in one gulp.

On the wall, the framed portrait of the white European mother being evacuated, weeping alone in the back of the United Nations armored van after they forced her to leave her Tutsi husband and children behind. Heartbreaking stuff, violent without showing blood. The story was offscreen, hidden in what was missing, what wasn't in the photo that should have been, like those 'find the difference' illustrated worksheets Rainbow brought home from school. Ronnie had always been bollocks at those.

She didn't love the photo. It felt too intimate, like something she didn't deserve to see. Give the poor woman some privacy in the worst moment of her life. War photography was a strange profession, making art out of other people's pain. It was ruthless, in a way, capturing and selling grief.

Nev had won awards for it. One of them lay taped to the back of the portrait. Ronnie had found it one night, snooping around while her boss was asleep.

She handed the empty glass back, kissed Nev on the cheek.

12

JUDAS MADONNA

TWO YEARS EARLIER

In October, Nev was quizzing eight-year-old Rainbow on spelling words out on the veranda of Stone House when her phone rang.

Bush fire at the Jacobsens. Again. Bloody hippy homesteaders with their twelve blond barefoot children, had a dry underbrush problem, never listened when she warned them to clear it out. Lovely people, always stopping by for a cup of tea.

Ron was inside playing the drums loudly with headphones on, rocking out.

She went inside where Ron could see her. Ron took off the headphones.

"Fire at the Jacobsens. Keep your phone on."

Nev drove alone up the access road towards the homestead on the hill, smelling smoke, seeing traces of it over the treetops. Sometimes, she forgot whether any of this was real. Reality had stopped making sense again when the State of Queensland revoked the Civil Partnerships Act a few months after it became law. Lawmakers had changed the words "civil partnership" to "relationship" and gotten rid of ceremonies. Nev had been used to the world not making sense, but that was over there; this was here.

Ron appeared half an hour, an hour later; Nev had lost all sense of time. Bush fire generated its own time zone, urgent and all-consuming. The Jacobsens were fighting the fire with water again. One of these days she was going to sit them down and force them to watch a video about firebreaks. Maybe the one with the farmer dragging the plough behind his tractor, corralling the massive wildfire in his neighbor's wheatfield like it was a hungry dragon tied up by a delicate silver chain. The fire stopped when it reached the bare earth. That only worked if the windspeed was mild or moderate.

Nev shouted commands with gestures.

The Jacobsens followed her directions like wide-eyed sheep watching a shepherd. Ron was scraping out the grass between the fire and the house with the Kubota. "Ron!" No answer. "Dain'y!" The kid looked up, looked where Nev was pointing. Nev pointed to the creekbed next to the drive, where small trees on either bank touched in the middle.

Ron went. The kid took the chainsaw from the tractor bucket and began clearing the bank on the fire side of the creek, felling the small trees without having to be told.

Afterwards, when the leading edge of fire had stopped spreading, and the rainforest uphill was crawling with firefighters, the Jacobsens gave them a cold beer on the veranda. Nev accepted a clean bandana, wiped soot off her nose and mouth. Her clothes were soaking wet, which felt nice, but the sun was setting and the temperature was dropping. She wanted a hot shower.

Mrs. Jacobsen reached over to clink Nev's glass. Finally not pregnant for once in her life, poor bugger. "You're a well-oiled machine! How many fires have you fought?"

Nev had to pause to think. "Counting this one? One."

The beer was nasty, home-brewed shit from the shed out behind the Jacobsen's pig shed. Why anyone would want to raise pigs was beyond her. But hey, to each their own.

"I can't believe you've never done that before."

"I have," she clarified. "Ron's first time."

Ron slouched in a wicker chair, glowing like a tomato, barely a hair out of place. Looked happy.

"You're a natural, Dain'y." Bone tired, shaking, back sore. "Go sleep twelve hours. See you Wednesday."

The neighbors knew all the words of the standard folk songs; even the toddlers clapped and sang along. They played 'Wild Rover,' jigs and reels. The Jacobsens danced, arm in arm, spinning around the garden without a care in the world.

She drove home in the dark, took a hot shower.

Slept like a baby.

Wednesday, lunchtime. Whistling, Nev assembled sandwiches while Ron studied the row of black and white photos in the hallway. Ron spent the most time on a photo of a European woman in a patterned sundress weeping in the back of a UN truck. In the bottom right-hand corner Nev had written *Judas Madonna* in the cursive she had learned at the Parisian all-girls boarding school, not her usual chook scratch.

"What's her story?" Ron asked.

"I didn't ask. The French and the UN evacuated Europeans."

"Operation Amaryllis."

"Look at you," Nev said, surprised that Ron had looked it up. "Curiosity killed the cat."

"She left her kids behind?"

Nev nodded. "In hindsight I would not have named it that." *Judas Madonna* was a preachy title, a short sermon positioning the artist above the subject.

"It's accurate," Ron said.

"Don't judge her." Nev wondered how to explain love to someone born after Live Aid. "She couldn't have saved them."

"What happened to her?"

"How would I know?" The woman probably went back to her parents' house and rebuilt her life from scratch or killed herself.

Ron pointed to the photo. "It's a self-portrait."

Nev frowned. She lifted Gumball's water gun off the table, pulled the trigger. Ron didn't flinch.

Afterwards, dripping, Ron held out her hand. Nev handed her the super soaker, contrite. Ron pumped it for a while, then soaked Nev's pants. Luckily the family room floor was tile.

"Are you done?" Nev asked.

"Are you?"

Nev snorted. "Don't you have something useful to do?"

Ron left.

Nev looked at the photo, studied the tiny reflection of herself in it, the image of the photographer clutching the camera, a young woman with long blonde hair and a black circle instead of a face.

13
LAWYER

Sunday evening in late February, the day before Ronnie was supposed to meet with the lawyer, she had Rainbow. She listened for the lightning that would electrify Reg's metal counters, vibrate the glass and shock the cousins through their chairs. Aunts, uncles and cousins sat at the long table on the veranda eating boiled dinner when spatters of rain ping-ed off the roof and a wall of water fell between them and the grassy yard. A waterfall from the heavens beat the grass, saturating the loam, filling it to overflowing.

Rainbow planted her fists on the table and howled. She blew out a whooping banshee cry, eyes squeezed shut, mouth wide in an "O" showing a perfectly round unchewed slice of salami. Ripping off her shirt, she jumped up on the bench and ran across the table whipping it in circles above her head. She stood in the grass grinning and catching rain on her tongue as more kids ran out tipping their heads back as the rain soaked their long hair and plastered it to their necks. The little cousins jumped on each other's backs and galloped out of sight up the jungle path.

Her uncle looked up from his card game. "That was you. You were like that."

. . .

The next dawn, riding childless again, lonely and relieved, she parked her motorcycle under the carport at Stone House and turned off the engine. Nev wasn't there, so Ronnie stood on the veranda under the eaves to wait. The older woman walked up the hill towards the house with the dogs in the rain. Nev looked like a shepherd in a waxed canvas barn coat, stick in one hand, other hand tucked in a pocket.

Ronnie watched the front door swing open at Nev's touch and followed her inside. Nev hung her wet Akubra in the mudroom and flicked on the electric kettle in the kitchen before leading her to a table in the family room covered with books.

"Big day, meeting with a lawyer. How do you feel?"

Nev offered her a plate of raw vegetables before biting into a thin slice of white radish that looked like a full moon. Nev ate them mandolined every morning from August to March.

"Good."

Ronnie picked one. It was wet with its own juice. Sunlight from the window illuminated it from behind, revealing inner patterns like the cratered surface of the moon. Rubbery, slimy, it had the surface texture of a carrot and mouth-feel of an apple. It was delicious. Peppery and surprisingly sweet. She swallowed it, took another.

Soccer practice was cancelled, so after work she drove back to her donga in Tinaroo, fed the dogs, reached under the kitchen sink and grabbed the box of garbage bags. She shook one out, then pulled it over the cast until her fingertips pressed against in the corner of the bag. She pulled the plastic taut, pushed her fingers through the thin black plastic one by one. She bit a rubber band, stretched it out with her free hand, pushed the cast hand through, then let it snap shut around the garbage bag at her elbow. She admired her homemade cast-cover, opened and closed her hand. It would keep the cast dry for a while.

The two-lane paved road north to Mareeba was slick. If this

continued, there would be washouts soon. News radio was all updates about the path of Cyclone Marcia. She had been upgraded to a category five cyclone off the coast sometime last night. She was making land now, near Shorewater Bay, north of Yeppoon, striking a relatively uninhabited area. The State Emergency Service (SES) was helping people evacuate from the path of the storm.

The lawyer's office was in a commercial building between a petrol station and an athletic field. Ronnie ran inside, head-down against a wall of water.

Inside the atrium of the office building she pushed down the hood of her sweatshirt. Indoor trees, some kind of ficus. The lawyer's office was on the second floor. The building smelled like a doctors' office. Soft jazz played in the elevator.

The secretary, older woman, handed Ronnie a clipboard with forms to fill out in the waiting room.

A middle-aged woman wearing a polyester dress that fit her like a glove, and high heels, came out and offered her hand. "You're Reg Madonna's daughter?"

"That's me."

"You work for the graziers? They'll be flooded. The Barron's about to jump her banks. All over the news. Gillies washed out yet?"

"Not yet. Thanks for taking my case."

"Pleasure to meet you. Come on in. A petition for a hearing is an easy process if you file jointly with the custodial parent. Have you asked your daughter's mother if she is willing to file jointly with you?"

The lawyer's office had a desk, a chair for clients, and a floor-to-ceiling window that was currently a view of the inside of a waterfall.

Ronnie shook her head.

The lawyer sat down behind her desk, sliding glasses that had been in her hair down to the bridge of her nose. She folded her hands on a manilla folder. "You can ask her to come in and meet with me, or I can send her a letter. It will go better if you talk to her first. Then she and I can arrange a time for her to come in and sign the first round of documents."

"Can you just call her?"

"I can if you prefer that, but I don't recommend it."

"Do that. Please." She watched the woman scribble on the legal pad. "How many rounds of documents does she have to sign?" She had a sinking feeling.

"Two. One in my office to file the joint petition, and another in the courthouse on the day of the hearing. If she expresses reservations, there are things we can try to ease her into it. Don't worry about that now. This meeting is for me to get to know you."

After some housekeeping about sliding scale hourly rates and confidentiality, the woman closed her laptop, folded her legs and pulled a legal pad onto her lap. "You assaulted your partner in '05. That's on the public record."

"Okay."

"This is confidential. Why?"

"Why what?"

"Why did you assault her?"

Ronnie sighed. There was no easy answer. "Self-defense?"

"Explain."

Ronnie rubbed her knuckles along her lips. "She was selling drugs. She had me shaking people down, roughing up dealers who owed her money. I never got caught. Neither of us did. She was my business manager."

"What sort of business manager?"

"Footy, music, other things. We thought we were entrepreneurs."

"How did that start?"

"She got shagged at church camp, started going on dates with older men she met online. She did that when I met her. She retired from that, moved to back of house, started setting up other girls."

The lawyer's pen moved across the yellow legal pad. "Your partner was a pimp?"

"You could say that."

"Was she your pimp?"

Ronnie hesitated. Wanted to laugh for some reason.

"How old were you when that started?"

"Fifteen. I only did it a handful of times."

"Is that how you became pregnant?"

Ronnie shook her head.

"How do you know?"

"I was doing handies, mate. Hand jobs."

"Did she make you do that whilst you were pregnant?"

"She didn't make me do it."

"How did Maude feel about the pregnancy?"

Ronnie shrugged.

"Bad for business?"

She nodded.

"Did she ask you to get an abortion?"

The nervous urge to laugh was gone. Ronnie nodded.

"Was she physically abusive?"

"She would say it was self-defense."

"She hit you?"

Ronnie nodded. "We beat each other regularly. It wasn't a one-sided situation. We went at it. Often it was foreplay."

"Does she still manage working girls?"

"No."

"Is she still selling drugs?"

"No. She tattoos tourists."

"Was the fight you had ten years ago your last?"

This woman was sharp. Ronnie smiled. "Next question."

The lawyer looked up from her legal pad, over her reading glasses, to study Ronnie. Awkward silence. Eventually the woman leaned back and sighed. "This isn't going to work. No judge will give you custody if you're beating this child's mother."

Ronnie flushed, angry. She scratched the cast. "I think you misunderstood." Her wrist hurt. "Can I call someone?"

The woman blinked, surprised. "Sure. You can step outside. I'll wait."

Ronnie pulled out her phone and dialed her dad.

"Do you want me to step outside?" the lawyer asked.

She shook her head as the phone rang on her dad's end. He could fix this. He was at work, but he answered.

"Hiya Brum."

"Hiya. I'm here in Mareeba with the lawyer."

"What's up?"

"It isn't going well."

"What can I do?"

"Talk to her, please?"

"Sure thing, baby. Put her on."

She handed the phone to the lawyer, who to her credit, rolled with it.

"Hello?"

Her dad talked the woman's ear off for a while. She couldn't hear what he said, but eventually the lawyer thanked him and returned the phone to her.

The lawyer scribbled in her legal pad, then looked up. "I'm sorry that this is still happening."

"No worries."

"I shouldn't have assumed. I've worked on cases like this with Blaise, through the nonprofit she works for at the Community Centre in Lionheart. I'm happy to work with you on this."

"Thanks. I appreciate it."

"No worries. Now, where were we? The fight that proceeded your arrest. What was it about?"

She shrugged. "I don't remember. We were arguing about money. Things got out of control."

"Did you try to leave?"

"Yeah."

"Why didn't you?"

"I wasn't thinking clearly."

"Drugs? Alcohol?"

"I never did those things whilst pregnant."

"After the police arrived, then what happened?"

Ronnie swallowed. She wasn't comfortable talking about this, but owed it to herself to try. "They arrested me because I look like this." Ronnie gestured to her six-foot-three self, including the black T-shirt, men's gym shorts and work boots. "They always assume the unconscious person is the victim." God, that sounded awful. She sounded like a dick.

Her eyes stung. She blinked. She wasn't allowed to cry here. "I don't think it was my fault."

The room became a sauna. Ronnie broke out in a sweat. She shouldn't have said it wasn't her fault. Now the lawyer would think she hadn't accepted responsibility or been reformed.

"She made it clear that she would, you know, nail everything we had done on me."

She winced. She could have walked out of Maude's house that night. She saw that in hindsight. She should have accepted Nev's offer to stay for chicken parmi. The solution had been right in front of her, but she hadn't been able to see it. Her life would have gone in a better direction if she had eaten that parmi.

"Shit messes with your head when you're a kid," she said.

"Did you gather evidence against her?" the lawyer asked.

Ronnie shook her head. "She was always gathering evidence against me. It never occurred to me to do the same. She's smarter than I am."

"Don't say that. We can't move forward without her support. Since you don't feel comfortable asking her, I'll call her and explain the situation, and then I'll be in touch to let you know what our next steps will be. Do you have a social worker on the case?"

Ronnie shook her head, palms sweaty.

"We'll need them to write a report. Start building a paper trail showing how often you care for your daughter, what you pay for, etc. We'll need a report from the social worker saying that you're capable of providing equal custody. The state will do a home review where they visit your house."

"No problem." She swallowed, feeling lightheaded. It occurred to her that she might faint. "Is it going to be a problem that I live in a donga?"

"Shouldn't be, if it passes inspection. The state will send their own person around to do that."

Numb, she shook the lawyer's hand, stood up, thanked her again, and left.

She got lost in the hallway, but eventually found the atrium with the indoor trees.

14
CYCLONE

Ronnie ran to her pickup in a downpour and drove home in a gale, wind howling, trees leaning sideways. Wipers swinging wildly barely dented the fingers of light and color obscuring her windshield.

Main Street in Tinaroo was under a shallow oily puddle. Traffic crawled. After the ice cream store she signaled and turned left down a gravel drive.

The sign for her mobile home village flapped in the wind. The shared drive along the back of the chain fence behind the Maccas car park bore a collection of potholes and puddles. Standing water already filled low areas between aluminum dongas, turning couch grass lawns, cement patios and gravel parking spots to blurry grey glass, dark mirrors reflecting storm clouds.

Minor flooding, so far, but if rain continued for days the water levels would rise. Water was the strongest thing in the world. Floods were the most expensive natural disaster in the state, causing billions of dollars of destruction each year. A river that jumped its banks was more destructive than wildfire. The Barron periodically wiped entire neighborhoods off the map, leaving behind nothing but mud scars and broken trees.

This neighborhood would need to be evacuated, or someone's

nan would cark it and be found weeks later sunk into a moldering mattress. Ronnie should have received an emergency text alert from the manager.

Dogs barked as she rolled down Lane B. The lawns between Lane B and Lane C were a pond. Neighbors' inflatables and kid toys floated up against chain-link fences, queuing like school kids.

Her side lawn was one with the neighborhood puddle. The patio she and Mikey had laid last time her friend visited was under water.

When she opened the door of her truck a wall of water instantly soaked her arm. She heard Matilda and Maya barking inside the donga. Hunched against the rain she fumbled with her keys, then edged through the door sideways so the girls wouldn't run out. They ran between her and the steel barrel where she kept their food.

"I already fed you, babes, but I know you've had a stressful day."

She scooped dog food into their bowls. Matilda and Maya leapt at their bowls like they hadn't been fed in days.

A flash of lightning, close, eerie like power flickering, then an ear-splitting crash shook the donga. Electricity hummed in the walls. Ronnie held her hands in the air, careful not to touch anything metal. People had been electrocuted during storms like this.

Where was Rainbow?

The dogs wolfed down their food and licked each others' bowls. Rainbow must be at school. Kids didn't get electrocuted at school. Rainbow would ride the bus home and run up the rickety front steps of Maude's white wooden Queenslander. Rainbow would spend the evening on the couch watching telly or reading in bed. Either way, she wouldn't be in danger.

Her worrying wouldn't make the girl safe. She could call Maude, but then what? *Please make sure my daughter doesn't touch any metal countertops or take a bath tonight?*

She opened the fridge, staring at the vanilla slice she had

bought for Rainbow yesterday. She had meant to send it home with her.

It stared back, sad and lonely. She ate it.

Another eerie flash of white light. The dogs tore through the donga, whining and shrieking like they had been kicked. They knocked over chairs in their hurry to scramble under the table.

The family room was a mess. The dogs had been panicking while she was in Mareeba. She picked up the chairs as she crossed the room. Wet carpet smell. The dogs had probably peed in her bedroom.

Ronnie flicked on the overhead light. Her bedroom carpet was under water.

Huh. Her donga was on cinder blocks. How high must the water be outside? It hadn't looked that high. Surely the water hadn't risen while she was feeding the dogs?

Ronnie shrugged into her raincoat. Her cast was too big. She cut the wrist of the raincoat with scissors.

She stuck her head out the back door, then took the plunge and waded barefoot through water up to her ankles. It was cool. Water in the back garden came up to her shins. If it had been moving it would have been dangerous.

She went back inside, threw Rainbow's clothes in a duffel bag, then loaded the dogs in the passenger seat of the truck, bribing them with strips of bacon. Her laptop, charger and phone she put in a garbage bag.

The office manager at the primary school in Atherton answered on the third ring.

"Ronnie? Is that you?"

"You all right?"

"We've got all the petrol for the generator. We haven't lost power yet."

"I'm assuming there's no sport this arvo."

"All afterschool activities cancelled. They're already talking about cancelling school tomorrow."

"Keep me posted."

"Cheers, love. Ta."

Next, she called her dad, who didn't answer. She called Blaise, who said he was at the fire station.

"Tell him there's heaps of rain headed this way."

She locked the door of the donga, then drove over to her cousin's house. His dog was out in the back garden, yapping his head off. She threw him in the truck with Matilda and Maya. The dogs wagged their tails and sniffed each other. She let herself into her cousin's donga, took his yappy little Chihuahua, too. The tiny one immediately started fighting all three of the others, as she had known he would.

Ronnie went down the line, knocking on every door.

A few elderly people were still at home.

She helped them call their relatives to come pick them up. A few of the elderly people didn't have relatives nearby, so she called 000 to come help them evacuate.

Women showed up in trucks, started moving boxes out of dongas.

Ronnie drove the dogs and a sweet old nan named Sheila to the farm. Sheila was at least eighty and deaf in both ears.

Nev's back door was unlocked. Ronnie held onto the white-haired woman with the walker so the dogs wouldn't knock her over, helping her shuffle to the kitchen in her slippers. "Make yourself at home, Sheila. I'm going back for another run." Ronnie grabbed a box of PG Tips out of the cupboard and filled the electric kettle. "Make yourself a cuppa. Eat anything you can find."

"Is this your house?"

"No. This is Nev Bickerman's place."

"I thought the view looked familiar. Right down the hill there was the old Shangri-La. Beautiful house. Burnt down in seventy-one or seventy-two. Such a pity."

Ronnie wrote the address on a piece of paper, and the phone number. She pointed to the landline. "You can use the phone." Then she hugged the elderly woman and went back out into the rain.

. . .

The clock in the empty truck glowed. Where had the last four hours gone? Ronnie turned right onto Boar Pocket road, then right onto the Gillies Range Road. It was getting dark already. Storm dark.

She had to turn on her headlights to see the road. Even then, with the wipes going at top speed, she had to crawl to stay in her lane.

The Gillies was the main road through the mountains, two lanes, on the edge of a sheer cliff. It wasn't uncommon on clear days to look over the side on a bend in the road and see a car upside down, caught by a tree.

Ronnie pulled over to check her phone. Missed calls from friends and relatives. She called Nev. No answer. She texted her about dropping off the dogs and her eighty-year-old neighbor, then pulled back onto the Gillies.

Fifteen minutes later she drove through Lionheart. The roads were puddles, but passable with four-wheel drive.

Ten minutes later she was back in Tinaroo at the donga village. Several more trucks had appeared: relies helping each other salvage what they could. She picked up where she had left off knocking on doors.

She dropped off a scared kid at the police station. That was hard, brought up memories. He looked like he was about Rainbow's age, but unlike Rainbow, he wasn't very talkative. He didn't know where his mum was. Ronnie could relate. She had been that kid. His mum would be frantic when she returned home and found her kid missing.

She drove back in the dark and left a note on the woman's kitchen table.

The next time she looked at the clock in the truck she thought it was wrong. Five hours had felt like two. There was still so much work to do. Neighbors were helping each other, though, so she felt all right calling it a night. The only people left in the mobile home park were a few random men moving boxes into utes, a strange man with a pet Amethystine python that probably wasn't legal, and some teenagers casing the place.

As she was leaving, a patrol car pulled in. Mouth suddenly dry, she gripped the wheel a little tighter.

The paddy wagon stopped in front of her. The driver was looking at her in the headlights. She forced herself to keep her eyes straight ahead, tasted adrenaline.

The officer stepped out of the vehicle. Ronnie swore. She rolled her window halfway down. Water poured in, soaking the inside of the door.

The officer shone a light on her.

"What are you doing, Peterson?"

She stopped breathing. *It's Madonna now, and you know it...*

The officer shone the torch into the passenger seat. "Running a dog-walking business now, are we?"

She swallowed. Brad Collins. She had met him when she was a freakishly tall teen with orthodontics who liked to party in the wrong part of town and fall asleep in random places. He had given her rides home on dark and stormy nights like this. Why was he in Tinaroo? Last time she checked he still worked for Lion-heart. Solid man. Married. Three kids around Rainbow's age. Nice guy. Too nice.

"Relax," he said. "How about this weather?"

The light turned off. She glanced in his direction. He was backlit. She couldn't see his face. She locked her doors.

He turned his head, disappointed. He was getting soaked.

"Are you stalking me?" she asked.

He laughed.

"You know I live here," she said. "You don't work for Tinaroo. You're out of your jurisdiction."

"I work for the county."

"Since when?"

"Why did you lock your door, Ronnie?"

"Don't. I've had a long day. I'm trying to help out some dogs."

"Owners left them?" He shone the torch in the truck again.

She looked away. "Is this because I called dispatch about python guy? Did your nan send you?" Peggy Collins was his grandmother. "I told her to send social services."

"Can't send Imelda in the middle of the night for psychedelic Steve-o, can she?"

Ronnie could hear "Crank That (Soulja Boy)" blasting from the camper van with the strobe light flickering in the dark window.

"That him?" Brad asked. "Lovely. How much do you know about scrubbies? They're constrictors, strong as. No shelter would roll that dice."

"Reckon he needs a motel."

"He can sleep with his girlfriend in a cage at Happy Paws." The animal shelter in Lionheart. Brad gestured to the ball of dogs writhing in her passenger seat. "Want me to take the kids to the pound?"

"What if their owners don't come?"

"Happy Paws."

His proposition was tempting. "You'll need food to tempt them into your car. Be nice to Steve-o."

Brad Collins walked away. The patrol car pulled up beside her passenger door. He got out again. Sighing, she unlocked the door. When he opened her passenger door all five dogs poured out. One by one they jumped in the back of the paddy wagon. He shut his door gently, then stood in the rain.

When he slid into her passenger seat and jerked the door shut she clicked on the overhead lights.

He offered her a cigarette. She shook her head.

"Trying to quit?" he asked.

"What do you want?"

He lit up, took a short drag, blew the smoke away from her. "You know what I need. I need to see my kid."

"Over my dead body." Boo hoo. She had no sympathy.

"Is that a threat?" he teased.

She spoke slowly. "I don't have beef with you. Don't start beef with me."

"I would never."

"I'm minding my own business. You do the same."

"Or else what? Look, Ronnie. I'm tired of being blackmailed by you."

She laughed. "You don't know what that means."

"I'm not ashamed of what I did. Everyone makes mistakes."

She saw black and red. A red streetlight two blocks away reflected in the water on the windshield.

"Let me put this in basic terms. You have something I want. You have all the power in this relationship."

"There is no relationship."

"I'm willing to compromise. You aren't. Eventually you have to meet in the middle. Fair's fair."

"You're making me uncomfortable."

"Sorry. I'll go."

"Now."

"I'm going. Think about it. That's all I'm asking."

He still had shiny bronze skin, freckles, smelled like cologne, and filled out his tight uniform in a way she liked. He still had acne on his neck and beneath the uniform a jagged scar on his chest shaped like Japan from the time a homeless kid, not her, knifed him.

I will never have a change of heart. Fifty percent of nothing is nothing. She isn't your daughter.

He opened his wallet, folded something, tucked it in her cupholder.

How many other fifteen-year-old girls he had slept with? She wondered where he met them. If he made them promise to keep it a secret. If he pressured them to get an abortion, then acted like he had no idea who they were, like they were strangers meeting for the first time, when they crossed paths in the check-out aisle at the Big W.

She sighed. "Does Rainbow have other half-siblings I should know about?"

He appeared genuinely surprised. "I told you. You were the only one."

"The only one who got pregnant?"

"I messed up one time. I've been faithful to my wife. I would pass a lie detector test right now."

She believed him. Brad was a selfish prick, but he had never lied to her. She hated how easy it was to forgive him.

She watched him get out of the truck, close the passenger door, and get into his squad car in the rain, then waited for him to drive off. He seemed to do the same.

She turned on the engine, glanced at the patrol car again out of the corner of her eye, then put the truck in drive. The patrol car flashed its headlights.

She stopped at the stop sign, counted to three in her head, then signaled right, let her foot off the brake and turned the wheel.

Two hundred-dollar bills.

Everyone's conscience manifested differently. He felt less guilty when he slipped her money. She didn't encourage him.

He did it for himself. It was cheaper than a therapist, and she imagined it made him feel like a big fucking hero.

The dickhead was blackmailing himself.

15
FLOOD

Back at Upsend Downs, Stone House smelled like something warm and fruity. Ronnie stripped the wet black trash bag off her cast, dropped it on the boot mat. It had been effective for a few hours.

She lifted her wet hat off her head and bent down to hug Nev, then gave her the usual peck on the cheek. "I need to eat a large amount of meat immediately."

"I know. I made *coq au vin.*"

"You're the best. Where's Sheila?"

"The woman you kidnapped?"

Ronnie stumbled into the family room and collapsed face-down on a beige suede couch.

"Sold her to the mob for five quid."

"No rape jokes, please. Not funny."

"What happened? Long day?"

Nev lit candles. Ronnie wolfed down two plates of red wine chicken with haricot verts and garlic mashed potatoes. Nev plugged an ancient blow-drier to an extension cord, then balanced it on a pile of books on a chair, blowing at the damp cast.

"That's a fire hazard."

"You're a fire hazard. Stop moving."

"Seriously, where's Sheila?" Ronnie asked.

"Imagine my surprise. I get home. Telly is on. I think nothing of it. I hop in the shower, come out naked as jaybird, find my house has been hoovered, bins emptied, floors waxed, two pies have been baked, and someone's granny is on the sofa knitting a jumper while watching The Price is Right turned up all the way."

"Did she see you naked?"

"She's nearsighted. Her daughter came and grabbed her."

Ronnie raised her eyebrows, then shrugged and returned to eating. She ate two slices of pie and a bowl of ice cream.

"You're not in a family way, are you?"

She ignored the jab. "I didn't eat dinner."

"How did the meeting with the lawyer go?"

"Fine, I think."

"Is she hopeful?"

Ronnie shrugged. "Fingers crossed." She took the bills Brad Collins had given her out of her chest pocket, laid them on the table.

Nev whistled. "What's this?"

"Guilt money from Rainbow's sperm donor."

Nev swore, flattened the bills. "Not feeling heaps guilty, is he?"

"Right? That's my feeling. What would you do with it if you were me?"

"Me?" Nev sounded incredulous. She looked at the ceiling for a moment and puffed out her cheeks. "Uni fund."

"That's what he wants me to do."

Nev nodded. "Shakespearean dramas have been written about lesser dilemmas. Is the right thing to do still the right thing if some dickhead wants you to do it?"

Ronnie smiled. Nev jiggled the blow-drier.

. . .

She watched Nev shrug into waterproof overalls and a canary yellow raincoat. The radio predicted heavy rain would hit the Tablelands in the middle of the night. Nev unplugged rechargeable batteries from the charger and tucked them under her arm.

Ronnie reached under the sink for a trash bag.

"No, Dain'y, you stay here."

"Cast is already wet." Her fingers stretched and broke through the thin plastic with a satisfying pop. She snapped a rubber band around the bag at her elbow again. She flipped through the coat closet until she found her old pair of rain pants.

"Fine," Nev said. "Stay where I can see you."

Floodlights mounted on the barns and shop buildings lit up the farmyard, but outside the circle of light the night was pitch. Wind was picking up, storm approaching. They drove down the gravel drive, trees groaning, wind howling, then parked in front of the horse barn.

Nev set two battery-powered lanterns on the table in the office. She turned on the walkie-talking that was sitting on the charger. Farm radios.

Nev held the radio to her mouth, pressed the button. "Kaz." They waited. After a minute Nev tried again. "Drover."

A rough voice crackled over the radio. "Balmy weather, eh?"

Nev sighed, straightening. "How are the girls?"

"Wet," Kazi said.

Ronnie chuckled.

"What can we help you with, boss?" Nev asked.

"I have Barney here. Keep the generator going if the power goes. We'll need it to run the telly."

"What are you watching?"

"The match."

"Beautiful. Carry on. I assume you're counting them."

"No point. They're behind the shed, not going anywhere. If they head for the hills, we'll find them in the morning. We run around the perimeter every two hours."

"Looking for what?"

"Beats me."

"Keep doing what you're doing. I have faith in you. If you need anything…"

"Ron there?"

"Yup."

"Little one called looking for her."

"I'll tell her. Love you," Nev said.

"Love you," the old man echoed automatically.

Ronnie raised her eyebrows at that sign off, had never heard the owner of Upsend Downs and the drover end a conversation that way before. Nev must be going soft in her old age.

The power flickered. She looked up. The lights cut out, leaving them in darkness except for the glow of the hand-held radio.

Nev handed it to her, then flipped on the battery-powered lanterns. Ghostly white light emanated from the center of the table, other-worldly. Nev lifted one. "I'm going to feed the machine." The generator. "Call Rainbow."

She watched Nev's light wobble away through the dark barn. In their stalls, horses whinnied. Dreadnought kicked the wall. She always did that when she couldn't see Brighty. True love was real.

The phone on the other end rang. Rainbow's voice, annoyed. "Mum, where are you?"

"At Upsend Downs. Where else would I be? Where are you, babe?"

"Why didn't you answer your phone? I've been worried sick about you." Rainbow sounded like a little mum. Oldest child for sure. Leader vibes. She would be a type-A chick, take the initiative on group projects.

"Been out in the rain with my phone off, babe, saving battery. Couldn't take it out of the ute or it would be fried. What's up? You alright? I'm sorry. I'm here now. It's been a day. I wish I was there with you."

"I wish I was at the farm."

"You're supposed to be asleep."

"How could I sleep through the worst cyclone in thirty years?"

"Is that what they're saying? They always say that, babe."

"Keep your phone on? Promise?"

"Promise. We lost power but the old lady's gone to start the generator, so we'll do. How about you? Lost power yet?"

"While ago, yeah."

"Lanterns and torches?"

"Yeah."

"You're not scared?"

"Nah. We're over at Nan's." Maude's mother's house. A faded pink house in a rose garden in Malanda. Full of rats. But charming. She tried to picture the terrain, remember whether it was higher or lower than its neighbors. "Is there water in the garden?"

"I don't know."

"Is there water in the house?"

"We've got jugs of drinking water and water to flush the dunny."

"Can I talk to your mama, please?"

"She's asleep."

"In the morning, if there's water in the garden, I want you to call Grandad. He's not far. He would come over and help. You girls could go stay with Grandad. Is that a good idea?"

"Obviously."

"Love you. You are strong."

"Love you, too, Mum. You're strong, too."

"Sweet dreams, baby."

16

FOOD BANK

Ronnie woke the next morning in the hayloft over the sheep barn. Kazi's bedroll was empty. The drover was already out moving the herd. He was an early riser, wasn't happy unless he was outside.

Kazi always wandered during storms. Like an old farm dog, he knew his way around, had his trails, his places he went. He couldn't get lost here. She knew that Nev, who lived in bittersweet premonition of all things ending, dreaded the day he became too frail to go up and down the barn ladder or flip the sheep on their bums. They couldn't put the soft-spoken man in a home.

Ronnie looked at his things in the hayloft since he wasn't there. He owned a handful of antique but functional tools with hand-carved wooden handles, a small pile of books, and clothes that could fit in a backpack. It was a painfully antiquated way of life. Poking through Spartan evidence of a life off the grid didn't give her nostalgia, but she knew it affected Nev differently. Nev didn't go up here.

School was cancelled. No one could go anywhere in a hurry until volunteers cleared fallen trees off the roads and the highway department fixed the washouts on the Gillies Range Road. According to local news radio, the Gillies looked like swiss cheese.

At a folding table in the front entranceway of the closed citizen center in Lionheart a coordinator recorded the names of locals volunteering to saw up the fallen trees blocking the roads.

Ronnie had left her Stihl in the cab of her truck, since it was raining and this wasn't a dick-swinging contest. The man at the card table turned her away when he saw the cast on her wrist. "Sorry, mate. Come back next time."

Life slowed. Energy companies preemptively cut power to the worst affected areas to avoid electrical fires. The town shut off public water for a week. Locals boiled drinking water and checked on their neighbors. Everyone had lost something. No reported fatalities, but almost three thousand people had requested help from the State Emergency Service and tens of thousands of homes lacked power.

The radio said the upper reaches of the Stanley River received more than 410 millimeters of rainfall in two days.

In Lionheart, storefronts remained dark. The local hardware store had a "sausage sizzle" to raise money for the food bank. People eager to fill sandbags had overwhelmed the depot team and were calling the Council asking for other ways to help. Since Blaise was a Shire Councillor, her phone rang off the hook.

At Upsend Downs, farmhands still had to feed the horses and move sheep from one muddy paddock to another. *The Express,* the newspaper that covered Mareeba and Atherton, featured a photo of Nev's neighbor's horses and chooks swimming in a paddock. "It's full on," the neighbor said in a quote.

Water permeated round bales left out in hayfields, left them sodden and moldy, worthless for animal feed. Ronnie knew that when the storm was over, agricultural insurance agents would drive from farm to farm tallying crop losses.

"Can we donate frozen lamb to the food bank?" she asked.

"Good idea." Nev helped her empty one of the chest freezers.

"This is the worst flooding I've seen in the twenty years since I moved here."

The town website listed addresses of food banks in Atherton, Lionheart, and Malanda accepting donations for displaced families. Ronnie jotted them down on the back of an old holiday card.

She delivered two crates of vacuum-sealed frozen lambchops to each of the food banks. They liked receiving donations of protein, frozen meat especially, because most people donated bags of rice or boxes of pasta. Lamb was expensive, felt special, would cheer people up.

Volunteers at the food banks laughed and hugged her. That felt good.

"It's from Nev."

The woman at the food bank in Lionheart had seen her on the telly helping evacuate the donga park in Tinaroo. "You're a hero, Ronnie. A real Good Samaritan."

She was surprised that someone had filmed that on their phone. There hadn't been any camera crews. She wondered if the boy she brought to the police station had been reunited with his mother. She hoped he had.

The volunteer followed her out for smoko on the veranda. They lit up next to each other under the eaves, pressed side-by-side against the building to stay out of the rain. It had been raining for eight days. Biblical. Flood waters rising.

The volunteer leaned against the cinder-block wall with a shy smile. Early twenties, pretty, high ponytail, T-shirt and jeans. They were always the most obvious, the ones trying to be discrete.

Her phone buzzed. It was her lawyer.

"Sorry," she told ponytail girl. "I have to take this."

She got in her truck and called the lawyer back.

"Do you want the good news first?"

"Always."

"Maude came in and signed the papers. She's filing for the hearing to give you joint custody."

Ronnie's vision blurred. Her breath caught, pushing a little high-pitched sound out of her throat that she had never heard herself make before.

She started to cry into the back of her cast, unable to stop the horrible noises that sounded like an injured sheep.

"It's all right, darling. It's good news. Congratulations. We're not there yet, but this is a good sign. Don't get your hopes up too much yet. We've got a date. The bad news is, it's in early October." It was March now. October was seven months from now, in the spring.

Ronnie swore. "I can't wait that long!"

"The magistrate's office is swamped. They have a backlog. I hear they took damage during the storm."

"Can we get on a waitlist or something?"

"That's not how it works." The delay wasn't personal.

It felt personal.

Seven more months of walking on eggshells.

She ended the call and did a face-dive into the passenger's seat, where she lay breathing hard, gasping.

17
MICHELANGELO OF MEAT

In late March, the autumn equinox marked the turning of the year for Nev. Yesterday, Ron had mustered the courage to ask the grouchy neighbor, Johnson, if he would sell her the open hectares of grazing land below Upsend Downs where he ran cattle, but he said no. This hadn't surprised Nev, but Ron had been visibly disappointed.

Accepting defeat wasn't in Ron's nature. After moping around for a few hours, lifting weights and blasting heavy metal, she had cheered up. "He'll change his mind."

Last night Ron had brought her down to admire a row of gnarled pomegranate trees in the gully behind Johnson's barbed wire. Ron had big plans for them. "You like getting attached to things that don't belong to you, don't you?" Nev had asked, rhetorically. Ron had smiled. What a dangerous way to live, with your heart on your sleeve.

Perhaps because she fell asleep happy, Nev dreamed of the time she watched the Tour de France from the Champs-Elysées in Paris.

The dream felt like a gift, a reprieve from the teenager with the machete and the cowering kids hidden under the floor. She hadn't seen them herself, but other people's memories had become her own.

She assumed they all died, but she hadn't heard the end of the girl's story, so she would never know. Women in the village had put the babies under the floor in an attempt to hide them, and the women had all been killed. What had happened to the babies under the floor? Did they meet the same fate as their mothers, the man with the machete? Or did they die of dehydration, later? She hoped someone had come back for them at night. Maybe someone had taken pity on them.

The pub looked half full: not bad for a Thursday night. In the corner a small stage held a drum set, guitar, fiddle and bass. She and Gunni drank a pint at the bar before the Wild Drovers played their weekly set list of classic covers.

Nev was lubricated and running her mouth. She saw Gunni turn with a bright grin and a "Hullo darling!" to welcome someone as a hand squeezed her shoulder.

Someone tall. A man. No, not a man, Ron. Ron bent to give their bass player a peck on the cheek, then squeezed Nev's shoulder again. "Have you done sound check?"

She nodded. "Did you close the gate?"

"Which one? Just kidding." Ron bent to give her a peck on the cheek like she had given Gunni. She was wearing one of Mattie's black Alien Weaponry band T-shirts with the sleeves cut off. She was vain about her arms. Dopamine released by lifting heavy weights hours every day was a kind of drug.

Ron sat down at the drum set in the corner and started warming up.

Nev carried her second pint over to the stage and set it down between her fiddle and guitar, then pulled her fiddle onto her lap. "How do you tell the difference between a fiddle and a violin?"

Ron was in a good mood. "I don't know. How do you tell the difference between a fiddle and violin?"

"You don't spill beer on a violin."

Ron laughed.

At Upsend Downs the next morning, Nev noticed a car parked on the grass at the bottom of the drive. Out of town girls got out and took selfies with the sign. Photography wasn't the elitist art form it used to be when she wore maroon Dr. Martens and smoked hash out of a whalebone pipe at Oxford in the early '80's. Everyone had a camera in their pocket now, every teenager was a documentarian.

She didn't know why the young women stopped, but cars had been doing that ever since Ron planted chrysanthemums in front of the azaleas. How did Ron know to do that?

Someone with the mind of a child had booby-trapped her kitchen. Pomegranates fell out when she opened the fridge door. They tumbled in groups, like penguins diving off an Antarctic ice sheet. She watched, amused, as they rolled across the tile floor in every direction.

A week ago, she had filed the agricultural insurance claim for the storm-ruined hay, and now waited for the approval of the insurance man, and tried not to think about it. She sang inside her head. *A live, a live-o, a live, a live-o, selling cockles, and mussels alive, alive-o...* Being judged by invisible strangers was not her favorite sensation; they had all of her information, but she had none of theirs.

Since the flood, Ron lived in a tent down in a clearing she had cut on the edge of Lazy creek, undaunted by wind, rain, high water, or electrical storms. Speak of the devil, there Ron was now, rolling up the drive on her retro black Kawasaki.

Nev envied her. Ron was a force of nature with her whole life ahead of her.

She wished she could enjoy camping the way Ron did, but sleeping in a tent always reminded her of the uprising in Mali in the early nineties that went on to become a civil war.

Ron's lack of housing was a problem. Ron needed to rent or

put a down payment on a property to create a paper trail to prove that she had stable housing. A tent didn't count as housing—neither, apparently, did crashing in a friend's guest bedroom.

On a whim, Ron had bought a used sawmill—a lumbermill that turned round logs into professional-grade custom boards. It was her new favorite toy. Ron thrived on routine, and exercise to the point of exhaustion, not unlike Gaia and Blair, so Nev wasn't surprised that Ron appeared to be living her best life in her lumberjack era at Upsend.

Nev sat on the grass to watch her work the machine. Ron knew how to use it from a summer spent milling wood for a church camp up near the Northern Territory in a previous life between age nine and fourteen. When she ran the sawmill she wore a safety helmet with a face shield, safety goggles and noise-cancelling headphones.

Nev watched the blurry blade, spinning disc with shark teeth, eat linear holes in one tree trunk after another, waited frozen by morbid fascination for the day Ron cut off her fingers. It looked like that would be easy to do. Ron always wore leather gloves and used safety equipment, rails and guide boards, but even so, it was only a matter of time. Sensible, intelligent people had accidentally lopped digits off.

"Quit," Ron said. "You're making me nervous."

"Sorry." That was Nev's cue to leave. "You could build a house, you know. If Johnson won't sell you a piece of his farm, I'd sell you a postage stamp at market value."

Ron lifted another log, set it down on the table, straightened it, fed it through the blade. She had lost weight felling trees, stacking them, milling them, and restacking them. More specifically, she had lost a layer of fat under the skin on her face.

"You're too generous, mate. I can't take your land. Breaking up a farm's like sacrilege. I'll find something. He'll come around." Ron had a lean, hungry look under the safety goggles, was probably dehydrated; most people were. "If he doesn't, one of the other neighbors will. Someone in Lionheart will sell to me."

"Have you scoped out 'For Sale' signs? Gone to open houses?"

Ron nodded. No takers, then. *Damn.* Becoming neighbors had been too much to hope for, given the price of real estate on the Tablelands.

As Nev got up to leave, she remembered what she came to say. "Chest freezer in the staff kitchen is empty again." They kept frozen meat in it for all the employees but really it was for Kazi, who otherwise survived off tinned beans and spam. Now even last year's leftover ground lamb was gone, eaten up by the lads one frozen half-kilo at a time in pasta sauce and burgers. "Next time you go hunting put some away for Kaz, eh?"

"Will do," Ron said, turning off the saw blade and taking off the ear protection. "Want me to fill the deep freeze?"

"If you like." Recently they had seen signs of feral pigs along the creek, bank churned to mud by hooves. The prints were too big to be sheep and too small to be brumby.

"I'll need your hunting rifle."

"Next time you're up at the house remind me."

Losing half the hay crop from flooding after the cyclone would not have been a problem if the taxes hadn't chosen that month to arrive in the mail. Life was a stack of bills. She had been late in paying an insurance bill before and nothing bad had happened, so she wasn't panicking yet. But... This situation had not happened before, with the hay, and the mortgage, and the taxes. This was uncharted territory. She tried not to catastrophize. Better to wait and see what the insurance company said.

Eight days left until her flight to Kigali.

Four days.

Two. She had plans to meet her Aussie colleagues from UNAMIR (United Nations Assistance Mission for Rwanda) at the hotel bar on the thirty-first. She was the only one who wasn't a veteran of the Australian Defense Force. Packing the dusty leather suitcase always gave her pause to wonder what she would regret leaving unfinished here on the farm if her Qantas flight made a ballistic dive into the Pacific or erupted in a karmic fireball. She would prefer not to leave Ron with a crushing amount of debt. Foreclosure would defeat the purpose of leaving her the farm.

She took a break from packing to ride the grey stallion Rainbow had named Unicorn. Before that his name had been Ned, but he didn't seem to mind the change. Horses were resilient, like children. They weren't neurotic like adults.

Barney was still fixing the baler. Ric-Rac mended fence. Kazi was out pinching the sheep.

Nev dismounted, tied Uni to a fence, walked over to join the old drover. She pinched the loose skin at the top of a lamb's shoulder-blades, felt the fat under the skin and wool, estimating the distance between her thumb and third finger. She and Kazi had been trying to fatten up the lambs. She was good at predicting what the marbling would look like by the feel of the back of the lamb's neck.

Kazi spat on the grass. Nev raised an eyebrow, disapproving. Chewing tobacco, nasty habit. Turned his teeth orange. It was a miracle he didn't have gum cancer yet. "Some of them are decent," he said.

She agreed. Most of them were. She had high standards. These animals would be perfectly plump by the time they went to slaughter in May, but the ritual worrying was what guaranteed they met the standard every year. Perfect marbling didn't happen by accident. She had to fuss over them this time of year.

Ron stood behind the shop butchering feral pigs, hosing blood off the concrete slab, spraying the color red downhill into the grass. She had three of the dead animals strung up in the doorway and was taking cuts off the carcasses systematically with an electric knife, like a butcher in a meat market.

Nev clicked her tongue and put Uni away.

The pigs all had a clean hole through the forehead, execution-style.

She set up another folding table near Ron's work station, ran an extension cord out from the barn, dusted off the old vacuum sealer and brought it outside. Watching Ron cut a tenderloin along the spine felt like watching an artist carve clay or marble. Ron knew exactly what was inside, had a picture of it in her head.

Nev cleared her throat. "This is a sentence I never thought I would utter, but you are the Michelangelo of meat."

Ron chuckled, head tilted in concentration as she worked. An earbud dangled precariously from her ear on a blood-stained white cord. "Years of practice."

"Be careful what you get good at, right? Any way we can monetize this?"

Ron snorted. Not a chance. Pity.

"What are you listening to?" Nev asked.

Ron held out the second earbud. Nev held it up to her ear, curious what kind of music the younger woman listened to when she was deep in the flow state of filleting.

She was listening to *The Lion, the Witch and the Wardrobe* by C. S. Lewis.

Nev felt her eyebrows rise. Unsure how she was supposed to feel, she returned to vacuum-sealing meat at the other folding table. "I admire how productive you've been since you bought the sawmill, but all work and no play makes Jill a dull girl. How is the housing search coming along?"

Ron put the second blood-smeared earbud back in and returned to carving.

Ron gave her hands a cursory wipe on the grass, lit up and puffed away, careful not to touch anything except the cig with her crimson gloves. Smoko time. Blood shrank when it dried, became tight, itched. It was impossible for her not to stare at her own wrinkled hand every time it approached her mouth. Blood lined the wrinkles, threw them in contrast.

Ron didn't appear to mind the mess. She probably didn't see it. It didn't remind her of anything other than what it was.

Maybe that was the secret to happiness, Nev mused. See things as what they are, not what they appear to be.

"I don't think the real estate agents in town like me," Ron admitted.

That was understandable given that they worked on commission.

"You could always buy another donga."

Ron shook her head, then blushed, took a last drag from her cigarette, dropped it on the dirt and crushed it with her boot.

Ugh... That answered the question of who to blame for the disgusting confetti of crushed filters littering the ground.

Ron glanced down at her face, reconsidered, picked up the butts and put them in a trash bin.

It was a shame that such a remarkable person who had lived so much in her years and had such an old soul was homeless again, and a shame that she wouldn't let Nev help her, but that was life. 'Such is life,' the outlaw Ned Kelly had said on the gallows. Pride bubbled up from beneath dirt like water from a desert spring.

18
MVP

Edmonton was an hour's drive to the north-west, past Gordonvale. Nev didn't want to go. A denial letter from the insurance company burned a hole in her pocket. She didn't know what to do. The last-minute decision to go watch Ron's AFL practice in Edmonton was Reg's fault. It wasn't that she disliked Aussie rules football. She had lived on the Tablelands long enough to become a devoted fan of the South Cairns men's team, the Cutters.

Cutters was short for cane cutters. The team logo was a cartoon drawing of a man holding a machete. You couldn't make this shit up. She followed the stats for the women's team but didn't attend games because that was Ron's thing.

In the stands Reg waved, gesturing for her to sit beside him in the direct sun. He had saved her a spot with his jacket. He was wearing a wide-brimmed kangaroo-leather crusher hat.

She worried that the popcorn she brought from home wasn't enough.

Reg leapt to his feet, hands braced around his mouth. "Let's go, cutter giiiiiiirls!" He sat down. "They're tight today." The South Cairns Cutters Women's team season started on the second Saturday morning in April, two and a half weeks from now.

Nev had to agree. This was the tail end of pre-season, so the players were physically in peak form. During the season each team fielded eighteen players with six substitutes. Tonight the team ran a practice match, shirts versus skins, ten to a side with four players waiting to sub in from the bench. Ronnie was running striker for the shirts, full forward, front and center, closest to the opposing team's goal. The other woman playing full forward tonight was also tall.

They watched Ron kick a goal, score six points. Nev clapped.

Reg jumped up, cheered. "That's my girl! Go Brum!" On the field Ron turned and waved at her dad while she jogged.

AFL was unique in that the teams played on an oval. It was a high-speed game, chaotic and violent. Players passed the ball with their feet or their fists.

After Ron's goal the teams reset. The ruck was the tallest player on the team, and a striker could roll into a ruck easily from the forward line. She and the ruck from the other side ran at the ball tossed in the air, jumping up to knock it down. Ron just edged it over the other ruck's hand, and the game continued, ball in play, runners hurtling down the pitch.

Nev watched, amazed. She had never had stamina like that. Every woman on the team had been the best player on her high-school team. They were all-stars.

She sent a prayer of thanks to whatever god had designed polyester footy shorts and footy players' thighs.

Ron wasn't wearing a black captain's armband tonight—older players than her would have seniority—but she scored the most goals: three, and tied for the most goal assists: two.

By Nev's maths, that made Dainty the MVP.

The night before Nev's annual flight to Kigali, Ron lingered late after band practice, in no hurry to leave, perhaps because she had nowhere to go, watching footy in the living room while Nev tried to avoid thinking about Rwanda by instead psyching herself up to do something else vulnerable that scared her. Distract and redirect. Look over here, not over there—one of the first horse training lessons Kazi had taught her. She took a long breath, then forced it out between pursed lips. She could do this. She had done harder things.

"Dain'y. I want you to see something."

She showed Ron the mortgage payment, tax bill, most recent farm account statement and the letter from the insurance company denying her claim on the water-damaged hay.

"You do the maths. Tell me what it means."

Ron went into the office with a calculator. Half an hour later she returned. Nev watched her. Ron carried herself differently. Something about her had changed.

A quote popped into Nev's head, *Render unto Caesar the things that are Caesar's...*

She apologized. "I should have been able to fix this. This was my job." This was way above Ron's pay grade, but of course the kicker was that Nev didn't draw a salary.

"How long have you been supporting the farm with your personal money?"

"I never thought of it that way."

"I know you didn't," Ron said gently, using her mum voice. Nev had overheard Ron use that patient tone with Rainbow when the girl accidentally broke something and then hid it out of fear of getting caught. "How much time do we have?"

That was decidedly not the mum voice. She preferred it over the mum voice. It was like a warm cup of tea. It sent shivers down her spine.

"How much have I got left? It's all there. It's all in the farm."

Ron rubbed her lower lip, but looked determined, like she had made a decision. "In the morning I'll go to the insurance place and talk to our agent. I'll get him to fix this."

"Good luck with that."

"There's a climate change disaster relief grant for farmers I heard about on the radio. You'll apply for that. The national graziers' association has an emergency fund, also. We'll apply for everything."

"Right."

"You won't like this," Ron said, "but how much are you spending on this trip?"

Nev blinked.

Silence dragged.

Nev left the room, stood alone in the dark kitchen. She had created a monster. *It's alive!* You can take the cat out of the box, but you can't put it back in. Now Ron would start noticing things, changing things. She would notice that Nev was an alcoholic, notice Nev still lived in 1994. The thought of being discovered frightened her, but it was also exhilarating.

She hadn't had a business partner since her father died.

She missed Emil. Missed his threadbare slippers and bathrobe, his old man smell, missed the way he looked at her and saw a child, missed being known. Missed the woman he had thought she was. Missed being his daughter.

She missed having a business partner. Making money multiply wasn't her forte. She invested in things that died. She'd rather run a bloody charity.

The question was, could Ron manage money?

She went back in. Ron put down her phone.

Nev perched on the edge of the couch, spread her knees, tented her fingers. "I'll make you a deal. If we don't get any of those fat checks, I won't go next year."

"Deal," Ron said.

Her guilt about burdening Ron with this boring adult problem lightened somewhat the next morning when she woke to find pomegranates in all the shoes: wedged deep inside the wellies under the bench in the mudroom, nestled in her sheepskin slippers under the bed, bowing out the sides of the white trainers by the back door, even plugging every last one of her dad's cowboy boots in the guest bedroom closet.

She hadn't gotten around to cleaning out that closet yet; it still smelled like Emil. The big man had small tastes. When he found something he liked he stuck with it. When she was younger she had dismissed that about him, written it off as a quirk, a fatal lack of creativity, but as she grew older she had come to admire him for it, even emulate him. Imitation was the highest praise.

He had left behind three pairs of black bootcut jeans and jackaroo boots, never worn, size Ron. Nev shook out a pair of pants, held them up to the window. She went to the kitchen, put the pants and boots on a chair for Ron. Then she finished packing her suitcase.

19
CRAMPS

Ronnie's drive home from footy practice in Edmonton felt longer than usual. She leaned out the window of the Ford to let the air cool her face. Up on the Tablelands, night air was chilly and humid. Judging by the mottled patterns on the road and the occasional sparkle of headlights on the pavement, it had sprinkled while she was at footy practice. Rain brought a familiar smell up from the clay.

In the middle of April, autumn, the night sky over Tinaroo's hills left a pale blue glow above the mountains. On the western horizon a dark line of clouds hung low, forming a shredded purple terrace that could have been a flock of cranes.

She had been feeling gross all day with period cramps. On Saturday her team had played and won their first match of the season: Round 1. She hadn't felt good then, either, but she had powered through and scored twice.

Cyclone season was officially over, and Nev had returned from Kigali—two more reasons to celebrate.

Her sports bag rode in the passenger's seat. She liked dog-sitting Gaia and Blair, and liked sleeping in Stone House, but looked forward to camping in her tent tonight so she could wake up to birdsong.

When Nev was gone the house didn't feel empty; the fridge still held the same half-full condiments and glass pitcher of iced tea, the bedsheets still smelled like cigar smoke and vermouth.

Physical therapy that morning in Atherton had gone well. The left wrist couldn't extend or flex as far as the right one but the range of motion was improving.

She reached the turnoff for Boar Pocket Road and turned right.

She passed Nev's drive on the right. A few minutes later she slowed down, signaling left, and turned left down toward the creek. Car tracks led downhill. She hugged the road back in the direction she had come. For a few minutes she drove towards Nev's house. Then she peeled away from the road and downhill to the right toward the trees and the creek. Gum trees. Dark forest.

A clearing appeared, then her campsite. She was fond of it, even proud of it. A blue tent sat under a grey tarp that she had strung on paracord between four trees. She parked her truck beside a barbeque and a circle of stones. The dogs jumped down, sprinted into the dark, chasing the scent of brush turkey, nosing among dead eucalyptus leaves for fresh pademelon scat.

An iron tripod stood over the ashes of her fire pit. Hanging from the tripod was a shiny tin can billy. The heart of the home was the kitchen, and the heart of the kitchen was the kettle.

The American turtle research intern she jokingly called her "karaoke boyfriend" because she sometimes hooked up with him behind the pub on Wednesdays had disappeared, unexpectedly flying home to the US without saying goodbye. She didn't miss him exactly, but she hoped he was all right.

She picked a newspaper from the pile, crumpled a page at a time, then tossed the balls into the center of the firepit. The headlines were about the banana blight. She arranged a circle of sticks in a cone shape around the newspaper, then lit the paper with a lighter. She added progressively larger sticks until the fire was big enough that she could add logs.

The fire cracked and popped. She fetched two spicy snags

from the esky in the bed of her truck, speared them with sharp sticks and roasted them. Being alone did not bother her. She wasn't afraid of the dark, or the outdoors. Nothing bad had ever happened to her when she was camping.

Five months until the custody hearing.

Five months until try-outs for the Brisbane Lions.

The next morning, she was still on her period and cramping worse than usual as she helped Nev replace the roof of the screen house down by the creek. She volunteered to go up on the roof. She always volunteered for the dangerous jobs, because she liked them. A cramp forced her to stop nailing plywood to rafters with the nail gun to wait for it to pass. It didn't, so she drank water. On one of the ladders, Nev paused with a hammer poised in mid-air. "Dain'y? If you're feeling unwell, get down."

"Cramps." Ronnie climbed down the other ladder and took an ibuprofen, then climbed back up the ladder, continued nailing plywood to rafters with the nail gun. Her boss, who excelled at detail work, carefully nailed a thin strip of metal flashing around the bottom edge of the roof.

After lunch her boss left to go pinch some lambs.

"Down, Dain'y."

"I will in a minute."

She used a measuring tape to check the size of a piece of plywood she had cut, then carried the plywood sheet up the ladder. If the ibuprofen didn't kick in soon, she would have to take a break and go find a hot water bottle.

Inwardly, she swore. Her period wasn't usually like this. Not since she was eleven or twelve.

She screwed the sheet of plywood in place. The nail gun felt heavier than usual, which was strange.

She climbed down the ladder.

A rubbery whirling noise in the bush grew louder before a tight clump of orange-footed scrub fowl materialized out of the underbrush and ran across the clearing. They ran in a line, in unison, heads up, necks extended, before disappearing back into the rainforest.

She found what she was looking for, the roll of weather-proof plastic paper, then carried it up the ladder. On top of the roof, she unrolled it and laid it out flat. She cut it with a Stanley knife from her toolbelt.

She carried the rest of the heavy roll under her arm down the ladder.

Lightheaded, she found the staple gun and plugged it into the same generator as the nail gun with a matching extension cord. The generator hummed.

She climbed up the ladder again, slowly this time, favoring her middle, then ignored the pain while she leaned on the roof with her left hand, stapling weatherproof paper in place with the staple gun in her right.

These period cramps were truly miserable. A bad one gripped her and twisted. The ladder wobbled, or maybe she did. She leaned closer to the roof.

A flash of pain doubled her over, pushing her chest into the waterproof paper. For a moment she thought she had stapled herself. Her right hand still clutched the staple gun. The other gripped the ladder.

She tried a deep breath. The pain pressed back.

Don't move.

She groped in her back pocket for her phone, almost dropping it. She stared down at her shaking hand. That was a bad sign. She didn't usually shake like that.

She weighed her options and decided to drop the staple gun, which hit the ground with a bang.

One bar of reception.

Lightheaded, she called Reg.

No phone service.

Below, the generator roared. She brushed the phone along her thigh, but couldn't find a pocket. Shivering, she started down the ladder.

She came to on the ground, looking up at the sky through tree branches. The sky was one of those tricky colors between indigo and white. Something bit into the middle of her back, behind her belly button, like a sharp stick. She explored with her left hand. No stick there. Nothing poked into her back. She must have pulled a muscle when she fell. She flexed both hands and both feet, relieved that she still could.

Not paralyzed, then.

The pain in her back and stomach grew.

Panic wouldn't solve this problem. She scanned the clearing, had to get to her truck.

Pain vacillated. When she moved it moved. It had a velocity, a direction. She groaned.

Waves of hot and cold, like food poisoning. She cradled her stomach and pressed her other hand to the ground. There was no way she could crawl to the truck.

Trees around the clearing danced. She waited for her eyes to focus, for her vision to clear. She turned her head. The truck was uphill. Dropping her phone had been a mistake.

Maybe her appendix had burst.

She lay on her side, knees bent.

Nearby in the clearing a radio played. The generator still roared.

"Help?"

Her hands and feet tingled. She would pass out soon.

Pressing her chest, she felt her heart drumming beneath her palm. Oxygen-starved lungs sucked air in and out.

Why can't anything be easy?

Then it was dark and Nev was repeating that word like a mantra.

· · ·

The generator had burned through its fuel and died. Sleep was close, a magnolia at night. She recognized it by the smell. It smelled like lanolin, the oil sheep secreted under their fleece.

She had the shakes, like after giving birth to Rainbow.

When she exhaled she bled sound, white noise. It felt good to vocalize, to push back against the darkness.

20

MATILDA-JANE

Morning in the trauma hospital in Cairns smelled like coffee, bleach, and formaldehyde. The last one was strange. Slouched in the stuffed chair, Nev ruminated on it over a paper cup of piss-weak coffee. Her underwear felt stiff, stuck to her legs and faded jeans. A burgundy stain like a cow's kidney covered her lap from pocket to pocket.

She would have bet her last dime it was a ruptured spleen, but no. Reg had guessed appendix. They had both been wrong. An ectopic pregnancy lodged in a fallopian tube had burst like a frangible bullet. Last night the emergency laparotomy, open abdominal surgery, had taken over two hours. The surgeon said the salpingectomy, removal of the fallopian tube, had been "complicated" and "a success."

Reg hadn't met Nev's eyes since nurses wheeled Ron away at sunrise for X-rays and an MRI of her spinal cord. Nev was less concerned on that front since she had felt Ron writhe around before the ambulance arrived, something quadriplegics generally don't do. Nev was, however, worried she might have cracked some of Ron's ribs doing chest compressions after Ron stopped breathing.

Nev was still shocked that it had worked.

After morning rounds, nurses moved Ron from the windowless post-surgical intensive care unit to a recovery room with a window. Ron lay drugged in the bed, tubes in and out, hooked up to machines, going nowhere fast. Pale and still, blue fingers and mouth, looked dead, but the dead don't shiver.

Ron had a line between her brows in the middle of her forehead. Was that new? Nev couldn't remember. She had a headache, needed a drink.

When Ron appeared to be snoring, Reg stepped out to make a call. That was when Nev oozed into the bedside chair like a guilty ghost, filling the void he had left.

She was careful not to disturb the other patients. She had been awake all night and was running on fumes. Adrenaline long gone. Stale sweat button-down shirt and dried blood jeans. That was the kind of person she was, she reckoned—she saved people by soaking up their blood like a sponge—that was her super power.

Of course, that was nonsense. That was the exhaustion talking. Ron's wound had been on the inside. Nev couldn't have stopped it. The blood on Nev's jeans was period blood, miscarriage blood.

Nev wondered where the blood on the inside had gone. When the surgeon had vacuumed it out of Ron's abdominal cavity, where had it gone? Was there a blood vacuum somewhere in the hospital with a blood vacuum bag in a closet somewhere? Did it clot, once exposed to air? Did it stink? Was that the sour formaldehyde scent she was smelling? The coagulating blood of all of these patients combined together?

Reg returned looking broken. His clothes were still immaculate. Green polo shirt and beige cargo shorts. Rolex watch and leather thongs. He sniffed. "Tilda-Jane is in the hall."

"You call her?"

He shook his head. "I don't have the heart to run her off."

"I can," Nev said, impulsively. It would be easy. If she could do what she did last night, she could do anything. God loved her.

Reg perked up. "Would you really?"

Nev nodded, stood. Reg squeezed her shoulder in thanks.

She opened the door.

Ron's mum waited on the other side, thumbs in belt. Matilda-Jane had given Ron her remarkable height, broad shoulders, narrow hips and long legs, but in everything else Ron must have been the clone of her unknown bio dad the way Mattie was Reg's clone. Neither of the Madonna kids looked like this woman.

With a frown, Matilda-Jane gave Nev a bored once-over, sizing her up, granting Nev permission to do the same. Pale blue eyes—Scandinavian, scary—long straight yellow hair, wide-brimmed leather hat, tanned, freckles, big tits, built like an Olympic rower if they were also a builder, an army commando and a bikini model.

"Who are you?" asked Outback Barbie.

"You know who I am."

"I'm here to see my daughter."

"Not a good time, love."

Matilda-Jane sneered. "Says who?"

"Says I, and Common Sense."

"I drove five hours to see her. You're a rando; they let you in."

Nev swallowed. Across from this paragon of posture it was painfully obvious that she slouched. She had inherited that unflattering habit from her parents as a trick to pass gently through the world. Strangers called her "sir" when she slouched, and treated her like she didn't need help, which she usually didn't.

This irrational urge to pull her shoulders back and puff out her chest, but then what? What was the end-game of swagger? Nev knew she couldn't maintain it. Courage had always been available to her in short flashes under pressure, like a combustion engine. "I'm not a random person."

Ron and Mattie's mother finally glanced down and noticed the dried blood on Nev's jeans. Her glare softened.

Pissing contest over, it felt appropriate to hug. They pulled each other into a rib-crunching embrace, not one of those loose back-patting deals Reg was guilty of forcing on strangers during rugby season. Matilda-Jane smelled like patchouli, cigarettes and dogs.

"How is she?"

Nev didn't say, because she didn't know.

"My mate at the station reckoned it was bad." Matilda-Jane rubbed Nev's arms. "How'd you know to go over there?"

"Lucky guess."

"An energetic thing?" Matilda-Jane nodded approvingly. "I'm intuitive, too. Thank god you went over there when you did. You saved her life. Did they say if she had organ failure? How's her brain? Did she have seizures? A stroke?"

Nev shook her head. "Not as I know. Seems she'll pull through."

"I had a mate who bled out. Late-stage shock. Lack of oxygen killed him. It's like drowning."

Nev winced. "I'm aware."

"Crushed under his own ute. Another mate bled out after a fall. Ruptured spleen. Fell asleep, never woke up."

Matilda Jane began to push open the door to Ron's room. Nev stopped the door with her boot.

"Sit down, poppet," Matilda-Jane said. "Don't mess with mama bear."

Nev frowned, crossed her arms. Matilda-Jane tried again to open the door. The door hit Nev's boot again. Matilda-Jane laughed and reached out with both hands.

"If you touch me, you will regret it."

"I'm only moving you off to the side, poppet."

"No, you're not." Nev regretted her empty stomach. She was too old and dignified to fight this voluptuous Viking like a school kid at recess. Surely. "If you manhandle me, I'll scream, and you'll be kicked out."

"Oh, I don't have to manhandle you," Matilda-Jane said cheerfully. "I only have to ask nicely."

"You're not listening."

"You're not in charge here, Neville. You may be god on your little dollhouse farm, but here you're out of your jurisdiction. You're only a bogan like me with bad teeth and too many dogs. I didn't drive five hours to be turned away. What are you afraid of? Afraid I'd hurt her in her sleep? How do you figure that? I don't know what she's told you, but I've never done anything illegal to her."

"Where have you been?" The question came out harsher than Nev intended. *How come I've never met you before? How come you haven't been doing your job?* "You created a vacuum when you left that no one can fill! I don't want to be your kid's mum! I want to be my fucking self, and live my fucking life, not be the solution to your lack of responsibility!"

"I've been trying to get back in with her for years! She doesn't talk to me."

Nev raised her eyebrows. *Whose fault is that?* "You should have had Ron's back. Kids need their mothers. They need to be able to trust them. You messed with her head. That fucked my life in ways you will never understand."

Matilda-Jane relented. "Let me see her while she's asleep."

Nev shook her head.

Matilda-Jane jerked the door again.

Nev kept her foot in front of the door. "Take a walk. I need a smoke."

Outside, lighting up together in the car park, Nev felt generous.

"She hates me," Matilda-Jane complained.

"Whose fault is that?"

Matilda-Jane perched on the edge of the curb with her heels

hanging in mid-air, then proceeded to do calf raises on the balls of her feet. "Don't judge me."

It was oddly familiar, talking to this older version of Ron. This lesser version. It was sad, really. She wondered what Matilda-Jane's childhood had been like. She had been a teen mother, a single mum, below the poverty line. Homeless, jobless, living out of a van. How the hell would she have learned emotional intelligence? From one of her redneck boyfriends? From the man who worked at the petrol station?

Matilda-Jane was smiling to herself at some private joke, for all appearances enjoying the weather and the day. She had snake-skin boots and a homemade wallet attached to a dog chain hanging out of a back pocket of her leather pants. It was like looking at a character out of a Mad Max film. Matilda-Jane was larger than life—not in a good way.

Nev took a drag from her cigarette, blew out smoke. She needed to quit, would quit this year. Matilda-Jane probably had a handle of Bundy in her van and wouldn't blink an eye if Nev suggested shots. Nev considered it, decided she would rather die. "You're exactly like they said you were."

Matilda-Jane snorted. "Did they say Crocodile Dundee?"

Nev nodded.

The woman tossed her cigarette stub in the bushes. "You're smaller than I thought you would be."

"That's what I hear."

Matilda-Jane ran her fingers through Nev's short hair. "This your natural color? It's nice. Like sand in Valencia."

"You go for the bullfights?" Nev asked.

"How'd you guess?"

"I've been," Nev admitted.

"Two types of people: those who like killing things and those who don't."

"That's more or less what Hemingway said." Nev had gone to Valencia to find out if she was a man or not. Real men, Hemingway wrote, loved the thrill of the dance, the communion between man and bull. Nev hadn't seen any of that, only a calf looking for kindness and finding none. She had stumbled out of the arena blinded by tears. Not a good day.

"What's your deal?" Matilda-Jane asked. "You a greenie tree-hugger?"

Nev shrugged. "Yeah, nah, that's Reg's deal."

"You got more money than god?"

Nev shook her head. "I'm land rich, cash poor. Nothing in the bank. Comes in and goes out."

"Well shite. What are you good for? Other than bossing people around?"

The woman had a point. What was she good for? Mowing grass. Making sandwiches. Drinking. Paying taxes. Judging people. Worrying about things that hadn't happened yet. Abstract existential horror. Pretending the world wasn't on fire. Dancing past graveyards. Playing the squeeze box accordion.

"I should teach music lessons," Nev mused.

"Christ." Matilda-Jane rolled her eyes and walked away.

Nev watched her climb into a white van and rev the engine.

Matilda-Jane drove by with the window down and her middle finger out, heavy metal music blasting. She held the horn down as she passed Nev. Matilda-Jane switched from the middle finger to a backward peace symbol, then wagged her tongue between her fingers suggestively. Bumper stickers on the back of the van read, 'Decolonize your mind,' 'Stolen Land,' and 'Jesus was a Boong.' Nev couldn't tell if the last one was racist or anti-racist, which made her uncomfortable, which was probably the point.

The van returned for a second pass. Nev caught the black leather hat tossed to her.

"Give that to Ripper. Ask if she opened my letter. Keep eating your Wheaties."

Reg sat by the bedside. He chuckled when he saw her face. "Explains a lot, doesn't it?"

Nev eased herself into the stuffed chair by the window, knees protesting. Matilda-Jane acted like a horrible teenaged boy.

"You must be a magician," Reg said. "She never does what I ask."

"I bored her to death. She's on to the next thing. Short attention span." Nev needed a drink but wanted a bagel. "I can't believe you dated that woman."

He smiled, looked down, shuffled his feet. "You know how it is when you're in love. We were teenagers." Reg sniffed. "She's a free spirit."

They both looked at Ron sleeping in the hospital bed.

Nev's chest squeezed. Today was still yesterday, not yet differentiated by the healing oblivion of sleep. Ron must have a guardian angel—a powerful one. The experience of the past twenty-four hours wasn't enough to make an atheist believe in god, but Nev had haggled.

An odd feeling, mercy.

It had been so pitifully easy for her to imagine that losing Ron was her own karma. She chewed her lip, then shook her head. She had cheated death before, but this felt different.

Reg hugged himself. He was having a hard time. She debated whether to put an arm around him. He was a grown man. No one had died. It was his kid, though. He was a wreck. She wondered why that was. It would be a crash, to come down to this reality, if you were happy ninety percent of the time. She could not relate. Perpetual satisfaction was not a problem she shared. Shit hitting the fan was just another day for her. Another iteration of normal.

Reg had been both mum and dad to his kids. Sensitive man like that had the skill set for it. He could talk for hours and he could listen. She imagined this barrel-chested bowling ball of a man sitting on the carpet playing with dollies and beanie babies. He must have.

He had never recovered from losing Ron when she was nine. Nev saw that now. He worried about his kids constantly. She wondered if each successive separation was easier or harder.

People like Reg made her grateful that she never had a child. She couldn't imagine loving someone that much, how he must feel, viscerally, missing a part of himself. She wondered if it was like the feeling described in books, like a string tugging from his sternum to his kids, tugging and stretching but never breaking.

Matilda-Jane had taken Ron away when Ron was the age Rainbow was now. Five years in a van in the desert with an adult child for a parent. What had happened during those years? More importantly, what had not? Nev knew the answer. Ron had been bored out of her skull. She didn't thrive in the nomadic lifestyle. She was a team player. She needed other people. Being alone was torture for Ron.

If attachment was a psychological response to abandonment, Nev was enabling the girl. That wasn't the right word. This wasn't the place to think about it.

A young nurse stuck her head in the room. Her eyes landed on Reg. "Are you the dad?"

He nodded, cleared his throat. "I'm the dad." Nev knew he had legally adopted Ron for times like these. During footy season she was accident-prone.

"The doctor reviewed the MRI of her spine, said to tell you it's normal."

"Thanks, mate. Appreciate it."

The nurse disappeared.

Reg bent over his sleeping kid. Nev stepped out into the hall to give him a moment.

When she returned, Reg was sitting down. She gave him a tissue. He blew his nose. He had been up all night with her. She pulled her chair next to his. He leaned over and cried on her chest.

That was different. She patted his arm awkwardly. He was heavy and smelled like cologne. If she relaxed, he would fall asleep on her. "Go rest. I'll stay."

"You need to change out of those clothes, mate."

"Gift shop opens at ten. I'll buy trousers." Chuck these in the bin. Outside the window it was raining. It had rained in Kigali and

Kibeho, too. April rain. Cold rain. Good for crops. Good for the grass. Autumn rain was not good for sheep. They got worms here when it rained too much in the fall.

"When do you cry?" Reg asked.

Good question. The ceiling tiles in the room were off-white, square, made of some kind of speckled Styrofoam.

"You don't?" he sounded concerned.

She didn't look at him. "Nah," she said. "Not about little stuff like this."

"You cry at movies?"

She nodded. "All the time. When I'm happy. If I cried when I was sad it would make me happy, which would be confusing. She'll be right." *I want her to wake up and be herself again...*

"Have you ever been pregnant?" Reg asked.

Nev looked down at her blood-stained lap. What an intrusive question. She wasn't sure how to answer.

Blaise was childless. Nev counted backwards in her head, trying to calculate how old Blaise must have been when Reg married her. Reg and Blaise might have lost pregnancies. She wouldn't ask. Had to be gentle with him just in case.

"You never can tell by looking at someone," she said.

"You would have raised this one on the farm."

She didn't have a response to that. "I'm not trying to steal your grandchildren, mate." She laughed.

Reg shook his head. "Relax. Listen. You don't need to... We're on the same team, mate. You know I consider you a part of the family."

She swallowed, studied the floor. He was only being generous with her because he was that kind of person, so it didn't surprise her, but it still hurt. No one since her dad died had found it necessary to say miserable bloody shit to her like, "I consider you a part of the family." It was probably the nicest thing anyone had said to her in ten years, and she hated Reg for it.

She licked her lips, rubbed the edge of the white sheet

between her fingers, wanting, feeling guilty for wanting. She needed Ron to wake up and Reg to disappear.

If he knew what she wanted to do to his daughter he wouldn't look at her like that...

"It's okay," Reg muttered. "I promise. We love you, and we trust you. I wish you would trust yourself. You don't have to be so uptight all the time. We're all a bunch of weirdos, mate. You know it?"

Nev didn't know what to say. Eventually she whispered what she was thinking. "I'm more weird than you."

Reg sighed. "Change out of those trousers before someone gets the wrong idea."

Nev didn't need to be told a third time.

21
HOSPITAL

The walls were white, sterile, meaningless. A hospital room, clinical, institutional. Ronnie was too weak to ask what had happened.

The bed bent like the letter N. The head of the bed was tilted up, the middle down, her knees pointed at the ceiling. She was folded up like an inchworm, trapped with pillows, on her back.

Reg brought her water, which she sipped through a straw. She had forgotten how much waking up from anesthesia sucked.

Nausea.

At least she was high on painkillers now.

Reg stroked her forehead while a nurse fiddled with one of her IVs. "There you are, Brum, all better. We thought we lost you. You bled out for a while. They took four liters of blood from your belly. We're lucky you're alive."

He appeared and disappeared when she opened and closed her eyes. She wondered who he was talking to. She was clearly still asleep. He carried on like a man talking to himself. Maybe there were other people in the room, sitting where she couldn't see.

.   .   .

A nurse came by to take her temperature. Ronnie shivered uncontrollably. Her skin was bloated, her belly especially. The pain in her abdomen was unreal.

Her body had changed shape while she was asleep. She had never thrown out her back before, but if she had, she imagined it would feel like this.

The room had a window. Light changed from one shade of cream to another, then passed through yellow and orange to blue.

Sleep eluded her. Nurses kept waking her up.

"Are you comfortable?"

No, I am not comfortable. I feel like I'm in labor with a demon that's trying to claw its way out of me. She rubbed her ribs, which didn't help, because some of them were cracked.

They gave her pills to swallow and clear liquids through an IV.

Absolute hell.

A whiteboard on the far wall said Thursday 16 April. A familiar man leaned over her, talking to her. Reg.

No, not Reg.

Mattie.

Ronnie furrowed her brow, confused. Her older brother only visited sometimes for Christmas, never during rugby union season. The Super Rugby round robin ran every weekend for twenty-one weeks. She couldn't remember whether his team, the Hurricanes, were playing tomorrow.

Mattie put his arm around her shoulders. She rested her head on his hand and closed her eyes. Someone made comforting noises, adjusted the blankets over her legs.

Gas bubbled in her gut, then grabbed and twisted. She blew air out in short puffs between pursed lips until the worst of it passed. She rubbed her sore ribs.

Reg came in.

"How is she?" he asked.

"Like me the morning after my birthday."

"Did she eat anything?"

"She's been sleeping."

"I'm awake." She didn't open her eyes. Reg was there. Mattie was there.

"How was the flight?" Reg asked him.

"Average."

"How's Luca?" Mattie's two-year-old son who lived in Madrid with his mother.

"Brilliant. I'll show you videos later."

"How's what's her name? Talk to them much? Have you tried to get back together with her recently? How's that going?"

"Is this a barbie or a sausage sizzle, because you're grilling me, old man."

She tuned them out and slept.

Her dad and brother waited in the hall while nurses removed her catheter, got her upright on the edge of the bed, then helped her shuffle to the bathroom with a pillow pressed to her incision. Walking felt dangerous. The room spun. Blood rushed out of her head.

The hospital had put her in the Maternity Ward, which might have been upsetting but wasn't. The staff had removed everything for newborns that wasn't screwed to a wall.

"I didn't want it, anyway," she said to no one in particular.

Nurses lifted her legs and arranged them on pillows, bent her knees, helped her lean forward while one of them put a pillow behind her back. The nurses did not appear concerned that she clung to them and squeezed their arms when they eased her down. They fussed with the pillows. She felt old, curled inwards on herself. She understood why grandparents sat in reclining chairs all day. She closed her eyes and focused on breathing.

She had a faint memory of gasping for air and mewling, begging Nev to stop the ambulance or something irrational like that. Now as long as she lay still her back was quiet, but the gas pressure in her gut only went away when nurses manhandled her into moving. Pick one. Drugs took the edge off, dulled the corners.

"Your old lady's back," Reg said.

She opened her eyes. Sunset outside. Nev sat on the hideous green couch by the window, overnight bag at her cowboy boots.

Oh wow... She came. Ronnie made an inarticulate sound that might have been a laugh, but wasn't at all like that, then sighed. Relief blurred the room. She was too tired to care, couldn't be bothered.

Reg looked relieved. He must have asked Nev to come. "They gave her something that helped with the gas. She's been quiet for a few hours."

Nev turned pink, which made her eyes blue. She had bags under her eyes and looked rough, but was too polite to do anything but sit and fondle her Akubra.

Ronnie tried to lift her arm, but it was heavy, and connected to the rest of her, so she gave it up as a bad job and panted for a while. She had forgotten how much cracked ribs sucked. It took a while to catch her breath. This ranked up there with the time she was hit by a car and left for dead between Bulloo Downs and Cunnamulla. When her lungs worked again, she found she could project her voice to the hideous green couch by the window.

"Come here, baby."

Awkward silence, ambient hospital noises growing louder as Reg, Mattie and Nev looked at each other. Reg and Mattie both pointed to Nev. Embarrassment mottled the already-pink face. For a moment it looked like she wouldn't answer to 'baby,' but then she stood, reluctantly. Nev approached the bed, hat in her hands, and stopped beyond the arm rail like a mourner at a wake.

Ronnie wanted a hug. "You look like shit. How many fallopian tubes does a guy have to lose to get a hug around here?"

Nev snorted. Ronnie saw the problem—Nev wasn't as tall as Reg or Mattie, so the side rail of the bed was in the way.

"There's a button to fold that down."

Nev lowered the siderail before leaning over her, reaching around without touching her, careful not to rest any weight on her. She smelled nice.

Ronnie pulled Nev's head down onto her shoulder, into the empty space on the pillow next to her left ear.

Nev's face tickled the side of her neck. The older woman began to shake.

Ronnie stroked her hair. "Shh..."

Reg and Mattie stepped out into the hallway.

"I'm alive. You did a good job. It's over. You did so good..."

Not many people knew that the owner of Upsend Downs was deathly afraid of blood.

After that, it wasn't hard to wheedle Nev into pulling over a chair. Nev surprised her by offering to show her pictures from her recent trip to Rwanda, which was exactly the level of distraction she needed.

She studied each image like a clue, trying to guess where her friend had been standing and how she had been feeling when she took each photo.

A fishing boat in a brown river with lush green banks.

An old tree. "What kind of tree is that?"

"Oak. In the villages people met under a tree like that to hold Gacaca courts after 2002, to try their neighbors for crimes committed in '94. They stopped last year. It wasn't perfect, but it was something. They had to process a hundred and thirty thousand alleged perpetrators."

"How often did they do that?"

"Every week."

"That must have been exhausting." And dangerous for the victims, Ronnie knew, who were afraid of facing reprisals from their neighbors if they testified or gave evidence.

Nev nodded. "They called it Reconciliation. It hasn't been a total failure. It let them return to village life. Society heals. It never ends. They forgave their neighbors but can't trust them. They'll carry that fear. The body remembers fear."

And guilt, Ronnie thought. "Will you take me someday? I could do a soccer camp for kids." She reached for Nev's free arm, found it, squeezed her hand. Nev's hand was cold.

Nev ignored the touch, but didn't move away. "Maybe someday. I need you to watch the farm."

Ronnie looked down at her friend's phone again. A church. Men with shovels standing behind a rectangular hole full of half-buried bones.

"They found that one recently. It had at least four hundred and fifty people buried in it."

Ronnie swore. *One murder is a tragedy, but a hundred is a statistic...*

"You must have pictures you can't publish." It occurred to her that the photos in frames on Nev's wall were only a fraction of her collection. Nev must have taken thousands of pictures before the UN forcibly evacuated westerners.

Nev raised her eyebrows, looked down at her phone. That was a yes.

"What did you do with them, the graphic ones, the ones you couldn't publish?" Ronnie imagined sinister cardboard boxes in the attic at Stone House. Photos that Rainbow must never, ever see.

"Evidence of war crimes I gave to the UN, who probably tossed them in the bin."

Ronnie's chest hurt. "That's hard." She breathed shallowly. Nev's cold hand felt nice, so she focused on that. "Were they all adults, or...?"

Nev looked at the window. Ronnie swore in her head. Nev had seen dead kids.

"No one wants to look at pictures of dead kids."

"You'd be surprised. The people who want to probably shouldn't, and the people who should probably won't."

She had so much respect for this woman that sometimes it amazed her—amazed her that a badass like that would be friends with her. What did Nev get from the relationship? What did Ronnie do for her that she couldn't do for herself?

"Were you shooting on film back then?" Ronnie asked. "Did you keep the film?"

"Negatives? Yeah. You're never going to see them."

"It must be lonely, not being able to talk about it."

Nev shrugged. She had captured evidence to give the dead a voice, ammunition for future prosecutors. When the Rwandan government released thousands of murderers and rapists back into the community, she must have been disappointed. Crushed. Betrayed. Neutrality in war zones must blow.

She tried to picture Nev as a bright-eyed twenty-something, hopeful and idealistic, with Joni Mitchell hair that looked soft and smelled nice, a ghost partially caught in the reflection on a bullet-proof truck window in a paper portrait behind glass on the wall at Stone House, so many layers removed from the person holding her hand now.

Reg and Mattie returned smelling like cigarettes. Their low voices made her sleepy.

"Rainbow wants to visit," Reg said.

Ronnie opened her eyes. The others were looking at their phones. Her hands were too swollen and numb. She swallowed saliva and listened to nurses debate whether it was time to try walking again. In the next room, a newborn cried and adults laughed.

"Do you want Rainbow to visit?" Reg asked.

Suddenly, it felt like someone had turned a hair dryer on her face. She leaned back into the pillow and focused on breathing. She was having some kind of blood pressure thing. *I can't deal with her right now.* She couldn't manage a nine-year-old's feelings when she could barely regulate her own. "I'll see her at the house."

"My house?" Reg asked. His eyes flicked from her to Nev, who remained silent.

"Of course your house. Where else?"

Black windows. Nighttime. Reg and Mattie took turns bending over the bed to kiss her on the forehead. Mattie hugged Nev, shrinking her down to child-size. "I'll be back in the morning. Text me if anything changes."

Ronnie lay with her eyes closed, waiting for sleep to swoop in and save her, carry her away from here. Machines beeped. Nurses crept around. Her friend lay facing the window on the couch that looked hard. She hoped her friend was asleep.

22

MORNING

The sun rose slowly all at once, lifting the hospital room high into the air over Cairns. Ronnie watched Nev watch the sunrise over the ocean from the floor-to-ceiling window. She couldn't see it from the bed, but could tell by her friend's expression that it must be magnificent. Ronnie couldn't be bothered to move—the most recent diagnosis was low blood pressure and anemia.

"I'm off for a walk in the park," Nev announced. "Need anything?"

"A winning lotto ticket?"

Nev reappeared later carrying a cup of coffee, then walked over to the window and gazed out at the Pacific again. It held power over her, more than a casual interest.

"Have you ever lived on the coast?" Ronnie asked.

Nev nodded.

"How was the park?"

"Nice. I see why people live here." Nev continued staring out the window at the ocean.

"Anything interesting?"

"A fleet of scuba dive boats preparing to ferry tourists out to the reef." The Great Barrier Reef. "Have you been?" Nev asked.

When she shook her head, Nev did too, which surprised her, because she thought Nev had been everywhere. "Gunni's been a few times." Nev stretched, then took the chair closest to the bed. Her voice softened. "How are you feeling? Knackered?"

Ronnie decided that was an accurate description. Nev touched her head, then gently pulled her hair. It took her a moment to realize that her friend was brushing her hair.

"That feels nice."

She went back to sleep, or what counted as sleep here. Nev would be the only one of her visitors to remember to bring a hairbrush. Nev thought of everything.

The bed inflated and deflated, making a noise like a washing machine. Cuffs on her legs did the same, squeezing, forcing blood through her heart and lungs, simulating life. Her feet and ankles looked like they belonged to someone else. The doctor called it edema, swelling from surgery.

"When was the last time you brushed your hair?" Nev asked.

Good question. "Maybe in school." No, that wasn't true, it was mandatory in the place down near Brissie. Everything there had to be tidy for daily inspection, like in the military.

"I run my fingers through it every few days." Her curls had broken every brush anyway.

"When I'm in New Zealand this weekend with Gunni, Blaise will wash your hair."

"Do you always think of everything?"

"Yes."

The ice packs on her stomach felt nice. Nothing to do now but sleep and wait for her body to heal itself. Full system reset. Unplug it and plug it back in.

"Not much petrol in your tank." Nev tactfully didn't mention the *recovering from a c-section* handout on the bedside table. That wasn't exactly the surgery she had, but someone here thought it was close enough. The pamphlet said, 'Five days in the bed, five days on the bed, five days near the bed.' Mattie and Reg had both read it to her when they were alone with her.

Nev had a thing about blood. One time when Rainbow was four, Rainbow cut her head falling off the monkey bars Nev built for her at the farm. Nev had run indoors to fetch a damp towel. While Ronnie cleaned Rainbow's face, Nev had been sick into one of two Japanese urns in the kitchen garden. The urn had been too heavy to tip onto its side and too deep to flush out with the hose.

Ronnie licked dry lips, stomach full of painkillers and apple juice, suspecting she might be sick again but hoping the nausea would pass. "Remember the time you chundered in the Japanese urn?"

"Hard to forget."

"Did you ever clean it out? Or just throw dirt in there and call it good?"

Nev chuckled. "Worms don't know the difference."

True. Judging by the sudden warmth between her legs that slowly turned cold, Ronnie suspected she had bled through another pair of maternity underwear. Nurses had taken the catheter out earlier and she hadn't forgiven them yet.

Two nurses appeared, undid the leg cuffs and set them aside, then moved everything off Ronnie's lap. She tried to help.

Linoleum was cold under her feet but she couldn't feel her toes.

She pressed a pillow to her incision the way the nurses instructed her, then eased more weight onto her left foot. She couldn't feel whether her right foot came off the ground. Still numb, then. Not a good show. The room spun.

Her center of gravity was off. Getting up had been a terrible idea. The nurses were patient. "Good job. Now move your left foot." She leaned to the right. Her left foot didn't come off the ground.

She swore. The women in pink scrubs appeared unconcerned.

"Relax. Deep breaths," one said. Her scrubs had alphabet blocks and teddy bears on them.

"Don't be tense," the other warned. Her scrubs had baby bottles and pacifiers.

A wheelchair appeared at her hip. Lowering herself down by the armrests strained her back, which spasmed, making her freeze despite her best intentions. "Ahhh, ahhh, ahh…" She couldn't be bothered to feel embarrassed.

"You're doing beautifully! You can do this!" alphabet blocks said. "You're already doing heaps better than you were yesterday!" Baby bottles pushed the chair into the bathroom.

She couldn't remember their names or faces—the nurses all blurred together into a laundry list of patterned scrubs. Kind, helpful people she would never see again.

In the other room, Nev said something about a transfusion.

The only bad thing about the blood IV dripping into her arm for four hours was that a nurse had to sit by the bed and watch the numbers on the machines for the first fifteen minutes. Ronnie wouldn't mind that if she was alone, but she could tell it made Nev uncomfortable.

The nurse stopped Nev from reading the bag. "Can I help you?"

"Whose blood is this?"

The nurse blinked. "We don't keep track of that."

"Yes, you do."

Bleeding into post-partum underwear that felt like a diaper under white hospital blankets, she watched Nev google the sea chantey festival in Christchurch. Nev remained trapped in the visitor chair across from the nurse because Ronnie wouldn't let go of her hand.

Images of Christchurch slid across Nev's dirty laptop screen. Ronnie had forgotten that her bandmates had plans to perform at a sea chantey festival in New Zealand that weekend.

When the doctor on call stopped by on her morning rounds, Nev stepped out into the hall.

"Questions?" the doctor asked.

Ronnie didn't have the energy to lift her head. "When can I play footy again?"

"After your eight-week check-up, if everything's healing."

"When can I ride a horse?"

"Same."

"What about work?"

"What do you do?"

"Farming and coaching football."

"You'll likely be able to return to coaching after a month, but take the full eight weeks off your manual labor job."

There went footy season. The primary school in Atherton must have noticed by now that she wasn't coming to work. She could call them today, had to try to remember. Maybe the fact that they hadn't called her meant that someone had called them already.

When the doctor left the room, Nev returned with Mattie.

She was relieved to see them, a little surprised that they were both still here. She pressed the down arrow on the remote that controlled the incline of the bed. "Did anyone call the school?"

Mattie leaned over the bed to kiss her on the forehead. "Dad did." Of course.

"Tell him I said thanks."

"Tell him yourself." Mattie felt her temperature. His palm was hot. "How did you sleep? You're looking better. Your lips aren't blue anymore."

"How's Rainbow? Has anyone talked to her?" she asked, feeling guilty that she hadn't asked earlier.

Mattie and Nev shook their heads. They hadn't called her. Maybe Reg had. Rainbow was in school now.

Ronnie would call her this evening. Had to try to remember.

23
BLUE QUANDONG

Three days later, when her blood pressure was stable and she could shuffle zombie-like to the toilet, the doctor let her go. Mattie pushed her down to the car park. It had rained overnight and earlier that morning. The air outside the hospital in Cairns smelled like wet asphalt, exhaust fumes, and the ocean. Nev ran to fetch the truck.

Her brother stood behind the wheelchair massaging her neck and shoulders. She always forgot he had a degree in sports physiotherapy. When he had told her he wanted to be a women's sports therapist during his off-season, she, along with everyone else, had written that off as a creepy excuse to get his hands on hot female athletes, but maybe she had been too harsh on him. Whatever he was doing to her back felt amazing.

The silver truck appeared, then parked in front of them.

Getting into it was a challenge.

When she finally sat breathless in the passenger's seat, safe from being asked to move again for at least an hour and a half, exhaustion made her cranky. She felt shitty about the fact that she hadn't called Rainbow yet.

The thought of calling made her emotional, and she didn't want to lean on the girl that way. Rainbow needed calm reassurance and lighthearted jokes, not to be traumatized by a half-dead parent. She couldn't project safety and stability if she was half-asleep or a weepy mess. In hindsight, not calling Rainbow was probably worse. She couldn't win.

Nev pointed to the seatbelt. "You got to wear it."

"I don't."

"Do."

"Make me."

They were still arguing when Mattie returned.

Nev shook his hand. "We'll meet you at your dad's in an hour. Have to make a quick pit stop."

Ronnie wedged her hands under the seatbelt to take pressure off her incision. She had lost the argument.

Wet highway, steam-clouds rising off shining asphalt in the sun. Who said roads couldn't be beautiful? Travelling west on the Gillies Range Road through the mountains was the same as before, but she noticed the scenery through fresh eyes. The view from the passenger's seat looked different than the view from the driver's seat. Angles and sight lines. Funny how such a small shift in location caused a dramatic change in perception.

Life was fragile and precious; she couldn't take it for granted, nor could she rely on always being healthy. She couldn't fight her way out of situations or run away. She needed someone like Nev to be a second set of eyes and ears, a second brain, asking nervous questions like, "Does she need a transfusion?" and "Where does this blood come from?" Selfishly, she liked the attention. Liked not being alone. "Reckon we ought to take better care of ourselves, eh?"

"Okey dokey." Nev squinted against the sun.

"We have to quit smoking."

Nev pulled down the overhead visor to shade her eyes as they went around a switchback. "I will if you do."

"Deal." Ronnie watched gum trees fly past the window. "I need to get back in shape so I can keep up with Rainbow."

"Being an athlete doesn't make you a better mum."

"Doesn't it?"

"Does it make Mattie a better dad?"

Point taken.

"Time together is the important thing for Gumball. That's all she wants."

That's not what you used to say... She turned toward Nev and narrowed her eyes. "What happened to 'it isn't the quantity, it's the quality of the time you spend with her'?"

"Yeah, well." Nev kept her eyes on the road. "That was back when you didn't have a chance." She frowned.

"What?" Ronnie asked. "You made a face. What are you thinking?"

"Nothing."

"Bullshit. Tell me."

Nev glanced over at her, then back at the road. "Have you heard from the lawyer yet? When you're feeling better, give her a call, check in. Have you talked to your ex about any of this yet?"

Ronnie shook her head. Since the frozen corn incident she had been avoiding Maude. Now Reg picked Rainbow up in Gordonvale and dropped her off. No contact. Easy Peasy, as Nev would say. "Not yet. I'm letting her get used to the idea first. I'll call the lawyer sometime. No news is good news." The lawyer hadn't met with Maude yet. If the woman in Mareeba had news, she would call.

Nev raised an eyebrow. "I don't know how to help with that, but if you need me to, I'll figure it out."

"Thanks, but I'll handle it. I think it's headed in the right direction. I mean, the lawyer said Maude was on board..."

"Don't worry about it."

"I wasn't. You're the one worrying about it. Jesus..."

Ronnie watched her boss shift the truck into park on the gravel in front of the plant nursery at Upsend Downs. Ric-Rac or Barney had given the sign a fresh coat of paint. The plant nursery was one of the beautiful parts of the farm, with wide views of rolling hills, hazy on an autumn afternoon, lavender fields, orderly and quiet, rows of silver gum trees, mahogany, bay laurels, and three hundred other species of native and exotic plants. Sometimes she and the other farmhands helped out here with landscaping, maintenance, or building repair when the seasonal staff were gone. Green hoses snaked and coiled between the rows.

Whenever she mowed the lawn here, she felt that something big was about to happen. The combination of orderliness and emptiness reminded her of a wedding venue before the guests arrive. That was a thought. They could become a wedding destination. Farms did that now.

Water evaporating brought a pleasant earthy smell up from the loam. Somewhere to their right a mister had been left on. Maybe it was on a timer. Nev opened the passenger door and offered her an upturned palm.

She took it, frowning. "Why do I have to get out of the ute?" Her friend didn't answer, merely snapped open the rented wheelchair. She gingerly lowered herself into it with a hiss. Nev pushed her towards the potted rows, slowly. She could feel how much harder it was for Nev to push the chair across crushed gravel than it had been for Mattie to push it across carpet and cement.

"Thought you might like to pick a tree to plant."

"Me? Now?" Ronnie asked, incredulous. *Oh, Nev... Nev, Nev, Nev, Nev, Nev...*

Her boss was often clueless in an adorably oblivious way, but didn't usually miss the mark by this much. Ronnie liked plant shopping under normal circumstances, with the thirty percent employee discount, but not on the way home from hospital. Maybe it was a surprise party. She hoped not. She wanted to lie down in a dark room, preferably with Nev and the dogs curled up against her, and sleep for a hundred years.

"Babe...plant shopping is not good right now."

"Any kind. Up to you. My treat. Remind me to pave these

walking paths. They lied to me when they told me this design was wheelchair accessible."

"Are you listening to me, babe? Stop. You're going to have to go all the way back to the car park, and I'm not getting any lighter, so if I were you, I would turn this chair around right now." Something was definitely up. "What is this? Please tell me it's not a surprise party."

Nev was a disembodied voice behind the chair. "Don't be angry."

"What did you do?" Her midsection burned, back competing with the incision scar for attention. "Come over here where I can see you. I feel like I'm talking to myself."

Nev came around in front of the chair. She looked guilty. "Nothing. I thought planting a tree might be a nice gesture..."

"Of what? A nice gesture of what?"

Nev's cheekbones and ears were pink. "It was just an idea."

The nursery was pleasant in the shade, here on the hill with the breeze—honeyeaters in grevilleas, two or three unwelcome rabbits peeking out from underneath the boxwood, azaleas in pots, pots in ordered rows—but Ronnie needed to take pills and sleep.

She gazed wistfully at the ute parked by the checkout kiosk. "Baby... I'm mostly dead. I know you're trying to do something nice for me, but I feel like I'm in a hostage situation and I have zero interest in whatever this is."

Why a tree? Why did Nev think she wanted to plant a...

Oh.

Right.

She swallowed, closed her eyes. The headache she had woken up with after surgery got worse in the afternoon. She rubbed her temples.

"Don't make this a big deal. Don't make it worse than it needs to be."

"I'm not arguing with you," Nev said. "If you're not interested, we'll go. I just thought it might be nice."

"Nice...?" Ronnie swallowed. "What part of this is nice? There's no part of this that I want to remember. I don't dwell on shit like this. Trying to forget about it and move on as fast as I can."

"I'm sure that's very healthy," Nev quipped. "You might feel differently about the ectopic in the future. Planting a tree would be a gift to your future self. Hedging your bets. If you never need it, grand."

"Grand? You're Irish now? Can you please just be a normal fucking person for one second, please? And not try to..." What was Nev trying to do? "This isn't the Titanic. I don't want flowers. I don't want a song. I want to..."

Bloody hell... Nev sounded like she wanted to have a funeral for the embryo. *Unbelievable...* Ronnie held her cracked ribs to make it easier to breathe. "You're not even religious! Neither of us are. It was never viable. It wasn't a person. I can't believe I have to say this."

The only baby I lost is Rainbow.

Nev crouched beside the chair, tearing apart a stray azalea leaf until it resembled confetti. "I didn't say those things. Don't put words in my mouth."

She knew Nev was trying to be supportive and she felt bad for snapping at her. She sighed. "I'm sorry. I have to conserve my fucks for living people who depend on me."

"By all means, do that."

"I will."

Clearly this meant more to Nev than it did to her. Nev had seen actual dead babies and Ronnie should give her more credit—the owner of Upsend Downs knew exactly what an ectopic was, but she had never experienced one.

Once Ronnie realized that this pit stop wasn't for her, she changed her mind. If planting something to watch it grow was important to Nev, Ronnie would do it, but she would complain the entire time. She rubbed her face. She hadn't bathed in a week and desperately needed something; she wasn't sure what. "Fine.

We'll do this faggy thing and never talk about it again. Call Gunni, he'll want to be invited. Play some Enya."

Nev stood up. "Forget it. Don't be a nong. That sounded like something your mother would say." Nev inhaled sharply. Ronnie watched her friend pull an almost empty carton of cigarettes out of a back pocket, put one in her mouth, produce a lighter, then catch herself. Nev returned the cigarette and lighter to her pockets before turning the wheelchair around.

Ronnie held her head. "I didn't mean it in a derogatory way."

Now Nev thought she was a homophobe, which was a new low. After making an arse of herself the least she could do was pick a shrub.

As Nev wheeled her between rows, Ronnie felt strange considering qualities of each young tree such as leaf color, shape, size, simple, compound, double-compound branching structure, projected height, and drought tolerance, looking for one that best matched the qualities of the embryo that had almost killed her. Nev was smarter than she was, so it must have occurred to her.

A large sapling in an unusual bright pink pot caught her eye. It was her height, or would have been if she was standing. She didn't need to look at the tag to know that they had bought it in as a tiny sprout from the non-profit native plant nursery for forty-nine dollars and now that they had kept it for years, priced it ten times higher. "That one."

"Blue quandong." Nev crouched to cut off the tag, straightened, then handed the plastic ribbon to her. "My favorite tree."

Ronnie laughed, then regretted it. "Ow. Is that a thing? Do people have favorite trees?"

"Rainbow does."

She frowned. When was the last time she thought about her daughter? She should have been thinking about her this whole time. Rainbow was waiting for her at Reg and Blaise's house at this moment, probably wondering what was taking them so long. Ronnie sent off a quick text to Rainbow using her voice to text ap.

> (Ronnie) Hey babe, stopped at the farm with Nev, be there in a bit. Can't wait to see you!

A moment later her phone vibrated.

> (Rainbow) Ok, see you soon. Me too!

The tag said it would be a large evergreen with buttress roots. The blue quandong was a native rainforest tree in a symbiotic relationship with the cassowary; the seeds of its giant, bright blue fruits weren't viable unless they passed through the gut of an enormous blue-headed bird. "The fruits are the same electric blue as the cassowaries," Nev added, cheerfully.

"I know what a quandong is."

Nev found a shovel and a wheelbarrow. "You have expensive tastes."

Ronnie chuckled. "Where will you plant it?"

"You'll see."

24
ABOUT MATTIE

On the road to Lionheart twelve grey kangaroos of various ages and sizes stopped hopping across a field to watch the silver truck speed by. The mob moved closer together, distrustful of the engine, then hopped along after the truck passed.

Ronnie reached for Nev's dirty hand, which helpfully came off the wheel and rested on the center console where she could reach it. The memory of the sapling surrounded by a ring of compost on the grassy slope behind the horse barn was oddly comforting.

"Thank you." She interlaced their fingers.

"No worries."

"That was really sweet." She kissed Nev's knuckles, then rested their hands on her thigh and watched window TV, letting the lights and colors wash over her. "I think I'm high."

Nev snorted. "Ding ding. Fifty points." She pulled off Pademelon Road onto the Bermuda grass in front of Reg's purple Queenslander and took her hand back to shift into park.

Ronnie's relatives were inside, which gave her a minute to adjust and transition into big loud family time.

Nev turned off the engine.

Lorikeets in the bloodwood tree that Rainbow called the vanilla ice cream tree. "Is that her favorite?" Ronnie pointed.

Nev nodded, put on sunglasses and unwrapped a stick of gum. "You good?"

Effortlessly mature and sexy. So annoying. Ronnie would have been turned on if she wasn't half dead. It would be a long time, yonks, before she got laid again. "Thanks for a fun date."

"You're welcome." Enigmatic behind Ray Ban aviators, Nev chewed the gum. "Something tells me it won't be the last time." Nev cracked an amused smile.

Relieved and grateful, Ronnie went in for a kiss, but Nev gave her a hug.

Ronnie wasn't offended. "Why do you do that?" she asked, curious.

Nev hesitated.

"Do you want to kiss me?"

"Um..." Nev licked her lips. "When you're older."

"How much older?"

Nev chewed the gum and hid behind the aviators. "A good wine takes decades to ripen. If you drink it too early, it's sour. Once you pop the top, you have to drink the whole thing in two days. It stops aging. You only get one chance to time it right. The longer you wait, the better the good ones get. You're not ready. I'm not ready."

Ronnie rolled her eyes. "M'kay."

Nev got out and walked around, opened the passenger door, then helped her down. Ronnie steadied herself against the truck door.

Reg and Blaise stood behind Rainbow on the raised Victorian veranda, next to the sign. Rainbow ran out screaming the way she screamed for ice cream trucks. Ronnie braced for impact.

Her daughter was gentler than the dogs would be, but not by much. Rainbow squeezed her around the lower ribs as if testing to see if she would break.

Ronnie held her breath, patted her daughter on the back.

Nev walked her to the veranda before handing her off to her relatives. Reg and Rainbow lifted her up the stairs.

She watched her swollen feet—numb meat balloons on stiff ankles—to help them find the steps. "Don't have unprotected sex, kids."

On the other side of the screen door Mattie laughed.

Nev didn't follow. She had hung behind and was leaning against her truck.

Ronnie paused and turned back. "Call me later?"

Nev shook her head. "Can't. Have to drive Gunni to the airport. I'll be back next week."

Ronnie swallowed. "Have a safe trip."

Nev touched the brim of her Akubra, tipping her hat in a way few people could without looking ridiculous.

Mattie's friend had given him a front-row ticket to the match, but if Mattie was disappointed not to be there, he hid it. The Madonnas cuddled on the couch while the Crusaders versus Chiefs super rugby round robin match played on the telly.

The hospital had told her to walk around as often as she could to prevent internal scarring. When she shuffled around the house, waiting for the older wallaby joeys that were loose in the family room to hop out of the way, Mattie and Reg spotted her like she was a midfielder they were guarding.

She rested on the couch, propped up with pillows under her knees on one of the coveted ottomans while her relatives pampered her and brought her random things they thought she might need.

That night, Ronnie was the only one who didn't cook something. The kitchen was in holiday mode—giggly excitement, everyone teasing Mattie, who teased everyone, and razor-sharp focus on what magic spell Nonna was casting in the big pot.

After dinner, which was pork roast, they let Rainbow stay up late watching movies, eating popcorn and candy, while Nonna retired with her boxed wine to her apartment in back, off the pool.

At eleven, Blaise turned off the telly and dimmed the lights. Rainbow opened windows and turned on fans, pausing to watch Ronnie shuffle to the toilet.

In the dark living room she lay on the fold-out bed beside her daughter and listened to a chorus of ceiling fans. In the wide old house, a central corridor caught the breeze. At night they slept with front and back doors open. Screens kept some of the mosquitos out.

Rainbow was all elbows and knees, in the midst of a growth spurt. The girl was already up to Ronnie's chest. She was pretty. Puberty would be a nasty surprise for the girl. There was nothing Ronnie could do about that, except love her and make sure she had clothes that fit.

"Did they take out your vagina?" Rainbow asked.

Ronnie laughed. "No. Did you learn about reproductive systems in school?"

"Can you still get pregnant?"

"They took out one of my two fallopian tubes. The other still works."

"Were you trying to have a baby?" Rainbow asked.

"No. I was trying not to. I'm happy with the one I've got." Ronnie tweaked her nose.

"I don't want to be an only child."

It hadn't occurred to her that her daughter might be disappointed.

"By the time you get married, all your eggs will be dead."

Ronnie laughed. "Nine-year-olds don't worry about that."

"I'm mature."

"Not that mature. I don't want to do the family thing again. We're a family. I'm never going to get married. Why would I? I already have you."

"Don't use me as an excuse to fail at everything. You're kind of a loser, mum."

Bloody hell... She wasn't thick-skinned enough to survive a tween. "Rainbow! That hurts my feelings. I'm not a loser. I'm trying extremely hard. We don't talk down at people."

"Sorry."

"It's okay."

Rainbow snuggled under her arm. "This is so nice. I love this."

What? "Really?"

To her surprise, Rainbow nodded. A minute later the girl rolled over and her breathing slowed. Ronnie was left wondering what had just happened and what she had missed.

Mattie appeared like a disembodied head, lit from below by the cold glow of his phone. He bent over the bed, patted Ronnie on the head like a dog. "Are you awake?"

Ronnie grunted, mentally walking through all of the steps it would involve to extricate herself from the pillows, sheets, and lukewarm hot water bottles.

Mattie bent over Rainbow, then picked up the girl and carried her into his bedroom. He returned carrying a pillow, tossed it on the couch, clicked on the overhead light. "I'm calling Luca. Want to say hi?"

Ronnie's cold dead heart melted. "Yeah." She checked the time. "Help me up." He helped her sit up and shuffle over to the other couch. She reached back with both hands, grasped the side and back of the sofa, then eased herself down gingerly. She was never going to take her abs for granted again.

Beside her Mattie held up his phone like he was taking a selfie. A tiny head appeared on the screen. A toddler's head bobbed at the bottom edge of the frame. Mattie's face broke into a wide grin. "Luca! My boy!" He began babbling in a mixture of English and Spanish.

Luca's face lit up and he approached the camera. He glanced up at someone off-screen, then back at them. Luca reached for the phone, held it upside down, giggled.

She and Mattie waved again, grinning. Mattie asked Luca about his day at school, which must mean daycare.

The toddler replied in near-perfect English and fluent Spanish. Luca was precocious. Ronnie had noticed that the last time she saw him. He had been born two months premature, spent two harrowing months in the Spanish equivalent of a NICU, and had cochlear implants that looked like external hearing-aids.

Luca showed them his toy dinosaurs and trucks. They oohed and aahed appreciatively. Mattie babbled on delightedly in Spanish about the various qualities of the t-rex and triceratops, front-end loader and bulldozer.

After a few minutes the toddler lost interest and wandered off, hunting for bikkies and milk.

Judging by the way yellow light slanted across the walls of the apartment it was late afternoon in Madrid. Mattie chatted with the elderly woman easily and affectionately. Luca's great-grand-mother's name was Firenza.

Firenza encouraged Mattie to buy an apartment in Bilboa. Ronnie nodded off against his shoulder.

Your sister is sick?

Mattie held her with one arm and the phone with the other, struggling to explain the ectopic in his limited Spanish.

"Pobre Ronalda," Firenza said. *So ugly, like my aunt. Everyone called her a lesbian. Send her to me. I will find her a rich husband in Bilboa. There are men in the city who like women who look like men. It is because of the French that they like ugly women.*

After Mattie ended the call Ronnie snorted. He chuckled. "It is because of the French that they like ugly women," he whis-pered, imitating the exasperated cadence of the old woman's voice.

Ronnie laughed silently, hugging a pillow.

In the morning, Reg and Blaise moved around the kitchen, frying sausages on the stovetop while talking in low voices.

Mattie joined her on the glider in the screen room, offered her a plate of snags and eggs. She accepted it, holding a hot water bottle against her incision with her other hand. She had seen her incision at the hospital when a doctor examined it yesterday; she would have a c-section scar.

She ate beside her brother in companionable silence. Today she felt better.

Nev had arrived in Christchurch and texted her pictures of the inside of a yellow house that looked like something out of a luxury lifestyle magazine, as well as a picture of white-haired Gunni double-fisting bottles of madeira.

"Where's this bloke so I can beat him up?"

She looked up from her phone. "Come again?"

Mattie gestured to her stomach with his fork. "Stop looking at pictures of Nev for a minute and tell me who knocked up my baby sister."

It took her a minute to figure out what he was talking about. "Julio?"

"By the laws of the Middle Ages I have to kill him now. Where is he?"

She looked down at her plate of eggs. "I don't know. We're not together."

"Were you?"

She shrugged without looking up. "He thought we were."

"Not into long distance? He bailed on you, eh? Are you going to tell him?"

She swallowed. The low-level headache was constant, distracting. Painkillers took the edge off but she still felt half-broken and half-dead. If she stood up, the room would spin. The lightheadedness was back. That was normal, given how much blood she had lost. She decided not to shake her head.

Mattie stared at her. "What?" she asked.

He leaned forward, waved a hand in front of her face. "Earth to Brum. What are you thinking about?"

Good question. What was she thinking about? More importantly, what should she be thinking about? "I don't know. Rainbow, I guess." Now that she said it, she realized it was true. "I miss being able to rock her and sing to her, and carry her around. I miss being the solution to all of her problems. I miss being able to kiss her boo-boos better. I miss being magical and god-like in her eyes. I miss the toddler who sucked her thumb and pronounced words her own special way. I miss the sound of her little girl laugh, that giggle. The constant hugging and touching, walking hand-in-hand everywhere. Putting her socks and shoes on. Filling sippy cups with milk. I even miss washing sippy cups with the sour milk that turns to cheese at the bottom. I miss having a little drunk stumbling around, giggling, bursting into song, enjoying herself, slurring her words. I miss when she called herself '*Wain-bow*' and tractors *duhwaduwuh*."

Mattie stood, stretched, and sat next to her on the glider again. It groaned under his weight. He sat sideways facing her, hairy ankle on bulging knee, cheek on his fist. "You can have another."

"Don't want another. I want the years that I missed with her." Her eyes burned. That was the problem, wanting something impossible.

Mattie nudged her.

She turned to look over her shoulder at the doorway to the kitchen. Rainbow sat at the kitchen table eating a bowl of cereal. The girl had headphones on.

"Oi. Did you hear that?" Ronnie asked.

The girl's dark eyes flicked from her to Mattie and back to her phone.

Ronnie swallowed. Mattie grinned.

Had Rainbow missed her when she was a toddler? Did Rainbow miss her at night in her dreams? Was missing her mother a part of Rainbow the way it was a part of Ronnie? She hoped it wasn't.

"Did your fallopian tube explode because you fell off the roof?" Rainbow asked.

Ronnie blinked, caught off guard. "No. I fell off the roof because my fallopian tube exploded."

"Do we live here now?"

"Until I get my own place."

"I liked the donga. And I like camping at the farm."

"That's temporary."

Mattie stood up and tapped the empty spot on the glider meaningfully. Rainbow came over and tucked herself under Ronnie's arm. The girl still fit against her side.

"Don't get after me about being a deadbeat, alright? I love what I do. Being a dropout doesn't make a person a loser. I have goals. I'm working towards getting us a place to live. Saving. Everything is coming together. I know it looks like I don't have my shit together, but I do. I've been working toward the same goals since you were born. I've had a purpose since you were born. I'm not using you as an excuse to slack off. It's the opposite. Does that make sense?"

Rainbow nodded.

Reg had come into the kitchen to get more ice for his tea. "You should have seen me when I was young. I was single and living out of a van on the Gold Coast. I didn't have a savings account or a degree. I was a swaggie. I didn't settle down until Mattie was born. Made an honest man of myself accidentally and here I am. I don't regret those wandering years. They made me who I am. Gave me appreciation for all this. Brum's light years ahead of where I was."

"Thanks to you," Ronnie said. "Also, you were raising two kids and had a full-time job by the time you were nineteen."

"My point still stands. You may not realize this yet, Rainbow, but your mum is a special lady. She works longer and harder than other people her age. She doesn't shirk or cut corners. She's kind of a big deal, your mum."

"Thanks, da," Ronnie said. "Love you. You're sweet."

Reg draped a kitchen towel over his shoulder and shifted the joey that had just finished drinking a bottle of formula under his arm into both hands. It was wrapped in a Moana towel and looked at her with round eyes like black marbles. "Sweet, she says? Strewth! Did you hear that?" Reg ticked her with the baby wallaby's towel, making her flinch away and Rainbow giggle.

"Stop!" Ronnie said. Rainbow shrieked with laughter.

"I can't hear you!" he teased in a sing-song voice, continuing to tickle both of them.

"I'll get you for this!" Ronnie said.

"In your dreams, Brum!"

"Ow, seriously, stop. I'm gonna pop my stitches."

Reg looked apologetic. "Sorry, Brum."

"No worries."

25
PERIOD

Reg dropped Rainbow off at Maude's on Sunday night, then Mattie flew back to Auckland the following Friday. Without them the house felt empty. Ronnie reclaimed Mattie's old room, then did her best to melt into the guest bed and rot.

Reg woke her up. She blinked up at him owlishly.

"Hey, baby," he said.

She went back to sleep.

When she opened her eyes again Nev was leaning over her. Ronnie drew a deep breath. "How was your holiday?" Nev had gone somewhere. Why was Nev looking at her like that? Did they think she was milking it?

"Did you take something?" Nev asked.

Ronnie didn't understand the question. "Like what?"

"I don't know. Drugs?"

Ronnie snorted. "No. Why?"

"Your dad was concerned. He hasn't been able to shift you out and about."

Ronnie frowned, confused. "I'm anemic. I lost four liters of blood."

"He was wondering whether you needed to return to the hospital. Do you?"

"How would I know? I'm just rotting here like a good doobie. I didn't take anything. The pills ran out on Sunday."

"What have you been taking since then?"

"Nothing."

"Not even over the counter stuff?"

"It wasn't helping."

"Right. Can you sit up?"

With help she was able to sit up in bed. A hot flash. She closed her eyes. Her mouth filled with saliva. Lightheaded. Nev helped her swing her legs over the side of the bed and put her balloon feet on the floor.

"You're still retaining water."

Ronnie shook her head. She knew her ankles and feet were twice their normal size. That was normal after the surgery. "They said it could take a while. What day is it?"

"Friday. You need to move around, get your blood flowing." Nev was frowning. Nev smelled like sheep, lavender and smoke. "This is my fault."

"How?"

"I should have come earlier to check on you. I thought they were taking care of you."

"They have been. They've been bringing me meals and watching telly with me. They've been wonderful. It's a long recovery. I'm not milking it. I think your expectations are too high."

Nev shook her head. "The doctor told you to walk around."

"Leave me alone. I'm doing the best with what I've got." She exhaled impatiently. "You could have visited me after you got back. I know I've been boring. I've also been bored. I don't want to be here any more than you do. I'm sure you have more important things to do."

"You're right. I should have visited earlier. I was being an idiot." Nev's eyes looked tired, like she hadn't been sleeping. "I didn't want to intrude."

"Into what?"

"I don't hang out with people in their twenties."

"You're my friend. I want you around. I like spending time with you."

Nev chuckled. "I don't have friends in their twenties."

Ronnie swallowed a lump in her throat. "Well, now you do." It was hard to imagine what would have happened if Nev hadn't found her that night. Nev had saved her life twice, both times at night, both times at the farm.

Nev drew a deep breath.

April was always touch-and-go. Every day was the anniversary of another massacre. Ronnie had researched it, had learned enough to wish she had learned less.

Nev's eyes were gentle.

April 25, Anzac Day. From her dad's couch in the family room she could hear Nev hoovering the bedrooms in an awkward attempt to be useful. Nev couldn't sit still and do nothing.

Being stuck on the couch with no abdominal muscles blew. Ronnie wanted to fast-forward eight to twelve weeks.

Mattie pontificated over speakerphone. "If you end up marrying a hot woman and wanting more kids, she can use my sperm. Up to you how it gets delivered."

"You're gross," Ronnie said. "Are you dating anyone?"

"Nothing serious."

"Are any of your teammates out? You can't be the only secretly bi one." Mattie wasn't out at work. People assumed he was straight based on his profession, the way they assumed she was a lesbian.

On the other end of the line, he chuckled. "Thanks for outing me."

Ronnie inhaled sharply, wincing at the twinge in her scar, pressing her belly below the waistband of her gym shorts. "You're not at practice. It's a holiday."

"You got me. It's not something we ruggers talk about. If they are, it hasn't come up."

"That's what she said."

"Mum?" A muffled voice from the bathroom.

"Yeah?"

"Can you come here for a minute?" Rainbow asked.

"Coming!" Ronnie turned off speaker phone and held the phone to her ear. Nev had reappeared from the bedrooms and returned the vacuum to the closet. "Gotta run. Talk later. Love you."

"Love you, too, Stinky."

Ronnie tossed the phone on the couch. "Help." She stood up and hissed, gently pressing her scar to hold her abdominals together. The room spun. She leaned on Nev.

"Easy," Nev warned. "You're milking it. I've told you a thousand times not to stand up like toast popping out of a toaster!"

Ronnie shuffled to the bathroom, knocked.

A soft voice said, "Come in."

Inside, Rainbow sat red-faced on the toilet, looking sick.

"What's up?" Ronnie frowned. "Talk to me, babe."

"There's blood."

It was too early for Rainbow's first period. She wasn't even ten yet. "That's alright, babe. No worries. That happens. You have other pants." She felt sick to her stomach. Don't panic. Pretend everything is fine. Project calm.

Rainbow moped, knees pressed together, eyes downcast. Ronnie wondered if this was the first time it had happened. It must have come as a shock. "Has this happened before?"

Rainbow shook her head.

"Right. Well. Congratulations. Welcome to the club."

"I don't want to be in the club. The club sucks."

"Right. Well." Ronnie looked at her watch. Too late to call Maude. "I have pads. I can teach you how to use them. How do you feel?"

"Stomach hurts."

"That's normal. That's called cramps." She handed the girl some over-the counter painkillers and a glass of water. "When I got my first period I was fourteen. Nana Jane gave me a new shot-gun. I'm not giving you a shotgun."

"I don't want one."

She searched for something meaningful to say that wouldn't sound trite. "Rite of passage." *Bloody hell. Rite of passage? What does that mean? Is that the best you could do?* "Do you have questions, babe?"

Rainbow shook her head. "Give me the pads, I'll figure it out."

She did. "Instructions on the box."

"You can go now."

"Right." She swallowed. "We can talk about it in the morning."

"Or not."

"There's nothing wrong with you. It's a little earlier than I was expecting, but that's okay. Drink water."

"Go away."

Ronnie left.

Nev was waiting in the passage. Ronnie wobbled between the wall and Nev's side. In the kitchen she gingerly lowered herself into a chair, knowing she wouldn't be able to get up again.

"Is she alright?" Nev asked.

Ronnie nodded. Her back hurt.

They exchanged a look. Nothing needed to be said. Nev rubbed her face.

"Ice cream?" Ronnie asked. She didn't have the energy to scoop it.

Nev ignored the hint. "Did you get her sorted? I bet she's scared."

Ronnie considered the possibility. Imagined ice cream sitting in a bowl in front of her. "Not visibly."

"She's your daughter."

Ronnie wondered what Nev meant by that.

. . .

Nev scooped two bowls of mango ice cream. "Bring these to her. While she's eating you can spend quality time. It doesn't have to be deep. Five minutes of sitting together."

Nev carried the bowls. Ronnie shuffled down the passage again, leaning on the wall with every other step. The pain in her lower back radiated down into her right leg and up into her shoulder and neck.

Outside the closed bedroom door she stopped to close her eyes for a moment, focusing on breathing slowly and evenly. When she opened her eyes she saw Nev twitch, holding bowls of ice cream and frowning. "Don't faint, for the love of... I don't have any hands."

Ronnie laughed.

"Seriously, Dain'y. If you faint, no ice cream. Ice cream goes boom."

Ronnie cackled. She forced herself to balance on her legs without the support of the wall. She could do this. Nev handed her the bowls and knocked on the door of the bedroom Rainbow had locked herself in.

"Go away," Rainbow said.

On second thought, Ronnie couldn't do this. "Ice cream?"

"Come in."

She sat on the bed beside Rainbow. They ate the ice cream.

When the bowl was empty she set it on her lap. "What was your favorite part of last weekend?"

"Talking at night."

It took her a minute to remember. "To me?"

Rainbow nodded. Ronnie was confused. "Why?" Their night-time conversation had been the low point of the weekend for her.

"I like talking to you at night. It reminds me of when I was a kid."

"You are a kid."

"Not technically. I could be a mum now."

What a terrifying thought. Ronnie snorted. "You won't be for a long time. Do you know what sex is?"

"Ew, gross."

"I'm serious."

"Stop."

"I take it you don't have a boyfriend."

Rainbow scowled and handed her the empty ice cream bowl. Ronnie set it inside her own.

"Good talk," Rainbow said.

"Do you feel better?" Ronnie asked.

To her surprise, the girl nodded. Rainbow surprised her again by leaning over and hugging her. Ronnie carefully wrapped her arms around her daughter. Rainbow's hair smelled nice, like conditioner and kid dandruff.

"How was school?" Ronnie asked.

"Good."

"I'm sorry I can't do fun stuff right now. I know you're used to when we cook, go on adventures, run around, and do cool stuff at the farm like ride horses, but I'll be better soon and then I'll make up for it, I promise."

Rainbow pulled back and gave her a look that melted her heart. It was the "I really like you" look from when Rainbow was little. It was generous and unexpected and Rainbow didn't have to look at her like that if she didn't want to.

Ronnie kissed her on both cheeks and both eyes like she used to.

Rainbow beamed, more patient that she had to be at her age. "I like hanging out here with you. It's cozy. It's not boring. I'm getting to do all the things I like that you normally never let me do, like watching telly. This is like a holiday. And since you're home all the time, I get you all to myself. You have to listen to me talk about whatever I want to talk about. It's like a slumber party. You can't run away."

Ronnie felt funny. "I guess I hadn't thought of it like that," she admitted. "I love your positive attitude. You're making lemons out of lemonade." Where had Rainbow learned that? "You're such a cool kid. I wish I had been friends with you when I was your age." Rainbow was smart, curious, bookish, skeptical, had strong critical thinking skills, knew right from wrong, liked following and enforcing rules, could do anything in life, be anything.

She made it to the kitchen by placing one foot in front of the other. Nev was playing solitaire at the kitchen table. The older woman glanced up as she set the bowls in the sink. Ronnie turned on the water and washed the dishes. She felt the approval, could hear it in the quiet snick of a card flipped over. The clock on the stove said midnight.

"How did it go?" Nev asked.

"You were right."

"Sugar and fat make everything better. She's always had a sweet tooth. Inherited that from her mother."

Ronnie leaned on a chair, needed to lie down. "It's late."

"I should go."

The chair protested as the older woman stood. Nev swept the cards into a pile, shoved them back into their box.

"Sleepover at dad's house? Quintessential gay teenage experience?" Ronnie bit her lower lip suggestively. They both knew nothing could happen tonight. If Nev slept over, it would be extremely platonic and dorky.

Nev downed a glass of water, set it empty in the sink. "What would your dad say?"

"We have mates sleep over all the time. What do you think the guest bedroom is for?"

"It would be weird." Nev was right, but Ronnie didn't care. Weird was in her lane. She liked things that took her outside her comfort zone.

"Mikey crashed here one time, and they didn't mind. She's my mate from juvie, my mum friend. She's also gay, but I'm not dating her."

Nev raised an eyebrow. "I don't want to make your dad uncomfortable. It's his house. Ditto Blaise."

"You're overthinking."

"Someone has to."

Ronnie slowly straightened, shifting her balance to take her weight off the back of the chair. She would fall asleep the minute she lay down. "Suit yourself."

Nev helped her shuffle to the bathroom, then the bedroom, then reheated the water-bottle for her while she took ibuprofen.

Ronnie was the little spoon.

26

TEA HOUSE

In the morning Ronnie woke first. The house smelled like milk and baby formula. From the family room drifted the sounds of the older joeys jumping around and rattling cages to Blaise's Jane Fonda jazzercise VHS tapes. Carefully, holding her middle, she rolled over. Hissing, she moved onto her back, then onto her other side. Her hands and feet were asleep.

She lay in bed, waiting for the pins and needles to fade from her limbs, watching her friend sleep.

She touched the scar on Nev's chin, wondered how she had gotten it, then studied the crows feet at the corners of Nev's eyes, realizing she didn't know if her boss had ever been in love. Had the owner of Upsend Downs ever had a partner? Had she lost someone she loved? Had someone broken her heart? It seemed more likely that Nev had broken hearts, given the wandering life-style she had lived. Did she ever wish she had found someone? Did she like being alone?

Ronnie ran the backs of her fingernails through the short hair at her friend's temple. Up close, Nev's hair was a mix of straw-berry blonde and white. Nev must have gone grey early, because her hair had been this color when they met. She hadn't aged. If anything, she appeared to be getting younger.

Pale eyes opened, blinked. Nev's pupils contracted, focusing. Ronnie watched, curious to see how her friend would react to waking up in an unfamiliar bedroom.

Nev subtly stretched her spine, which cracked, then smiled. Nev freed her arms, then lifted one off the mattress, making her invitation clear.

Ronnie scooted closer, closed her eyes and relaxed again, exhaling deeply. Her hands, pressed against Nev's chest, found their way out and around in a symmetrical loose embrace. She relaxed again.

Nev's breath slowed and became even.

Ronnie didn't have anything to compare this to. It wasn't like any romantic relationship she had known. She wasn't even sure if it was romantic, but hoped it would be. Nev would be a gentleman in a way that none of her previous partners—male or female—had been.

There was a reciprocity to it, a hesitancy, like climbing a tree and testing every branch.

The next time she opened her eyes the sun kissed the curtains and Reg stood in the doorway. "Knocky knock. Wakey wake."

Nev, who lay curled facing Ronnie on the side of the bed closer to the door, stretched and rubbed her face, then groggily muttered, "right, what?" before immediately falling back asleep.

Reg grinned and made a heart shape with his fingers, which was something Mattie would have done. "The rest of us are driving to the Tea House at Lake Barrine for brunch. They have the fresh scones with jam and clotted cream that you like. Keen to tag along? My sisters are coming. They want proof of life. If you don't go, they're threatening to come over after."

"Is Rainbow going?"

Nev blinked, rolled over, spotted Reg in the doorway, then covered her eyes with her hand like a kid trying to make someone disappear.

"It was her idea. You're invited, too, Bickerman. Morning, cougar. Where's my shotgun? Never mind, I haven't got one."

"Don't make fun of me," Nev muttered.

"You? Never," Reg teased. "You two bogans coming? Does Brokeback Mountain do brunch?"

Ronnie took stock of the sensations in her body. Stiff. Sore. "Five minutes."

"Get dressed, have a wee. We'll meet you there." Reg disappeared but left the door open.

She watched Nev reach for a shirt and shrug it on with an effortlessness that made her jealous. The sheep farmer had slept in matching grey cotton panties and bra—duplicates of the same ones Nev always wore. One-type-of-undies, one-type-of-socks basic bitch, like Ronnie. Reg had reacted exactly the way she had known he would. He didn't care what she did so long as she was safe and happy.

Nev cleared her throat. "I expect you forgot all about this because it was a while ago, but I finally got around to mailing that climate change emergency relief grant you told me to apply for after the flood. It was a pain in the ass. Maybe the greenies who work for the state will throw some money at us for the moldy hay. Worth a shot. Thanks for suggesting it. I'm no good at asking for stuff like that."

Ronnie held out her fist. Fist bump. "That a girl! Leveling up in life."

"More like plumbing new depths of humiliation."

Sometimes it was the same. "You miss 100% of the shots you don't take."

Rainbow walked in without knocking as Nev was buttoning her jeans. Nev didn't blush, didn't run away—that was new. The girl looked like a tween in a white tank top and cut-off shorts. She approached the side of the bed and loomed over Ronnie, frowning. "Are you sick?"

Ronnie pulled the sheet up to her chin and sighed. "No, but I would like privacy while I get dressed, if it's not too much to ask."

She didn't want the girl to see the bruises. They looked worse than they were.

Rainbow turned her judgement on Nev. "What are you doing here?"

Nev respectfully ignored her.

"Try that again, but in a nice way," Ronnie said. "You can say, what a pleasant surprise! I'm happy to see you here! She's going to brunch with us."

"Why are you still here?" Rainbow asked Nev.

"Your mother asked you to do something. Did you hear what it was?"

Rainbow stared at Nev like she had two heads.

Ronnie closed her eyes. When she opened them again Rainbow was gone and the door was closed. Nev helped her sit up. Ronnie hissed, wincing, holding her incision. Slouched on the edge of the bed, she took a minute to catch her breath. The room spun. A wave of nausea came and went. She swallowed a mouthful of saliva, then opened her eyes again.

"Can I ask a question?" Nev asked.

"Shoot."

"Does your ex know you had major surgery nine days ago? Isn't Rainbow supposed to be with your ex this weekend? Why is she here?"

"I don't know. No one asked me. I don't mind. I like having her here." She didn't say Rainbow's name in case she was listening outside the closed door.

"What will you do after I leave?"

"Watch movies."

Nev blinked once, slow. Disapproval.

"And walk multiple circuits around the garden." When everyone else was gone she would be bored out of her mind again.

"You need hobbies," Nev said. "Like reading."

The last time she had been forced to stay indoors this long she had exercised hours a day in her cell, gotten high off endorphins, bulked up.

"Can you hold a guitar?"

"I think so."

"I'll teach you to play."

"Really? That would be awesome. I would love that."

The Tea House, built around 1930, was a charming historic building with a long green lawn and several daunting front steps. As soon as they reached the carpark at Lake Barrine and she saw the walk to the front door, she knew she had overestimated her stamina. Nev seemed to agree, based on how slowly she walked around the truck to open the passenger door. Ronnie psyched herself up to step down from the truck.

Hissing, she unfolded herself slowly.

"I don't like this," Nev said. "I have a bad feeling about this." An enormous amethystine python lay half-hidden along the edge of the carpark where the lawn hit the pavement and created a natural curb.

On the round crater lake, an old-fashioned white paddleboat chugged across like a trolley or a toy. She wanted to ride it, but had to stay focused on reaching the front door. She took her hand off the side of the truck, swearing under her breath.

"How do women with C-sections take care of babies?" Nev asked.

"Beats me. I can't imagine taking care of a newborn right now. Breastfeeding..."

"Did you...?" Nev steadied her when she stopped. "Right, my nerves are shot. We should get you home before you fall and hurt yourself again."

"It's not bad."

Nev laughed.

Inside, Ronnie headed for the table where her relatives were sitting. She hugged her aunts and uncles before sitting in one of the two empty chairs, feeling eleven pairs of eyes watch her lower herself with her arms.

Nev held the chair steady, pushed it in, then sat in the other one. "G'day, g'day."

Ronnie's aunt with the purple hair began. "G'day, g'day yourself. You look a dog's dinner!"

"Thanks, auntie."

"She lost four liters of blood," Reg said, almost proudly, as if surviving was an accomplishment.

"How do you feel?" her aunt with the purple hair asked.

"Alive."

Reg interjected. "If the ambulance had arrived ten minutes later, she would have had been dead or brain-damaged!"

"Is that all?" her uncle asked, unimpressed. "Doesn't sound too bad, does it? Could have been ebola, eh? One of those flesh-eating bacterias."

"Ebola's not a flesh-eating bacteria," Rainbow muttered, nose in a book.

Reg patted Nev's shoulder. "This ugly piece of shit saved her life."

Her aunt with the nose ring frowned at her across the white tablecloth. "Crikey, Brum... Can you still have children?"

Ronnie sighed. Coming here had been a mistake. "Yes, and no."

"How likely is it to happen again?" her aunt with the nose ring asked.

She picked up a menu and pretended to read it. "More likely."

"You'll have to do IVF?"

Ronnie glanced down at the menu, hoping they would take the hint. "Not planning to have any more kids come out of me. What's new with you?"

"You can't wiggle off the hook that easy. You're the news. Everyone wants to hear about your near-death experience. Did you see a white light?" her uncle asked.

Rainbow sucked loudly on her straw. She had already finished a glass of lemonade and the ice at the bottom rattled around under the suction from the straw. "They're sleeping together."

Ronnie's aunts and uncles gasped. Nev blushed. Ronnie touched her arm so she wouldn't run away.

"Rainbow..." Ronnie warned.

"Ron's a nun," Nev muttered. "There's a kilometer of surgical thread holding her together. She'd ooze out like a bowl of spaghetti."

"Yuck," Rainbow said, making a face. "What's a nun?"

"Me," Ronnie said.

"A woman married to Jesus," Reg said.

Rainbow frowned, skeptical. "You're not married to Jesus."

"I could be."

"Don't joke about that, you'll offend someone," Nev muttered.

Ronnie muttered under her breath. "You're the one who said it!"

"Can't distract us that easily," the aunt with the purple hair said. "I need details, Rainbow, show us the receipts."

"They slept in uncle Mattie's bed with no clothes on."

Ronnie shook her head. "Whoa, not true, big exaggeration—we both had underwear on, nothing happened, lot of people do that, it's totally normal, let's keep this rated G, please."

Nev eyed the exits.

Reg touched his sister's shoulder and shook his head.

"Have you ordered yet?" Ronnie asked, picking up the menu again.

Nev was beet red.

"Who's the baby daddy?" her aunt with bracelets asked.

Reg chimed in. "She says it was another one of those so-called American college students at the center for rainforest research. She's always getting knocked up by conservation biologists. Why is that? Are they super fertile? Or super sexy?"

"Dad!" Ronnie glared at him and gestured across the table at Rainbow. The girl still had a book over her face. Smart girl.

"Like the last one, who may or may not exist, he buggered off back to the states," Reg continued in a stage whisper. "I gather it was more of a casual hookup situation."

"End of your party days, then?" her uncle asked. "No more wild oats?"

Nev coughed, and went in search of the toilet.

Ronnie watched her go. "You're making her uncomfortable. She's not used to being teased in public. Her family didn't do that. She's had a traumatic experience, probably drank a liter of my blood when she was trying to inflate my dead meat suit, and now she's turning into a vampire, which must be difficult. It's bringing up stuff from her work in Africa with the UN."

Her relatives agreed.

"Obviously, we've got something going on, right? I'm really into her, 'cause look at her, she's bloody hot, but she's kind of aloof and says I'm too young for her. She's extremely skittish for whatever reasons, it doesn't matter, and I'm trying not to scare her off, if you don't mind. If I wanted you guys to talk about it in front of her, I would broach the subject first, but I didn't, so don't. She and I are just good mates."

Several of her aunts and uncles made air quotes with their fingers and winked theatrically at each other across the table.

"Back to what your dad said, I reckon you're too old to be sleeping with Americans," her aunt with the purple hair said.

Ronnie's eyes widened. "No one says that to Mattie!"

The relatives responded in a chorus. "Yes, we do!"

Blaise patted Ronnie's arm. "We do."

"I don't believe it," Ronnie said.

"Let her be," Reg warned. "Nev's harmless. I think it's sweet."

"Don't make it weird."

"Sleeping with your boss is...a choice," her uncle said. "None of us are surprised. This is very you, Brum. Reg, I'm surprised you don't have anything to say about this."

He shrugged. "I'm more concerned with how she's going to find a place to live so she doesn't take up my guest bedroom for the rest of her life. If she moves in with Nev, at least she won't be my responsibility."

She couldn't lean around the empty chair to whisper in his

ear, so she touched his shoulder. "Don't talk like that in front of Rainbow. She doesn't know you're joking."

"Who says I'm joking? I want to put roadkill babies in there! Am I the only one thinking about the wallabies?"

"Yes!"

The waitress came by. "Sleeping with our boss, are we? Who is?"

The relatives pointed at Ronnie, who folded her hands over the menu. "I'll have two orders of scones with clotted cream and jam, please, with a side of eggs. Do you have cheerios?"

"Fresh from the Toowoomba butcher this morning. How do you want your eggs?"

"Not exploding," her uncle said.

"Over easy, please."

"Cheers, love."

Everyone else's food arrived. Nev returned from the bathroom, then reached for the black coffee that had appeared at her spot and downed it. Ronnie put her arm around her friend's chair. "It's an ambush."

"I should go," Nev said, setting the empty white mug down on the white tablecloth.

Everyone at the table protested loudly.

"You can't go! We need you to tell us about all the sheep things you're doing on the farm! We love sheep, don't we, Kevin? Tell us a yarn! Not the one about brain worms, though, since we're eating."

Nev caught the waitress's eye, mouthed, 'to go,' and mimed the shape of a takeaway box.

"Can I ride Brighty?" Rainbow asked. Ronnie wiggled her pointer finger.

Ronnie's aunt with the purple hair said, "Nev, I always knew you were a lesbian because you look like Tig Notaro."

Relatives burst into an argument over whether this was accurate or not.

"What's a lesbian?" Nev asked.

The Madonnas stared at her. In her usual uniform of bargains from the men's clearance rack at the farm supply depot, she was the butchest person Ronnie had ever seen, and Ronnie had been to pride.

Ronnie patted her friend's shoulder.

"I could be straight or bi for all they know."

Ronnie refrained from mentioning the dog-eared copy of *Stone Butch Blues* on Nev's bookshelf. "We can talk about this later. No one's trying to out you."

Nev frowned.

Ronnie felt guilty. She reached for her friend's hand, but stopped herself. Nev was already embarrassed. Ronnie noticed everyone watching them. "In other news, Rainbow's on the rag."

"Mum!"

Aunties erupted into gasps and cheers, clapping wildly, leaping up out of their chairs and hugging the girl. All conversation turned to Rainbow, who found herself in the hotseat.

Nev stood, reached into the back pocket of her jeans for her wallet, dropped bills on the table. Ronnie swiveled sideways in her chair and pushed herself upright with her arms.

They slipped out. It wasn't a fast escape. Ronnie had to stop several times to catch her breath, but was relieved when they were finally alone in the truck. She slumped sweating in the passenger seat, laughing.

Ow... Laughing hurts...

She watched Nev put the truck in reverse, back out of the parking space, then put it in drive and turn left onto the Gillies Range Road west towards Lionheart. Nev rummaged behind the seat before handing her a cold Fanta.

"Bless you," Ronnie said, cracking it open.

"Don't get used to it. I'm nursing you back to life."

"Yes, and. Lean into that."

"You threw your kid under the bus."

"She deserved it," Ronnie said.

"That's debatable." Nev kept her eyes on the road. "I like your family."

"But?"

"Are they always that open?"

She thought about that for a minute. "Yeah, generally. I'm guessing your family isn't."

Nev shook her head. "Less so now that they're dead."

"That'll do it." She watched her friend drive. "Why did you get offended when they asked if you were a lesbian?"

"They didn't ask. They assumed. It's rude to out someone at brunch."

"I mean, yes," she agreed, "but do you think you're not out?"

"Are you asking if I'm straight?"

"This conversation is so weird."

"Obviously I'm a lesbian."

"Thank you. They were trying to be nice."

"The allyship flag was waving loud and clear. And yes, I'm mixing metaphors intentionally."

"You're in a mood."

To her amazement, she realized her friend was happy.

27
ANOTHER LIFE

Ronnie shuffled outside, cupped her hand around the phone. "Oi. Can you pick me up?" Reg helped Rainbow with her math homework at the dining room table. Rainbow corrected him every time he solved an equation differently than Nev would have.

Nev sounded exasperated. "Gumball has to be your priority right now. Stop calling me."

"After she falls asleep."

"What do you imagine life will be like if you get every other week with her?"

"I'll get used to it."

"Stop running away from her."

"I'm not. I'm here all the time."

"Don't perpetuate the cycle of abandonment." Nev was right, as usual. Irritating. "Go play with her."

She can be kind of a lot, if you haven't noticed. "Being around kids is exhausting."

The familiar roar of the large Kubota's engine carried through the phone. Nev was riding a tractor. Probably fertilizing the hayfields with lime. "Wait until she's a teenager. I've been meaning to ask. When you sleep over at my place, is it a Freudian thing?"

Ronnie swallowed, looked out at the pool and the dry grass in her dad's garden. She puffed out her cheeks, made a popping sound with her lips. She scratched a bug bite on the back of her arm. "What is that again?"

"Never mind," Nev said. "I don't want anyone to get their feelings hurt."

"I like you. It's not that complicated." She winced. "Am I taking advantage of you?"

Nev snorted. "Pretty sure it's the other way around."

Ronnie didn't know what that meant, only that Nev wasn't coming.

Saturday night, after Rainbow fell asleep, Ronnie texted Nev a picture of Rainbow asleep against her side. The girl was wearing pale purple pajamas with fluffy white clouds on them.

> (Nev) Good job, mama.

> (Ronnie) What's on for tomorrow?

> (Nev) For you, nada. I'm driving up to Mareeba to meet a potential buyer and give them a test bale. I'll leave after smoko. Might pay some bills. Could take Uni out if it doesn't rain, check perimeter fence for fallen trees. If it rains, I'll change the oil on the Kubota.

> (Ronnie) My hero

> (Nev) Go to sleep.

> (Ronnie) Miss you

> (Nev) No you don't. I don't do codependent shite.

Ronnie didn't answer. Eventually her phone vibrated again.

> (Nev) Sorry. There was nothing wrong with what
> you wrote. I miss you, too. Ennio Morricone and
> champagne make me emotional.

> (Ronnie) What's the occasion? Are we
> celebrating?

> (Nev) Not exactly.

Oh right. May was dicey for Nev, a continuation of April, heavy with anniversaries. The genocide had lasted one hundred days. Ronnie had read that somewhere.

> (Ronnie) Sorry

> (Nev) No worries.

> (Ronnie) Wish I was there

> (Nev) Enjoy your kid. She's growing up too fast.

> (Ronnie) Love you

Ronnie waited, holding her breath, resisting the urge to touch the black screen in her hand until after it vibrated. She felt silly for waiting. Her brain felt like a free throw from the sideline, frozen in mid-air. Her phone buzzed.

> (Nev) Love you.

The ball unfroze, play resumed.

Reg came in and kissed her head. He had been doing that lately, which would annoy her normally, but for the moment it was nice. "Who are you texting?"

Ronnie set the phone on the bedside table.

"Ah," Reg said. He sat on the bed. "We like her. Is she emotionally available, though?"

Ronnie shrugged.

Reg rubbed her feet. "You guys talk about ex-boyfriends or girlfriends?"

She shook her head.

He raised his eyebrows. "Friends talk about that stuff."

"Nev doesn't."

"Maybe she's asexual."

"I doubt it."

"You might want to ask her. Before you go too far down that road."

Ronnie shrugged. Her dad hadn't grilled her like this about any of her casual hookups.

"You guys have been getting a lot closer recently. You've been focusing on her instead of asking Maude how she feels about giving you your parental rights back. It's a distraction. You're procrastinating."

She frowned. "I think, in another life, she and I would have been together."

Reg blinked, then laughed awkwardly. "That's some depressing shite."

Her face burned. "I just meant..." What had she meant, exactly? "I want to find someone exactly like her who loves me the way she does. I want to work with her forever. Or at least see her every day. Ideally, we'd live together."

Reg chuckled. "I hope this is your way of saying you have a crush on her, not internalized homophobia that's gonna haunt you for the rest of your life and prevent you from ever finding true happiness."

"Um, no," Ronnie said. "The first one."

He looked relieved and let out a deep sigh. The foot massage he was giving her felt nice. "Talk to her. Relationships don't have to be murky. They can be straightforward and out in the open. You don't have to sneak around."

She hadn't experienced a healthy relationship like that. She had never brought a partner home to her parents. Maybe Nev would be the first, if that was the direction this was headed.

Reg was right. She should find out.

"Call Maude," he said.

"I will." *Eventually.*

Tuesday night Nev picked her up and drove her to a theremin concert at the Anglican church. The woman playing the theremin was a middle-aged white woman in a yellow sundress and a grey shrug. Without smiling, she raised her hands in the air like she was a conductor and the audience was the orchestra. The instrument was a metal stick protruding from a wooden box plugged into the wall with a bright orange extension cord half-hidden by a rug. Her hands hovered, one at chest-height, the other a little higher. One was closed, as if pulling an invisible string, the other open, pushing something away. It reminded Ronnie a little bit of the tai-chi she had seen older people doing at parks near the beach.

The audience watched, transfixed, as the woman used her hands to make the instrument, which must have been some kind of receiver, howl and warble. The sound was more like music than Ronnie had expected it to be. It was actually pleasant, like watching a magician play an invisible harp. It sounded like a flute or a bird, mixed with a synthesizer. It peeped and trilled, but most of all it whooped and whipped up and down the scale like a slide whistle.

Most impressive, though, were the times when the musician hit clear single notes, on key, not pitchy at all, without a trace of a slide into true. She must have known exactly where the notes were in the air, the way violinists know where to put their fingers on the strings. Precision like that took practice.

During the intermission, concertgoers milled around the church cemetery at dusk.

"My dad likes you," Ronnie said.

Nev pulled overgrown grass from around a random headstone. "Oh?"

"He respects you."

Nev lit up, then offered her the pack.

Ronnie shook her head. "We're quitting, remember?"

"After this one."

She held out her hand for the lit cigarette, then stubbed it out. "The pack." Nev handed it over reluctantly. Ronnie threw it in a waste bin. "Healthy living from now on. We're reformed."

Nev said nothing, continuing to weed the gravestones from the 1800s, revealing willow trees and winged death's heads, angels of death.

"Looking for anyone?"

"No."

"Are you asexual?" Ronnie asked.

"Not as far as I know. Why?"

"My dad was wondering."

Nev snorted. "You told him."

"What?"

"That we spoon. Is he creeped out?"

"No. Why would he be?" Ronnie asked. "He likes you."

"You tell me. It's creepy. I'm your boss."

"Yeah, but you're not like that kind of boss," Ronnie said. "You're not like, in a position of power. You don't manipulate me or make me do things for money." Gravestones of a family. Mother, father, and three children. Influenza epidemic, 1919. It had unfairly targeted the young. "Why do we never talk about personal stuff?"

"What do you mean I'm not in a position of power over you? I have more everything than you do. This isn't an equal dynamic. I wish it was, but it isn't. We're not in the same stage of life. We're not holding the same number of cards."

"I think you're wrong about that. You're like, skint, and have no friends, mate. You're not some big CEO with a corner office, babe. My dad thinks it's odd we don't talk about sex."

"Why would we?"

"I don't know. Friends talk about personal stuff."

"We talk about personal stuff." Nev laughed nervously.

Ronnie scuffed the grass with the toe of her Blundstones. "I have a crush on you."

Nev frowned, pink rising through her neck and ears.

Ronnie picked a blade of grass that had gone to seed, chewed on it. "Do you have a crush on me?"

Nev looked like she would rather be getting a root canal. "Jesus Christ, Dain'y." The Tablelands were open-minded on account of the rich greenies who retired here from Sydney for the weather and waterfalls, but Queensland was still the most conservative state. "If I did, I couldn't tell you because of workplace ethics. But I'd probably act the way I'm acting now, so conclude what you will."

Not direct enough.

"Have you ever been in a relationship?"

Nev nodded.

Thank god. This would have been awkward if she hadn't.

"I'm guessing you've been in the closet your whole life."

Nev shrugged. "I was and I wasn't."

"You have zero interest in this conversation."

"Correct."

"With anyone or with me?"

"What are you asking, Dain'y? How is it your dad's business what we talk about, hmm? Am I talking to you or your dad?" Nev wasn't usually defensive; something Ronnie said must have struck a nerve.

Ronnie felt bad. "I don't usually tell him things." *I don't tell him everything.*

Nev rubbed her forehead, then folded her arms, looking miserable. "I'm not asking you to keep secrets from him."

Don't freak out. It's just me.

"He doesn't want me to shag you," Nev said.

Peggy Collins chose that moment to walk up the stone steps into the chapel. Nev held the heavy door for her. "G'day, engaged lady."

"Thanks, darl'." The old woman leaned on Nev's arm to stage whisper. "This is the twenty-first century, love. Life's too short to worry what some man thinks."

Ronnie turned away, stifling a laugh. When they were alone again, she leaned against the iron railing. "Have you ever—"

Nev interrupted. "Intermission's over."

Inside the church, classical music resumed.

They returned to their seats for the second half of the concert. Ronnie sat with her jeans touching Nev's in the wooden pew. The theremin joined the string quartet. It made sounds like a giant flute, then like a human voice, making an open-throated *oooo, woop, woop, oooo.*

Like a Sarus Crane on the banks of Lake Tinaroo at dusk.

In the truck on the drive home, Nev said, apropos of nothing, "Your mum calls you Ripper."

"Rip. Ripper. Jack the Ripper. My initials."

Nev's gaze remained fixed on the road. Ronnie knew her friend couldn't open up yet—maybe never would. Part of her must be tempted, or she wouldn't look like this.

"It's good," Ronnie said, like reassuring a wild animal. She had to be so careful with this one. "I liked the concert." They rode in companionable silence.

Nev drove back to Stone House. Ronnie watched her pour herself a drink and swallow a pill before feeding the dogs.

"Want to have a fire down by the creek?" Nev asked.

"Good idea."

They walked downhill with head lamps, carrying bedding, eaten alive by mozzies.

The screen house loomed over them in the dark. If they finished fixing the roof, she could sleep there. While she was gone, a scrub fowl had made a large nest in the clearing out of leaves and a few sticks. A circle two meters across and half a meter high. Nothing was in it. Maybe it had been there before, but she hadn't noticed it.

Beside the campfire, Nev finished her beer, cracked another

one. "After University my line of work wasn't conducive to long-term relationships."

Ronnie melted into her camping chair.

"I travelled between assignments. Work had me moving around countries in Asia and Africa, never staying in one place longer than two months. I had relationships with women who were in the closet, for one reason or another, which ended. None of those relationships were great. The ADF, Aussie Defense Force, overturned their gay ban in ninety-two, but people were reluctant to come out for career reasons, and because so much of the work was overseas in places where it would have been dangerous to show PDA. The Americans started 'Don't Ask, Don't Tell' in ninety-three."

"How many lovers have you had?"

"No comment."

"When was the last time?"

"Oh, a fair while ago."

This did not surprise her. Nev seemed like someone who hadn't been touched in twenty years. "How do you feel about BDSM?"

"Rough stuff? Not my cup of tea, but if it's someone else's that's fine. Why? You like getting spanked?"

Ronnie chuckled. "Shut up." She sipped her beer and slouched in her camping chair, slapping a mosquito on her arm. People assumed she liked to be in control because of the way she looked. Usually, she didn't bother to correct them. This was why.

"You don't like the word 'spank.'"

"No. I don't. It's an instant turn-off." It sounded silly.

"Good to know," Nev said.

Ronnie sipped her beer.

"Do you feel different?"

She shook her head, then realized that wasn't true.

"You have changed, you know," Nev said.

"How?" She tried to remember how she had felt before, couldn't.

"You're more open. Your voice is softer."

"Really?" She found that hard to believe, but the more she thought about it, the more it felt true. She felt more receptive now, more sensitive to changes in ambient temperature. With only a limited amount of energy to draw from, each movement had to be intentional and serve a purpose. Before the accident, she would have been multitasking right now, tending the fire, searching the forest for dead branches to burn, cooking, listening to a game on the radio, texting someone, and running her mouth about god knows what, analyzing the next stages of the roof repair project, without paying attention to anything she was doing, because her mind would have been somewhere else.

Now she was content to watch flames lick wood.

She remembered cutting down that dead tree, chainsawing up the limbs, carrying them behind the barn in the front bucket of the mid-sized Kubota tractor, splitting them with the wood splitter, stacking them behind the barn. She sipped her Carlton Mid, watching Nev crouch beside the campfire to add another log.

"Who made the firewood before I came?"

Nev looked surprised. "We didn't really have fires before you came."

What?

"What? What do you mean you didn't have fires before I came?"

Nev shrugged. "Camping is your thing. Kazi and I never did this. Rick-Rac and Barney go home at night."

She tried to imagine life without campfires, couldn't.

"What's the point of living on a farm in the bush if you don't have fires?"

Nev looked sheepish.

Ronnie felt warm and tingly. The invisible cricket bat she carried around inside her for emergencies was gone, maybe forever. She moved differently without it, cautious, compensating. Her center of gravity had shifted. She would be slow until her abdominals grew back.

"Your eyes," Nev said.

Ronnie might have been horny and felt drunk, but her friend was actually drunk. An ant crawled along the back of Nev's hand. Nev took her guitar out of the case and taught Ronnie how to play a C chord, G chord, A minor and F chords.

Ronnie closed her eyes, inhaled weightlessness.

She felt somewhere between a steam engine with a red-hot boiler and a spitfire pilot who had just landed in the dark without wheels or landing gear; bruised, shaking, adrenaline-sick but clear-headed and sharp—lucky, sensitive, nervy and ready, one length ahead of the lightning, locked-in, unable to fail…

"All right?" Nev asked.

Ronnie kept her eyes closed. "Yeah." Being back here was triggering her old stuff from ten years ago.

"What do you need?"

"Nothing. Give me a minute." She did deep breathing, asked her body what was wrong. The guitar was something solid to hold onto. Smoke from the fire kept some of the mosquitos away. No wind.

Cold.

She shivered. The aircon inside the place had been icy the night Rainbow was born. The connection made sense now. She opened her eyes. Nev lay beside the fire, hand behind her head, ankles crossed. Ronnie slid closer to the fire, wincing, then warmed her long arms and legs as if she was giving the fire a hug. Immediately she felt better. The clearing smelled sharp and sweet, like eucalyptus.

"I'm back. Sorry, what were you saying?"

"We don't have to sleep here," Nev said. "I don't actually want to, if I'm being honest."

Ronnie's incision itched. Under the skin tugged.

"Let's go home," she said.

The walk up the hill in the dark took longer than the walk down had. Nev carried the sleeping bags and guitar.

Back at Stone House, in the glass and marble guest bedroom

bathroom Nev had remodeled nine years ago into an accessible bathroom for her aging father, Ronnie checked the wound below her waistband in the mirror. She had overdone it tonight and was lucky that it hadn't reopened.

She ran a shower, waited for hot water. Lights danced in the corners of the room.

A soft knock on the door.

"Come in."

Nev stepped in, sized up the situation, and shut the door behind her. "Can I join you?"

"Please."

Nev undressed, folding clothes that smelled like woodsmoke and lining them up on the bench smallest to largest. Ronnie stepped into the steamy shower and turned the heat down from scalding to hot before Nev joined her. They took turns under the stream, keeping a respectful distance apart, not touching. Ronnie averted her eyes like she would if she was showering with a friend in the locker room after football practice.

In the master bedroom they sat in the big bed under the fluffy white duvet and listened to Chopin. Women's football on the telly, muted, with subtitles. Ronnie sprawled on her back with her head on her arm.

"Is this all right?" she asked. As she asked, her phone vibrated. Incoming call from Maude.

Nev glanced up from her book, watched her send the call to voicemail, but made no comment. "Do you need anything?"

"I'm good. You sure you don't mind?"

"What do you need?" Nev asked.

"Nothing."

"Tell me if that changes."

Ronnie took over-the-counter painkillers, drank water. "You didn't like being down there."

Nev shook her head. Ronnie hadn't either.

The older woman set her phone on the bedside table and slid her reading glasses up into her hair.

Ronnie put a hot water bottle on her stomach, Nev's hand warm on her knee. There was still so much they were not saying, maybe never would say about that night down by the creek. The night she almost died. Technically, maybe she had died.

It wasn't clear why Nev had reacted as if the loss was her own. That was Nev's personality, to be responsible for things.

Like a nocturnal animal, the older woman wasn't always there in the day, or if she was she wasn't always on the right foot, but she was there at night, in the ugliness and pain. Nev was the veteran in the darkness, found it beautiful, saw more clearly at night, knew all the hidden paths and ways. When traveling in a foreign country, hire a local guide. Nev was that interpreter.

Ronnie's phone rang. It was Rainbow's number. Ronnie answered. "Hiya, babe. What's going on?" She glanced at Nev, who was reading a James Baldwin book.

Rainbow's voice. "Hi."

The burn started in Ronnie's chest, then travelled to her throat and eyes. She cradled the phone against her ear. "Everything good?" She really needed to figure out video calling.

"Are you feeling better?"

"Much better today. I'm at Stone House with Nev. We went hiking." *I'm sore but it was worth it. Worth it to feel human again.*

"Where?"

"Down to Lazy Creek. We had a fire."

"You shouldn't have done that, mum. Don't do too much. You're not superwoman. You need to take it slow."

"Thanks, babe. What did you do today? You had school? What did you do in soccer practice?"

"Drills."

"Which ones?"

"Lots of stuff. Foot work. Sprints."

"Was it fun?"

"Yeah."

"Everyone nice to you?"

"Yeah."

"Did you play a friendly? Score any goals?"

"Four."

"Good onya! That's my girl! How did it feel?"

"Normal. What did you do today?" Rainbow asked.

"Nev and I went to a theremin concert. Have you ever seen a theremin?"

Rainbow had never heard of it and didn't believe it was real. "Can I talk to Nev?

Surprised, Ronnie handed the phone over. It was sweet how much Rainbow liked Nev. "Rainbow wants to talk to you." Hopefully, Rainbow had gotten over her prudishness and forgiven them for sleeping in the same bed at Reg's house. Rainbow got upset easily but forgave just as fast.

Nev took the phone without hesitation and put it on speaker. "Hey Gumball."

A woman's voice came over the line. "Who is this?"

Nev frowned and shot her a look.

She froze. "It's Maude," she mouthed. "Say something or hand me the phone."

Nev handed the phone back. "She hung up."

Ronnie stared at the home screen, feeling like she was falling up.

Nev clarified. "She hung up on me, not on you."

She called Maude back. It rang once, then went to voicemail. She swore. This was not good. She stared at her home screen again, which was a picture of Rainbow as a baby. A shiver ran down her spine.

"Oi," Nev warned, watching her. "It's late. Maybe it's past her bedtime."

She shook her head. "She's never hung up on me when I'm talking to Rainbow... She's never cut me off before..."

Is Rainbow upset? Does she need me? Obviously, she needs me. Do I need to go over there?

"Relax. She's not upset with you. She doesn't know who I am. She's doesn't want her talking to strangers late at night. You'll finish your conversation soon. This is not a big deal. It's not going to change her decision about giving you equal custody."

Ronnie didn't know if it was a big deal or not. That was what was so terrifying—she never knew what was a big deal with Maude. One thing Nev was wrong about, though.

"She knows who you are. Rainbow talks about you all the time."

Nev's eyebrows rose.

Ronnie called again, no answer.

"Give it a rest." Nev pulled her laptop onto her lap and opened a website, scrolled down to pictures of sheep. "Look at these gorgeous rams. Let's make up names for them and rank our top three choices for next year. You love that."

"What if she's in trouble? She had something to tell you. What if it's important? What if something bad happened? What if Maude's been...giving her a hard time?"

"That's a lot of what ifs."

"Should I go over there?"

"No. That would be a terrible idea. You could get in a lot of trouble for showing up uninvited. Don't even think about it."

Nev tapped her laptop screen, drawing Ronnie's attention back to the rams. The rams had been photographed against blurry green backgrounds by people with expensive camera lenses. Nev could do that: take glamour shots of livestock, make them look like movie stars. "What about that one?" Nev said, pointing to a Border-Leicester ram with a majestic profile and a bald head. "What's his name?"

Ronnie pulled the computer onto her lap to get a closer look. She said the first word that came into her head. "Blue." Nev's eyes were a sort of pale sky color that changed depending on the light.

Nev accepted her laptop back.

"True Blue. That's the best I've got. I like Border-Leicester and Southdown. I'd also be fine with Dorset, White Suffolk or Corriedale. You pick."

Nev looked disappointed. "I thought we agreed to make the

lambs less cute and fluffy next year so we wouldn't grow so attached to them."

"That plan is flawed, mate." They would grow attached to the lambs regardless of what they looked like. All lambs were adorable.

Ronnie called Maude. The line rang. Maude answered. "Hello?"

"Please don't hang up again."

"Sorry about that. I wasn't trying to. Rainbow and I had to have a talk about mobile phone safety."

"I thought we agreed she could call me any time."

"She can. I didn't know she was talking to you. It's after her bedtime. She's supposed to be sleeping right now. Let me bring her the phone."

She drew a deep breath in, then let it out slowly. Maude wasn't angry. Everything was fine. False alarm. Over the phone she heard Maude walking up the stairs and could picture the antique wooden staircase with the Victorian railings and redwood banisters, so out of place in the otherwise dumpy old Queenslander. She swallowed. "You've been trying to call me? I saw I missed a call or two."

"You've been avoiding me."

"Sorry, babe. Sometimes I turn it off at work. I'll keep it turned on."

"I thought you were on medical leave?"

"I am."

"You're hanging out at the farm not working."

"Um, yeah?"

"What happened? The rumor mill about you is wild right now —I keep hearing stories about you getting hurt at work. Are you all right?"

She couldn't explain the ectopic to her ex over the phone right now. "It's a long story, but I'll be fine. I can't lift anything for eight weeks."

Maude swore. "That sucks. Can you drive?"

"Not currently."

"Maybe we should hold off on you taking Rainbow until you can drive again?"

Ronnie's stomach dropped. *I need to see her.* "My dad or Blaise have been picking her up and dropping her off, so nothing has changed from that perspective."

"If you think you're up to it. I feel bad for sending her with you two weekends in a row. I wouldn't have if I had known you were laid up. Can you still supervise her properly? I don't want Nev driving her around. Like, that's a red line in the sand for me."

Ronnie stole a sideways glance at her friend. Nev was still oogling rams.

"She doesn't."

"I know you're like the friendliest person ever and haven't experienced stranger danger, but we're still on the same page about not letting her be alone with people outside of nuclear family members, right?"

"Right. Still on the same page."

"Good. Here she is."

"Hi," Rainbow said.

Ronnie felt her shoulders drop and her body relax. "Hi, babe. Everything okay?"

"Yeah."

"How are you doing? I know the last three weeks haven't been easy for you."

Silence. Rainbow didn't want to say. Talking about feelings was awkward.

Ronnie swallowed. Now is when she would have given her daughter a hug if she could. "I'm hugging you through the phone. How have kids been at school? Have your mates been there for you? Do you talk to them about stuff?"

"Yeah."

"I emailed your teacher. She seems nice."

"Do you know if it was a girl or boy?"

What? "Who?"

"The baby."

Oof... Ronnie was not prepared for that one. "It was too early to tell, babe."

"I dreamed about him."

Bloody hell... Ronnie glanced over at Nev, who had closed her laptop and was reading James Baldwin again. "Right. Sometimes things like that happen in dreams. What was he like?"

Rainbow hesitated. "His name was Riley. He was cute."

"That's..." Ronnie swallowed. "You know I'd never in a million years have named it Riley, right?"

Rainbow snorted.

"I have to stick to the theme. It has to sound good with your name."

Rainbow chuckled. "Can you take me to the mall?"

"You know I hate the mall, babes."

"I need pants."

"Mama doesn't buy you clothes? Fine. If you go to the aquarium with me."

"Deal."

"Will you go to the aquarium with us?" Ronnie asked Nev. Nev shook her head. Ronnie turned back to the phone. "You're a great kid. I'm so lucky to be your mum. I'm sorry this happened. There's no right or wrong way to feel. It was super early, and it was never viable. It wasn't in the right place so there was never a chance it would develop. Some people in this situation are sad about it. Others don't think about it that much. Some people brush it off. And that's all right, too. You can be sad about it or not. Does that make sense?"

"Yeah," Rainbow said.

"What are you feeling?"

"It's a lot."

"Yeah."

"It was scary."

"Scary as hell."

"Will it happen again?"

"At the moment there's zero chance of that."

Rainbow's voice became quiet. "I want a brother."

Aww... Sweetheart...

"I know having a sibling would be fun, wouldn't it? You want a brother because I have a brother? Your mates all have little siblings, don't they? That isn't in the cards at the moment. I'm not in a position to have a baby right now. I would be a single mum again, which is hard. I would want to be in a relationship first, and have saved up a nest egg. Getting equal custody of you in October has got to be my main focus now. No distractions. After that, hopefully everything will settle into a rhythm and feel more relaxed. Good plan?"

"I want to live with you."

"Ditto, baby. Your mama will still have you half the time. We'll live at grandad's while I look for a place. We have to think about what's best for you long term. Who can provide the best resources for you, what school you want to go to, that sort of thing. I might have to buy cheap land further out in the Outback, who knows. I might not be able to stay in Lionheart forever." *The closest professional footy team's two hours away.* "The judge might ask me to take parenting classes or something for all I know. We'll see how it all shakes out."

"Are you changing your mind?"

"Not at all. I'm all in, babe."

"Why can't we live on the farm?"

"I said 'a farm,' not 'the farm,' babe."

"But I want to ride Brighty..."

Nev pointed to her watch. It was midnight.

"You have school tomorrow," Ronnie said. "I have to let you go."

"Awww..."

"Call me any time. If I don't answer, call back. Goodnight, babe."

"Tell Nev I say goodnight."

She turned to Nev. "Rainbow says goodnight."

"Tell her I say tootle-oo."

"Nev says tootle-oo."

"Love you, mum."

"Love you."

Ronnie felt lighter after she tossed her phone on the duvet. Rainbow had named the embryo Riley of all things. The ectopic was a distraction, but it had reminded her how precious this relationship with her daughter was. Rainbow was the ball and the goal.

Time to move past the lost years, let go of what had been stolen from her, and focus on making the most of the years they had left. Rainbow wouldn't be a child much longer. Puberty was a critical time in a girl's life. She would be there for her daughter in a way her own mother hadn't been.

"You look like you figured something out," Nev said.

"She's so great. I love her so much."

"She's a keeper," Nev agreed.

"So are you." A vision of the future she wanted, shifting into focus. "You're my person. You're not a substitute or a placeholder. If I was dating someone, I'd still be here with you right now. You're my bezzie. This is where I want to be. I don't care if it's childish to have a best friend. I don't ever want to stop doing this. There's things I share with you that I wouldn't share with a girl I was dating. We're past that. We're approaching family territory."

"Wow. Okay."

"Now you say something."

Nev looked at her, then licked her lips.

"You think I'll disappear as soon as I start dating again?"

"That's generally how this goes."

Damn... Objective fact stated without judgement: a masterclass in maturity. Nev continued. "I'm supportive of you. I don't have an opinion. I'm not allowed to have an opinion."

"What do you mean?"

Silence.

"Am I way off base here?" Ronnie asked.

Nev shook her head.

"Is it cringey when I call you my best mate?"

Nev shook her head. "I wouldn't use those words, but I don't mind if you do. You're so young. I don't want to rub off on you."

"You think because we keep this on the DL that there's something wrong with it, something icky?"

"We haven't done anything, Dain'y. Not embarrassed. Not a secret."

"I'm not embarrassed either. I don't think we need to put a label on this."

"Don't overthink it, Dain'y. I love having you in my life—but this isn't a relationship. Besides, talking about feelings kills them."

"It is a relationship. You don't actually believe that."

"I guess not. I guess I'm full of shite."

"We have a tree baby," Ronnie said. There. She had said it.

Nev blushed and rubbed the side of her nose.

Ronnie laughed. "We're tree parents."

"It sounds ridiculous."

"I'm not kidding."

"There's an element of magical thinking involved," Nev said.

"Not really. This relationship has value and deserves to take up space. I factor you into my long-term plans. If we ever start to hate each other, we'll go to counseling together."

"Wow, okay. You're doing some unhealthy codependent thing. Let's not micromanage this to death. It needs to breathe. Friendships evolve. They're organic. Friends go through seasons of intimacy and distance. That's healthy. It doesn't have to be prescriptive. There might be years when we don't see each other."

"When? The only time we don't hang out is when you're in Rwanda. Are you planning to move away?"

"No. That was hypothetical."

"Why would we not see each other?"

"Relax. Your hormones are all over the place. Your body thinks you gave birth. Your estrogen is up and your testosterone is down."

Ronnie sighed in frustration. "You have no idea what you're talking about. I still have valid thoughts when I'm hormonal. You're on the same roller coaster I am."

"I didn't have major surgery on my reproductive system. You're more hormonal that I am."

"Stop talking about it, please."

Nev looked like she hadn't been sleeping well. Ronnie knew her friend had been staying up late drinking and waking earlier than usual, burning the candle at both ends.

"Lie down," Ronnie said. The older woman's shoulders and upper back were full of knots. Nev's fingers were work-scabbed on the forefinger knuckles, rough from a quarter century of farming without work gloves.

Nev turned out the light. "I have to work in the morning."

Ronnie closed her eyes, exhaled. She felt old, but not in a bad way. Had to protect Nev from Nev's demons; working too hard and being too generous. It sounded like a beauty pageant answer.

"Old lady," Ronnie muttered.

Nev's breathing changed. Stopped. Resumed. Ronnie's hand came to rest on Nev's arm. After a while she touched the back of Nev's head, scratched her scalp where columns of muscle from her neck met her skull. She fell asleep with her hand on the back of Nev's head.

She woke up in the dark to the smell of sweat.

Nev sniffled, congested, an allergy sound. Nev didn't have allergies.

Ronnie let her breath slow and deepen, let her chest expand with each inhale. Nev's sadness would pass. Ronnie felt tenderness for her friend, the sort you feel for a past or future version of yourself.

When Rainbow cried, her pain was chaotic, urgent, coupled with fear and helplessness. Her daughter's tears physically hurt some muscle in her chest. Child pain was sharper than adult pain.

Adult pain was always secretly about something else, something that happened before, some secret hurt from ten, twenty, thirty years prior. Distance dulled it. Adult pain could be stopped and started. It came when one was alone. It stopped when someone else appeared, put back into the box.

The taxidermized barn owl observed from her perch in the corner.

Maybe Nev missed her parents. Had Nev been with them both at the end? Ronnie realized she didn't know. What else had happened during the lost years, the two years they never talked about?

From now on Ronnie wouldn't date anyone who didn't want kids.

How would Nev fit into that? Would Ronnie tell her future partner that Nev was like a sister to her? That Nev needed her? That she needed the older woman more?

Would she still work for Nev a decade from now?

She was outgrowing the farm labor around Upsend, aging out of mucking the horse stalls and filling water buckets when there were teenagers for that. She could become a barn manager or a mechanic, make a higher hourly rate somewhere else. Nev had been trying to promote her, but accepting a raise was a commitment to stay.

She couldn't stay here at Upsend Downs forever, much as she would like to.

Moving into Nev's screen house down by the creek might have been a possibility before she fell off the roof, but had become dramatically less appealing.

"We're okay." She rubbed Nev's warm back, hoping it was true.

28

PROCRASTINATION

The only downside of being a soccer family was that since Ronnie coached Atherton, she had never been able to attend Rainbow's soccer matches for Gordonvale.

Where life closed a door, it opened a window. On Saturday morning, she tagged along with Reg to Rainbow's match since she wasn't supposed to drive herself yet. In early May, sugarcane flowered in the fields along the road to Gordonvale. She couldn't wear anything with a waistband yet on account of the bloating, so she wore one of Mattie's old Alien Weaponry hoodies and baggy gym shorts he had left behind in the dresser in his room.

She cheered when Rainbow scored a goal. Five minutes later the nine-year-old scored another, fist-pumped, then high-fived her teammates.

Ronnie cheered, hooting.

It happened again.

Unbelievable. Rainbow was a ringer.

No one in the stands acted surprised. Reg clapped, but he didn't jump up and down or throw his hat on the ground the way she expected he would if he was as shocked as she was. Why had no one told her how fast Rainbow was? Or that she was the star player on her team?

"Dad! Rainbow's a ringer!"

Rainbow's footwork was clean—she controlled the ball whenever her boot made contact with it. "How'd she get that good? Her coach is terrible."

Reg squeezed her shoulder, grinning. "All those lessons you gave her. It's a Madonna thing. You were like that at her age."

She didn't know how to feel about this revelation. Her daughter was a whole other person on the pitch: confident and bossy, ordering her teammates to get open, pointing them to where they needed to go in order for her to pass to them. Rainbow looked like her tiny clone, except for the fact that Rainbow's ponytail was high and had a bow in it.

Sun shining, freshly-cut Bermuda grass, happy crowd, happy daughter. *This feeling, bloody hell...* Better than anything she could have imagined when she was fifteen.

What a perfect day...

As that thought crossed her mind, she noticed Brad Collins in the stands on the other side, cheering for the Lionheart girls with his wife and twelve-year-old son. His nine-year-old daughter, Lacey, was on the field playing for Lionheart.

He flashed her a double thumbs up.

She ignored him.

Beside him in the stands, his aunt Debbie and grandmother Peggy clapped. They were cheering for Rainbow.

Ignore him...

Inside the pocket of her hoodie her phone vibrated—incoming call from Maude. She hesitated for a moment, looking down at the screen, before she answered. "How ya goin'?"

"Where are you?"

She squinted against the sun. "At Rainbow's game. What's up?"

"I heard from your lawyer."

Ronnie swallowed. She shifted on the hard bench, suddenly uncomfortable.

"You're doing that thing you do. You're avoiding talking about this," Maude accused in a light voice.

Next to her, her dad ate peanuts and dropped the shells.

She cupped her hand around the phone. "I'm listening."

"We need to have a sit-down with her. Who's paying her bill? It better not be me."

"I am."

"On your salary?"

Ronnie snorted. *As if tattooing paid better...* "Did you talk to her? What did she say?"

"I met with her at her office. She seems nice. She walked me through everything I have to do and what would change."

When will the other shoe drop...

On the other end of the line Maude's high voice sounded relaxed. When she was in a good mood, her rural Queensland accent all but disappeared and she sounded urban, like a woman from Sydney. "Can you handle this right now? Are you emotionally mature enough and financially stable enough to take care of a human being? You can't even take care of yourself. You're a mess."

Ronnie swore inwardly.

Maude continued. "But Rainbow adores you, and she trusts you. She thinks you're god. You've always been so good with her. I keep expecting you to stuff it up, but you haven't. Not with her, anyway. Having two supportive, loving parents would be better for her in the long term."

"Thank you? I think so." Maybe this bullet was going wide. She got up and walked down the grandstands.

Maude plowed ahead with her lecture like she thought she might not get another chance. "She has self-confidence issues and anxiety about the fact that you gave her up. She thinks you didn't want her."

She could relate. "Right."

"If I give you custody back, you have to be one hundred and ten percent reliable. Do you understand? You can't be unpredictable or fun. You can't be the fun one. You have to be a responsible adult. You're dealing with a traumatized child. This can't be about you and your baggage, or about what's best for you, it has to be for her, and what's best for her."

"I am. I am good for her."

"If you get your shit together and don't stuff this up, I'm open to it."

Ronnie laughed, tingling. Adrenaline rush, full-body chills. "Thanks. I appreciate that."

"I have conditions."

The bottom dropped out of her stomach. "Right."

"Do you want to meet up to talk about it?"

"No, not really. Could you email the list to me? That would be easier. Maybe email it to the lawyer so she can forward it to me?"

"You want to pay a woman a hundred dollars to forward you an email?"

"I'm supposed to keep a paper trail of everything. Trying to do everything right."

"Better late than never, I guess. It's not a long list. I'll email it to the lawyer. You'll see. It's all normal stuff."

"Thanks." She felt hot, like she might be sick, and tried to imagine what someone smart would say. "Did you want to schedule a time to meet with her together?"

"Maybe later. The hearing's not until spring. My list will give you something to work on. At some point we should sit down with Rainbow and explain it to her."

That sounded like a terrible idea, and also completely unnecessary. Having her and Maude in the same room unsupervised could go south fast. "I would need the lawyer to be there."

Silence on the other end.

Next to her, Reg had started listening in. He had figured out who she was talking to.

"Still there?" Ronnie asked.

"I'm still here."

"She's our lawyer. She represents both of us."

"Don't be a bitch about this."

"I'm not. This is important to me. I don't want anything to go wrong."

"Don't blow it."

"I won't." Ronnie had to keep her ex happy. If Maude walked away now, Ronnie might never get another chance, and Rainbow would end up in court petitioning for emancipation, becoming a bitter, disgruntled teenager. "Thanks for doing this. Thanks for helping me."

"I'm doing this for Rainbow, not for you."

"Right."

"Kisses."

"Bye." She hung up and slid the phone back into the pocket of her hoodie.

Reg held out his hands expectantly. "What did she say? Is it still a yes?"

Ronnie nodded. "Yeah."

Reg whooped and jumped to his feet, pumping his fist. He looked like Mattie.

In May she resumed coaching her primary school girls, the Wattles, belly-laughing at their dancing, ponytail flips, cheers, cartwheels, dribbling and passing, the routine of it, the smell of freshly mown grass, amazed and grateful that this ridiculousness was her life.

Her back ached. She had been ignoring the letter from the Lions. By October she would be strong enough to play for her local amateur team, the Cutters, but would she be fast enough to survive try-out camp week in Brisbane? Standards were higher at the pro level. If she wasn't scoring tries by the spring, there would be no reason to fly to Brisbane.

Trying out for a professional team three days away wouldn't demonstrate commitment to parenting. But weren't self-care and self-improvement parts of being a good parent? Playing pro footy would be good for her.

What kind of role model would she be if she didn't pursue her dreams? What kind of role model was she now? A high school dropout working a dead-end minimum wage job?

"Which way are you leaning?" Jackie Collins asked on the sidelines of the Atherton primary school athletic fields.

"Leaning toward taking the free vacation. Realistically, they won't pick me anyway."

After practice she high-fived her Wattles, girls pink and sweaty now in yellow school uniforms, then took the public bus back to her dad's purple Queenslander in Lionheart, feeling old, watching FOR SALE signs for properties she couldn't afford float by along the roadside, wanting two mutually-exclusive things.

29
RAINBOW'S BIRTHDAY

On Rainbow's tenth birthday, May twenty first, Ronnie lay in bed alone, looking out the screen into Blaise's native plant garden. No rain again last night, cooler morning, mist rising off the mountains, autumn transitioning into dry season.

Quiet outside.

Reg's flag hung limp. The ocean would be glassy, not even enough wind for mush burgers. Nature felt less alive this morning, except two small brown honeyeaters in the bottlebrush grevillea cheerfully took turns whistling "tyzuit."

Next weekend they would pretend it was Rainbow's birthday, decorate a cake, sing the song, blow out candles.

Feeling hollow, she lay in bed staring at the ceiling. An empty anniversary. Memories echoed in the closed zoo sounds of her dad and stepmom's empty house. Wallaby water bottles rattled in the family room. Matilda and Maya's nails clicked over tile as they padded around the kitchen.

When she closed her eyes, she saw her fingers delicately caressing the tiny lavender body. Rainbow had been the size of a footy ball when she was born, a squishy alien with fat belly and skinny frog limbs. Nothing had prepared her for that moment—

suddenly being responsible for a helpless creature who owed her everything and nothing.

Ronnie had labored quietly. No one had known she was in active labor, alone at night in her cell. Slow at first, then fast and bloody. Those first miraculous moments as a duo had been wild. No audience. She had pushed out an organ, watched it come to life, breathe for the first time, flail her arms and legs for the first time without resistance, had seen Rainbow as she had been inside her: her-shaped, a piece of her attached by what looked like a white telephone cord.

Immediately after birth, Rainbow smelled like roast beef.

The first time Ronnie held her in her arms and hugged her to her breasts, Rainbow had relaxed. Home. It felt like she had always been there, like she had never left.

Ronnie's womb was on the outside now, perched on top of her round postpartum tummy. Squishy mama shaped to hold a squishy newborn.

Rainbow opened her eyes.

Ronnie sang to her.

Rainbow's wrinkled hand gripped her finger.

No one had warned her about the placenta. At first, when she labored to deliver the thick organ at the other end of Rainbow's umbilical cord, she thought Rainbow had a twin.

After the placenta came out, she had fallen asleep holding her daughter against her chest in the silence and the dark, had woken alone in light and deafening noise.

A decade later, after years of therapy, she still missed her baby.

Ten years old. How was that possible?

In the kitchen, she stuck a pink and white candle in a banana, found a lighter in a drawer and lit it, careful not to burn her thumb.

The flame flickered, then held steady.

Happy birthday, Rainbow. I would be with you if I could.

She blew out the candle, thought about making a wish, but didn't. Asking would jinx it.

It took everything she had not to jump in the truck and go to her, scoop her up in her arms and take her away, the way Matilda-Jane had disappeared her into the Outback in that goddamn white van.

A familiar truck engine outside jarred her back into the present. Nev knocked on the front door, whistling, carrying an esky. "Happy days." Nev hung her Akubra on the hat tree and toed off her boots on the mat inside the door.

"You're in a good mood."

She watched Nev stack frozen packs of lamb and mutton from last year in Reg's freezer like bricks. Nev must be clearing out to make space at home, and that was why she was whistling. A new batch was coming to fill the freezers at Upsend Downs. She must have deposited a fat check that morning, hence the whistling.

Yesterday, Upsend Downs had sent eighteen hundred lambs and two hundred ewes to slaughter—the fruit of a year's labor. Nev and Kazi had driven them on horseback to a neighboring farm to be butchered. Ronnie was a little disappointed that she had missed it.

"How did it go?" she asked. Droving days were her favorite.

"No problems," Nev said, pulling groceries out of the cooler she had brought. "I came to cheer you ladies up."

Nev slowly covered Blaise's kitchen counter with produce, then proceeded to cook snails and amuse bouches, new potatoes, carrots, lambchops, rocket and toasted pecan salad.

For dessert she made lemon custard tartlets with strawberries and crème brulée. Nev ate the green tops of the strawberries. While she cooked, she sang along to Madonna's "Material Girl" in a gravely alto with perfect pitch. She had brought three wines that paired with the courses. A French country dinner party.

Ronnie had no appetite, but kept her company while she

cooked. The spread on the dining table after Nev plated all the courses looked like something out of a magazine.

Reg took Nev's picture before shaking her hand. "Mate. I know this isn't for me, but I'm thanking you anyway."

"You're welcome." Nev dug in, serving herself.

Afterwards, telly blaring in the family room, joeys wrapped in warm bath towels sucking bottles of milk on everyone's laps except Ronnie's, she accepted the steaming mug of tea from Blaise with a grateful, "Thanks, mum." The word sounded twee from her mouth, but "step-mum" was too formal.

Reg grinned. He noticed that shit. She did it for him.

Nev perched on the arm of the couch. She scratched Nev's back through the thin flannel.

After a while Nev stood behind her and massaged the tight muscles at the base of her neck. She closed her eyes. Another birthday in the books. On days like this it was tempting to be cynical, to lose hope.

The state had tried to sever the maternal bond.

But it had failed.

Her phone vibrated in her pocket. An email from the lawyer, originally from Maude and forwarded. "It's here," she said. "The list of conditions from Maude."

Reg and Blaise crowded around her to read it over her shoulder.

a. **Do the social worker's home visit at your parents' house**

b. **My parents want to have a chat with your parents**

c. **I need to meet Nev. My parents want to see the farm.**

Within minutes, Reg called a social worker to schedule a home visit, Blaise called Maude's mother, and Nev was on the phone with the lawyer, talking over the logistics of what a supervised visit from Maude and her parents would entail.

When Ronnie woke from a nap, sunlight on the wall was warmer, golder, and her dad played folk songs from the sixties and seventies on guitar on the back veranda with Nev—Phil Ochs, "There But for Fortune," and Gale Garnett, "We'll Sing in the Sunshine."

She listened for a while, then walked to the kitchen to fix herself a plate of leftover lamb.

She walked out onto the veranda, sat across from her dad and Nev. They had been smoking cigars and drinking whiskey.

Cold slices of roast lamb were delicious.

After a few rounds of darts, Nev left in her silver pickup truck and Reg's brother arrived.

Local news came on the television. She muted it. Her dad and uncle talked politics while older orphaned rock wallabies and pademelons hopped around the fenced garden. They would be ready to release into the wild soon. The rescue had a system to reintroduce them into the wild gradually, involving progressively larger pens in the yard.

Reg voted with the Green party. He read all the political news articles, knew all the voting histories of the state and local candidates on Aboriginal issues as well as the Environment. She voted for whoever he supported.

A news anchor holding a microphone stood in front of a brick building with a shallow-pitched red metal roof. Behind him rose a cloud of black smoke. Burning tires? The building or something in the courtyard behind it must be on fire.

Ronnie reached for the clicker, turned the sound on.

Prisoners at the Youth Detention Centre down near Townsville were rioting. The campus was on lockdown. An unknown number of the kids had escaped their cells. The news station broadcasted footage from a helicopter circling the facility.

Ronnie felt sick.

Reg stood behind her. Her uncle looked at her, then back at the news.

Someone could get badly burnt, or asphyxiated by smoke if they were trapped in a cell or a wing of a burning building on lockdown.

The kids must be scared. The guards must be scared. Adrenaline on both sides. Staff worked there, cooks in the kitchen, janitors, nurses, women volunteered there as counselors or teachers.

Was anyone trapped inside?

Hopefully the standoff de-escalated before anyone got hurt.

"Reg, turn it off," Blaise said.

If he did, Ronnie would turn it back on.

It was May, autumn, Second Term in the school year. Was the fire near the library? Would all of the books be ruined? Or was the fire near the dormitories? Was it in the male or female dormitory?

Men in black uniforms pointed machine guns at the doors and windows. She hoped people who complained Queensland was "soft on youth crime" were watching this shit. They must be satisfied to know that their tax dollars were paying for grownups to point loaded guns at kids.

Reg went outside on the patio to take a phone call.

Blaise stood watching from the kitchen. "We don't have to watch this. It's upsetting Brum."

News anchors repeated old information but didn't say anything new.

"I have to see what's happening inside." She needed facts, details, not random people's conjectures about what might be going on behind locked doors.

"This will be on the news all day," Blaise warned.

Ronnie's phone vibrated. Call from Mikey. She answered, leaning forward and gingerly sliding to the edge of the couch. "Mate."

"Mate. Are you watching this?" Mikey was an auto mechanic in Townsville.

"Unfortunately. Are you all right? How's Jesse?"

On Mikey's end of the line an engine revved. "We're all right, other than the landlord situation." Mikey was still looking for an apartment in a safe neighborhood with a landlord who didn't hate her. "How about you and Rainbow?"

She and Mikey didn't get together as often as they should, but when they did they bonded over their kids. Ronnie was one of the lucky ones from juvie who hadn't been nailed for anything since they let her out. She credited that entirely to her dad.

"She's good, I think. I've been better. I'm at my dad's. Have you heard anything about what's happening inside?"

"No, I wish. I was going to ask you. Looks heaps bad. I feel gross."

"Me too." She figured out how to stand up from the couch and took the phone outside.

"Have you found out if you need a character witness for the hearing?" Mikey asked.

Ronnie rubbed her forehead. She had completely forgotten. "I'll ask."

"If you need someone, I'll take time off work."

"You're the best."

"Shouldn't you be at work?"

"I'm not in ace shape right now. Recovering from a thing."

"Another half pipe injury?"

"Fuck off."

Mikey snorted. "You don't have Rainbow today, do you?"

Ronnie inhaled slowly, then exhaled. Her friend knew it was Rainbow's birthday. Mikey had been with her when she started having contractions, early labor, and had been there when she returned from the infirmary alone.

"Man," Mikey said. "That sucks. If I was there, I'd give you a hug."

"Thanks."

"Tell her happy birthday for us. We have a present for her. We'll give it her next time we see you. Come visit."

"I want to. I've been thinking about driving down there again. I can't right now, but when I get over this thing I will."

"Tell you what." Mikey was always so thoughtful and kind—a better friend than Ronnie. "Why don't you pick me and Jesse up a few days before the hearing? The kids can play together and I'll be there for moral support, even if you don't end up needing a character witness."

That was a fantastic idea. She wished she had thought of that. "You're seriously the best. Are you sure?"

"Of course. We have to get your daughter back."

"Partially back."

"Same thing."

30
BACK TO WORK

On June first the note from Ronnie's doctor clearing her to return to work finally appeared on her online health portal. Ronnie let out a sigh of relief, printed it out to show to Nev, then began hunting down work clothes. It took her an age to figure out how to pull on boots. Her back had mostly healed, but she still had no core strength when she was bent over.

She drove herself and the dogs to Upsend Downs mid-morning in the truck. Driving was uncomfortable, but that was allowed. On either side of Boar Pocket Road the neighbors' paddocks looked dry.

She had been to Stone House a handful of times since the accident, not as often as she would have liked, but she hadn't set foot on the public side of the operation. The lads hadn't seen her in six weeks.

Nev stood out front waiting for her. That wouldn't have happened before. Ronnie's stomach tightened into a knot. She turned off the engine.

Nev opened the door of the truck.

Ronnie's cheeks burned. "Bloody hell. Don't look at me like that." She swallowed.

"Like what?" Nev asked.

Her boss unfolded her from the seat the way Rainbow unfolded origami dream-catchers—lower lip between her teeth, cautiously optimistic, already knowing what was inside.

Kazi, Ric-Rac and Barney came running when Nev radioed that she had returned. Ronnie was deeply moved by how relieved they were to see her. They took off hats, ran fingers through thinning hair and gave her one-armed hugs as if she might break, which made her throat tight. She wanted them to squeeze the breath out of her, manhandle her and wrestle her the way they used to.

The lads presented her with a pavlova while singing "For She's a Jolly Good Fellow" loudly, off-key.

Nev's sleeves looked tighter. Either her shirts had shrunk or she had been lifting. The thought of the older woman working out on the free weights behind the barn made Ronnie smile. Nev didn't own gym clothes.

The bin in the staff kitchen in the barn contained an empty box of nicotine gum. Someone was trying to quit.

In the barn office a letter addressed to Ron Madonna sat face-up on the desk. The return address was TAFE North Queensland in Atherton. She ripped it open. Inside was a formal-looking letter printed on corporate letterhead from the post-secondary adult education campus.

She carried the letter out into the open center of the barn where the two halls crossed. Barney was outside hosing down horses. The animals flicked their tails placidly while he bathed them with a giant soapy sponge.

Letter in hand, Ronnie went back inside.

Nev was angrily cleaning out a chest freezer.

"What's this?" Ronnie asked.

"Tell Barney he's sacked."

"Why? What did he do?"

Nev had rubber gloves, a spray bottle of bleach, and was scrubbing out the inside of the deep freezer. Buckets nearby were full of defrosted packets of lamb. By the smell, Ronnie guessed they were not good anymore. Dog food, maybe. She swore.

"How long was it unplugged?" Ronnie asked.

"Long enough."

Barney walked over to see what Ronnie was looking at. He peered into the buckets, watched Nev scrubbing the bottom of the chest freezer. He took off his hat, scratched his head. Nev straightened, threw a wad of blood-soaked paper towels in the bin, glared at Barney. "You're sacked."

Barney looked around, startled. He touched his chest. "Me? What did I do?"

Nev disappeared over the edge of the chest freezer again.

Barney swore, scrubbing both hands through his hair and taking a step sideways. "I thought I plugged her back in! Truly! I only unplugged her for a second when I was hoovering with the shop vac like you asked me to..."

"Yup. I told you what would happen if you buggered something again. You're done."

Barney chuckled nervously. "Mate..."

Nev straightened, fixed him with a glare. He swallowed. He turned and walked out of the barn. Nev bent over the chest freezer again, reaching into the bottom corner with a fresh wad of paper towels. "This wasn't the first thing he did."

"He means well. It was an accident."

Ronnie jogged after Barney. Outside, he looked like he had seen a ghost. He looked sick. He lit a cigarette, sucked on it in the shade against the side of the building, calming his shattered nerves. She walked over to him. The hand holding the cigarette was shaking.

"Mate," he muttered.

"You're not sacked. I'm re-hiring you."

"Can you do that?" he asked.

She didn't know. "Take the rest of the day off, eh? Wait for her to cool down."

"Bloody hell... Thanks, mate. Owe you one."

"No worries. What did you break while I was gone?"

Barney's shirt said *Love Fast, Die Sprung,* around a cartoonish drawing of a snake. "Nothing, mate. She didn't like the way I mowed the grass." He sucked his ciggie. "She's mental."

"Mate. Anyone else would have sacked you day one." They had all been guilty of leaving tools out in the rain once or twice, but Barney had a special gift for buggering the machines. He had the touch of death, but that wasn't his fault.

While she waited for the computer in the barn office to boot up she tossed back a fistful of party-colored chocolate candy from the jar. According to the letter, TAFE had received letters of recommendation from two of her references. This had to be a practical joke from her dad. Another heavy-handed attempt to help her rebuild her life.

She pulled up the website for the adult education center. *"Certificate IV in Adult Tertiary Preparation."* According to Google, tertiary meant third. That answered no questions. She read the smaller text below. It was a year twelve alternative, and ran for a year out of the Brisbane campus. There was an option to do the course online. *"Gain access to university or other tertiary education institutions."* On the right side of the page four price options ranged from $0 to $5,000.

Interesting. As far as she could tell, the material was only reading, writing, and math. She could do this. It would give her more opportunities. It would give her the choice to go to uni someday. Most high-paid jobs on the Tablelands required a professional diploma, certificate or degree.

She didn't seriously want to do manual labor for the rest of her life, did she? Surely that wasn't sustainable long-term?

She drew a deep breath, puffed out her cheeks, let out the air with a fart sound.

The car park at the public boat launch on the east side of Lake Tinaroo was full. Winter was tourist season. Number plates from Queensland and the Northern Territory. Ronnie parked on the grass. The door of the truck thudded shut behind her. She lowered dark sunnies over her eyes. A sign at the end of the public dock said "Tablelands: Shire of Diversity."

Nev stood behind the sign, throwing brown bricks into the lake. One landed with a splash and floated away.

"That's gonna upset some people, babe," Ronnie said.

Nev snorted. "Feeding the barra." Barramundi. "Can't eat dogs, can I?"

"No," Ronnie agreed, peering into the half-empty esky of rotten lamb from the defrosted chest freezer. "Need a hand?"

"I got it."

Ronnie watched her friend toss another slimy brown block into the lake. "If you could have any job, what would it be?

Nev hesitated, squinted against the sun. "I don't know. This one isn't too bad." She looked down. "How about you?"

"Women's pro soccer coach."

"You need a master's degree."

"I don't want to travel for work."

"That eliminates pro sports, Dain'y."

"I like working for you."

"But I made that job for you," Nev said.

"That's why."

"What part of working here do you like?"

"The people," Ronnie admitted.

"If we were all dead, hypothetically, how would you make your living?"

Ronnie was silent for a while, then smiled. "I'd flip real estate."

Nev tossed a towel at her.

31
FOOTY

The third Monday night in June, Ronnie's therapist—black cardigan, cheeseburger and rituals lady from Kuala Lumpur—thought Ronnie had anxiety about the upcoming custody hearing and told her to join a mum's group. "You need to talk with women who have had similar experiences. Reg and Nev are not mums," the therapist had said, as if that should be obvious but wasn't.

"They kind of are," Ronnie said.

She was too busy. She had sent in the application for the TAFE online school program that started at the end of September.

On the drive back to Lionheart she stopped at a doctor's office to pee in a clear plastic cup. She watched a bored-looking phlebotomist draw a vial of blood from the inside of her elbow, label it, then set it aside to send to the state for the drug screening a judge had ordered.

She was grateful that she had never become addicted to drugs. Every time she broke a bone and the hospital gave her painkillers she thought about all the people out there addicted to fentanyl or oxy, and it gave her pause.

. . .

When she stepped onto the footy pitch in Edmunton that night, her teammates knuckled her head and crushed her in a hug that lifted the toes of her cleats off the grass. It felt good to be wanted.

Night footy had its own feel-good magic, when the lights were bright and the passes were clean. Of the twenty-four women on the roster this year, only two had children. Most mums couldn't sacrifice every Saturday morning from April to October and two weeknights a week. Most mums had to watch their kids after work.

If Ronnie hadn't lost custody of Rainbow, she wouldn't have been able to play.

They ran a ten-on-ten scrimmage with four subs on either side.

Her teammate Ginny scored the first goal on a pass from her teammate Jay. Ginny sprinted by with a huge grin on her face, then screamed like a banshee and fell to her knees, eyes closed, mouth open, fists pumping.

Violent joy.

Ronnie had missed seeing it and feeling it. People who didn't play competitive sports didn't know what they were missing. What a rush it was to celebrate your victories loudly and unself-consciously, to scream your success and be loved for it.

The best players on the team belonged to everyone. Their individual victories belonged to the team. Collective victory was a beautiful conceit. Footy was a game, but after a few minutes on the pitch Ronnie forgot.

Being here on the pitch under the spotlights felt like a homecoming, but she didn't enjoy the scrimmage as much as she used to. Her body was out of practice, her footwork clumsy and slow.

The coach pulled her off to the side. "Come to night practices, but we're going to keep you out of Saturday morning matches until mid-July."

Before the accident that would have devastated her. She had things to do on Saturdays, like email landlords and try to find someone who would rent her an apartment or one side of a run-down duplex. Footy season wasn't as important now that her team wasn't depending on her to win the championship.

The social worker had sent in a letter of recommendation for her, which her lawyer had submitted to the judge. Ronnie had to keep her head down and stay out of trouble.

Her teammates stole the ball from her without breaking a sweat. Footy wasn't as much fun when her back hurt and she sucked. She frowned, stretched for the umpteenth time, drank water on the sideline. She needed to be stronger.

Yesterday, Rainbow had announced out of the blue that she was switching schools from Gordonvale to Lionheart. Maude would hate that idea; it would mean more driving for Maude. The prospect of her upset ex sabotaging her custody hearing over something as petty as commuting was all she could think about. Worrying sucked. It didn't come naturally to her.

At the beginning of July, she watched Mattie's rugby union club team, the Hurricanes, play the Super Rugby Final against the Highlanders on the overhead screens at the pub alongside everyone else in Lionheart.

Mattie's team lost. It was a Friday night, so Barney's band played on the other side of the pub, in the quaint wooden function hall with the timber rafters and high windows. He and his bandmates played "Edge of Seventeen," then the 1977 album *Rumours*, which Nev took as a personal affront, because that was the Wild Drovers' thing first. "Bloody hell. This town isn't big enough for two Fleetwood Mac cover bands. He's doing this to spite me."

Ronnie nursed a frothy golden pint of Carleton Mid, her first in a long time. "I hope you know how silly you sound right now."

Gods, she had missed beer; it was like drinking bread. She took another sip, bubbles on her tongue. She set the pint glass down on the bar. When was Taylor's graduation? Nev's little sister was graduating the University of Auckland in early September. They had to make a plan for Ronnie to farmsit while Nev hopped over the ditch again.

"Are you going to Taylor's graduation?"

Nev shook her head.

"What? Why not?" Ronnie frowned. "You have to go. Your mother's dead. You're all she's got."

Nev scoffed. "She has heaps of family over there." She was drinking mid-range whiskey. "Besides, I can't." Nev looked around as if checking to make sure someone wasn't there. "I promised to take Gunni to a doctor's appointment."

Someone else could do that. "I'll take him."

Nev shook her head.

Ronnie had a sinking feeling. "Why? Is it bad?"

Nev nodded. Ronnie swore. "Don't tell anyone I told you that," Nev said.

"I won't." The idea of their elderly German bandmate being sick distressed her, but she hadn't given up on convincing Nev to go. "Kazi could take him."

Nev tilted her head. "He doesn't drive."

"You can't miss your only sister's graduation. You'll regret it forever. If it was me, I would want you to be there."

Nev rested her hand on Ronnie's shoulder.

Ronnie blinked back tears, didn't know where that response came from.

Three days later, New Zealand's national rugby team, the All Blacks, went on to play a gorgeous away game against Samoa. The island nation shut down for this national holiday. Reg and the rest of the Madonna relatives bawled their eyes out unselfconsciously at the pub—proud of Mattie and the All Blacks, but more proud of Samoa. Everyone loves an underdog with self-respect and something to stand for.

Samoa put up a hell of a fight. The talking heads on the telly agreed it was an historic game. God bless sport, religion of Queensland.

32
LAMBING

A thousand ewes could drop two thousand lambs. At the moment, the ewes were heavily pregnant. Kazi had separated out the ewes that looked like they were about to lamb and brought them into the sheep barn.

Monday morning, Nev carried two cups of coffee out to the sheep barn. Ron had a large bandage on her neck again. She must have had another laser session to remove the fading KITTEN tattoo.

"How much did that cost?" Nev asked.

Ron peeled back the bandage to show off the blistered pink skin underneath. It looked like it hurt. Nev winced.

"You don't want to know," Ron said.

Noted. Nev didn't have any tattoos, which might be a sign that she feared commitment. "Did you do something nice for your dad yesterday?" Yesterday was Father's Day, September 6th.

"Took him fishing."

"Good onya. Catch anything?"

"Barra." Barramundi.

"How big?" Nev asked.

Ron held her hands shoulder-width apart. Coffee sloshed onto the barn floor.

"Niiiice. Sleep in the barn last night?" Nev asked. Ron moved into the loft with Kazi during lambing season.

Ron nodded, sipping from the mug, gazing out distractedly at the pregnant ewes that milled about restlessly. One bleated. They'd drop lambs any hour now.

"How's Kaz?" Nev asked.

"In his element. What time are you leaving?"

"Noon tomorrow. You sure you don't want to come? She saved you a seat at the thingy." Nev didn't say graduation, because she didn't want to see the look in Ron's eyes after. It was true, though, that Taylor had sent Nev two tickets. That girl didn't miss a beat. Their mother had been thoughtful like that as well. Pity Taylor didn't remember her.

Ron shook her head. "I have Rainbow Friday."

"Fly home Thursday."

Ron looked skeptical. "I shouldn't. Nervous about the hearing."

"Don't be."

"Can't help it."

Nev tugged a lock of Ron's hair to make her smile. Worked every time.

"I'll get her a card and a present," Ron said. "What do you think she wants? What is she into?"

Nev puffed out her cheeks. "Hell if I know. You're closer to her age, you tell me."

"I don't know what college girls like. Journals? Gift cards? What are you getting her?"

"Haven't thought about it."

"I'll buy something from both of us."

"Thanks. I have wrapping paper, you know where it is, behind the door in the office. I can wrap it," Nev said, on second thought.

Ron left after breakfast to cut hay, but Nev stayed to help Kazi with the ewes.

Once in a while a young first-time mother who didn't understand what was happening rejected her newborn lambs, kicking them off the teat. When that happened, Kazi intervened to swoop the unhappy trio into a small blue lambing pen with one corner fenced off so that the lambs could get away from their mother if she head-butted them. If the mother continued to reject the tiny newborn lambs he let the ewe out into the field, put her ear-tag number on the cull list to be slaughtered with the lambs next May. Farms couldn't afford to keep bad mothers.

Nev watched the old man rub a towel on a ewe who had lost her lambs. That happened sometimes; lambs were born dead. This particular ewe, number three-eighty-seven, would need to be milked by hand or adopt lambs soon or else she would get mastitis.

"Need a hand?" Nev asked.

Kazi shook his head. "Nope." He carried the dirty towel over to the lambs who had been rejected by their mother. He crouched. One of the lambs was black, the other white. He rubbed them both with the towel that smelled of the ewe. If he was lucky, the ewe would smell these lambs and think they were her own. Worth a try. The old man carried the lambs, one under each arm, little hooves dangling front and back.

There was nothing quite as precious as newborn lambs, probably because they were so floppy and fluffy, squishy and eager to press soft white noses into the hands of anyone who approached them. Lambs were gentler than puppies. They would have been ideal pets if they didn't grow into sheep.

Nev held the side panel of the ewe's pen open, then slid it shut behind him. The ewe watched as Kazi set the lambs down beside her on the hay. "Go on, then." Kazi climbed out of the pen. They watched, side by side at the rail, as the ewe sniffed the tiny white and black lambs. Nev held her breath. It didn't matter how many times she had seen him do it, the anticipation still got her. The ewe, number three-eighty-seven, rubbed her nose against the black lamb's side, gently pushing it towards her. A hopeful sign.

She licked the lambs. Then, forcefully, she head-butted them towards her udder. Success. She had accepted them.

The lambs were rooting around under her belly in the wrong place, not finding her teats. Kazi went back into the blue pen to guide the bumbling little muppets' noses under the ewe's udder to smell the warm milk. Lambs weren't born knowing how to nurse, but they sure sorted it out quick. He held their noses to the hairless pink udder. They squirmed against his hold for a minute, then relaxed, opened their mouths and latched onto the ewe's fat, finger-like teats.

Nev loved watching the moment lambs tasted milk for the first time. The lambs crouched down and wagged their fluffy white tails in the air in obvious pleasure, the way dogs do. Without letting go of the teats they head-butted the ewe's udder, which encouraged milk to come down and squirt into their tiny pink toothless mouths. It was all so very instinctual. Primal. *I can make sweet milk come out of this squishy blob!*

To every newborn lamb it was an epiphany.

33
HIGH SCHOOL EQUIVALENCE COURSE

Nev returned from Auckland on Saturday.

She found Ron in the sheep barn, a bandage taped to her wide neck, hay in her long black curls. The sleeveless Alien Weaponry T-shirt may or may not have seen the inside of a washing machine in the five days since Nev left. Nev handed her a steaming cup of tea and new earbuds.

Ron carefully took the hot mug and jammed the earbuds down the neck of her baggy shirt. "How'd you know I know I lost my old ones?"

Nev suspected she had been up all night helping Kazi deliver lambs. Ron had definitely slept in the loft over the sheep barn. She looked tired but happy.

"Where's our girl?" Nev asked.

"At a birthday party."

Good. That meant Gumball would probably be over later for dinner. Nev missed her. "You better not have been up all night."

"Not all night, no." Ron set the tea on a shelf and returned to what she had been doing when Nev arrived: bottle-feeding orphaned lambs.

One of the ewes had died shortly after giving birth. Internal hemorrhaging. The ewe had flopped over dead while the vet was setting up an IV. Tragic business, but Nev was more or less numb to it now, having seen it so many times over the years.

At the moment, Ron only had the two bum lambs that Kazi hadn't been able to graft onto another ewe. She was bottle-feeding them formula from an old water bottle with a screw-on red rubber nipple. She would fall hopelessly in love with them and want to make them pets. Ron fell in love easily—too easily. If Ron asked, Nev wouldn't be able to say no.

"You enjoy this, don't you?" Nev asked.

Ron shrugged. Nev wondered why. Did Ron not know she was glowing? Was she afraid to jinx it by sounding boastful? Or was Ron just physically incapable of admitting out loud that she was happy? Or was Nev projecting her own feelings? "Why do you do that?" Nev asked. "Why do you shrug instead of saying "yes"?"

Ron sat on the floor with the lamb on her lap, petting it while it drank from the bottle. It was the cutest thing Nev had seen since last lambing season. Any of them could have set up a milk dummy bucket, hung it upside-down on the side of a lambing pen, let the lambs suck on that, but none of them had, because Rainbow had been two the first time Ron was allowed to feed her.

Ron glanced up, then back at the suckling lamb who was rocking its little body back and forth and wagging its tail. "I assumed it was a rhetorical question."

Fair enough. "Being busy makes you happy."

"What about you? What makes you happy?" Ron asked.

Nev considered. *This.* "Passive income."

Ron laughed.

It was the first day of spring.

The first laugh.

That was how Nev knew she was in too deep. Love made everything new again.

"Did you hear?" Ron asked. "Queensland introduced a bill to Parliament to reinstate civil partnerships."

Nev's eyebrows rose. "Oh? When?" She only asked to be polite. The bill would probably fail. Conservative bloody pricks.

"Mid-September. They still have to debate it. They might vote on it by the end of the year." She had been paying attention, which meant she cared about it. She only paid attention to things she cared about.

"Took them long enough, eh?" Nev knew the younger woman expected a more celebratory response. "Hopefully they pass it again and don't take it away this time."

Ron ignored her cynicism. "We'll get gay marriage after that."

"Likely in your lifetime." Nev couldn't allow herself to feel anticipation after the whiplash of gaining and losing the right to have civil partnerships in 2012.

Progress would always be an uphill slog.

"By the way," Nev said. Ron looked up. Nev nodded. "Thanks for encouraging me to go to Taylor's thing. It was a big deal." It had been important to Taylor that she was in the pictures. Nev had been the only relative there representing their mother's side. Taylor had been excited to show her where she went to school and introduce her to everyone.

Ron looked surprised. "I told you it was a big deal."

"You were right."

The defeated look in Ron's eyes was still there, but softer.

By September thirtieth, the day Ron's online course started, lambing season was trailing off. The year twelve equivalence program at TAFE was supposed to take twenty hours a week, but it would take Ron closer to forty.

Nev regretted encouraging her to do this. Ron still bottle-fed orphan lambs every three hours at night. Ron insisted she could do the coursework after work, but that seemed naïve.

Nev read the homework out loud to her at the coffee table in the family room with the television muted. Wordy and convoluted, the assignments used three paragraphs to explain a prompt that should have been summarized in a sentence. Nev couldn't tell if Ron understood how to get a passing grade.

Together they researched what homework help was available at the TAFE student center in the school library an hour away.

On the website they found a tiny link to *Accommodations and Accessibility*. Ron didn't click on it and Nev bit her tongue. Frowning, Ron shut the laptop.

Nev pointed to the words printed on Ron's shirt: *Success won't be won inside the comfort zone.* "In school, were you ever assessed for learning differences?"

Ron's face went blank.

Nev watched her try to sip from an empty water bottle and wordlessly got up to refill it. She handed the full bottle back to Ron and returned to her chair at the head of the table.

"I learned other things."

Like how to be the Michelangelo of meat.

"Did they say you were dyslexic?"

Ron shook her head. No telling what they had diagnosed her with or if it was accurate.

"You could get educational services. Extra time on assignments. A tutor."

Ron smiled, but not with her eyes. "Not right now. But I appreciate the offer."

34
ONE HOUR

On Nev's request, the lawyer arrived first, parking under the Moreton Bay fig tree in the gravel carpark between Stone House and the horse barn. Maude's terms included a one-hour supervised workplace visit, for which Nev paid the lawyer, holding out a check-sized envelope the moment the woman from Mareeba stepped out of her Toyota Camry. The tweed skirt suit and high heels looked out of place on the farm.

"Make sure it's enough."

"I'm sure it is." The lawyer shook Nev's outstretched hand. She had a light grip, soft hands, and was over-dressed. "Ms. Bickerman, I presume. Call me Karen."

"Nev."

"What's that short for?" the woman asked.

"Niamh." *Neeve.*

"That's a pretty name. Irish?" The lawyer surveyed the farmyard as she chatted, no doubt filing observations for later. "Are you Irish? You look like you could be. Is that a sunburn, or does your skin always look like that?"

Nev hated this already. Internally, she was debating with herself if there was an upper limit to what she was willing to do to help Ron get parental rights back. "I have barn boots you can borrow." It was likely murder, the upper limit. She couldn't see herself committing murder for this project. She still had morals. That felt good.

The woman smiled. "Brought my own, thanks." She took muck boots out of the trunk of her Camry and changed. "My uncle has a farm out in Chillagoe."

"Not much water there. Bit dry." Closer to the Outback, dusty roads, desert. Red dirt.

"Your grandfather had a tin mine. What town?"

"Ravenshoe. Forty-five minutes south of here." Nev jammed her hands in her jeans pockets. Had debated dressing up for this meeting, had decided not to. "Everyone's coming?"

The woman nodded. "Except Ronnie, who wasn't invited."

Good. This would be harder if Ron were here. Without her, nothing could go wrong.

"Thanks for arranging this, Karen."

"No worries." The woman checked the contents of her purse before closing the Camry door. A custom pink Chevy Silverado turned off Boar Pocket Road and rolled up the long gravel drive towards them. Nev felt like she might throw up. *Easy...* She gentled herself in the same voice she reassured the horses she trained. She could do anything for one hour.

"That must be Maude," the lawyer said.

Nev nodded. They watched the obnoxiously-bright truck approach.

The lawyer scribbled something on a legal pad. "You've never met her before."

"Nope."

Nev's heart raced like before a gunfight. She would be the sound of one hand clapping. She could be the perfect host.

The lawyer turned to her with a frown. "Before she gets here, I want to say how much I respect you for doing this."

Nev blinked. "Least I can do." The gravel had worn thin in places, she realized. She scuffed the dirt with the sole of her boot.

The lawyer lowered her voice. "If she starts acting erratic, I'll wrap things up early and get her out of here. If you can't stand her, don't say anything to her, catch my eye and tap the top of your head. I'll make up an excuse to end the meeting early and she won't know it was your idea."

Nev was impressed. "You've done this before."

Karen unbuttoned the top button of Nev's shirt and fluffed up the front of her hair. "There, much better. Hands out of your pockets. Don't slouch. Everything will be fine."

A boxy white Kia parked next to the pink truck and two middle-aged people who must be Maude's parents got out. From the pink truck emerged a pretty young woman with heat-straightened hair and Rainbow.

Nev's heart skipped a beat. "Is she supposed to be here?"

"Yes. The social worker is here to observe how Rainbow acts."

At first glance, Maude looked like a teenaged babysitter. Long, straight, auburn hair too perfect to be real. Maybe it was a wig.

"You must be Nev." Urban accent, upper class, almost British, vowels breathy and open. Fringe that draped stylishly on either side of wide, startlingly green eyes. Mesmerizing. Pouty pink lips, plump face, slender limbs, like a doll.

Jesus Christ...

Maude was not what she expected. How the hell had Ron bagged this ten when she was fourteen?

Nev shook the limp outstretched hand the same size as her own. The two of them were the same height. Maude knew she didn't need to introduce herself. Her last name was Green, the lawyer had told Nev over the phone.

Rainbow hugged Nev around the waist. "Hi Nev! The turtle I found last week laid an egg!"

"That's exciting. You got to let it go."

"The dog ate it."

"What, the egg?"

"No, the turtle."

"Whoops. Well, maybe look up how to incubate a turtle egg. Probably too late now, though."

Maude's parents stood behind Rainbow. Nev extended her hand. "Mr. and Mrs. Green? I'm Nev. Welcome to Upsend Downs."

Maude's father had hot hands, and her mother had cold ones. The woman smiled anemically. "Thanks for letting us drop by."

"No worries."

"We're waiting for the social worker," the lawyer said. "That must be her now."

A green minivan pulled up the drive and parked beside the Kia. A woman with braids and carrying a sparkly clipboard stepped out of the car.

Rainbow's eyes shot to the clipboard. Sparkles were like crack for kids. She went over to the social worker and touched the polymer clipboard. "This is cool. Where did you get this?"

When the social worker hugged the girl against her blouse Rainbow sank into the woman's soft body. "Rainbow girl! Long time no see, darling! Like it? There's a new art supplies store in Atherton. I bought one in every color. How are the hermit crabs?" This must be a social worker who had worked with Rainbow before.

Why the hell did Rainbow need a social worker before? What happened? No one tells Ron anything. I get fifty percent of that, if I'm lucky.

"They're all dead," Rainbow said.

Nev frowned.

The social worker looked unconcerned. "I'm so sorry to hear that, darling. Hermit crabs don't live very long."

"I left the cage in the shade in the greenhouse, but then the sun moved, and they cooked. At least I think they cooked. It could have been dehydration that killed them."

Morbid, much?

"Oh, what a shame," the social worker said. "I'm so sorry. Tell me more about it after, darling. I'd love to hear about it after the meeting." Her voice was deep and warm. "Is this your friend, Mrs. Bickerman?"

Rainbow hugged Nev around the waist again. Nev reached as

far as she could to shake the social worker's outstretched hand. "You can call me Nev."

The woman held up a phone. "Mind if I take pictures?"

"Go ahead."

When the woman pointed the phone at her, Nev schooled her expression to look approachable and law-abiding.

The lawyer stepped forward. "Thank you all for coming. You all know why we're here. The Green family is excited to finally meet you and is looking forward to seeing the farm where Rainbow has spent so much of her childhood since she was four." The lawyer consulted her notes. "Approximately one day every other week."

"Since she was two," Nev corrected automatically. She hoped that wasn't a secret. She didn't tell them that Rainbow had been here in utero because they didn't need to know that.

The lawyer and the social worker scribbled notes on clipboards.

She hoped she wouldn't accidentally say something that would get Ron in trouble.

Rainbow led the farm tour. Nev was only along for the ride, which in this case, was exactly what she wanted. Less pressure on her to entertain. They could have done the tour without her. The lawyer led the group from building to building, while Rainbow told random anecdotes about things they lingered next to, or saw, and the social worker dictated into her phone everything the girl said only slightly wrong. Rainbow's lack of filter was like a truth serum.

In the barn: "This is where I brush Brighty, my pony."

Smiling, sidelong glances among the adults.

In the house, more specifically the kitchen: "This is where we eat dinner and where Nev helps me with my homework."

Approving nods from Maude's parents.

In the family room, Rainbow pointed to Nev's guitar case and Ron's drum set in the corner. "This is where we jam."

Maude glanced at the hall where the bedrooms were. "Do you ever sleep here?"

Rainbow nodded cheerfully. "Yeah. Heaps."

"Where?" Maude asked.

Rainbow led the group down the hall into the guest bedroom. Nev followed the others. The social worker took pictures of the bed and the bathroom, which thankfully Nev had cleaned last night in a fit of paranoia. The social worker wrote on her clipboard. "How many times have you slept here?"

"At least a million."

"Where do your mum and Nev sleep?" the social worker asked.

Of course, this whole thing was a setup to eviscerate her. *Here it comes...* Nev held her breath and jammed her hands in her pockets.

Rainbow looked around the guest bedroom, then pointed to the bed. "Mum sleeps here with me. Nev sleeps in her room."

Nev exhaled, unable to believe she would be so lucky as to dodge that one.

"They don't sleep together when I'm here."

Rainbow was only trying to do her a solid, to protect her. Heart racing, she walked to the kitchen and filled a glass with water from the fridge. This had been a terrible idea. Why had she thought it would be all right? Why did humiliation still sting? She leaned on the counter. They had come here to gather evidence against her. Well, everyone except Rainbow. And Karen.

The lawyer peeked into the kitchen. "Everything all right?"

"Peachy." Sarcasm was creeping back. Not good.

"They're not going in your bedroom."

Nev finished the water and set the empty cup in the dishwasher.

The lawyer looked sympathetic. "Let's continue on, shall we?"

The next stop on the tour was the sheep barn that they used

for lambing, which was empty now. Maude walked alongside her. "I'm sorry for embarrassing you."

"Not embarrassed," Nev lied.

Rainbow wanted to ride Brighty so they all walked back to the horse barn. The spring sun was hot, but inside the barn was cooler from fans whirring overhead. Rainbow showed off how she could saddle and tack Brighty, which made Nev unreasonably proud.

"What do you like about horses?" the social worker asked Rainbow.

"Nev's going to be my mum someday," the ten-year-old announced.

In other circumstances, Rainbow's prediction would have made Nev feel pretty good. Nev half-turned her back on the others and lowered her voice. "You are so sweet."

The girl hugged Nev around the waist, asking to be picked up, which seemed babyish for her, so Nev ignored her. The girl was persistent, continuing to try to climb Nev like a tree, as if it was a game. The other adults politely acted like nothing was happening. Maude covered a smile. Eventually Nev couldn't take it anymore, so she picked her up.

"Do you feel like a parental figure?" the social worker asked.

"I don't know how to answer that. I don't have anything to compare this to."

"Are you in love with my mum?"

The girl was on a streak.

"Everyone's in love with your mum."

The social worker said, "Awww..." in a high voice.

Maude cleared her throat. "I'm not."

Maude's mother chimed in. "You're so good with her, Nev, helping her with her homework. Rainbow adores you. Will you be a stable part of her life? It sounds like you don't know what's going to happen with Ronnie, which, to be fair, no one ever knows what's going to happen with Ronnie, but we need to know that Rainbow will be safe here. You don't drink or do drugs?"

"Um," Nev said. "Not in front of her."

Maude frowned. "Do you mind if we run a background check?"

"Go ahead." There was nothing in her record but a few old DUIs.

Maude snapped pictures of Rainbow with Brighty. "We want what's best for Rainbow."

Maude's dad agreed. "You've built a nice place here."

"I don't take any credit. All I do is try to stop it from falling down."

Maude's mother touched Nev's arm. "She's lucky to have you. If you and Ronnie break up, we hope you'll stay in touch. Rainbow cares about you and she loves coming over to ride the horses."

Nev felt strange. She swallowed. "Rainbow is always welcome." She licked her lips. "She always will be."

"Don't say that unless you mean it," Maude warned.

Nev still held Rainbow, who was getting heavy. She tried to think of something nice to say to the woman she considered her arch nemesis. *Thank you for helping Ron.* No, she couldn't say that, it would sound forgiving, permissive.

"I've been wondering, what do they do for you?" Maude asked. "You cook for them, do laundry for them, help with the schoolwork, entertain them, you do everything for them, and what do you get out of it? What do they do for you?"

Nev blinked. Maybe Maude had never loved anyone other than herself. She ran her tongue along her lower lip. "They don't have to. That's the point." She didn't understand why they thought there was anything unusual going on. "There's no greater privilege than to take care of other living things. The farm is..." What was she trying to say here? "The farm is its own reward."

"I'm not talking about the farm."

Nev shrugged. "It's not different."

"For what it's worth, you probably deserve parental rights more than she does," Maude said. "You're in the most vulnerable position, and you're not asking for anything. You can't ask for anything. When Ronnie breaks your heart, don't disappear. You have our contact information. We like you, and we think you're a good influence for Rainbow. We haven't decided what we're going to call you, but you're something."

Nev swallowed. "Right."

"You have permission for whatever this is."

Maude's mother chimed in. "We agree with everything she said. This is unexpectedly wholesome."

"Bit early to jump to that conclusion, love. I don't need your permission to—"

"Well! Look at that! That's time!" the lawyer interrupted, tapping her watch. It had been an hour. "Isn't this a little slice of heaven?"

Maude pulled her aside, out of Rainbow's earshot. "I mean this in a respectful way, so don't be offended, but are you on the spectrum?"

"Not as far as I know. Do you want me to be?"

"I don't care. I'm just glad you're not her usual type. She's dated some real assholes. You're the safest person she's shown interest in."

"She did date you, after all. We're not... But thank you for bringing all these people into my house to laugh at my friendship with your daughter, to try to put a box around it, to make it something they can understand."

"Be careful," Maude warned. "I'm not the one who's going to hurt you."

35
CRANE COUNT

Friday night the South Cairns Cutters Women's team battled it out in their finals round one match against the Manunda Hawks for a place in the semi-finals. Nev watched the match on telly at the pub in the Lionheart Hotel with owner Peggy.

It was Debbie's night off and her nephew hadn't arrived so Nev was bartending.

The camera crew and whoever was editing in the booth that night had a bit of a spank on Ron; the camera loved her. It kept catching her at just the right moment, sliding a daisy cutter to steal the ball, running backwards or sideways, winning a ruck by slapping down the ball over her opponent's head. Ron looked good in a uniform, but she looked especially good in her footy uniform because it showed off her knees.

Nev was not disappointed when the Cutters lost, because now Ron would have free time again.

As usual, eighty-year-old Peggy wore a sleeveless purple batik sundress down to her calves. Nev refilled Peggy's plastic cup with the cheap rosé they sold at the pub. "On the house, engaged lady."

"Cheers."

"Have you an idea what song you want us to play when you

walk down the aisle?" The Wild Drovers had volunteered to play her wedding for free as a present to her and her fiancé, Tom.

Peggy's eyes got a misty look in them, and she touched the back of Nev's hand. "Do you know the Scottish folk song, 'Mairi's Wedding'? My parents walked down the aisle to it eighty-four years ago."

"Of course."

"They were a beautiful couple. He was a pilot, you know, died in the war. RAAF. Such a shame. It's always the good ones. My mum never remarried. Mother-in-law planned my first wedding sixty years ago. I always said if I married again, I'd have that song."

"You got it, sweetheart. You'll have a gorgeous day." Peggy deserved a perfect wedding. She deserved a good man like Tom, the retired corporate man who now painted ceramic figurines of mice for a hobby, after her first husband brought an explosive temper back from Korea.

The next evening, a warm breeze stirring the new grass in the pasture, Nev walked down from the lower paddock through waist-high sedge until she reached the edge of the lake. Reg's annual Crane Count team stood gathered in one of Johnson's cattle pastures. Towering over the others, Ron was impossible to miss. This was not their first time counting for the conservation survey, but it was the first time they had invited her to join them.

Luckily, she had remembered binoculars, and to jump over the barbed wire fence. Lake Tinaroo looked odd—as the manmade product of a dam it wasn't strictly speaking supposed to be there—but what the human eye found strange about it was that it was young. Sixty years hadn't been long enough for erosion to shape the banks, so where the field met the water flowed as seamlessly as a dream. There were no real edges to this lake. It looked, Nev decided, like lowland that had been flooded. It looked temporary. Perhaps that was why it was so beautiful.

Climate change made storms stronger and more unpredictable, floods in Queensland bigger and more destructive every decade. It was dangerous to live near the Barron River, which flooded December to March.

Ron and Rainbow sat on either side of her in the tall grass. Rainbow clutched the binoculars Ron had given her for Christmas. The four of them waited statue-like for sunset to fall over the western mountains, forced by the covert nature of their mission to admire the scenery in silence.

Cloud-split rays moved across the valley until grass warmed like glowing blond hair.

In 1959 the Queensland State government completed construction of a forty-five-meter concrete dam on the Barron River, raising water levels forty-two meters. Water inundated the valley so rapidly that the flood swallowed heavy construction equipment, including trucks. In the center of it all, the small township of Kulara disappeared under the surface of the lake. A few hundred villagers had relocated to the nearby town of Lionheart.

Tinaroo lay bright and still as a mirror. Like the wreckage of some sunken fleet, the gum trees of Kulara broke the water's golden surface with hundreds of crooked black arms. Kulara's underwater forest would be rotting and reaching for the sky as long as Nev was alive.

The hillside leading down to the lake felt like a graveyard—not a crypt, but a cool breeze and a final resting place, no souls in sight save Johnson's cattle and a lone pelican on a dead tree.

Suddenly the valley became dark and cold.

Sunset. A line of solid-looking grey clouds rose behind black mountains like a higher horizon. In some places Nev saw four, five horizons, and in those places clouds and mountains became indistinguishable. Above the fierce yellow cloud-outline the sky glowed orange. She stared through binoculars at the ribbon of light where warm wet currents met cold dry air, blinking and breathing for the Sarus she hoped to see fly into breeding grounds for the night.

When they pierced the clouds they were so small she barely recognized them.

Standing six feet tall, the world's largest flying bird emerged delicately through marsh grasses, blood-orange red crown leading a graceful straight neck, light grey body and cautious pink legs. With its rope-thin white neck and sleek teardrop body, it looked like something the Queen of Hearts would have used as a mallet in a deadly croquet match.

The *whoop whoop* sounded like what would happen if you cut an old tire into a thin strip and then spun it around above your head as fast as you could like a helicopter.

Rainbow said it sounded like the lake was laughing.

"More cranes than last year," Reg said, smiling, visibly relieved.

Rainbow snuggled in her mother's oversized sweatshirt on her mother's lap. Ron looked like she didn't feel the cold.

Nev's phone vibrated. New voicemail. Missed call from an unknown number. Most likely spam. She got up and walked to the top of a low hill where she wouldn't disturb the Madonnas.

The voicemail was soft and breathy, high-pitched.

"The background check came back. Call me."

Nev swore.

How had that woman gotten her phone number? Was it still on the farm website? She thought she had taken it off. Ron wouldn't have given it to Maude, neither would the lawyer. The fact that Ron's ex had a direct line to her pocket made her squirm. This didn't feel like the kind of call she could put off until the lawyer's office reopened on Monday.

She pressed call.

Maude answered. "You're an alcoholic."

She couldn't let Maude use her as an excuse to sabotage the

custody hearing in three days. If it fell through, Ron would be devastated.

"Nah, yeah. That was a long time ago. I assume you're talking about those DUIs."

"You lost your license."

"I got it back."

"Some of these are from twenty years ago and others are from ten years ago."

None after the night Ron appeared. She had been better since then. She had to watch what she said. A little flame burned in her chest, warming her cheeks. She wasn't drunk, but she wasn't sober, either.

"Every ten years is a pattern. You're due."

Nev swallowed.

"Does Ronnie know you're an alcoholic?"

The silence lengthened. She didn't trust herself to speak.

"She deserves to know," Maude said. "If you're in recovery, you shouldn't have enough liquor in the kitchen to open your own pub. Your recycling bin had too many bottles in it, even with two people. Ronnie doesn't drink. She doesn't like the taste. I'm not trying to scare you. I'm not threatening to blackmail you. She's not observant enough to notice. How do I say this? She's the moth to every flame. She doesn't know when to stay and when to run. She stays when she should run and runs when she should stay. You're enabling each other."

"Maybe."

"If you've got a dark side, she'll strap a turbo engine to it. She's an adrenaline junkie. I can't believe I'm about to say this... She can't you-know-what unless someone hits her. Mentally, she's still in the van, waiting for MJ."

Nausea in the pit of Nev's stomach. "Is that all?"

"I take back what I said about you."

Nev covered her eyes with her hand. "What was that?"

"You are her type."

Nev hung up, then blocked Maude's number.

Heart racing, face hot, hands cold, she wondered if she was having a heart attack. *Get yourself under control...*

Not good. She recognized the feeling of being caught. Dull panic. The game was up. She could deny it, but no one would believe her. She rubbed her jaw. She turned and walked uphill toward Stone House, lawn dead from the drought.

36

TOWNSVILLE

Two days until the hearing. Five o'clock alarm. Ronnie emerged from her tent down by the creek, ran around the perimeter trail, then lifted weights behind the barn for an hour. The blue quandong sapling hadn't died from neglect yet. Someone must water it. She still felt tight beneath the incision scar. Exercise cleared her mind.

She drove up the hill past brown grass and sun-scorched orange clay to Stone House as the sun rose. Barefoot, she pressed the gas pedal and rolled up the gravel drive. A few hundred ewes looked up from grazing.

She left her dogs at Nev's, filling her water bottle from the sink on her way out. Maya and Matilda darted about the house like kids in a bouncy house. Nev was still asleep, but Gaia and Blair wagged their tails hopefully. Nev's black collies looked eagerly between Ronnie and the metal bin that held their food.

On the Bruce Highway south, radio news personalities chatted about the sugar harvest. Cane harvesting season, what locals called "the crush," had begun.

She arrived in Townsville by noon. She parked at the beach, eager to get on the swell now that she could see it. It was a bigger day. The Great Barrier Reef made this part of the coast bollocks for surfing, but she was in luck; rough weather here yesterday made the waves larger. From the car park she could already see surfers riding two-meter swells. Good intervals today, not too close together.

The sun was out. Blue skies, turquoise water, couldn't ask for better weather. She wrestled into her wetsuit, waxed her longboard. She loved the smell.

Hot sand underfoot, then wet sand along the waterline. Water was colder than air, a shock to her bare feet and ankles, then felt nice.

Holding her board under her arm, she jogged out past the first wave, then paddled out to where the other surfers were. She had been worried about the paddle out, but it wasn't bad. The wetsuit insulated her core and kept her warm.

Surfers out on a good day with clean break. She spotted Mikey, paddled over, then sat next to her, boards side by side. They rode sets while their other friends arrived.

They took a break in the early-afternoon to eat falafel from a food truck on the beach, hit the public toilets, then went back out on the water again.

Ride a perfect set in, paddle out, spot another set on the horizon.

The golden hour before sunset, sky on fire. Saturation dialed up all the way.

Orange and pink clouds, rainbow sherbet.

Sea on fire, burning waves.

The board bobbed up and down beneath her on the waves like Dreadnought walking. She let it carry her toward land, toward the dark shore.

Mikey bobbed next to her, straddling her own board. "Nervous about the hearing? It's so soon."

Her back hurt. "A little, yeah. Thanks for volunteering to come to the courthouse for moral support. You know I haven't been in a courtroom in ages. I'm glad we're hanging out today. I won't be able to talk much the day of the hearing. I'll be disassociating and trying not to poop my pants."

"No worries, mate, I've got your back. Least I can do, as her fairy godmother." Mikey had been by Ronnie's side every day in juvie before Rainbow was born and had been with her the following day, when she didn't have a baby anymore, and the day after when her milk came in. Mikey had been with her through the mastitis. Worst two years of her life.

The sunset was pretty, but they should probably start paddling in before dark. "I'm thinking of buying land in Lion-heart, or maybe a little further out where land's cheaper. If I build a house and start my own farm, you two should come live with us. It would be fun for the kids. Rainbow would love that. She's been after me for a little brother."

"Aw, really? That's so sweet. Jesse would love that. Sure, maybe. I don't see why not. If you're serious, ask me again."

"Totally."

After sunset, they paddled to shore in the dark.

She imagined sharks watching them from below. Surfers ignored sharks the way farmers ignored fires and floods. You could be a smarty pants and plan, but in the end the elements controlled your fate. Danger was the price of admission.

She moved her truck to a different parking spot on the Strand, then lay down in her sleeping bag in the bed. She loved how soft and warm nights were here as opposed to up on the Tablelands in the mountains. Her lower back kept her awake. She stretched until the painkillers kicked in, then drifted off to the sound of waves, nose and lungs full of sticky salt air, sand between her toes.

Safe.

At dawn a cop woke her by squeezing her shoulder. "Oi! Oi!" The officer ordered her to move along.

Nowhere was perfect.

Dawn at the beach—pale pink, pearlescent. Ocean spray on her face a mist like horizontal rain, cold as her dream of flying. Mikey sat on the back of her camper van, smoking. Ronnie walked over and joined her in looking out at the waves. Mikey passed her the joint.

Low drone of waves crashing on the shore, eternal white noise machine inhuman, older than life. Ronnie envied people who lived near the beach.

She relaxed. She had pushed herself yesterday, so her lower back hurt, but that was part of the healing process. She hadn't done any permanent damage.

Mikey took the joint back, gesturing to Ronnie's longboard. "Want to go for a surf?"

She studied the ocean. Glassy offshore. Two-foot-tall, short-period waves breaking softly and slowly. "Mush burgers?" Kiddie stuff. It wasn't stinger season yet, so she could get by without shoving herself into a damp wetsuit.

Mikey killed the joint, slid heavily down from the van and stretched with a loud groan. "Rock and roll." Ronnie's mom friend who worked as a mechanic hadn't been athletic ten years ago, but had joined a gym and had been working out. Mikey appeared to have more energy this spring than she had last summer.

Mikey was kicking so much butt in life, showing what a badass a single mom could be.

When Ronnie returned wet to her dented F-150 later that morning after surfing and rinsing off in the public showers, the side doors of her friend's van were open and her friends were inside smoking. As she walked closer, she smelled pot.

Reg stood chatting with her friends from juvie, his hairy arms crossed. His truck sat parked nearby.

She pulled the hood of her sleeveless hoodie up against the midday sun. "What's up?"

Reg's face brightened when he saw her. They hugged.

"Everything all right?" she asked.

"You didn't answer your phone, kiddo."

She pointed over her shoulder towards her truck.

Reg had shadows under his eyes. "Big day for the family tomorrow; everyone's on edge, mum reglazing windows, Blaise blasting ABBA..."

The man drove ten hours round-trip to check on her. He thought she would do something stupid.

"You worry too much," she said.

"I know. It's a problem."

"I'll be there. Trust me."

Reg deflected. "You're my baby girl. It's hardwired into me. Don't forget you have that suit fitting in Cairns at four. It was big of your brother to set that up. He doesn't like to throw his weight around like that, so show him that you appreciate it by not being late, eh?"

Godlike Mattie, the perfect son.

"I'll be there. I have another thing at two." Tattoo removal appointment. What time was it now? She needed to jet.

"Better leave now, or you'll be late." Reg looked guilty, rubbed his nose. "Listen. I brought Nev."

"What?" Ronnie walked over to the passenger side of her dad's truck. Nev looked up from her phone and waved. Dark sunglasses made it difficult to tell if she was there voluntarily or if she had been kidnapped.

Reg was in full papa-bear mode. She didn't know why she was surprised.

"Thought you might want company on the drive," he said. Not quite an apology, but almost. Reg glanced out at the ocean. He thought she was going to stuff this up between now and tomorrow. That hurt.

She stared at him in disbelief. "You brought a babysitter?"

Nev got out of Reg's truck. She had showered and combed her hair. She looked fussy and posh in her jackaroo boots and button-down work shirt, and frowned. "I've been demoted. Don't look so excited to see me. I got roped into this. Did I miss surfing?"

Ronnie laughed, then felt self-conscious about how grunge she must look barefoot in board shorts. Her wet hair was a mess, and she had sand in her arm hair.

"Hiya babe." She squished Nev against her chest, accidentally drowning the shorter woman in boobs. "Come meet my mates."

Nev shook hands with Mikey. "G'day, g'day. How ya going?"

Mikey looked impressed. Some of the others smiled. One snickered.

Nev jammed her hands in her pockets. "Did you tell them about the thing?"

Ronnie was confused until she remembered.

"I have a hearing in front of a judge tomorrow." Why was it so hard to talk about? "I'm trying to get more time with Rainbow. They might give me my parental rights back. You know, legally."

Her friends stared at her blankly for a minute, then jumped up grinning when they understood. "Aw, mate! Good luck! You've got this!" They piled out of the camper to hug her. They were big on bear hugs.

"I'll let you know how it goes."

Mikey had to pick up Jesse and decided to drive her own car to Lionheart.

Nev held out her palm for the keys. "I can drive. I'm fresh."

"Nah, that's all right," Ronnie said. "I like to."

Nev tossed her a bottle of ibuprofen from the passenger seat. "How was church?"

In the driver's seat Ronnie's back was making it hard to think, but other than that she was high on happy brain chemicals from pushing her body past the point of exhaustion two days in a row. She searched for words to explain this feeling to someone who had never surfed before.

"It was exactly what I needed. The ocean puts shit into

perspective." The ocean was scary, but it wasn't stressed. It was peaceful out there, even when it was about to crush you, rip your board away, snap it in two, drown you, or eat you alive. "No one explained to me what was going on when I gave her up. I feel like they tricked me."

Nev frowned at the road.

"I knew I was in a shitty situation. If she was adopted, she would be safe with a family screened by social workers. She'd grow up better than I was. I thought I could save her from something, like a real mum would, you know. I thought she had a future with Mr. and Mrs. big house in Brissie. When they asked if I wanted to apply to keep her with me in a different detention facility, I thought... I don't know what. I thought she would be better off outside, I guess. I should have kept her with me. If they told me she would be with Maude, I would have kept her with me and gone wherever they were threatening to send us. At least we would have had each other."

"Pull over," Nev said.

Ronnie parked in the breakdown lane. Nev stepped out, lit up.

Maude won. She always said she would.

Not being able to protect your kid was hell. There was nothing rational about it. Ronnie had gotten better at pouring sand into a sieve. Therapy helped.

Nev got back in the truck, smelling like an ashtray. Ronnie checked the mirrors and eased out into traffic. "Sorry for over-sharing."

Nev watched the cars. "A lot of people made mistakes."

"Budget cuts," Ronnie said.

"Budget cuts," Nev agreed.

"I should volunteer at a place like that, coach soccer or some faff. I would, but I'm too much of a coward."

"It's five hours away."

The closest one, usually. At the moment one was fifteen minutes away. "It's still bad there. Kids are neglected. When you're inside, the world is a cement wall. Home isn't necessarily something you want. The government is the ultimate arsehole authority figure." An abstract idea. "Queensland incarcerated you. Queensland is rehabilitating you. Queensland will give you another chance. Queensland has procedures in place to support you after your release... I didn't want to live here. I didn't think I belonged anywhere. They really mess with you, make you think you shouldn't exist."

"You belong everywhere, Dain'y. Home is a feeling you carry inside you."

"I know that now." At the moment, driving in the truck with Nev, she felt fine. "I think I'm an anarchist," she decided, eyeing the sign on the highway for the exit that led to the Youth Detention Centre outside Townsville. "Is there an organization I should join? What do anarchists do?"

"Do I look like I know? They distrust organizations. You might be an activist."

"Greenies who chain themselves to trees?" She signaled and took the exit.

"Your dad's an activist. Someone who protests. Usually, the work is disappointing because it fails. I've dabbled. They burn out. The only sustainable form of activism is singing and dancing. That way, if you lose, at least you had a hell of a party."

"You're more of a Pete Seeger type than I am."

"They're not all like that. Nobody likes being oppressed." Nev's head swiveled as the petrol station went past. "You missed it. There's a place to turn around up ahead."

"Taking a detour."

"No," Nev said. "None of that."

"It won't take long," she promised, turning down an unfamiliar two-lane suburban road.

"Your dad will kill me."

"Not if you don't tell him."

There was the sign. Behind it, a car park, flood lights, giant black metal fence, and a complex of ugly buildings made of glass, brick, and cement. No one was outside. No sign of fire damage from the riot. The place looked abandoned, but wasn't. Recent reports of human rights violations inside and overcrowding.

The front door wasn't what she wanted, so she turned the truck around and went back to the road, then drove around the far side of the complex, looking for an outdoor recreation area. Those were always on the back side. She was considering blasting music and dancing on the roof of the truck. Kids liked that.

The layout here wasn't the same as the one in Brisbane. The perimeter fence was set back farther from the main buildings, and the recreation area wasn't visible from the public road. No one in sight. Pity.

Disappointed and relieved, she turned and headed back toward the Bruce highway north.

"Does it look the same?" Nev asked.

"I wasn't at this one. They only started sending girls here in January. Before that, they used to ship all the Queensland girls to Brisbane." Three days drive away. Too far for most of the girls' families to travel. She hadn't had a visitor for two years. The only person who would have been allowed inside to see her couldn't be bothered.

She swallowed. "It's good that girls can come here now." Instead of being sent halfway across Australia.

"There's only one kid waiting for you, and she's in Gordonvale," Nev reminded her.

The tattoo-removal office south of Cairns was a brick building attached to a carwash. Ronnie signed papers, paid a few hundred dollars, then lay on her stomach on a padded table while a technician with black gloves used a laser to burn off another layer of skin on her lower back.

The laser stung like a bee. It hurt more to remove a tattoo than to get one. Tomorrow the skin would be bright red and blister. Depending on how deep the laser went, it would be wet and scab over or feel like a sunburn, peeling and itchy while new skin grew underneath.

She listened to Maori heavy metal in her earbuds and closed her eyes.

The men's luxury clothing store was inside an upscale mall in downtown Cairns.

Ronnie tried on designer suits while Nev sat outside the changing room reading a newspaper. Mattie had arranged for the store to stay open late.

She decided on a black button-up shirt and a tailored cobalt suit that fit her like a glove.

Nev handed her a white shirt.

Ronnie returned it to the rack.

"This is court, Dain'y. The goal is to look young and guileless. The black one makes you look like you're in the mafia."

Ronnie snorted. "Maybe I am. I'm also wearing it to Peggy's wedding."

"No, you're bloody not. We're performing, remember? You can't play guitar in a Tom Ford that costs six thousand dollars."

Good point.

Her phone vibrated. Text from Mattie.

(Mattie) Nev with you?

(Ronnie) Yes

(Mattie) Make her pick one for herself. I'm buying.

Ronnie held up two colorful suits, size tiny. "This is what he likes to spend his rugby money on, women and cars. What color is your old suit?"

"If you're the woman, I'll be the car. Light grey. You've seen it."

"It wasn't memorable."

"Good thing I'm not a phone number."

"You look good in mauve."

"What do you think mauve is?" Nev showed Ronnie a color on her phone halfway between pink and grey. "That's mauve."

"Fine. You look good in green."

"I don't own anything green."

Ronnie sighed, exasperated. "What color is that linen shirt you always wear? The long-sleeved one?"

"Pastel Aqua. You want me to find a suit the color of toothpaste?"

Nev only tried on one—Ronnie suspected it was the cheapest she could find in her size—a baby blue linen three-piece with a tag that said 'wrinkle-proof, no ironing.'

Mattie arrived an hour late. Sales associates crowded around him for selfies. He signed autographs and flexed his muscles, flirting shamelessly with the staff.

Ronnie rolled her eyes and crossed her arms.

Stylish female sales associates laughed at everything he said while he posed in his boxers.

Mattie tried on candy-colored suits that looked expensive and tight on him. He was the same height as Ronnie, but stockier across the hips. His neck and wrists were thicker. Suits which had hugged Ronnie in all the right places would need to be tailored to fit him.

He worked the crowd, let them vote to help him decide. The staff chose a blue suit for him that was almost the same color as hers. A beautiful elderly woman—the owner—arrived and began hemming Mattie's sleeves. Mattie chatted with the owner, in no rush to put clothes back on. One of the employees handed him a sweating tinny of beer.

"Thanks, sweetheart. This place is the best. You girls are

lovely. Did you pick one?" he asked Ronnie. "Put it back on, give us a fashion show."

"They want to go home."

"Come on, Stinky!"

She went into one of the changing rooms and put on the cobalt suit. When she came out, Mattie catcalled and rubbed his hands together in the gesture for throwing dollars. "Damn, we have good genes!" He fist-bumped her and they did the one-armed bro hug. "What do you think? Like it?"

"I picked it out, didn't I?"

Mattie turned to the owner. "We'll take it wrapped. She has a big day tomorrow. It's her wedding."

"Congratulations," the owner of the shop said.

"He's full of shite," Ronnie said.

Mattie paid for all three suits. She overheard Nev remind him to leave a tip.

37
CUSTODY HEARING

The courthouse in Atherton had twenty-one steps. The atrium floor looked like white marble laced with dark veins. Madonnas arrived wearing the polyester-blend outfits they wore to funerals and weddings. Ronnie hugged them one at a time, absorbing anxiety from concerned upturned faces.

Nev wasn't coming to the courthouse—something about the bank and visiting a neighbor. Mikey and Jesse had slept over with Ronnie at the purple house on Pademelon Road last night and had carpooled with Reg and Blaise this morning. The stocky mechanic looked handsome in a suit and tie, short brown hair combed to one side. Mikey and Jesse wore matching green bowties. Mikey's strong, solid energy made Ronnie breathe a little easier, as did having two-year-old Jesse there.

They filed into the courtroom where the judge, a woman Ronnie had never seen before, was presiding over other people's problems. On a long bench near the back, she sat down between her dad and her lawyer, then dissociated while she waited for her case to be called. Nothing good had ever happened to her in a courtroom. This was the place you went to be slapped in the face in front of a crowd of onlookers; a stage of public humiliation.

She recognized the back of Maude's auburn hair in the second row. Her ex had arrived early, which she told herself was a good sign.

Rainbow's little head next to Maude's shoulder. Dark pigtails.

She couldn't let herself think about Rainbow now, but couldn't look at anything else.

So much trouble to get back the best part of her.

Someone in the row behind her flicked her earlobe. Mattie.

Reg put his arm around her and squeezed. Her rock. "Breathe." They had met all of Maude's requirements and checked all the boxes on her list. They had done all they could do. Now it was out of their hands. "It'll be fine. You'll see." So long as the social worker for the state agreed that living with Ronnie was best for Rainbow's wellbeing, the judge should approve their joint petition.

It was a good sign that Maude had brought Rainbow.

Their lawyer from Mareeba had submitted proof of Ronnie's income and housing ahead of time. The state had done a safety review of her dad's house, which he said had gone well. She assumed she had passed the drug test.

When it was their turn, the court officer called their case. "Madonna and Green?" Strangers from the previous hearing filed out. Ronnie and her lawyer walked up the aisle to the front, joining Maude, and followed her through the little gate to the front half of the room with the magistrate.

The judge addressed basic administrative questions to Ronnie's lawyer first, then to a woman in a suit dress who must represent the state of Queensland.

Ronnie's stomach burbled and her mind went blank. Her face tingled and her chest felt tight. She hoped she wouldn't faint.

Her lawyer confirmed the judge's statements. "Correct, your honor."

The other lady confirmed similar statements about documentation and approvals that went over Ronnie's head. Everything sounded mechanical and impersonal. She had no idea what they were talking about. No one looked at her. She couldn't believe they were talking about her.

It didn't feel real.

Poor Rainbow sat beside Maude's parents in the front row, biting her nails, looking worried. Ronnie wanted to go to her, put her arm around her. She felt guilty for subjecting her to this. She never wanted Rainbow to know the stress she had known, didn't want her daughter to grow up shell-shocked by legal spaces and afraid of sirens.

The grey-haired judge shuffled papers around her desk.

Ronnie cracked her knuckles. Her hands were sweaty. The judge looked at the woman in the navy skirt. "You received the fax from the social worker?"

"Yes, your honor."

"No problems?"

"No, your honor."

"Does your office have concerns?"

"No, your honor."

Ronnie held her breath. That sounded good. Like, 'game over' good.

"Any limitations your office would like to add?"

"None, your honor."

The room faded. She inhaled. She had to stop holding her breath or she would actually pass out. Mattie squeezed her shoulder. She hoped she didn't get bubble gut from the stress and have to run for the bathroom. Courthouses gave her the runs.

"In that case," the judge said, shuffling papers around, "petition granted."

Reg sobbed big man sobs, loud and urgent, but Ronnie could barely hear him. The courtroom frosted over.

She settled back into her body with a hot flush, drunk with relief. All around her, smiling people touched her and patted her arms.

On autopilot, floating above the courtroom, she hugged her

dad and kissed the top of his head. He was the reason she was a halfway functional human being.

Ronnie's lawyer shook her hand. "See how easy? I told you not to worry."

"Is that it?" Ronnie asked.

"That's it," the lawyer agreed, shouldering her purse. "Shared parental responsibility means joint custody. You got equal time, which is what you both asked for. Go home and celebrate."

Blood rushed out of her head and back in. She held onto the back of the bench. "No conditions?" she asked, unable to believe it. This whole thing disoriented her. Nothing had ever gone her way before. She wasn't used to it. She wasn't used to anything being easy.

The lawyer shook her head.

Ronnie hugged her. "Thank you." Hopefully this would be the last time she saw her. She never wanted to step foot here again.

Maude and Rainbow had already slipped out through the crowd. She didn't blame them. She wanted to get out of here.

She put her arm around Mikey, then followed the tide of smiling faces out of the courtroom.

She couldn't wait to see Rainbow. Hoped her daughter was happy.

Please let this be as good for her as it is for me...

Out in the hall, Maude walked over alone and hugged her. Maude had dressed the part of the sophisticated urban professional in a tight shirt with a plunging neckline, short black pencil skirt and heels. She smelled like vanilla. Maude pulled back first.

Ronnie straightened. "Listen." She swallowed. She needed to get this off her chest. It was now or never. "That time you squashed me with the frozen corn, my wrist was broken. You probably didn't know that."

Maude's expression fell. "No, I didn't."

"You scared me. You shouldn't do that to people. It was really upsetting."

"Sorry. I had no idea. I feel terrible." Maude's neck flushed and her eyes got a glazed look in them. "I was joking around. I thought you could take it. You should have said something. You were acting tough and macho, like riding a kid's board wasn't idiotic, and I wanted to teach you a lesson. People pretending they're fine when they're not is one of my pet peeves. I had been drinking wine and arguing with my mother. I'm sorry I over-reacted. It won't happen again."

Reg inserted himself between them and led Ronnie away towards the open doors. With her peripheral vision she saw Maude say something to Mattie and receive the cold shoulder.

Finally, there in the bright lobby, she saw the reason for all of this—wearing a sparkly purple mermaid backpack. Her favorite person in the world.

She picked her up.

Rainbow hugged her around the neck.

She carried her across the marble floor covered in dark veins, out of the courthouse and down the twenty-one steps.

38
RIND EATER

Ronnie wanted to apologize, but didn't know how. Rainbow rode beside her in the passenger seat. Ronnie didn't know how to say *I wiped shit off your bum for years. My shirt is how you wipe your hands. I'm your crust eater, your rind eater, your cereal milk drinker.* She was also the perpetrator of a violent crime. It would have been selfish to ask for forgiveness now.

"This is the second happiest day of my life, after the day you were born." It sounded trite, but it was true. She felt free for the first time in over a decade. She had been minimizing the hearing in her mind, afraid to admit how life-changing getting her parental rights back would be. She was a mother again on paper. Until today, she and Rainbow hadn't legally been related. She could have been arrested for kidnapping her own daughter. Surreal.

This must be how Reg felt when he adopted her when she was eighteen. She understood now why he was so overprotective.

"Can I have a dog?" Rainbow asked.

"I don't see why not."

"Can I have a pony?"

"If you muck out its stall."

"Can I have a pool?"

"No. You can swim in the creek or over at Grandad's."

"Maude said violence is a disease. That some people are born with it."

Ronnie's hands tightened on the wheel. "That's a depressing thought."

"Do I have it?"

She shook her head. "No, baby. You don't have it."

"Uncle Mattie hits people."

"He's a rugger."

"Women aren't supposed to be like that."

"No one is supposed to be like that."

"Boys are allowed to hit people."

"Not legally, but you're right that there's a double standard."

Gum trees and jacarandas flew by the passenger-side window.

"Were you scared?"

She hesitated. "When?"

"In juvie?"

"No. You were my whole world."

"I don't want to be your whole world."

"I'm your mum."

Rainbow glared.

"You're done talking about this," Ronnie guessed.

If Rainbow ever ended up in that place Ronnie didn't know what she would do. She could handle it happening to her, but she couldn't handle it happening to Rainbow.

On the Gillies Range Road she let her hair down, working knuckles through tangles and knots.

"Nev coming to the party?" Rainbow asked.

"She's bringing Gunni." Their third bandmate often rode with Nev.

On Pademelon Road, the trees dripped with fruit bats. A hundred flying foxes as big as Chihuahuas hung upside down from the branches, flapping translucent wings backlit by the sun, touching each other with fingerlike claws.

Cars and pickup trucks covered the Madonnas' front lawn and lined the driveway down to the road. She found an open strip of grass to park on in front of the purple Queenslander.

Nev answered the phone. "Congratulations, Dain'y."

"Thanks, babe. I'm here. Are you by the pool?"

"Yeah, why?

Ronnie loosened her tie. "Did you bring your bathing togs?"

"Should I have?"

"Don't put your phone back in your pocket. Set it down on a table."

Ronnie hung up. She took off her suit jacket and leather shoes, leaving them in the truck.

"What are you doing?" Rainbow asked, suspicious.

She took Rainbow's hand. Someone at the party was blasting Mary J. Blige's "Family Affair."

They walked hand in hand up the front steps. "You're plotting something," Rainbow said. "You've got that look."

Ronnie laughed. "Want in?"

Rainbow's face lit up.

Nonna dropped chopped onions into a beef stew simmering on the stove. Ronnie bent to give her a hug. The smell of the stew almost but not quite masked the faint background smell of animal poop and baby formula. In the family room, five orphaned baby wallabies peered out at them from inside wallaby pouches made of old blankets sewn into bags and hung from the ceilings of their cages.

Out back on the veranda, she saw Nev lounging next to Gunni in a white plastic lawn chair, sipping a gin and tonic in the shade while Mattie and the cousins played touch rugby on the lawn. Relatives who had come from the courthouse still wore suits and fancy dresses, while neighbors with rugby shirts and mullets had been pregaming.

Her middle-aged bandmates had come dressed for a classier party, in tasseled loafers. When they saw her they stood.

Nev looked handsome in a pale button-up shirt, Akubra tilted rakishly, looking like a time traveler from the 1920s. "Oi. Proud of you. You've worked hard for this."

Ronnie patted down her friend's pockets, confirming that they were empty. Nev raised her hands in the air, smiling indulgently.

When Ronnie and Rainbow picked her up, Nev made a delicious little sound in surprise, then passed her hat to Gunni so it wouldn't get wet.

Giggling, they carried her to the pool, where they hugged her between them and counted down, "3, 2, 1..." before jumping into the deep end with a splash.

Dripping wet, she and Nev made sandwiches at the kitchen bench beside Nonna, who continued concocting her stew according to the secret family recipe.

Nev didn't have tan lines because she often skinny-dipped in Lake Tinaroo and was a believer in topless tanning. "Totally acceptable in parts of France, I'll have you know. Nudity only became sexualized and demonized in the past fifty years. Before that it was completely normal for families and friends to swim naked."

Ronnie spread Vegemite and thin slices of cheddar on whole wheat bread. Nev cut the onions and tomatoes into rounds, laid them on top. Ronnie snagged a can of pickles and a bag of chips.

Wet cotton didn't keep secrets. Nev was remarkably well-preserved for forty-six, like a cucumber pickled in brine. Flat chest, flat abs, so far she had escaped gravity's more noticeable effects. No visible scars, neat little feet. In some ways, her compact body looked more youthful than Ronnie's because she had never been pregnant.

They ate sitting on the glider, watching Rainbow swim underwater from one end of the pool to the other.

Ronnie sipped lemonade through a straw. "If we dated, people would say I was taking advantage of you."

Nev snorted.

Ronnie glanced at her, then back at Rainbow, supervising with half her attention. Several people around the pool were lifeguards. Blaise blasted ABBA in the kitchen.

Ronnie took another bite of sandwich. "Anyone in their right mind would be attracted to you. You have a dynamite personality and you'd be my number one pick in a bar fight."

Nev chuckled. "I'm flattered and slightly concerned."

Nonna beckoned Ronnie into the kitchen. "Offer her something to drink."

Ronnie stuck her head out the open door. "Booze?"

Nev tossed ice on the lawn, then handed her the empty glass.

When she handed the glass back full, her friend looked guilty. "I have to tell you something. Promise you won't be angry."

Ronnie grinned. "What'd you do? Buy another tractor? More cute animals at auction that we don't need?"

"No, but good guess. Maude dug up dirt on me."

"No...!" Ronnie smacked her forehead. "You didn't give her money, did you? Please tell me you didn't. What did she dig up on you?"

"DUIs from years ago."

"That all? How much did you give her? You got played."

"I didn't give her anything."

"Now she thinks she owns you."

"She doesn't. She can't make me do anything I don't want to

do. She can't control you, either. Any leverage she had over you evaporated in that courtroom."

Ronnie was still trying to process that. It hadn't sunk in yet. "Don't ever let anyone blackmail you. I'm the last person who will judge you. We're a team. I've got your back."

Nev sipped the rum and coke. "Same."

39
JOHNSON

The following day, Ronnie's phone rang while she was under the large Kubota changing the oil. Incoming call from unknown number. Assuming it was Nev calling to tell her that she had lost her phone again, Ronnie jammed the phone between her ear and shoulder. "Oi."

"Hiya Ronnie, it's Taylor, how ya goin'?" Nev's kid sister who had just graduated from the University of Auckland.

"Hiya, good to hear from you." Ronnie stood up and wiped her hands on a dirty rag.

"Congratulations! I heard you guys got Rainbow back! She's your daughter, now, officially?"

"Yeah. Thanks. I'm really happy."

"Did you have a party to celebrate?"

"Yeah. How are things with you?"

"This is the best. You two are such good mums. Listen. I need you to do something for me."

"What?"

"Nev's refusing to get the testing done to see whether she has the gene our mum had. I need you to help me pressure her."

"What?"

"You know, the breast cancer gene. I thought she told you."

"No, she didn't." She could already tell Nev wouldn't get the test. "Would it change anything?"

"They can do preventative things."

"I'll talk to her. No promises."

"Thanks. Congratulations again."

Ronnie added Nev's sister to her contacts, then opened a bag of potato crisps. Nev must have given Taylor her number when she went to Auckland for the graduation last month. She was flattered that Taylor thought she could make Nev do anything she didn't want to do.

Another incoming call. This time it really was Nev.

"If you're driving, pull over," Nev said.

"I'm here at work, at your house. Where are you?"

"Down at Johnson's place. Your luck's turning. He wants to sell those scrubby hectares he's been grazing cattle on."

"Johnson? Don't joke about that."

"The place is a dump. It isn't worth a penny over forty."

"Hand me over," she said.

A pause, then a deeper voice. The grouchy neighbor. "Madonna?"

"How much do you want for it?"

"For the lot without the house or barn, fifty. No inspection. As is."

"I'll take it. I'll go to my bank in the morning."

"Livestock not included. What bank do you use?"

Ronnie told him.

"I'll meet you there at ten," he said.

Nev's voice again. The neighbor had handed the phone back. "He would have given it to you for forty."

"He still might."

The next morning, she took Nev with her to the bank for moral support.

It turned out that wasn't necessary. A man in a tie said she qualified for a loan. She thought she had misheard him. This week kept getting better and better.

A bigger man in overalls arrived in the conference room behind the bank. She recognized him, had seen him riding his tractor down the road. He had short grey hair and a gut, looked like he had been out riding the tractor earlier that morning. Johnson had one of those closed, judgmental faces that she could imagine muttering nasty things.

He shook her hand. "Can you pay?"

She could.

She played hard ball. He cracked, gave it to her for forty, without inspection or ecological review.

In the truck, Nev took the papers from her lap, then read them out loud before starting the engine. "Look at you, adulting."

Ronnie leaned forward in the passenger's seat, head in her hands, then burst out laughing. "I feel like I just robbed a bank."

"More like the other way around."

Butterflies in her stomach as they drove towards her new property.

Her friend turned off the Gillies onto the unpaved Boar Pocket Road, then stopped in front of a rusty cattle gate beside a boulder that faced the road. Two vertical iron pipes with a third welded across the top flanked the old gate.

The entrance was overgrown with lantana and mile-a-minute vines.

A flock of lorikeets flew overhead, pink and blue.

Ronnie unlatched the gate, which had a dummy lock, pushed it open on its wheel across the remains of a dirt road. "Ever snuck in and poked around?"

Nev shook her head. "Other than that time you showed me the pomegranate trees, no. This is all floodplain. A geologist would charge thousands of dollars to tell you that."

She wiped red clay dirt onto the thighs of her jeans. "Good for grazing sheep, though."

"We'll see. You might have better luck selling dirt."

A well beside a burnt-out concrete foundation appeared to be in good condition, relatively new judging by the lack of rust.

"Did you know there was a well?" Ronnie asked.

Nev shook her head. "This is where they moved the original Madonna house before they built the dam and flooded the valley." Concrete outline of old ruins. The clay soil around it was flat.

Over the top of a line of gum trees Nev's red tile roof was visible, as were the lavender field and plant nursery up on the hill. The lowlands would need work before they could return to use as hay fields or sheep pasture. Thickets of wild brambles spotted the dusty fields. Clearing it would keep her busy for years.

Grass, lantana, wattle, eucalypts. A haven for wildlife, but a challenging ecosystem for humans.

She would put up a barn first.

The stainless-steel pipe topped by a red J-shaped handle stuck out of the ground. She pumped the handle to see if it still worked. Nothing came out.

Nev fetched a plastic water bottle from the truck, carefully poured water into the hole at the top of the well-head where the handle joined the shaft.

"You have to prime an old well first."

This time when Ronnie pumped the handle she felt resistance deep inside, could hear and feel the lever catch on something heavy. She kept pumping. The pipe breathed, gasping for air.

Several pumps later, clear liquid gushed out and spilled onto the dirt.

It smelled like nothing.

Nev cupped her hands, tasted it.

Ronnie released the handle. Her friend pumped while she cupped her hands under the flow. It tasted like the tap water at Upsend Downs.

She laughed. "That well's worth at least ten grand."

Nev offered her palm. "Welcome to the neighborhood. Bail me out during fire season?" It was fire season now, but hopefully they wouldn't have another bushfire like the last one here for years.

Interestingly, land liked to be burnt—fire was good for native species.

She shook Nev's small hand. "What about you? Return the favor?"

"Always. I'll help you build a house. Reckon you'll put it here, where it won't flood during the wet?"

Ronnie had plenty of lumber. She had milled enough to build a tiny house and a barn. "I'm leaning toward putting up a barn first. That way I can rent out stalls and get an income stream going while I work on the house."

"Practical. Good girl." Words like a warm hand running down her back.

Ronnie shivered. "Oi." She scratched her neck where the ghost of KITTEN itched. "Taylor called. She wants you to get tested for that thing."

Nev frowned and crossed her arms.

"I told her I'd talk to you, but no promises."

Nev raised an eyebrow. "She shouldn't have bothered you."

"You gave her my number."

"I get mammograms."

"You don't want to know if you're a carrier?"

Nev shook her head.

"It's your call." Ronnie let it go. For now.

40
TEASE

Hot nights during fire season were dangerous. In October, the Cape Cleveland bushfires tore through the Townsville area burning rainforest, farms, RV parks, and houses.

Nev listened to radio coverage of the bushfires while baling hay on the largest Kubota tractor, pulling the hay wagon behind her with Ric-Rac and Kazi in it. "Yeah, nah, mate," the man whose house had burned told a reporter on the radio. "Me and my wife, we beat it out of there, went to me brother's house. Couldn't enjoy the game, understand? Ruined it for me."

Nev had been drinking water, but spat it out. The laugh caught her by surprise.

Queenslanders cared more about rugby than life itself. Ron would get a kick out of that.

The next morning, skid marks in the grass near the Upsend Downs sign made her frown.

Three pickup trucks sat in front of the machine shop. Barney, Ric-Rac and Ron blasted punk rock inside and may or may not have been doing anything useful. Nev tossed her keys on the shop bench. "Oi. Who skidded into the ditch after the sign?"

"What sign?" Barney asked. He was still here, on what Ron called probation.

She looked at Ron. "Please tell me you haven't been whipper-snippering with your tits out again."

Ron grinned. Guilty. Unrepentant.

"When I said take a course on marketing that was not what I meant."

"You're the one who taught me about topless tanning."

Barney and Ric-Rac laughed. Nev frowned as blood rushed into her face. *Relax.* Too early in the day for this shit.

"How are third quarter sales?" Ron asked innocently. Cheeky. She knew sales at the plant nursery had doubled. They had been inundated by soccer mums of late. Nev hadn't known why. Now she suspected it had to do with Ron landscaping the verge every morning with her top off.

She sighed.

The lads snickered. Ron lifted her shirt and flashed her tits.

"I could fire you for sexual harassment," Nev said, matter-of-fact, in the same flat tone. They all knew it was an empty threat. None of her farmhands looked concerned. They didn't take her seriously anymore, not since Ron talked her into letting Barney back. They knew she was wrapped around Ron's little finger.

Barney and Ric-Rac lifted their shirts, flashed their tits, too. "I am Spartacus!" Barney said.

"I am Spartacus!" Ric-Rac said.

"If you sack her, you have to sack us, too!" Barney said.

"Understood, thank you." Nev tossed her work gloves on the shop bench next to her keys. She felt strange this morning, tight, impatient. Normally she would laugh it off, ignore them, but she didn't feel like being the butt of their jokes today. She didn't feel like being the butt of jokes in general.

"Go on then. Give us another show," she said.

Ron lifted her shirt obligingly. As an athlete with a weight-lifting habit bordering on obsessive, she should have had not much there. Genetics dictated otherwise. The undersides were perfect half-spheres.

"May I?" Nev asked, flapping her upturned palms. She squeezed the air, giving the old *honk honk*, the way you would toot an old-fashioned horn. She was taking this joke too far, but that was the point.

"Knock yourself out. They're all natural, baby."

Nev cupped Ron's breasts. The soft weight of them felt nice. Ron's skin was cool.

Barney and Ric-Rac stumbled over each other running for the door. They were smart enough to get the hell out of there.

Nev dropped her hands and took a step back. "Don't tease me at work."

"I wasn't."

"You were. It's unprofessional. I don't advertise what I do in my free time. Now everyone in town will laugh at me about topless tanning."

"No one's laughing at you, mate."

"I have a reputation to maintain, a reputation as a serious person. My role in the community is a professional one. If people think I'm a loony tune they won't respect what we do or value our products. We'll lose customers. The farm can't afford that."

"Serious people don't announce that they are, they just are. Having a hissy fit about how people perceive you does not prove your point." Ron crossed her arms, smiling. "You're cheeky today. I don't know what's gotten into you, but I like it. You feeling all right?"

Anxious and horny was a dangerous mix. "I think I've explained myself."

Ron spat her gum in the bin before she stepped into Nev's personal space, crowding her against the shop bench. On the ancient CD player, Stevie Nicks' moody "Edge of Seventeen" droned.

Nev gently pushed her away. "Snap out of it. You're being a nympho."

"You got me excited, mate. I'm keen."

"Not here," Nev said.

"Where?"

It was a sincere question. Nev gave a flippant answer. "Tomorrow." By tomorrow Ron would have forgotten about this and be on to the next thing, like her mother at the hospital. Easily distracted. Peterson women had short attention spans.

"Now," Ron muttered into the side of Nev's neck, breath hot.

"Tonight," Nev compromised.

Ron's eyelids were at half-mast. "Take a shower."

Nev swallowed.

41

STRANGLER FIG

Don't worry about logical things when you summon magic. When you head into darkness to cast a spell, cast aside all rationality.

———

Ronnie rode her mare Dreadnought a few horse-lengths behind Nev's white stallion that Rainbow had re-named Unicorn, following her friend downhill along bush trails between low-hanging lantana vines at dusk. Nearby, in the rainforest, a lyrebird mimicked the sounds of a chainsaw and a whipbird, alternating between low and high-pitched sounds.

October, springtime, ripe for new beginnings.

Despite the gathering gloom, Nev didn't seem to be in a rush. Nev hadn't said much since they left the barn at Upsend half an hour ago. Two large barn brooms lay tucked where Nev had strapped them to Uni's saddle like hunting rifles. Ronnie had no idea what they might be for but was eager to find out.

Nev had silently taken charge of organizing this when she consented to it, which was a relief to Ronnie, because it took the pressure off her and decreased the chance that she would accidentally mess it up.

If Nev felt as excited as she did, she hid it better. Nev kept Uni to a leisurely pace. No moon tonight, too cloudy. It might rain on them. Rain would be good for the grass. It felt good to be outside, in the bush, at the mercy of the weather. If there was a god, it must be weather.

Within the hour it would be slow dark, torch dark.

Nev turned Uni down the trail that led to the giant strangler fig. Ronnie sat up straighter, hoping that was where Nev was taking her—someplace dignified and old.

Next to the towering wooden waterfall, Nev dismounted and tied Uni to a gum tree. Smiling, Ronnie followed suit. The hollow behind the vines looked black as a tomb.

This is exactly where I wanted this to happen, Ronnie realized.

Ancient vines had fused together in a tree-shaped lattice, engulfing a giant tree, weaving a living basket around it and then strangling it to death. A fatal, parasitic hug. The original tree had rotted away to nothing, leaving a hollow chamber as wide across as Ronnie was tall that extended up to the sky. As a kid she used to climb it like a ladder and eat a bagged lunch among the high branches.

She followed Nev inside, discovering that it was harder to squeeze through now, and knelt in front of her on the wet leaves. Nev threaded a broom through both sides of the tree above her head, then played Madonna's "Like a Prayer" on her phone.

Several times since coming home from the hospital, alone and bored, Ronnie had daydreamed about unbuttoning Nev's trousers and pulling them down over narrow hips. Nev stopped her.

"Get up," Nev said. "There's leeches."

In the heat of anticipation, Ronnie had forgotten that the forest floor crawled with the little bloodsuckers. She unbuttoned her work shirt.

Her phone buzzed. She ignored it. The vibration in her pocket felt nice. Cool night air became warm and sticky, subtropical. She watched Nev thread the second broom through the tree at knee height.

Nev pointed at the low bar.

Ronnie stepped onto the lower broom, which bowed slightly but held her weight. That brought her shoulders up to the higher broom. Moonlight filtered through wet leaves, dappling them like a disco ball that jiggled instead of spun.

She laughed. "I'm glad we're doing this." She hadn't trusted someone to do this to her in a long time. "I hope this will be kinky."

"You like it?"

Ronnie perched on the lower broom. "It's headed in the right direction."

She wrapped her arms around the broom behind her shoulders and watched Nev take off the Akubra. Nev had brought a rope. Ronnie grinned, watching her unroll it.

Nev remained fully dressed. "I call this the Strangler Fig Special."

Ronnie would take whatever Nev was willing to give her at this point. Nev didn't jump into new things willy nilly—she would take it slow and be a perfectionist. She approached this the way she approached everything else around the farm when she was sober—frowning in concentration.

Maybe Nev was a virgin.

Ronnie wished she had loosened her up beforehand with shots. Probably too late now—she hadn't brought any alcohol.

Ronnie stepped down off the broom, resting her hands on Nev's narrow shoulders, then leaned down to nuzzle her cheek and breathe against her ear.

"Go on," Nev said. "Get back up there facing me and grab hold of the tree behind you."

Ronnie did. Reaching behind her head, she found fused vines that fit her palms like the handles of her motorcycle. Snake-trunks tangled upwards in a wall of knots. Fig bark was smooth and cool. The broom pressed her upper back.

Nev stepped up into the tree and reached around Ronnie to tie her wrists.

Ronnie's cheeks hurt from smiling. "You got me excited when I saw the brooms, mate. There's other things you can do with them, you know, just saying. I wouldn't mind. This is nice, though. Relaxing."

Rope tightened around her wrists. Near her cheek, Nev snorted. "I knew you would be hard to please. What you want is more than a reasonable person can give." Nev was probably right.

"I appreciate that you're willing to try to meet me halfway, babe. No one's done this for me, like, ever."

"I believe that," Nev said. Ronnie watched Nev drop the coil of excess rope, heard it hit the ground. "Abuse isn't consensual power play. In a minute you'll step down off the bar. Your feet won't touch the ground. The broom will stay there the whole time. I'm not going to take it out. If you start losing feeling in your hands, or if you want to stop, step back up onto the broom. You can pull your hands free from up there. I didn't tie you tight."

Ronnie looked down at her Blundstones on the lower bar. She still had her jeans and workboots on. "Got it." The feeling she wanted would come from her own weight when she stepped down off the lower bar. That would be a yummy stretch.

Nev stepped closer, hair silver in the moonlight. Cool hands slid down Ronnie's sides and rested on her lower back. "Comfortable?"

Ronnie's smile widened further.

Nev's eyes were dark. "You like being uncomfortable."

Her friend's face was annoyingly far below hers, handsome and kissable. Ronnie licked her lips. "I want to snog you."

Nev exhaled in a snort, palms warming on Ronnie's lower back. "After." Moonlight confetti mottled Nev's flushed neck and ears.

Ronnie grinned. She wanted to watch Nev turn into a little Napoleon, drunk on her own power. Wanted to go on that haunted house ride with her, to watch Nev lose control, to create space for Nev to feel limitless. "Go on, then. Do whatever you've been fantasizing about."

Nev ran her hands down Ronnie's back again, which felt amazing on her bare skin, then frowned.

Ronnie sighed, impatient. "Babe..." She wiggled her elbows on either side of her ears. "I don't have all night. I've let you tie me up inside a tree and I've indicated that I'm keen. This is all very vanilla for me. Cut to the good part. The cat is out of the bag. We've already crossed the big scary bridge of no return. I understand that you want to talk about everything first, but that's not necessary for me. You are the sweetest fucking loon and whatever it is you've been fantasizing about can't hurt me. I love that we're doing this. I have a high pain tolerance. The only thing that I wouldn't like is poop stuff."

"That hadn't crossed my mind."

"See? That's why I trust you. You don't know about poop stuff."

Nev touched her.

Ronnie's body responded involuntarily. As a bored adolescent, she used to touch electric fences for fun. Whatever kind of bogan that made her, she was still that. She drew a shaky breath, willing herself to relax. Electricity lit a small fire in her belly. Touch awakened her skin.

She slipped her right foot off the bar then dropped, tension starting in her wrists and shoulders. She slipped her left foot off the bar, hung in midair.

As more muscles engaged, breathing became difficult. Warmth spread through her shoulders and migrated between her shoulder blades. She imagined a burning ball of light on her trapezius where the bar left little red kisses when she went for a PR in squats.

She hung there, letting her body get used to the tension in her shoulders and the burn in her belly and glutes.

Nev looked up at her. "Does that feel nice?"

"You have no idea."

Ronnie inhaled, expanding her chest, rocking her hips to see what that added. Moving felt good. She closed her eyes.

"Still all right?" Nev asked.

Ronnie's breath caught. She couldn't speak, so she nodded.

She felt hands unbuttoning her jeans and opened her eyes to watch Nev unzip the zipper and tug the loose denim down a few inches, stopping at her hips.

Nev froze.

Panting from the strain of holding herself up with her arms, Ronnie wondered what was taking her friend so long. She needed to be touched.

Nev stared at the newly exposed skin.

Nev was beautiful—not feminine or masculine, but herself. If Ronnie's hands had been free, she would have sunk them into Nev's short hair, would have given her something tangible to bring her back and keep her tied to the present.

She wasn't offended that Nev appeared to be having doubts. Nev's idiosyncrasies were part of her, part of the package. There was no button to press to return to factory settings for either of them. If there had been, she wasn't sure she would have pushed it.

Whatever this was felt real. Nev wouldn't judge her and wouldn't leave—Nev couldn't leave Upsend Downs. She might second guess shagging Ronnie and decide she wanted to be friends without benefits, but she would still be there in the morning.

Ronnie leaned forward and looked down to see what had made Nev stop. Ronnie's abs looked shredded from this angle.

Nev was kneeling, staring at the scar.

Ronnie relaxed and let gravity lengthen her spine, detaching her vertebrae like plastic beads on one of Rainbow's elastic bracelets.

A riflebird called through the dark like a whip snapping.

Nev appeared deep in silent conversation with the line of scar tissue that ran above the zipper of Ronnie's jeans, studying it the way she had the ocean in Cairns, the way she stared at the sheep.

Ronnie felt like she was intruding.

She cleared her throat. "That's cool that you're into scars."

"I don't like it." Nev's accent was always so sexy.

It took Ronnie a moment to decipher what her friend had said. *Liar,* she thought. *You wouldn't look like that unless you did.* Ronnie's tongue separated from the roof of her mouth with a click and she exhaled through her nose. It was too dark to see Nev's eyes.

Relaxing her arms, she let her weight hang from the ropes. She would have bruises on her wrists tomorrow.

Nev licked a line down the scar, tracing one end to the other. It tickled, followed by a cold line spreading horizontally.

Nev was not indifferent. She was doing the telltale hand thing, when someone's hands got big and grippy and squeezed her like a meal.

Ronnie closed her eyes and let her head fall back. Hanging in a community theater passion play position, it was hard not to feel like she was being worshipped.

Something gave inside her.

Surprising herself, she stepped back up onto the broom and wriggled her wrists out of the rope, then threw herself on the leaves with Nev beneath her. The ground was pliant, springy with deep layers of leaf detritus and moss. Nev's breath rushed out with an, "Oof!"

Ronnie groaned, straddling her friend and sinking her knees into the loam. "God, yes... I want leeches..." On impulse, she tossed fistfuls of dead leaves in the air, provoking a startled giggle.

High on freedom, she pressed her forehead to the ground and her arms around her tiny, androgynous, ageless, mercurial sprite who still suffered the misconception common among farmers that she could own something warm-blooded without it owning her back.

Nev chuckled. "Crushed by an angel..."

Ronnie let Nev hold her and touch her, and everything was soft and nothing hurt.

. . .

After, but not long after, lying pressed together in the circle of leaves inside the strangler fig, lights dancing inside Ronnie's eyelids, Nev played "Because You Loved Me" by Celine Dion on her phone.

Ronnie winced in a good way, furrowed her brow and shook her head. "Yes! Slow it down, Celine! Preach!" She knew all the words and sang along, pretending Nev's hand was a microphone.

Reunited with her shirt and phone after thorough inspection found zero leeches, singing under her breath and doing a little shimmy with her shoulders, Ronnie checked her messages. Thirty missed calls from Maude.

She swore and called her back.

Car crash. Had to be a car crash.

When Maude answered the phone, she sounded frantic. "She's missing! She won't answer me. She'll answer you."

"Right. Bye."

Holding her breath, Ronnie dialed her daughter's number. It rang.

The line picked up. "Hi." It was Rainbow.

Ronnie sucked air into her lungs, then sank onto a nearby log. "Where are you, babe? At a mate's?"

"I'm at Charlotte's house."

"You can't go off grid like that. Your mama's been worried sick about you."

"Sorry."

"She needs to know you're okay. Call her."

Ronnie called Maude to let her know Rainbow was at her friend's house, then hugged Nev with a shaky laugh. "I'm buzzing. That was terrifying. Everything's fine. Feel my heart racing. I'm shaking. I almost had to go looking for her. Can you imagine?" Nev would have gone with her. Total nightmare.

"Shh, it's all right. Karma owes you a few good ones. Now you say it."

"Karma owes you a few good ones."

"Cheeky."

"If it's true for me, it's true for you."

Horses waited for them in the dark rainforest. Bush stone curlews wailed like ghosts. Refreshing drop in temperature, like jumping into the lake. Dreadnought followed Uni back to the barn. Ronnie felt raw in a good way—sensitive and sore.

Spotted catbirds meowed and night cicadas droned.

They had left the barn light on.

She hung up Dreadnought's leather tack while Nev returned the brooms to the wall. Alongside Nev, Ronnie put away saddles and brushed horses, preoccupied by memories of nights in small towns in hotter, drier parts of Queensland—visions of the Outback, gum trees that looked like these...

They walked the horses into stalls.

"I used to go on walkabout when I was her age," Ronnie admitted.

Nev was only half listening. "That tracks." She disappeared into the barn office, emerging holding an Outback hat.

Ronnie recognized the style of the black leather crusher. It looked like the one her mother had worn. She turned it over in her hands, found the small hole. It was the same hat.

"She asked me to give it to you. I forgot."

The white lie uttered as an afterthought was so obvious that Ronnie understood it was an apology.

She showed Nev the puncture near the band from the time she had hung it from a road sign and used it for target practice to sight in a Tikka Super Lite. "You met my mum. When did you meet her?"

Nev jammed half a flake of hay into the empty haynet on the wall of Uni's stall. "She tried to visit you in hospital."

Ronnie shuddered.

"We should have asked if you wanted to see her, but it felt like emotional heavy lifting."

"Good call." Conversations with Matilda-Jane always disappointed her. Her mother and Maude were in the same category as Eastern Brown snakes and car accidents. Rainbow's behavior tonight unsettled her more than she cared to admit.

"What is it?" Nev asked, partially backlit by the barn light. She cast a shadow on the barn floor.

"Rainbow's making my mistakes."

"Nah, she's making her own." Nev's face was closed, her feelings guarded. In the fever-dream inside the strangler fig Ronnie had forgotten to kiss her on the mouth. Rectifying that omission now, she leaned down.

Nev's lips were soft.

It was a closed-mouth kiss until it wasn't. Ronnie's shirt chafed her chest. An invisible string drew tight. She hummed.

She felt where Nev's little belly touched hers through her clothes. Ronnie's breath slowed. Warm in all the right places, happily exhausted.

Nev barely moved. "I love you."

Ronnie recognized the wide-eyed look of a bandicoot in headlights, frozen, unwilling to save itself. You feel bad for it and slam on your brakes. She licked her lips, then straightened with a smile. "That's random, mate, but I love you too." Words they had said to each other a hundred times before to mean goodnight or goodbye.

She put on the hat.

Nev flushed. She looked angry, but no, that couldn't be right. Probably embarrassed.

Ronnie tried to set her at ease. "I had fun tonight." She rolled her shoulders. "Tomorrow's a leg day."

Two spots of red appeared on Nev's cheekbones. "Hat looks good on you."

Ronnie winked.

42

HIGHER STANDARD

Colorful musicians and vendors descended on the Lionheart market grounds and main street the weekend of the Tablelands Folk Festival. The weekend in late October had long been Ronnie's bandmates' favorite. It was the only weekend a respectable person could buy three-dollar margaritas from noon to midnight from a food truck parked outside the Opal Museum.

All weekend the Wild Drovers jammed on the shaded wooden veranda outside the historic pub, the Lionheart Hotel, with its wraparound second story and 1950's-style faux-arched pillars.

Ronnie wore the jackaroo boots Nev had given her, and her mother's Outback hat completed her metamorphosis into a bogan. Whitebeards outside the pub, senior bogans, wore kangaroo-leather and faded jeans. She tucked a black shirt into bootcut jeans. Owning land made her a forever kind of local. Wearing all black was an homage to New Zealand's national rugby team.

Once in a while, a fellow musician or pedestrian in the street below complimented her drumming with the Wild Drovers. No one complimented her guitar strumming, except Nev.

. . .

All the barstools in the pub at the Lionheart Hotel were taken, standing room only. Ronnie stood next to Reg's elbow at the bar. He nursed an amber schooner of Carlton Mid as he watched the game. Mattie was on. It was hard to spot him until the camera zoomed in on him in his black uniform with his number on the back. He had gotten a trendy haircut since she saw him on the television two weeks ago. He looked good.

She wondered if it would always be like this. She could see him but he couldn't see her. He would never move back to Lionheart now that he had kiwi citizenship. He had confided in her that he felt safer in Auckland as a bisexual man than he did here. She teared up every time his team performed the haka on the field. She didn't want him to move back.

No one had been surprised that the All Blacks made it to the semi-final match against South Africa of the Rugby Union World Cup. Mattie's team were arguably the best starting lineup of the best team in the history of rugby union. They had won the previous two World Cup finals.

If they won another, they would set a world record.

"Go Wallabies!" her dad's friends shouted, taking the piss out of Reg. Everyone in town was rooting for Mattie to bring home the $100,000 bonus that he would earn if his team won the Final.

Reg glanced at her between plays. "Where'd you get that drover hat? Your mum had one like that."

Ronnie tossed a handful of bar nuts into her mouth. "What would you say if I became the new drover at Upsend Downs when Kazi retires?"

"I'd be disappointed," he said, eyes glued to the telly behind the bar.

She chuckled, assuming he was kidding. She put her arm around his shoulder.

He gave her a disapproving look. "Real talk. Now that you're adulting, I'll hold you to a higher standard. Raise the bar. You leveled up in life. You've got responsibilities now, a mortgage to pay. You're my princess, but that's not a real job."

"What? Droving?"

"Kazi's not a drover, he's a bum who lives in a barn. You need money to build your house for you and Rainbow. Don't limit yourself. You're smart. Smarter than you pretend to be. It's time to stop playing the dropout card. You're past the age when you can use that as an excuse. You are as capable as anyone else at anything you set your mind to. Keep your options open. You're all Nev's projects there. She's farming you more than she's farming the animals. She's posh and bored. She doesn't even like sheep. It's a lark to her. She's a nihilist. Don't ask me how I know. Someday you'll step out of her shadow and strike out on your own. If you stay there, you'll turn into Nev."

"That wouldn't be so bad, would it?" Why was he going off about her job now? Ronnie bristled. She couldn't believe he had insulted the farm. She thought he liked Upsend Downs. He had never said anything dismissive about it before. What was making him a critic all of a sudden? Was it the fact that Mattie's team was ahead in the World Cup semi-final? If Mattie won this match, Reg would go home and buy tickets to London.

Mattie scored a try. Everyone cheered and thumped the bar. Soon they would be jumping up and down hugging each other. "My shout," she said, reaching for her wallet. Her dad shook his head and slid a hundred-dollar bill across the bar towards the bartender, paying for the next round.

"Da." She took off the hat. "I don't want a lecture from you."

Reg glanced at her and back to the game, contrite.

She turned the hat over in her hands. It wasn't like they spent all day braiding each other's hair and singing kumbaya around a campfire. Was he making fun of the fact that they had a folk band? Or was he making fun of the fact that they were single and didn't have traditional families? Either way, it hurt.

It had never crossed her mind that people looked down at her for working there. Those people would look down at her for working on any farm. If she continued working at Upsend, this was the price she would pay. This was what Nev had been so agitated about—people in the community not seeing her as a serious person with a real job.

"I'm not Mattie."

"I didn't say you were."

"Stop comparing me to him."

"I never have."

Debbie Collins set an overflowing frothy pint on the varnished mahogany.

"My version of success looks different. I can take care of myself."

Reg studied her during a commercial break. *Can you really?* his eyes seemed to ask.

"I don't need a degree for my career."

"Is it a career?" Reg asked.

She gave him a look.

"Fine," he said. "Do your thing, if it pays the mortgage. Are you going to Brisbane to try out for the Lions? That's coming up soon."

She had been thinking about it. Tickets were more expensive the longer she waited. If she was going, she should have bought them by now. She was doing that thing she did where she made a decision by not making a decision—a bad habit that she needed to break.

"No," she said. "I'm too busy, my game's off, and everything I need is here."

Reg nodded. "That makes sense."

"There is something you could help me with." Figuring out how to build a barn. She had already milled enough lumber. "Who do we know who can organize a barn-raising party?"

She returned to her new campsite down on the far side of Lazy Creek to the welcome sight of a Lumholtz tree kangaroo curled up in a furry ball in a high fork in a blackbean tree, long tail dangling, and an email from TAFE.

She brushed her teeth, then curled up in her sleeping bag to read it. The director of the program tersely informed her that she was failing all of her classes and advised her to come in for a meeting.

She skimmed an email from her English instructor explaining what a five-paragraph essay was. The small words on the screen blurred together. Maybe she needed glasses. She hoped not. They wanted her to rewrite her personal essay comparing and contrasting her childhood to the childhoods of the Aboriginal Australian man and the Asian immigrant family in the readings. "The strongest part of your essay was the sentence about collecting cans and trading them for candy bars, but your essay was only ninety-six words, when the assignment was four hundred."

The Marie Kondo book Blaise had given her was still in her truck. *If it doesn't bring you joy, get rid of it.* She Marie Kondo'ed the emails from the school, then logged into the website and Marie Kondo'ed the course.

It felt like the right thing to do.

Life was too short to beat a round peg into a square hole. She was ready to focus on things she was good at, to lean into things that made her feel like a badass. Work that made her sing.

43
BAND PRACTICE

Ronnie almost stepped on a Hercules moth under the porch light at Stone House. Another one clung to a window. They were light brown, approximately twelve centimeters across the wings, hairy, with long, feathery antennae.

She shut Nev's front door behind herself, toed off her Blundstones and hung her leather hat on a brass hook. Nev hunched towards the music stand, pencil tucked behind one ear.

"The ceremony's outdoors on grass?" Gunni asked.

Nev nodded. "They won't be sprinting, either."

Inside Stone House was cool. Peggy Collins' wedding was the day after tomorrow.

Nev had set up three music stands in the family room instead of the usual two.

Gunni kissed Ronnie hello on the mouth, but Nev only hugged her. That was new. Ronnie didn't like it. They sat down. Ronnie unpacked her guitar.

Gunni held his bass between his legs. Nev held her guitar, though she was not playing on this song. They had given the guitar part to Ronnie, who was also on backup vocals.

"The guests want it drawn out so they can take photos," Nev said. "We'll keep it light and airy." She played the chorus through once on the guitar, then began to sing the chorus and play the fiddle. Ronnie attempted to copy the guitar strumming Nev had done.

She stopped when Nev and Gunni stopped. "That was good," Nev said. "A little faster with the guitar." They began again, Nev singing the verse alone in a Scottish accent, Ronnie and Gunni accompanying on guitar and bass.

Nev stopped again. "It's not a dirge. Keep up."

A minute later Nev stopped to drink water. "That time you were ahead." Nev lifted something off the piano, set a metronome on the floor, opened it and turned it on. It clicked away, setting a steady pace.

"Are you serious?" Ronnie asked, offended.

Nev demonstrated the guitar part in time to the clicking metronome.

"My voice is the metronome," Nev said. "You follow me. Guitar follows vocals, not the other way around."

Ronnie flushed, aroused.

Nev was in a mood. "Also, it's Mairi with a soft "r", not a hard "r.""

Ronnie lost her patience. "I don't see why it matters."

"The hard "r" sounds Australian."

"We are Australian."

"It sounds better in a Scottish accent."

"Says who?"

"Says I."

Gunni was smiling, brows knit together. "You two out of sorts with each other?"

Ronnie pretended to study the sheet music. It had been Nev's idea to teach her guitar.

Nev sang the chorus in her normal accent to prove her point.

Something inside Ronnie relaxed. "I love your accent."

Nev frowned. "This isn't your wedding."

"It isn't yours, either." Ronnie swallowed, flushed. Her chest burned.

"At your wedding, I'll sing it however you like," Nev said. "This time I sing it my way."

Ronnie excused herself.

In the bathroom she splashed water on her face. Her cheeks were pink.

When she returned to the family room Nev was hunched over, elbows on her knees, head between her hands. Ronnie shivered, feeling Gunni's hand scratching Nev's back. She wanted to be the one doing it.

"Everything good?" she asked.

"Peachy," Nev said.

Ronnie hesitated with her guitar on her lap, wondering how to finagle it so that Gunni went home and Nev invited her to sleep over.

"Gunni, are you staying or going?"

The white-haired German looked at her and raised his eyebrows.

"Don't talk to him like that," Nev muttered.

Ronnie itched to tell her that she had dropped the course, wanted reassurance that she had made the right decision. Nev hid a lit cigar in one hand. She didn't resist when Ronnie took it and dropped it in Nev's beer glass.

"Fuck you," Nev muttered.

Ronnie squeezed Nev's shoulder before hugging Gunni. "Love you."

"Love you," Nev and Gunni said at the same time.

The fact that Nev had cold feet shouldn't surprise Ronnie as much as it did. Every new thing had growing pains. *Progress wasn't achieved inside the comfort zone.* Hopefully in the morning Nev would feel better and get over whatever mental block this was.

"Dress code: vest and tie," Nev said.

Ronnie turned, guitar case behind one shoulder. "Can I raid your closet?"

Nev's bedroom was dark. Ronnie felt the owl watching her as she touched the light switch. The same ironed shirts, slacks, neckties, bow ties, and the new baby blue linen suit Nev had loaned to Mikey for the hearing. She ran a finger down it. Soft as an old T-shirt. She wondered if Nev hadn't come to the hearing because she loaned her only formal outfit to Mikey. That was something Nev would do. She chose a black vest that had been Nev's father's, then pushed the light switch.

She had to pass through the family room on her way out. Gunni tapped Nev's arm. Nev looked up, guarded.

"Don't you want to ask which one she picked?" Gunni asked.

Ronnie held up the black vest, feeling childish.

Nev glanced at it. "Don't wear a black shirt with a black vest. That defeats the entire purpose of wearing a vest."

Gunni chuckled. "She looks good in black."

"Everyone looks good in black," Nev said.

Outside, honeyeaters and rainbow lorikeets warbled urgency in the grevilleas. The avian chorus sounded like a mixture of nails on a chalkboard and a crowd shaking sleighbells.

The next morning Ronnie biked to the boat launch on the east shore of Lake Tinaroo near where they had done the crane count with her dad earlier that spring.

Nev swam in goggles and nothing else.

Ronnie piled her clothes on a rock before wading through waist-high grass to the water's edge, then ran in, splashing.

The water grew colder farther from shore. Ronnie ducked under, then popped up. She treaded water while pushing wet hair out of her eyes.

Nev looked silly in the goggles. "That night in the strangler fig was magical for me."

"Same," Ronnie said.

"It was more magical for me."

"Pretty fucking magical for me too, babe."

"I don't want to do it again."

Ronnie's heart fell. "Why the hell not?"

Treading water made Nev pink. "The way you trust me and ask me for things makes me feel like I'm worth something."

"You are," Ronnie said.

"If we slept together again, it wouldn't be casual for me."

"Me neither."

"I don't want to date you, Dain'y. You're a shitty girlfriend, no offense."

"None taken."

"I would be jealous and miserable," Nev said. "We would drive each other crazy."

Ronnie wanted to say that was paranoid, but Nev was right. Ronnie would anticipate sex and be disappointed if it didn't happen. She would feel annoyed when Nev didn't invite her to sleep over. She would start to read silence as rejection, and make it a personal challenge to get Nev to orgasm every time they hooked up. If Nev didn't, Ronnie would feel like a failure.

She would try to cheer Nev up, to fuck her depression away, to be the drug that mellowed her out at night instead of the gin, which wouldn't work. It would never be as magical as it had been the first time in the hollow tree. She couldn't solve Nev's problems with sex. It wouldn't fix anything that was broken, but it might break something that was whole.

"You've never had a healthy relationship," Nev said. "I haven't had one that lasted longer than three months. We don't have the skills to date each other. Maybe someday we will."

"It's not rocket science. We'd figure it out," Ronnie said. "People do this all the time."

"People break up all the time. I can't break up with you. I would rather..."

"Don't be melodramatic." Ronnie sighed, exasperated. *Come here and stop talking.* The idea of never touching Nev again felt like a tragedy.

Nev looked sympathetic.

"Don't get in your head about it," Ronnie said.

Nev chuckled, out of breath in the dark lake. "I live in my head. It would be more mental work for me."

"Live a little."

Nev treaded water. "You're bigger than me on the outside. I can't lift you. Along those same lines I wouldn't ask you to lift what I have going on up here." Nev touched her head. "I'm bigger on the inside."

"That's insulting," Ronnie said, "and frankly not true."

"I have twenty years more life than you do. What do you think life is? That's twice as much shite to process. Twice as much stuff going on up here."

"I'll text you my therapist's number."

"Are we good?" Nev asked, reaching out and touching the side of Ronnie's neck where the tattoo from juvie had been.

It wasn't what Ronnie wanted, but maybe it was what she needed.

"You don't have to be in control all the time," Ronnie said.

"Feelings are the one thing I can control."

"You're repressed."

"Good talk." Nev disappeared under the surface and reappeared a few meters away. "Pain and pleasure have always been linked for me. I don't know if that's other people's experience. The way I feel about you is better than sex. Feelings are the only thing you own at the end of the day, the only thing that belongs to you," Nev said. "You can't keep anything else. You can't take anything else with you."

Back on the boat ramp, they dried off and shrugged into comfy clothes. Ronnie lifted her bike into the bed of Nev's silver truck and snapped up the tailgate with a satisfying thud. Nev drove with one hand on the wheel. Ronnie resisted the urge to touch her.

They rode uphill past a local family that was hauling a motorboat full of inner tubes. "Is the possibility that you might be a carrier of that gene the reason you don't have kids?"

Nev watched the back of the car in front of them. "No." At the intersection she signaled and looked both ways before turning onto the Gillies Range Road.

They didn't know if Nev had it. Maybe she didn't. "How old was your mum's mum when she died?"

"Fifty-one."

"Was it...?"

Nev nodded.

Ronnie swallowed. "Right." So it ran in the family. That didn't mean Nev had it or that she would get breast cancer. "Has Taylor been tested?"

Nev nodded. "She's negative."

Ronnie sighed. "Thank god. That's a good sign, right?"

"Don't worry about it."

"Oh, I'm going to worry about it."

Nev ran her hand through short, wet hair. "I don't lose sleep over it. It's not one of the top ten things I lose sleep over. There's nothing I can do about it." Ronnie knew about white noise, how it faded into the background. You get used to not knowing.

"It's not the death sentence it used to be." A white T-shirt was a good look for Nev.

"I wish you didn't have to deal with this."

"Everyone has something."

"Carpe Diem, right?"

"I happen to like living alone."

"You get what I'm saying though? You're a catch. Seriously."

Nev's ears turned pink. "Enough."

"You should go on dates. If not with me, with someone else. Put yourself out there."

"I'd rather not."

"You want to end up like Kazi?"

"Best-case scenario."

"You're not an old man."

"Not yet."

"I want to be an upstanding member of the community, like my dad. I want to stand for something. I want people to know who I am, and faces to light up when I walk into a business downtown. I want to be the one people call when shit hits the fan. I want to get married and have more kids." Ronnie hadn't meant to say that, but realized it was true. "I want a home like my dad and Blaise's place, with open doors and relatives coming and going, but with fewer wallabies." She wanted to be a leader. An all-around decent, regular bloke. Unpretentious. Aggressively middle class, with thick skin and good humor for armor.

Nev parked in front of Stone House. "Sounds like a plan for you." She patted the front pocket of her shirt where Ronnie knew she used to keep an emergency cigarette, but apparently there was none.

Ronnie rested her hand on the knee of Nev's sweatpants. "What about you? What do you want?"

Nev hesitated. "I don't know, Dain'y. I guess I'd like to be the person you think I am." She parked in front of Stone House, got out and shut the door.

44
SINGLE PEOPLE

The morning before Peggy's wedding, Ronnie woke damp with dew, serenaded by cockatoos, riflebirds, bowerbirds, chowchilla, and scrubwren.

Before she opened her eyes, she knew where she was from the sound of running water shushing in rills over rocks, and from the smell. Moldy wet leaf detritus, rotting logs, tree perspiration, fresh wood shavings. If her mother was here, she would be able to identify each tree species Ronnie had milled into boards from the scent.

She opened her eyes and sat up in her tent. Outside, a clearing lay shaded and hidden between silent ferns and mossy stones.

Behind the horse barn at Upsend Downs, the blue quandong sapling had grown since they planted it six months ago. Someone had hammered metal t-posts around it and strung chicken wire to save it from the slasher. No one but Nev would have thought of that. No one else knew it was there.

Tracey Chapman on the radio. Honeybees in the clover, grass gone to seed glowing backlit in the distance. Golden lawn, dusty haze, blue mountains, cerulean sky. Barney must see it when he mowed the nursery. What did he think when he saw it—a lone sapling on an otherwise barren hillside that rolled down into a wet ditch? The boss was not prone to whimsy or sentimentalism on the public side of the farm.

The quandong was now as tall as her chest. She pinched it gently near the top where it was no more than a leggy twig, careful not to damage it, unlike the other thing, the thing that came before. She was irrationally fond of it, was glad they had planted it here where no one else would see. Someday it would be a shade tree. It would look like it had always been there.

If anyone saw Ronnie she would blush like a kid caught misbehaving. It was always a mistake to become irrationally attached to things.

Nev seemed committed to protecting the quandong if the fence was any indication. Would she plant a new one if this one shriveled and turned brown? Ronnie suspected the older woman would replace it without telling her, like a parent replacing a beloved goldfish or budgie. Did that make it immortal? Would there always be an iteration of it here as long as Nev was alive?

Ronnie wanted to be that type of person—tending a perpetual flame for no reason other than that it seemed like the right thing to do.

The ectopic might have been her child but the tree was Nev's.

With her outfit for Peggy's wedding in the backseat of her truck, she drove to the house at Pademelon Road—humbled, bruised, but stronger. She had lost a round with Nev, but lived to fight another day.

She felt lighter.

The fact that she owned property still felt miraculous.

She remembered why she liked being single: more solitude, more time to muck about in gyms and watch sports, no one to nag her if she ate greasy takeaway on the couch with her fingers, like she was planning to do today.

The Rugby World Cup was tomorrow, October thirty-first. On the radio a sports commentator said, "If they win, this roster will be the fifth-best rugby team in history."

Reg's front door was unlocked. She let herself in. Reg's dogs jumped on her, sniffing her and licking her hands. "Good morning." She used an empty yogurt container to pour scoops of dog food into metal bowls on the kitchen floor. While the dogs ate, tails flapping, she opened the fridge and poured mango juice from a plastic bottle directly into her mouth. Cold juice woke up her tongue.

Reg and Blaise had flown to London to watch the game. Mattie's son, Luca, would be there in the stands with his mother, the coffee barista social media influencer from Barcelona who lived in Madrid near the Prado. The All Blacks were defending their title against the Wallabies.

Her brother had not offered her a ticket.

She hoped he won and got the hundred-thousand-dollar bonus so that he could buy a house. Mattie spent money as fast as it came in, but he needed to plan for retirement. At twenty-eight, his prime wouldn't last forever. The gravy train would dry up unless he made a sound business plan and courted sponsors, brand endorsements. He could advertise deodorant, she mused, punch the television camera.

Her phone vibrated. A photo of Nev smiling in her car. Her smile was unusually lopsided.

(Nev) YOU'RE SINGING TOMORROW. CAN'T WHISTLE WORTH SHITE.

Nev had been to the dentist that morning.

(Ronnie) Dentures?

Her phone vibrated again before she could return it to her pocket.

Ronnie frowned.

At five o'clock, Ronnie dressed to go dancing at the pub. Barney's band was playing tonight—Fleetwood Mac hits again. She was loving her Johnny Cash era, leaning in. Black pearl snap shirt from the men's section that fit like a glove tucked snug in Nev's father's jeans. Silver belt buckle with her initials. Black hat, boots.

The car park was full. Inside the Lionheart pub, locals with mullets, sunburns, and crooked teeth packed the room. She had to take off her hat to fit through the door.

Heads turned. The warm buzz of noise in front of the bar grew quiet, then loud again as people returned to their conversations.

Maude and Rainbow sat at a table with Maude's parents. Ronnie couldn't remember the last time she had seen Maude's father. They waved her over, toward an empty fifth chair, which they must have put there for her. The invitation from the Greens had come as a surprise. They had never asked her to join them for dinner before, let alone out in public. That was something family did.

Maude looked clean and well put together. Ronnie knew her ex had spent an hour putting on makeup to look like she wasn't wearing any. Now that she and Maude shared custody, Ronnie discovered she was no longer terrified of her.

The Greens stood and took turns hugging her, which wasn't as awkward as she expected. Rainbow was nose-deep in a book about pirates. Ronnie leaned down to kiss her on the head. "Hiya, baby. Good book?"

Maude's parents talked about the big match tomorrow. They were going to a barbie at Maude's aunt's condo in Cairns, which sounded like a terrible idea because of traffic, but they were bringing the pavlova and were certain the traffic would be fine.

When they moved to the dance floor Ronnie followed.

Maude's parents danced together in front of Barney's band.

Maude turned toward her, asking with a half-smile before raising her arms to reach for Ronnie's shoulders. Maude's palms were cool on the back of Ronnie's neck. "Are you disappointed you're not going to London?"

She shook her head. Everything she needed was here.

She wasn't attracted to Maude.

They danced to Cyndi Lauper's 1983 hit, 'Girls Just Wanna Have Fun,' which made her sleepy. Maude turned away.

Ronnie hugged the shorter woman from behind, swaying in time to the music. Things would never be comfortable between them, but neutral was good enough. This was a kind of a tenderness. Rainbow tied them together. They were family in a way.

Maybe if she didn't date anyone for a while, if she spent time with herself, worked on herself instead, she could sort out how to be the best version of herself.

Rainbow deserved that.

She and Maude danced face to face again. She spun Maude around, out of step with the music. The dance floor at the pub was hot and crowded. She loved her eccentric, close-knit town.

"You clean up nice," Maude said.

"So do you."

"The farm looks good on you. You've grown up."

"Oh?"

"You look ten years older. It's wild. You're giving dorky dad energy now."

Ronnie was a little softer around the middle than she had been last year, and better dressed. Not trying to impress anyone.

She taught Rainbow dance moves, the lasso and the fishing rod.

She understood why Nev made the commitment every day to be with herself, content with herself, a unit of one. She respected that. It surprised her. Now that she had seen it, it seemed so clear.

It was a privilege to be single. A gift. Selfish, in a way. People pitied single folks, but they had the best deal. They had figured out something and they weren't letting the secret out. They were the lucky ones, the people who loved themselves.

45
PEGGY'S WEDDING

The next morning at the wedding venue the last empty parking spot was directly in front of the door.

Ronnie jogged down the lawn.

The stage was a Persian rug. Nev and Gunni sat on folding chairs. Nev fiddled with the sound system at her feet. Someone in a STAFF T-shirt miked Ronnie and explained where the stationary mikes were while she took her guitar out and tucked the case behind her chair.

Nev had dressed all in cream from head to toe to make a point; shirt, vest and slacks, with a black silk ribbon tie that made her look like a reenactor. Her mouth was symmetrical again.

"Where's your straw hat?" Ronnie teased.

Nev pointed under her chair.

Ronnie ran a hand through her hair. She was wearing it down today. If it got sweaty and stuck to her neck she could always tie it up later.

"Sorry I'm late. What did I miss?"

"You're on time," Gunni said. "We were early."

Nev held her guitar. "Can I show you the opening bars of Mairi's wedding again?"

Ronnie propped her guitar on her knee, put her fingers on the strings. Nev played the opening. She copied it.

"Good." Nev put her guitar behind her chair. "How'd you sleep last night?"

"Good." The question touched something tender, but didn't sting. "You?"

"Like a baby."

"A baby who sleeps through the night or a colicky one?" Ronnie asked.

"Option one."

They were learning the new shape of their friendship, figuring out where the boundaries would be. Her friends smelled like cigar smoke. Ronnie would win that battle, but not today.

Brad Collins was in the crowd, his face etched into her memory like a tattoo she would remove if she could. She almost pointed him out to Nev, but decided it wasn't worth troubling her. All the Collinses were there.

Ronnie waved to Nonna, who waved back in a pale pink dress and matching hat, rosy like the inside of a seashell.

The officiant nodded to Nev, who nodded to Ronnie, who started playing the opening bars of the reel. In front of a crowd music came easier and faster—electric, alive—almost an out-of-body feeling, as if it was playing itself.

Nev sang more expressively in front of a crowd.

Now that Ronnie was in a flow state, she easily followed Nev's pace. The moment the wedding party began walking down the aisle there was nothing outside the song, the lawn, and the crowd. The whole world was here. Everything else disappeared.

A wedding in motion had the inertia of a spherical stone rolling down a steep hill. The show would go on until the last slice of cake was boxed in the freezer, the hall floor swept, and the lights turned off. The processional was the carpet on which the wedding walked. They walked because of the song, and she played because the people in pastel dresses and suits walked.

Strumming and harmonizing happened instinctually.

Rehearsal did that. All the clumsy work they had put in transformed into something spontaneous and ecstatic, water tumbling over a rill. The song came without thought because she knew it by heart.

Peggy's elderly fiancé Tom shuffled arm-in-arm with his daughter. A woman walking her father down the aisle—already not a dry eye in the crowd.

Everyone turned to watch Peggy. Peggy had answered the phone of the police department since before Ronnie was born. She carried a long-haired dachshund and glowed, barefoot in one of her batik sundresses and a wide straw hat. The crowd oohed and aahed, filming on their phones. Peggy shimmied and danced her way down the aisle.

She deserved a good man like Tom. Her first husband had been a monster.

Peggy walked arm-in-arm with her son, the District Commissioner, Brad's father, who was a real bastard. With any luck he would retire soon. Both were crying. Michael Collins sat down in the audience and Peggy took her place across from her fiancé Tom in front of the officiant.

The ring exchange drew a laugh from the crowd. The octogenarians hammed up the fact that their knuckles were too swollen and arthritic, until with the help of butter, both rings slipped on.

"About time," Nev whispered in Ronnie's ear. "I was about to fetch the lube from my glove box."

The laugh relaxed Ronnie's stomach, released the tension in her shoulders. "I love it when you talk dirty to me."

Peggy kissed Tom, and the white-haired couple were married.

Rainbow's secret great-grandparents.

Nev stood with her guitar across her chest, then put her straw hat on. She walked behind the couple and played as they shuffled away down the aisle.

When Nev began to sing the recessional, Ronnie recognized the Robert Burns poem her mum used to sing to her on brisk nights camping in the Outback, staring up at stars thick as sand on a beach.

Careful not to make a sound, she slid her guitar back into its case. It had been generous of Nev to let her play lead guitar on the processional. Nev could have easily played and sang without her, like she was doing now. But that was Nev in a nutshell: patient, understated, generous with those less skillful than herself.

Straightening, she noticed two late arrivals walking across the lawn.

Maude and Rainbow.

Ronnie raised a hand. They waved back.

She checked her phone. Two missed texts from Maude, saying that she was dropping Rainbow off.

Maude waved again and headed back towards the car park. Rainbow continued alone. Ronnie beckoned her closer.

Guests trapped in their seats until the closing music ended watched as the newlyweds shuffled up the aisle towards the country club, arm in arm, leaning on each other and giggling like kids.

Across the lawn, Ronnie saw the moment Rainbow decided to sit in the audience. Helpful neighbors pointed her toward the last empty seat.

Ronnie sat frozen as Rainbow squeezed between rows of knees to take the seat next to Brad Collins.

Carefully, Ronnie sipped from her water bottle and rose to her feet. Everyone else was still seated. The tacit cue to rise had not been given because Nev was still singing, but it would only be a few more bars now, and then everyone would make a run for the reception and the open bar.

Nev glanced at her, seemed to notice her standing there motionless and caught her eye. Ronnie stared back, clutching her water bottle. Nev turned to see what she had been looking at, while continuing the last verse.

Nev's voice faltered. She stopped picking the guitar. She had seen what Ronnie had seen. It was impossible not to notice the resemblance between ten-year-old Rainbow and the man seated next to her.

Nev laughed. It was not a pleasant sound, like a branch breaking.

Nev played a closing chord on the guitar with a flourish. The crowd exhaled, released from the spell. A hundred warm bodies stood at the same time, stretched, turned to their neighbor and resumed chit-chatting.

Ronnie jogged over to Nev halfway up the aisle and put her arm around her. "It's cool, babe. Be cool."

Nev's eyes were blank and her face was flushed. Ronnie swallowed. Nev handed her the guitar, then the straw hat. "Take Rainbow," Nev ordered.

"Leave him alone," Ronnie said.

"Like he left you alone?"

Ronnie had no response to that. "He's a cop."

"I didn't hear that. Scram."

This was spiraling out of control faster than Ronnie could think. She had to fix this before Nev did something she would regret, but her brain wasn't working. Magic words to calm Nev down...

Rainbow appeared, clutching pink backpack straps. Her converse trainers and lilac T-shirt with snapping turtles on it looked jarringly out of place. "Hi," Rainbow said. She blew a bubble with her gum, brown hair shiny on either side of a severe part made with the tip of a comb. Ronnie used to wear her hair like that when she was ten. Long curly pigtails.

What would Rainbow think about herself if she knew Brad was her dad? Would she be ashamed? Would she feel less-than his 'real' daughters? He wasn't her dad in any meaningful sense of the word.

"Run and jump in the ute." Ronnie tossed her keys to Rainbow.

Rainbow caught them. "What's wrong? Did someone die?"

Nev walked across the lawn in the direction of the pub where the reception was.

Ronnie handed Rainbow both guitars. "Put these in the ute, please. I'll meet you there in a minute."

She caught up with Nev behind the white tent at the back of the building. "Don't make the mistake I did."

Nev checked her phone. "This isn't about you. I should have done this years ago."

"Violence is never the answer. Believe me. Do I have to pick you up and throw you over my—"

"Go home, Dain'y!" Nev roared, red-faced. Guests in pastel sundresses turned to stare. Nev raised her hands. "You left the oven on!" Concerned onlookers relaxed, smiling, turned away.

Ronnie drew a shaky breath. Right. Nev needed to break something. This wasn't about her. "Rings count as a weapon. In sentencing."

Nev tucked her rings in her vest. Maybe that's all life was, a series of small gestures of care or neglect. The worst sins were unassuming, forms of negligence.

"Neighbors will call about hay." They called Nev because she would cut them a deal and Ronnie wouldn't. "Don't be a hard-arse."

Nev had calmed down, as if someone had flipped a switch. Ronnie suspected her friend was doing that on purpose to reassure her. It was working.

"See you back at the farm." Nev said.

Ronnie jogged to the carpark.

She tried to remember what was on Nev's calendar for the next few days.

Rainbow sat waiting in the truck. Ronnie tugged open the door, swung into the driver's seat. Key already in the ignition. She turned the key. The engine purred.

"Where's Nev?"

"We drove separately." Ronnie put the truck in reverse, backed out carefully. "There's something she has to do." When the truck was lined up with the road she put it in park and turned to Rainbow. "Would you mind sitting in the back seat?"

Rainbow looked suspicious. "Why?"

Ronnie blinked.

Her daughter frowned, then rolled her eyes and climbed into the back.

"Thanks, baby." She waited until the girl buckled her seatbelt, then pulled out onto the road.

Was this subconsciously what she wanted? Had she manifested this?

She turned the track on the CD player to Stevie Nicks singing "Edge of Seventeen."

She had no idea what Nev would do. She wanted to be that type of person, someone who wasn't afraid. Ronnie would go berserk if anyone messed with Rainbow the way people had messed with her. Nev had a thing about protecting kids. Maybe Ronnie did, too. Maybe that was called being a decent human being.

She wiped her cheeks with the back of her hand. By the time they turned east onto the Gillies Range road through the mountains her shirt was wet.

She should have fought Brad instead of Maude ten years ago. She had overreacted that night at Maude's house because she had underreacted to him. Pent up energy will break free inappropriately in other situations.

No one had ever stood up for her before. No one had pressed charges against Maude or Brad. She hadn't asked anyone to. Filing a report would have been her responsibility. She had been too embarrassed.

Her mother should have protected her. Even Reg, who would walk across broken glass for her, acted like he didn't know Brad Collins used to rescue her from dangerous parties at night and take her to the Lake Barrine car park, down that long, dark road, kiss her gently, say he loved her, and keep the uniform on because she asked him to. Nothing to do about that now.

Nausea came in waves. *Please don't let Nev make a scene...* Today could still end the normal way. Nev's truck could roll up to Stone House and her friend could knock on her own door, hands jammed in pockets. They could go back to this awkward phase of whatever they were doing, growing older side by side but not together. Life would change now that Nev knew, but most things would stay the same.

She turned left onto Boar Pocket Road.

Her phone vibrated.

Like inside the strangler fig, the buzzing didn't stop. Lump in her throat, she pulled over. This time it was all texts and calls from relatives and friends. She laughed.

46
HOME

Ronnie tossed the phone into the passenger seat, shifted the truck back into gear, signaled with her blinker, then merged onto the empty road. Neighbors were all home watching the rugby final. Her phone continued vibrating as calls and texts poured in.

Bloody hell, she actually did it.

She wiped her face with her shirt, amazed that someone cared.

No one had ever defended her honor before. She hadn't had any. That invisible thing that didn't exist.

It should have felt silly, but didn't. Nev took it seriously; it must be serious.

Why had no one been outraged before? They must have known. Lionheart wasn't a large town—the half-sisters played soccer together—people looked the other way to protect his career.

The past was all around her. If she stayed here on the Tablelands, where each soft green place, swimming hole and tourist attraction reminded her of childhood—for better and worse—she would always live in that magical state of perpetual youth, simultaneously all the different ages she had been, carrying those girls around inside her, a family of little Ronnies. That's the best and worst part of staying in the small town where you grew up.

Saltwater, nature's soap. Amazed, she cradled to her chest the lost thing Nev had found, picked up, brushed off, and returned. It felt soft and wobbly, fragile and precious.

At Stone House, she parked on the grass, cut the engine, and answered her phone. Nev's collies tore barking across the lawn to greet Rainbow as she hopped down from the truck. Stadium noise in the background—Reg was in London at the Rugby World Cup. He shouted. "Brum! Where are you?!"

"Is Nev all right? Have you heard from your mates at the police station?" she asked.

"Where are you?"

"At the farm."

Rainbow bent over to pet Gaia and Blair, whose tails wagged.

"Was she drunk?"

Ronnie hesitated. Information like that could be evidence. She might be called to testify. "I'm sure they'll breathalyze her. Is he pressing charges?"

"Dunno. Nonna called me. Poor Peg. I thought Nev liked her. Why would she start a barney at Peg's wedding reception? It's not like her at all. Everything good between you and her? You're two aren't fighting, are you?"

"We're good." *Best we've ever been. That's my bezzie.*

"What did Brad do?" Reg asked through the phone.

"Underage stuff."

She heard her dad swear. "What? When? To who? How'd Nev find out?" The World Cup stadium was loud on his end. Maybe he didn't know. Maybe he hadn't known this whole time.

"We can talk about it when you get back. Focus on Mattie's game. Enjoy it."

"Wish I was there with you, Brum."

"Grateful for you, Da. If I wanted to bail her out, who would I call?"

"Crikey, not Peg, eh?"

They chuckled. He screamed "Goal!!!" and hung up.

Next to her, Rainbow glanced up from scratching the dogs behind the ears. "The game started. Can you play it on your phone?"

"I don't know how to do that," she admitted.

"Can we watch it in the house?"

"Sure."

"Here's the plan," Rainbow said. "We'll order takeaway and watch the game on Nev's telly. During commercial breaks you'll tell me what happened. We'll eat the choccies she keeps hidden in the dishwasher. Sound good?"

"Ripper." Needless to say, Ronnie's version of the story would be redacted for ten-year-old ears. Some things she could tell her now.

Stone House was locked.

"I have a better plan," she said, improvising.

They made a bonfire, roasted snags and mallows, then watched stars come out.

Ronnie remembered she had drums in the truck. They drummed at the old ruins beside the wellhead where the barn would be. Mozzies buzzing. Spring night, cool damp air swirling in. Fireflies low along the bottom paddock, down in the scrub along the edge of the creek.

They howled at the moon with the dogs in the dark.

Gunni and Kazi materialized out of the mist, drawn to the fire like white-haired spirits. They drank and told stories and drummed late into the night. Time stood still in this other world, this world of fire and shadows.

In the morning Ronnie and Rainbow played tag in their pajamas, black T-shirts with the sleeves cut off, through their campsite down by the creek, passing time while they waited for news. Already that morning a customer had called inquiring about hay, but no call from Nev. Ronnie had that kicked ball feeling—she wouldn't be able to think clearly again until she heard her friend's voice and knew she was all right.

Rainbow started to roam further afield like a feral home-schooled child who had grown up off the grid. The girl showed her all the special places under the bushes where she would build forts and pens for the koalas, quolls and brush turkeys she thought she would catch.

The campsite must feel vast, mysterious, and full of potential to her. Ronnie let herself imagine she didn't know where the fences were. She had chosen a nice spot. They could spend years exploring nooks and crannies, mossy rocks and shaded glens along the serpentine creek. Universe in a nutshell.

She loved that the creek was hers now, as much as anyone's, and that it would be Rainbow's. It felt like a safe place here. Rainbow would grow up with roots to the land, not homeless and drifting from sheep station to sheep station.

This was only temporary, but that didn't mean it wasn't real. It was good enough until she built a house on higher ground.

Wet from a dip in the creek and half-dressed, hair down, she nursed a cup of tea. As she returned her toothbrush to the truck, she noticed the manilla envelope from her mum sticking out of a bag of important papers she had rescued from the flooded donga. Impulsively, she ripped it open.

It was empty.

When she shook the manilla envelope a business card fell out.

Matilda-Jane Peterson
Battlers' Rattler etc.

Ronnie hesitated for a moment, then typed the number into her phone. Her finger hovered over the call icon.

Talking to her mother always made her feel like shit, but it had been a long time, and people changed.

She could press call. Try again. Maybe it wouldn't be disappointing.

What was the worst that could happen? Homophobic slurs? Ableist and racist language? Her decision became easier.

Not yet. Maybe after she finished building the barn, when things were more solid. She slid the phone back into her pocket.

That door would be open when she was ready.

At the moment, Rainbow wanted to watch cranes.

First, there was something they needed to do. They took a can of white paint up to the top of their drive, where they wrote BRUM'S on the giant boulder.

In the horse barn at Upsend Downs, under the mops and brooms, they returned the half-empty can of white paint.

Rainbow perched on her shoulders, legs dangling. Both of them silently stared through binoculars out past land covered in sheep, at enormous grey Sarus cranes. The birds looked ancient and eternal—guardians of the lake—elephants of the avian family. When they talked to each other they made a strange warbling rubber sound.

"I liked what you said last time about it sounding like the lake was laughing," Ronnie said.

Rainbow was tall for her age, but her feet still fit comfortably in Ronnie's armpits. Human backpack. Full-grown, she would tap out at Ronnie's chin.

Through the binos Ronnie spotted a mother crane with chicks weaving around her feet. "Look, chicks!"

A long silence, calibration, like a game of battleship. Ronnie held the cranes in her line of sight. "Underneath the willow tree that looks like a lima bean, just in front of the patch of sunlight, two thumbs left of the dead tree stump…"

"Got it. Aww… They're so cute!" Rainbow said.

Two little grey fluffballs pecked at the grass, looking for seeds.

Wrong time of year for seeds. Ronnie wondered if they ate grass. What did chicks eat? Surely they didn't drink milk?

"What do chicks eat, Gumball?"

Rainbow hummed. "Bugs and grain."

"Their parents don't feed them?"

"Not once they've left the nest."

"Where do they nest?"

"Marshes. Their nests can be two metres in diameter and a metre high."

"Did you read that in a book?"

"Encyclopedia." So nonchalant.

"Proud of you, kid."

"Love you, mum."

"Love you, baby."

The kid-sized motorbike helmet Ronnie ordered had arrived in the mail. She walked toward Rainbow with the helmet tucked behind her back.

When Ronnie held it out, Rainbow squealed, jumping up and down. Ronnie crouched to show her how to put it on, teaching her how to widen the straps, pull it on over her head, then make sure it sat level two finger-widths above her eyebrows. Satisfied, she patted the top of Rainbow's helmet. "What do you think, angel? Want to go for a ride?"

The Kawasaki sat in the machine shop at Upsend Downs where she had left it. She straddled it now and rode it out onto the lawn, then idled with the motor running, playing Fleetwood Mac's "The Chain" over the bike's speakers while Rainbow climbed on behind her.

"Let's go to the lake and get ice cream!"

"Rock and roll. Hold on."

Rainbow's arms tightened around her waist.

"Don't let go."

Careful not to go too fast, Ronnie cruised down the gravel

drive and out onto the country road. Far above, a V-formation of migrating Sarus cranes trailed them like a kite.

———

Pickup trucks lined either side of Ronnie's drive. Relatives had come for the barn raising, even Mattie, who flew in from London two days after winning the Rugby World Cup. Ronnie's footy teammates—half the South Cairns Cutters Womens and a handful of friends from the men's team—helped volunteers from Lionheart assemble wooden arches flat on the ground. Jack Collins, the boys primary school soccer coach, worked alongside his wife and kids.

Debbie Collins ran kegs off the back of a ute under a waratah with blossoms like bush fireworks. Blaise and Nonna blasted ABBA, keeping volunteers fed on bratwursts and burgers while two of Reg's firefighter recruits ran the grills.

Rainbow and her friends picked wildflowers, then discovered a dirt pile to run down. Two-year-old Jesse followed Rainbow with wide eyes as she alternated between holding his hand and carrying him around on her hip.

Ronnie gave the signal to the crew to raise the first arch. Sweaty volunteers pulled on long ropes and hauled the frame upright with her. She pulled as hard as she could, rope biting into her hands through work gloves. As giant beams rose magically off the ground, it looked like they were erecting an upside-down ship.

Still no sign of Nev. According to the grapevine, the police station had released her after twenty-four hours, but Peggy had kidnapped her for 'Collins family bootcamp,' deep cleaning the pub in exchange for Brad not pressing charges. If Nev had been there, she would have shaken hands and chatted with everyone, drank too much coffee and whiskey, or played the fiddle.

Their houses would be close as the crow flies, but to drive there on roads they would have to trace the outline of two lungs or a mishappen heart.

At sunset, Mattie whistled from where he sat perched atop the timber roofline a few ribs away from the cross-joist Ronnie was hammering snug into a beam.

She turned to see what he was pointing at. Shading her eyes, she squinted against the sun. Up on the hill, silhouetted against the horizon, a figure on horseback wore an Akubra hat.

Relief.

Euphoria.

Her favorite feeling.

"The Night We Met" played on a radio below the unfinished barn, bringing her back to the night she played Russian Roulette with post box numbers.

She had replayed that scene in the broken room over and over, trying to get it right. Each time she did something different. Each time Nev did something different. It could have gone down so many ways. On the best nights Ronnie stayed. On the best nights she didn't drive off into the darkness alone. Rainbow was born on the farm.

One part of the dream never changed, a memory so deep it had become part of her. When Nev locked eyes with her above the shotgun's mouth, Ronnie's soul flew back into her body and every atom in her danced.

She looked around for the nearest extension ladder, spotting one at the end of the beam with an unfamiliar queasy feeling in the pit of her stomach. The distance to the ground made her slightly dizzy, like a spin on a merry-go-round, as she calculated how to reach the ladder. This new fear of heights would take getting used to. She hadn't been up this high since falling off the screen house.

On the next beam, Mattie waved his hands in the air before cupping them around his mouth. "Neville's back!"

Ronnie scooted on her bottom down to where she could reach the framing below with her feet, then carefully slid the sole of one boot after the other down the rafter toward the extension ladder, all while hugging the beam. "Don't call her that." *That's the woman I'm going to marry.* She froze, halfway to the ladder. The thought surprised her, but she knew it was true the same way she knew anything. A laugh burst out of her, once, loud, then kept coming. Once she started, she couldn't stop.

Oh, man. This will be fun.

New mission: convince Nev. She had no idea how she would do it.

AFTERWORD

Queenslander deals with intimate partner violence. According to domestic violence statistics, one in four women in Australia experience violence from an intimate partner. LGBTQ and gender diverse people are particularly vulnerable.

If you have been affected by intimate partner violence, please tell someone you trust, find a therapist, and reach out to the appropriate resources, like https://whiteribbon.org.au in Australia, or the National Domestic Violence Hotline in the United States, www.thehotline.org, or the equivalent resource in your country.

THE SEQUEL:
QUEENSLAND MADONNA
COMING FALL 2026

Now that Ronnie's life isn't a hot mess anymore she knows what she wants—to settle down at the sheep farm with Nev and have a second child—but Nev is being squirrelly about their relationship status.

When Ronnie's ex returns to Lionheart, an impatient Ronnie decides that platonic co-parenting with him would solve both their problems.

Nev has to make a choice: watch Ronnie build a life with someone else, or overcome her fear of letting Ronnie in. When bushfire hits Upsend Downs during the drought, will Nev finally swallow her pride and admit she's hiding problems? Nev must admit she's a fraud or lose a love she never thought possible, and the motherhood she thought she sacrificed long ago.

QUEENSLAND MADONNA is about second chances and small-town resilience in the face of climate change.

ACKNOWLEDGMENTS

I would like to thank my editor, Ann, and my developmental editor, Leslie. I would like to thank my thesis advisor at Wesleyan University, Krishna, who read the earliest draft of this book way back in 2010 when it was the capstone for my English and Environmental Studies majors.

I would like to thank the School for Field Studies for the magical experience they gave me and my fellow American students studying abroad in the rainforests of Far North Queensland. This semester changed my brain chemistry, introducing me to a biodiverse landscape of dynamic opposites, including ecosystems with scars from colonialism, agriculture, deforestation, and climate change. The rural communities we met were diverse, resilient, and hilarious—if you met them you would fall in love with them, too.

I would like to thank the friends and sensitivity readers who read drafts of *Queenslander*: Emily, Katie, Rachel, Jacob, Stef, Candice, Alaina, Erin, Tia, Jake, Carly, Maggie, Ellen, Charlie, Alexis, Sarah, Terry, and Alice.

I couldn't have done it without my creative writing group in Portsmouth: Jim, Alexis, Tia, Caroline, Carly, Jake, and Leslie, my creative writing group in Newburyport: Donna, Tessa, Marcel, and Sandy, and my writing groupmates who I met through Grubstreet: Aisling, Lauren, Ledyard, and BB.

Thank you to the Grubstreet community of Boston, especially my mentors Milo and Leora.

I would like to thank my newsletter subscribers who support me on my Substack "Writing in Work Gloves"—your financial support made this possible.

I would like to thank Wesleyan University for the Olin fellowship for creative writing that paid my bills for a summer, Harvard for the fellowship that paid my bills for three years, and Writer's Digest for the award. Cash prizes allow writers to continue doing what we love.

I would like to thank all the people from GCLS, you rock! My GCLS fam, you know who you are.

I want to thank all the people from small presses for your advice as I navigated ways to publish this series.

I want to thank all of my author friends who inspired and supported me along the way, too numerous to name, especially Cheyenne in Queensland.

I want to thank my bookstore owner friend, Meg, for cheering me on every step of the way and for organizing my launch party, and Elizabeth for helping.

And last but not least, my partner, Donnie, a cowboy from Oklahoma and the sweetest, gentlest person I know.

ABOUT THE AUTHOR

Laura Garden raises sheep and is a flower grower. She studied conservation biology in Yungaburra, Queensland with the School for Field Studies, where she fell in love with Australia. Garden is passionate about sustainable agriculture and conservation. She has won several writing competitions, including an award from Writer's Digest, as well as fellowships from Wesleyan University and Harvard University. She was longlisted for the Minds Shine Bright Prize in Melbourne. She runs the substack "Writing in Work Gloves." She has a Masters from Harvard University and lives on a farm in Massachusetts.

You can follow her at
Instagram @lauragardenwrites
Bluesky @lauragardenwrites
Facebook: Laura Garden Author

Sign up for her newsletter at her website
www.lauragarden.com for updates, publishing news, etc.